Praise for *A Glitter of Gold*

"What a spellbinding book. . . . Throw in a little bit of romance and learning to overcome the shame of past mistakes, and you have the makings of an intriguing, well-written story."

Bookworm Banquet

"Fun, witty, charming, and pirates make for the best kind of summer story."

Write-Read-Life

"*A Glitter of Gold* has all of the classic hallmarks one would look for in a great story—pirates, hidden treasure, secret diaries, and romance. Yes, indeed, this story has a little of everything."

Compass Book Ratings

Praise for *A Sparkle of Silver*

"Johnson pens an evocative tale of family intrigue and dashing romance sure to delight fans of Melody Carlson and Susan Anne Mason."

Library Journal

"This is a sweet story with likable Christian characters and chaste hints of romance. . . . Johnson's many fans and all gentle romance readers will be delighted."

Booklist

"A mystery, a treasure hunt, and a split-time romance—all set within a beautiful chateau on St. Simons Island during its 1920s heyday and its beautifully restored present. What more could we want? Especially as Liz Johnson also delivers a sigh-worthy ending. Enjoy!"

Katherine Reay, author of *Dear Mr. Knightley* and *A Portrait of Emily Price*

"This sparkling tale of mystery and romance will delight fans of Liz Johnson!"

Denise Hunter, bestselling author of *Honeysuckle Dreams*

Books by Liz Johnson

PRINCE EDWARD ISLAND DREAMS

The Red Door Inn
Where Two Hearts Meet
On Love's Gentle Shore

GEORGIA COAST ROMANCE

A Sparkle of Silver
A Glitter of Gold
A Dazzle of Diamonds

GEORGIA
COAST
ROMANCE

A DAZZLE *of* DIAMONDS

LIZ JOHNSON

a division of Baker Publishing Group
Grand Rapids, Michigan

Published by Revell
a division of Baker Publishing Group
PO Box 6287, Grand Rapids, MI 49516-6287
www.revellbooks.com

Printed in the United States of America

Library of Congress Cataloging-in-Publication Data
Names: Johnson, Liz, 1981– author.
Title: A dazzle of diamonds / Liz Johnson.
Description: Grand Rapids, Michigan : Revell, [2020] | Series: Georgia coast
    romance; 3
Identifiers: LCCN 2020001217 | ISBN 9780800729424 (paperback)
Subjects: GSAFD: Love stories. | Christian fiction.
Classification: LCC PS3610.O3633 D39 2020 | DDC 813/.6—dc23
LC record available at https://lccn.loc.gov/2020001217

ISBN 978-0-8007-3859-4 (casebound)

Scripture quotations are from The Holy Bible, English Standard Version® (ESV®), copyright © 2001 by Crossway, a publishing ministry of Good News Publishers. Used by permission. All rights reserved. ESV Text Edition: 2016

Published in association with Books & Such Literary Management, 52 Mission Circle, Suite 122, PMB 170, Santa Rosa, CA 95409-5370, www.booksandsuch.com.

20   21   22   23   24   25   26   7   6   5   4   3   2   1

For my sweet readers.

Your letters and messages inspire
and encourage me.
May you always search for God
as for hidden treasure.

If you call out for insight
and raise your voice for understanding,
if you seek it like silver
and search for it as for hidden treasures,
then you will understand the fear of the LORD
and find the knowledge of God.

Proverbs 2:3–5

ONE

Penelope Jean Hunter loved every wedding she'd ever been to. Except her own.

Oh, it wasn't the colorful tulips in every bouquet and centerpiece or the peach and lavender bridesmaid dresses. They were sunny and bright and perfect for spring nuptials in Georgia.

It wasn't the chocolate ganache cake with raspberry filling. That had been sublime. She would know—she'd eaten half of the top layer in one sitting. In the middle of her living room floor. Surrounded by the fluffy tulle of her gorgeous dress.

It had been perfect. It had all been exactly as she'd pictured it as a child.

Her wedding had been pure magic. All except for one thing—or, rather, one man. The groom.

Who hadn't bothered to show up.

Who now stood in the entrance to her office beside the prettiest woman Penelope had ever seen.

"Hello." The woman rushed forward, her smile broad and her eyes filled with the unmistakable glow of a soon-to-be bride. "I'm Emmaline Adams. We spoke on the phone." Emmaline reached out her hand, and Penelope had no choice but to shake it, even though her gaze never left the man trailing behind.

Emmaline followed the direction of her eyes and pointed with her chin. "This is my fiancé, Winston St. Cloud."

Oh, no need for introductions. The only problem was Penelope didn't know if Emmaline was supposed to know that. She didn't know how much Winston had told Emmaline about their past, about the previous wedding he helped plan.

All right, that wasn't entirely fair. He hadn't done a single thing to help plan that wedding.

Penelope couldn't read his face beyond the surprise written across his raised eyebrows and unblinking eyes. He clearly hadn't known he would run into her here. And she had no desire to reveal their history thirty seconds after meeting the poor bride.

Well, she did *want* to say just what she thought of Winston. But that was no way to keep a job she loved. Just because *her* wedding had been an unmitigated disaster didn't mean she would ever do anything to jeopardize other marriages she helped launch.

"Winston." She nodded in his direction, but she couldn't force herself to reach out to shake his hand. He didn't seem to mind, as rigid as a statue.

Emmaline's smile dimmed, in fragments first and then all at once. "Do you . . . ?"

Penelope put on her very best smile and ushered the other woman deeper into the office. "We used to be friends. A while ago." Three years, one month, and four days, to be exact. Not that she was keeping count. And technically, she'd seen him three days after that. He'd wanted to apologize. She'd wanted to shove his grandmother's two-carat diamond ring up his nose. But that's not what Southern ladies did. So she'd pulled the rock off her finger and thrown it at him.

And now Emmaline Adams was wearing it.

Eyes closed, Penelope took a deep breath. She could be civil. More than that, she could be professional. She was completely over Winston St. Cloud. She rarely thought of him anymore. Except in those fleeting moments when she wondered if she'd missed her last chance.

Her smile still pasted in place, she opened her eyes just as Winston opened his mouth.

"How have you been?" His voice was still deep, but it held a note of uncertainty.

"Fine. Great, really. Everything's going really well." She stood up a little straighter. That had sounded pretty believable.

Good. It was the truth.

"I didn't know you worked here."

Her eyes darted around her office before it clicked that he meant he hadn't known she worked at the Savannah River Hall. "I'm sure you didn't." What else could she say? He wouldn't have sought her out. He wouldn't have come looking for her. She'd started as the event manager at the Hall after their would-have-been wedding.

Shaking off every memory and trace of bitterness, Penelope looked directly at Emmaline. "So . . . let me show you around."

Emmaline nodded eagerly, grabbing Winston's hand. She was either unaware of the strain in their interaction or willing to overlook it. Penelope would too.

Waving her hand toward the door from her office, she ushered them into the event space. "This is such a unique venue—right on River Street and in the heart of Savannah's history." She marched down the short hallway that connected her office to the venue and then stepped out of the way as she swung the door open.

Emmaline's mouth dropped open as she walked into the cavernous room that had been decorated for the next day's event. "This is . . . so much bigger than the pictures. Winston, look."

He nodded.

Penelope strolled in behind them, waiting for him to say something. When he didn't, she pointed out a few of her favorite features of the room. "We can customize décor to your theme, like the Hollywood letters across the front, or we can do something gentle and feminine. The cement floors can be dressed up or down, and we have all the furniture pieces you'll need—up to twenty round tables, plus a dance floor. If you can get Winston out on it, that is." She chomped into her bottom lip and shook her head quickly. She should not have said that.

Emmaline's eyebrows rose, but a sweet smile danced across her lips. "Oh, we're taking lessons."

Of course they were. Winston had refused to take even a single foxtrot class with her when she'd asked. She'd missed that and a dozen other warning signs that he didn't truly love her. At least not in the way he loved Emmaline. That was more than clear as he squeezed his fiancée's hand and stared into her eyes.

The phone in her pocket rang, and Penelope snatched it free. Anabelle Haywood, president of the Ladies' Historical League of Savannah. Who was just about to confirm a weeklong charity event at the Hall.

Penelope gave Emmaline a brief smile. "Take your time and look around. I'll be just a moment."

Emmaline nodded as she sashayed farther into the room, and Penelope scooted back toward her office. "Mrs. Haywood. How can I help you?"

"Well, I heard the most awful rumor today, and I just had to call and see if there was an ounce of truth to it."

Penelope's stomach lurched, and she leaned against the ancient brick wall, her throat dry in a split second. "Why, I'm not sure what you mean."

"It's about that man—your friend, the one running for sheriff."

"Tucker?" That didn't make any sense. There weren't any rumors floating around town about him. In fact, he was actively sequestering himself to keep any from sprouting up. Work, home, and campaign events only. Especially after he accidentally got his name on the ballot for the special election in the first place.

Anabelle tsked. "Do you have more than one friend running for office?"

Penelope scrambled for a response. "No, of course not. I'm just . . . well, I'm surprised. What is it you've heard?"

"You know that I'm not one to gossip."

That was not entirely true. By the end of their first encounter, Penelope had learned all sorts of things she'd never wanted to know about the self-proclaimed caretakers of Savannah's history, the women of the Ladies' League.

Sure enough, Anabelle required no push to continue. "But there's been some talk about your friend Tucker's family."

"His family?" Tucker was the only child of a well-respected doctor and a beloved elementary schoolteacher. They'd both retired in the last year. And she would know if Tucker's relationship status changed.

"Yes." The word came out a near hiss. "Apparently they were involved in . . . well . . . some traitorous acts."

"Excuse me?" The words popped out much louder than she'd anticipated, and she peeked over her shoulder to make sure Emmaline and Winston were still otherwise engaged. They were spinning slowly in the center of the dance floor.

Please, Lord, let them find another venue.

"Well, they certainly had some plans for that treasure."

She bit her tongue to keep from repeating that last word, but she couldn't find a response. What treasure? She'd know if the Westbrooks were hiding a treasure. After living next door for most of her childhood and twenty-five years of friendship, they were nearly family.

"And you know the good ladies of the League can't be affiliated with anything like that."

"Of course not. But . . ." Anabelle had made a jump that Penelope couldn't follow. There wasn't a connection between Tucker and the Ladies' League, except . . .

"I'd hate to have to find another location for our event. But with all this nonsense with Tucker and you being on his campaign committee . . . well, I'm sure you understand my predicament."

A heavy silence more than implied the threat in her words. If Penelope didn't fix this—whatever it was—she would lose a client, an event, and probably her professional reputation.

"I'll take care of it."

"See that you do, dear. Quickly."

"Yes, ma'am." That was the only appropriate response when she'd been scolded at twelve, and not much had changed in more than twenty years.

Anabelle ended the call, and Penelope could only stare at the screen of her phone as it dimmed and then went to sleep. It provided no answers and no clear direction, and for a moment she couldn't formulate her next steps. She needed a plan, a checklist.

But first, she needed to know what *nonsense* Tucker had landed in.

"I really love it!"

Penelope jumped, pulled from Tucker's nonsense back to Emmaline and Winston, who were thinking about starting the rest of their lives in this very room.

Forcing a smile, Penelope turned toward them. "I'm so glad you like it."

"We have one more venue to look at later this week. We'll have at least two hundred guests, so we might need more space. But I'll call you as soon as we decide."

With a brief nod, Penelope pressed her hand to her stomach. She tried to smile, but it wasn't easy to cover the war within. She needed to fill the Hall for the summer. She also needed to keep her sanity, and having Winston close for the next few months was not conducive to that.

This day was not going as planned. First Winston's return and then Tucker's mess.

Tackle the first thing first.

That was her motto when the lists got too long. And the first thing she had to do was make sure her job was secure. Then she'd figure out how to keep Winston out of her space and off her mind this summer.

Tucker Westbrook glared at the newspaper on his office desk and growled low in the back of his throat.

"You okay in there, boss?" Betty Sue Templeton sang her question but made no move to get up from her desk in the front office to check on him.

"Have you seen the newspaper today?"

"Yes, sir. Did you forget to tell me something?"

No. Yes. Mostly no. "Maybe."

"That's a pretty big picture of you in the paper for a 'maybe,' boss."

Yeah. He knew it too. The headline also seemed twice as big as all the others on the op-ed page. Maybe that was just because his name jumped out from the print. Or maybe it was because he couldn't stop staring at the black-and-white picture of himself. It was his official work photo, the one on his company's website, and about four years old—pre-beard. But it was unmistakably him. And the question below the image couldn't be missed.

A Traitor on the Ballot?

The good people of Savannah could forgive a lot, but Confederate traitors? Well, that was asking too much. Even 150 years after the war had ended.

"Good morning, Penny. He's in his office." Betty Sue's greeting was warm as always, but Penelope Jean's response was little more than a mumbled grunt. "Boss, you have a visitor."

By the time Betty Sue's voice reached his office, so had PJ. A decidedly scowling and cranky PJ, her nose red and her arms crossed. "You didn't answer your phone last night."

"Good morning to you too."

She sighed and shuffled across his office, dodging a couple stacks of file folders on the floor and sliding into one of the empty chairs on the other side of his desk. "I'm sorry. How was your day?"

Somewhere between not great and terrible. But given the frown that had replaced her usual toothy smile, it was possible hers had been worse. "How was yours?"

She frowned harder than before, wrinkling the corners of her lips. "Terrible . . . and confusing."

"All right. I'll bite. What was so terrible?"

"Winston came into the Hall yesterday."

The words were a punch to his gut. He'd been relieved to see that selfish jellyfish slink out of their lives. He'd hated that PJ had been hurt, but he'd never thought Winston worthy of her particular brand of verve and humor.

"He came to see you?"

She shook her head, the corner of her eye twitching as she ran her fingers through the end of her long brown ponytail. "He came in with his new fiancée. He's helping to plan *their* wedding."

Tucker's mouth slowly dropped open, and he leaned his elbows on the overloaded desk before him. He tried to find a response, but there was none. What was he supposed to say when the guy who had broken his best friend's heart casually strolled back into her life? He could think of a few choice words, but they were all ones he didn't let his staff use on the job.

PJ waved her hand through the air like it didn't matter. "They're thinking about having their reception at the Hall at the end of August."

"This August?" It seemed an insignificant detail, but it was the only thing he could latch on to.

"Yes. This August. As in three months from now. As in, if they decide on the Hall, I'm going to have to put in extra hours to get all the details in place in time."

Tucker pushed himself from behind his desk and walked around to meet her. Tugging on her arm, he pulled her up and into a tight hug. "I'm sorry. This stinks."

"I know." Her words carried a slight tremor, and he could visualize the quiver in her full lower lip without even seeing it.

"Can you convince them to have it elsewhere?"

She nodded into his chest. "I'm going to try."

"So what was confusing about yesterday?" He almost didn't ask. He couldn't handle it if she confessed to being conflicted about her feelings for Winston. It had been bad enough watching that jerk crush her spirit once. Tucker would rather spend another summer in the Middle East than see her go through that again.

She wiggled out of his embrace and looked him in the face. "I got a weird phone call. About you, actually."

"Me?"

"Anabelle Haywood, from the Ladies' League. She said you're in some—and I quote—'nonsense.'"

His stomach sank, and he couldn't keep his face from folding. "Have you seen today's paper?"

With a hard shake of her head, she shot him a look that said he should know better. "Only retirees read the actual newspaper. Well, retirees and you. I wait for Instagram and Facebook and *Southern Weddings* to tell me what I need to know. Why?"

He couldn't hold back an eye roll. "Nice. Way to be an

informed citizen. Don't you know there's an election coming up?"

She pursed her lips and narrowed her eyes—a scowl fully implied. She'd been shooting him the same look since he'd stolen her after-school snack in the third grade. "Hey, I'm just helping you plan your campaign events. I'm not your political advisor or campaign manager."

All the same, he nodded toward the desk and the open paper atop the reports from the night before.

She leaned over his desk, snatched up the local newspaper, and scanned the headlines. Her eyebrows drew tight, and the tip of her nose wrinkled as her eyes darted back and forth. When she looked up, fire filled her eyes. "What is this supposed to mean?"

"What do you think it means?"

"I think Buddy Jepson is trying to discredit you just to win the election."

The letter was unsigned, but that didn't mean Buddy's prints weren't all over it.

Tucker crossed his arms as he strolled across the room. Leaning his hip against the windowsill, he stared across the square. Outside, the city was rumbling to life, vendors already setting up for the City Market and praying toward the overcast sky that the rain would hold off until night.

When PJ heaved a short breath, he glanced back over his shoulder. "No *just* about it. He wants to win, all right, and he'll do anything to make it happen."

"But how can he accuse your family of being part of some hundred-year-old conspiracy without proof?" She waved the newspaper. "He can't do that."

"Hundred-and-fifty-five-year-old conspiracy."

She rolled her eyes, her heels clicking across the wood floor, and smacked the paper against his shoulder. "I'm being serious."

"I am too. But it doesn't make any difference. The writer says he has proof that names my family among smugglers and thieves."

"But . . ." Her face turned red, her fist wrinkling his black-and-white picture at her side. "But what about the Marines? I mean, everyone knows you served two tours in the Middle East." She waved her hand around his office. "And you provide security for half the businesses this side of Abercorn Street. Plus this is just in the op-ed section. No one would believe this . . . this . . . *nonsense*." Her voice rose with every word, until he could hear Betty Sue stirring in the outer office.

Her steam gone, PJ dropped her chin and gazed up at him through black lashes. "They wouldn't believe it. Would they?"

Her question went down like bad catfish and limp potatoes, yet he had no choice but to swallow it. He'd faced worse than Buddy Jepson before. And he wasn't afraid to stand up for what he believed.

The problem was, there was no winning this fight.

Tilting his head back, he stared at the exposed ventilation duct that ran the length of the room and let out a slow breath. "Anabelle Haywood called you about it yesterday?"

"Uh-huh."

"Then half the city knew before the newspaper even ran the op-ed."

She leaned toward him, reaching out like it was her turn to hold him, but then she pulled back. "Will anybody care? I mean, really? Maybe this will all blow over in a week."

"And maybe Mrs. Haywood will cancel her Fort Pulaski Remembrance Picnic this year." Yeah, that wasn't going to happen. Not after thirty-plus years of hoop-skirted Southern belles serving sweet tea and cherry punch to a packed audience, with Anabelle Haywood holding court at the entrance.

PJ rolled her lip beneath her teeth, her gaze targeted somewhere near his feet, her hands still balled into fists at her sides.

Maybe he was the one who needed to be comforted, but he wanted more than anything to pull her into his arms, take a deep breath of her citrus shampoo, and know that everything was going to be all right. Because it always had been that way. As long as they were together, they'd been able to conquer the world. Even when he was halfway around the world, she'd known to tuck gummy worms and caramels into his care packages. And she'd never sent one without a handwritten note. It was never long or boring, just a reminder she was there. They would get through it together.

But this was uncharted territory.

Dropping his chin to his chest, he sighed. "I'm going to figure out how to fix this."

"What? The election?"

Lifting one shoulder, he turned his gaze back to the buzzing market just opening for business. "There's no coming back from an accusation like this." She opened her mouth, but he held up a finger. "People here still care about the Civil War. They may know that the outcome was best for our country, that it put an end to a terrible wrong. But they care. They love this city and this state, and their history. They brag about being the only city Sherman didn't burn in his march to the sea. They can trace their lineage back to

19

soldiers who fought for this city, for the Confederacy. So can I. So can you, for that matter. Whether it's right or wrong, this city thrives on Southern pride."

"We could, you know, *fix* it."

He reached for something to throw at her, but her face broke into a wide smile before he could find anything he was willing to lose.

"Kidding, kidding." She held up her hands and laughed it off. "No election tampering, I promise. But maybe there's another way. Maybe your family was really smuggling to support the South."

"Well, that would be great. One way, the majority of the town—including the wealthy donors I need to finance my campaign—refuses to support me because they think my ancestors were traitors. The other way, transplants—who don't give a lick about Southern pride but still vote—find out my family was going above and beyond to break the law, and my entire security platform is called into question. I'm having a hard time seeing how either way is going to lead to a win."

"Is it too late to back out?"

He pinched the bridge of his nose between his thumb and forefinger and squeezed his eyes closed. If only. If only he hadn't let Buddy Jepson get him all riled up at Maribella's—in front of a reporter. He should have just gotten his cup of coffee and chocolate croissant and walked out. But no. He couldn't let Buddy jaw on and on about how no one needed to rush to make changes in their county.

Tucker knew the truth because he'd installed a new security camera at the county jail and had immediately seen how an updated system would improve security for guards and detainees alike. And the whole city had seen how woefully understaffed the sheriff's department was in the aftermath of Hurricane Lorenzo the year before. The department had done their best, but Tucker had some plans that would make them more efficient until he could convince the county to hire more deputies. The county needed to make some changes for the sake of its residents and local businesses. Buddy might not care about them, but Tucker sure did.

He'd told Buddy as much in the middle of the coffee shop. And his words had ended up in the newspaper nearly verbatim. Before Tucker knew it, he'd landed on the special election ballot—about ten years ahead of schedule.

"If I back out now, I doubt this community will give me another chance." He didn't have to tell PJ that wearing a sheriff's badge had always been a dream.

"All right then. Can't back out of the race. Can't afford to be branded a traitor or a thief. You're just going to have to prove you're not." She whipped the article back in front of her face. Silence hung for a long moment except for the crinkling paper. "'It has come to the attention of this local resident that the long line of Westbrooks may not have been as loyal to the great state of Georgia and the good people of Savannah as one would hope, especially when one of those Westbrooks is running for sheriff.'" She let out a disbelieving puff, and he could practically see her rolling her eyes behind the newsprint. "*Local resident*, my eye."

PJ straightened the paper and started reading again. "'A recently discovered letter from a high-ranking officer during the height of the war proves the Westbrooks were involved in undermining the Southern cause . . .' Blah, blah, blah . . . 'It suggests a missing treasure, one smuggled and stolen by the Westbrooks to support Grant and his men, that may not have reached its intended recipient.'"

His heart slammed against his ribs, and he shoved himself off the wall, staring hard at her even as she droned on, reading those insipid lies.

When she finally dropped the paper, her blue eyes were bigger than usual and filled with pity. "This is ridiculous."

"Is it?"

"Of course it is. I mean, you can't prove a negative. What are you going to do?"

A grin tugged at the corner of his mouth. "Well, if there's a treasure out there, let's find it."

Her arms fell limply to her sides. "A what?"

"You read it. There was a treasure that was supposedly lost. If we can find that, maybe we can find the truth. And if we know the truth—what my family was really involved in—then at least we know what we're fighting."

"Okay." She nodded slowly, thoughtfully. He could practically see her mentally constructing her list. "The only person I know who knows anything about finding a lost treasure is Carter Hale at the maritime museum. Want me to call him?"

Tucker didn't even pause to consider. He couldn't fight what he didn't know. But if he didn't fight, he was bound to fail.

"Do it."

TWO

ucker bounded up the cement steps of the Savannah Maritime Museum, checking his watch again. Two minutes to spare.

The front windows were always bright against the two-story gray building that had been the home of a wealthy Southern banker before the war. Even after almost two hundred years, it was as beautiful as ever, green ivy snaking up the corners and wrapping around the trellis along the adjacent wall.

Pushing the wooden door open with his shoulder, he stepped inside. The entryway/gift shop was empty, the rooms beyond silent. PJ had texted him to meet her here, but she'd offered exactly zero details.

"PJ? Carter? You here?"

Carter Hale, museum director and local treasure-hunting hero, materialized from the darkness of the room off the entry with a smile and quick handshake. "Thanks for meeting me. Is Penelope coming?"

"I think so." He looked over his shoulder like she might

appear, but the doors remained closed. "Do you have something for me?"

Carter's smile dipped. "I wish I had better news."

"I'm here. I'm here." PJ's voice arrived before she opened the door, out of breath and panting. She swung inside like she owned the place, her arms packed with colorful file folders and her ever-present spiral planner. Thumping her load onto the wooden counter and wiping her forehead with the back of her hand, she blinked at him and Carter. "What did I miss?"

"I just got here, and Carter was about to share his bad news."

PJ's hopeful smile flickered, but her cheeks bunched as she fought to keep it in place even as her blue eyes lost their glow. "Really? It's not good?"

Carter shook his head. "I'm sorry, but I saw the letter. Mr. Jepson brought it in for authentication."

"It can't be real." PJ shook her head like she refused to allow such a monstrosity to occur. Not on her watch. And certainly not when it ruined her plans.

Tucker reached for any hope. "Were you able to confirm it?"

Carter shifted his weight from one foot to the other. "I don't have the kind of equipment needed to authenticate the letter, so I sent him over to the university for that. But whether true or faked, there's definitely a letter that drags the Westbrook name through the mud."

"Westbrooks in general?" Tucker asked.

"Daniel Westbrook."

Tucker's gaze darted to PJ, whose eyebrows had bunched together across her porcelain forehead. "Daniel is a family name. He's my fourth great-grandfather, I think. I'm pretty sure. My aunt Shirley would know for sure. Either way, it's my family."

Carter sighed. "I'm sorry."

PJ tapped her finger against her stack of folders, her nail ticking like a clock that promised there wasn't enough time in the world to fix this. "Can you tell us what it said? Exactly?"

A grin popped into place, and Carter said, "I'll do you one better. I made a copy." He disappeared into an adjoining room, heading toward the offices in the back and the new addition being built onto the house following the discovery of a 250-year-old sunken ship the year before.

Tucker leaned his elbows against the counter beside PJ, resting his head in his hands, wishing he could soothe the thunder inside. "So there really is a letter."

She patted his arm, but the action didn't match the question that followed. "Did you think there wasn't?"

He let that question bounce around inside him for a few seconds. Had he thought that? No. But he'd allowed himself to hope so. Evidence changed everything.

Her hand was small on his back, but there was a fierceness in her stance, her shoulders square and unrelenting. "I'm really sorry. But we're just getting started. There's so much we can do."

"Let me guess." He pushed himself up enough that he could look down at her. "You have some ideas."

She let out a giggle. It was more self-deprecating than nervous, but she didn't look up at him as she shuffled through some of the papers in her folder. "I had a few."

A piece of yellow legal paper got loose and fluttered to the ground. He stooped to pick it up, only glancing at it for a second. Until Winston's name caught his eye. That deserved a closer look.

The top of the page showed a line in all caps in her distinctive penmanship: OP KMJ. It was followed by three lines, each beginning with a box yet to be checked:

☐ Fix Tucker's nonsense

☐ Have a backup—several large events at the Hall

☐ Backup to the backup—Winston and Emmaline's wedding

"OP KMJ?" he asked.

Her cheeks flushed a deep pink, and she bit her lips together so long that he thought she might not answer him. Finally, she shrugged. "Operation Keep My Job."

"You really think you might lose it?"

"I think if Anabelle Haywood decides to move her event, Madeline won't hesitate to show her displeasure. Even if she just cuts my hours, I won't be able to pay my rent."

He suddenly felt a little sick to his stomach. "Which is why I'm at the top of your list."

She nodded, the pink in her cheeks fading until her skin took on a sad pallor. "We have to fix this."

"But if we can't . . ." Her list said it all. She had a couple backups.

"We're going to fix it, but it might . . ." She sighed, picking at the corner of one of her folders. "If it takes longer than a week, I have to be ready. I can't give Madeline any reason to let me go."

"So you're going to try to get Winston to have his wedding at the Hall?"

Her smile looked like it took every ounce of effort inside her. "Yes."

"No." He pushed himself off the counter and waved the ridiculous checklist in her face. "I won't let you do this. This is my fault. My election. You don't have to be wrapped up in this."

"I don't think you have a choice in the matter. Unless you want to call Mrs. Haywood and convince her that we're no longer friends."

The paper crinkled in his fist. "I could do that. I can be very convincing."

She wrapped her silky fingers around his clenched ones, slowly releasing his hold and recapturing her list. Then she patted his arm like a mother comforting her child. "Thank you for offering, but you've been my best friend for twenty-five years, and I expect to get at least another twenty-five years of friendship out of you. I'm not going to let an old biddy like Mrs. Haywood tell me I have to change my plan."

"But Winston—"

She cut him off with a raised hand. "I'll figure it out. I'll make it work. I mean . . . it's not . . . I'm not looking forward to it."

He could see the truth written in her eyes. Dread. She'd rather meet up with a rabid raccoon than have to see Winston and his new fiancée. But she'd do it. For Tucker.

"I can't let you do that."

Her eyebrows nearly reached her hairline. "*Let* me? *You're* not going to let *me*?"

He sighed, holding back the urge to shred her list. Instead, he scrubbed his hand over his hair. "You know what I mean. You're trying to help me, and it's making your life miserable."

"Ha!" She laughed in his face. "Thank you for trying to be all chivalrous, but I'm not doing this for you. This is the price I'm willing to pay to keep a job I love. Would I rather not have to see my ex-fiancé on the regular? Yes. Am I willing to? Yes. Because I'm fine. I'm over him."

He squinted hard at her, wishing he could know for sure if that was true.

As best friends, they talked about nearly everything. But somewhere around the start of high school they'd come to an unspoken agreement—boyfriends and girlfriends were off-limits. That was probably around the time Tad Andrews had asked her to the homecoming dance. Tucker had been pretty vocal about his disapproval. Worse, he hadn't known why it bothered him.

So after Winston didn't show up on her wedding day, Tucker had done the only thing he could. He'd held her.

They'd never talked about it again. Not using words, anyway.

"You would know," he said.

She stiffened, her eyes scorching him. "Yes, I would. And I do. I am just fine." She plucked a piece of paper from one of her folders and waved it in his face. "But you are not, so I'm going to help your sorry little self."

He nodded quickly, because determined PJ was not to be trifled with.

When she slapped the paper on the counter, he got a good look at her handwriting again. She had scribbled "Op Fix Tucker's Nonsense" across the top of the page. Below it, three unchecked boxes sat in a neat column. The rest of the page was empty.

"So, you're going to help me, but . . ." He waved at her page.

"But what? I'm going to help you. The plan is . . . in progress." She put her hand on her hip and glared at the empty page. Her dark brown hair was pulled into a ponytail, but an escaped strand curled over her ear. Undoubtedly, she'd twirled it around her finger during moments of frustration earlier in the day. Her blue eyes narrowed to focus on the single page, and her full lips pursed then relaxed several times in a row. Her thinking face.

It was one of his favorites. Although her someone-kicked-a-dog avenging face and over-the-moon happy face were pretty fantastic too.

She rubbed her hand over the waist of her black skirt, and he couldn't help but follow the motion with his gaze. The fabric sat snug against her hip and followed the line of her leg to her knee. There was some word for the design. He didn't know it. He didn't need to. He only knew that whenever she wore skirts like this, it made him look a little too long at her legs, a little too close at the dimple on her knee.

"What are you staring at?"

He jerked his gaze back to hers. "Nothing. Just thinking."

"I'm going to get this list fleshed out. I hope Carter can help with that."

Tucker nodded. Better that she thought he was thinking about the letter than what was really going through his mind. Which he should not—would not—let happen again. So what if PJ had a set of legs on her? He needed her in his life as a friend, and she'd never given him any indication that she'd thought of him as more.

Penelope spun at the sound of Carter's return, shooting one more questioning glance in Tucker's direction. His furrowed eyebrows hung heavy across his face, weighing down his usual smile, and she had a terrible suspicion that it had everything to do with the return of Winston St. Cloud.

"Sorry about the wait. My assistant, Hazel, decided I needed a cleaner desk and moved the letter, but I've got it here." Carter held out a sheet of white printer paper tucked inside a plastic protector. The curled edges of the original page had been captured in the copy, the scrawled handwriting slanted heavily to the right.

She reached for it at the same time as Tucker, and with a glance she asked if she should read it. He nodded. Leaning into him, she pinched her side of the page with two fingers and tried to ignore the earthy scent that wrapped around her like an embrace as she read the words aloud.

Colonel Covington Knowles
Richmond, Virginia
January 4, 1865

My investigation has met with a brick wall. I have turned over every rock in Savannah, but evidence of the thieves dissolves as soon as it appears. It seems to be as real as the ghost stories that swirl through the streets at night, and I am no more able to latch on to it as to the mist in the morning.

The cargo to have been delivered this November past has vanished. A ship's worth of gold and jewels and arms from

France was taken and has disappeared into the night, surely scurried away by the traitors among us. They can have only one intent, to hinder our Cause and injure your good self. Whether they seek to send all support north or arm themselves for an internal uprising is unclear. There are still Southerners about the city, though men in uniform are absent save the Yankee invaders.

I have identified the leader as one Daniel Westbrook. I am certain he is involved, as he led a band of thieves and smugglers about town in the wee hours of the night. Several locals have confirmed his involvement, but there is no evidence of the missing cargo and no sign of the deserter. Westbrook sits piously in church every Sunday, hands folded and head bowed. 'Tis a ruse of the worst sort.

I will watch him relentlessly. I must believe that his stolen gain is still within Savannah, for he has yet to pass it off.

I will see this treasure restored and put to its rightful use, and I will see Westbrook hung for the traitor he is.

> For the Cause
> and Confederacy,
> Fox

Tucker sighed. "Well . . ."

Penelope fought to find the right sentiment, but words escaped her. In the end she reached around his waist and hugged his side. He returned the embrace, his breaths coming out in strained, controlled gasps.

"I'm really sorry about this, man." Carter shoved his hand through his already wild brown hair.

"And you don't have any idea where it came from?" Penelope hated the desperation in her voice.

Carter shook his head. "But I'm pretty sure Buddy is going to try to get it shown somewhere. He asked if I'd put it on display here."

Tucker's back tensed before he stepped out from her encircling arm. "You turned him down?"

"Of course I did. I'm all for showing off history, but that letter hasn't been authenticated. And I'd never add a piece to my collection that would tarnish someone's reputation."

Tucker sighed, his shoulders relaxing and his eyes closing for a moment.

Until Carter continued. "Even if I have been trying to put together an exhibit on Civil War smugglers."

Tucker jolted, his eyes now open and his mouth agape. Penelope wasn't struck silent though. "You've been researching smugglers in this area? You can help us find the treasure. That'll prove the Westbrooks weren't involved."

With another shake of his head, Carter dashed her hopes. "I'm just getting started on my research. I don't have much—definitely not anything as interesting as a lost treasure."

"Do you think it's out there?" Tucker asked.

Carter crossed his arms and bowed his head, seemingly studying the carpet between his feet for a long moment. "I don't know. The Civil War was a long time ago."

"But you found a ship that was way older than that." Penelope squeezed her hands together at her waist, praying for a scrap of good news.

"Yeah, well, it was under 150 feet of water. It was a lot easier to hide for so long. And most of those looking for underwater treasure don't have the right equipment. It's a lot easier to find treasure when all you need is a map and a shovel. The smuggled treasure mentioned in the letter could have been found a hundred years ago and never recorded."

The wind left Penelope's sails, and she sagged against the counter as Tucker shoved his hands into the pockets of his jeans.

"It's worth looking for," he said. With a shrug, he added, "I've got a shovel. Too bad I don't have a map."

"I don't have one either," Carter said. "But I'm happy to offer you the only thing I do have."

Pushing herself off the countertop, Penelope leaned forward. He'd been holding out on them. "What's that?"

"Jethro Coleman."

Tucker raised his eyebrows, and she was pretty sure her face mirrored his response. Jethro Coleman wasn't known for being particularly useful. Not since his wife had passed and he'd picked up the bottle, anyway.

That didn't stop Carter from scribbling down a phone number on her legal pad. "Call him. He knows more about Georgia's Civil War history than nearly every historian in the area—combined."

Mentally scratching the number from her pad, she shook her head. "I think we'll—"

"Call him." Carter's eyes lost that chummy look, the dimples in his cheeks disappearing. "If that treasure was ever found, he'll know. If it wasn't, he'll know where to start looking."

Tucker nodded, held out his hand, and thanked Carter for his help. Then he ushered her from the building and down the steps, his hand hovering at the small of her back—completely normal. Except for a strange feeling deep in her stomach.

It had to be the shrimp she'd eaten for lunch.

Around the corner he stopped to face her, his eyebrows drawn tight. "What do you think? Should we talk with Jethro?"

Everything inside her wanted to scream that it was a fool's errand. Jethro wouldn't—couldn't—help them, even if they pumped a carafe of coffee into him.

But Carter had found his own treasure.

He'd had a diary for that though. He'd had his family history spelled out for him. Right there on the page.

"That's it." She snapped her fingers, and Tucker snorted.

"You forget to share something with me again?"

She shoved his immovable arm and continued. "Carter had a diary from his family. Maybe we don't need a Georgia historian. We need your family historian."

A smile broke across his face. "I'll call her in the morning."

THREE

"That man is a pompous, arrogant, conniving imbecile."

Penelope's gaze jerked up from the binder on her desk, straight over the heads of the couple sitting across from her. But she still caught the surprise in Emmaline's eyes and the immediate tension in Winston's jaw.

Tucker's head, bowed over the phone in his hand, entered her office first, followed by his square shoulders. "He won't even—" Lifting his gaze, he made eye contact with her and froze. "Pardon me." He tipped his head toward Emmaline. Winston didn't get the same treatment. "I thought we were having lunch."

It took everything inside her not to stare pointedly at Emmaline, who had wanted to see every inch of the property again. "We're running a little long. Can you give me five minutes?"

"Of course." Tucker began to back out of the door. "Sorry to interrupt."

But Emmaline was clearly curious. "Well, who's this?" Her stage whisper stopped Tucker in his tracks, and Penelope crossed and uncrossed her legs beneath her desk, carefully keeping her eyes focused anywhere but on Winston's face.

"This is my— Have you not met Tucker Westbrook? He's running for sheriff, and I thought he'd met the whole town by now."

Emmaline popped from her seat and smoothed her perfectly coiffed blonde waves with one hand, holding out the other as though she was a queen accepting a kiss on her ring. "Emmaline Adams. It's a pleasure." Batting her thick lashes at him, she offered a demure smile. Totally appropriate. A little sickening.

Tucker took her fingers in an awkward shake and nodded. "The pleasure is all mine."

Pressing a hand to her stomach, Penelope choked back the fullness rising in her throat. She tried for a smile not unlike the one Emmaline had just given. She was pretty sure she failed. Badly. "Emmaline is marrying Winston."

Tucker finally gave the other man a brief glance. "St. Cloud." His voice was more growl than usual, and his eyes narrowed, but Penelope might have been the only one to notice. Then again, a solid assessment of Winston revealed his hardened posture and tight lips.

The two men had never gotten along. No matter how hard Penelope had tried, they'd barely been civil toward each other all through the two years she'd been with Winston. Of course, that meant she'd had an understanding shoulder to cry on when she needed Tucker. A strong, broad shoulder.

It seemed not much had changed in three years, and the thunder crashing between them was nearly audible.

"I'll just let y'all finish up here." Tucker pushed the door open behind him and caught her eye. "Let me know when you're ready."

The moment he disappeared, Emmaline slipped into her seat. "Oh my." Her neck and cheeks flushed. "Well, he's quite a presence. How long have you and he been . . ." She let her raised eyebrows finish her question.

Penelope immediately looked at Winston, her own cheeks burning. "Oh, um . . . We're . . . It's not . . ."

But Winston didn't give her a chance to finish. Pushing himself up, he reached for Emmaline's elbow. "We should get going. I have to get back to work."

Penelope jumped from her chair, following them across the room. "So should I prepare the contract?" There was more than a note of pleading in her voice, and she could just about bite off her tongue. Clearing her throat, she tried again. "I'd hate for y'all to miss our last open weekend in August."

Winston's gaze narrowed, but the firm line of his lips didn't move. If she was a betting woman, she'd wager that he'd yet to tell Emmaline about their past. Had he even told her that he'd been engaged? Promised another woman she was the one? Ruined another wedding?

Emmaline was oblivious, tugging on his arm and gazing into his face like he'd invented buttermilk biscuits. Running a bright pink nail down his arm until she clasped her hand in his, she blinked lashes so long they had to be fake. "What do you think, babe? I really love it."

Penelope held in a full-body shudder and forced her smile to stay put. Her prayers vacillated between asking that he'd agree and begging for him to run.

He looked at his betrothed and then glanced back at Penelope. She could read the doubt in his eyes. But when he turned back toward Emmaline, the tension in his jaw leaked away. "Whatever you want, sweetie."

Emmaline dipped at the knee and squealed her delight. "We'll take it!"

Penelope nodded, forcing her smile to show her teeth. "Wonderful. I'll get the contract put together, and we'll need the fifty percent deposit when you sign. I'll call you in a couple days."

Emmaline's smile dimmed. "Oh. I'm going out of town tomorrow. But Winston can drop off the deposit and sign the contract, right, honey?"

Perfect. Just perfect.

"Oh, I think we're going to have the best time planning this wedding." Emmaline let go of her fiancé and grabbed Penelope's hands, squeezing them with surprising strength. "I can tell already we're going to be wonderful friends. Maybe we could even double-date. It's so hard to find couple friends, you know?"

Nope. Penelope didn't know. Finding friends had never been her problem. Staying a couple had been.

Penelope nodded anyway, mumbling a maybe, ushering them toward the door, and not daring a look in Winston's direction. Then they were gone, promising to wait for her call.

And she was left to wonder why she hadn't denied her relationship with Tucker. Why wouldn't she? There had never been anything more than friendship between them. Except for that crazy semester when she had hoped and prayed that he'd take her to the junior prom.

That was long gone and forgotten, and she'd never even told him about it. Which left too many questions to answer about why she had let Emmaline—and, moreover, Winston—believe otherwise.

The man in question waltzed back into her office. "Listen, I'm sorry about that." Tucker waved in the direction of Emmaline and Winston's retreating figures. "I didn't realize you had an appointment."

She smiled as she leaned over to open her bottom desk drawer and pull out her purse. "You never do."

He shrugged. "I guess I figure if your office door is open, you must be taking visitors."

Patting the palm of her hand against her sticky forehead just enough to remove the dew there but leave her makeup intact, she laughed. "Or you could remember that the AC in my office is still on the fritz."

"I could fix that for you."

She stepped around her desk and led the way out of the office. "Right. And risk Madeline's wrath that an unlicensed unprofessional touched her precious AC unit?"

He lifted his shoulders again, and the half grin she knew so well danced into place. "I'm willing if you are."

Locking the door behind them, she debated actually taking him up on the offer. But he had more important things on his plate. He hadn't planned on this election business, and neither of them could have predicted Buddy Jepson's ridiculous accusations. That was probably why Tucker had been so worked up when he'd first arrived at her office.

He didn't motion in the direction they would go. He didn't ask where she wanted to get lunch. They simply started walking. Together. The shadows of the trees were the same as they always were in May, and she sighed as she stepped into the shade, a brief respite from the early summer sun. It would only get worse, but for now it was bearable. For now she wasn't turning into a puddle. This was flowy-skirt weather, breathable-cotton temps.

She adjusted her pencil skirt and wiggled against the pool at her lower back, a reminder that she still didn't know why she hadn't told Emmaline the truth. She wasn't dating Tucker Westbrook. Not now. Not ever.

She hadn't been planning to stomp her high heels against the uneven sidewalk, but suddenly everything about her outfit and this day felt off. So she did, the clack echoing off the brick buildings surrounding Ellis Square. Whether Tucker had been staring at her before her little outburst or not, she wasn't sure. But he was sure looking at her now.

She cringed. He only raised an eyebrow.

"What? I'm just . . . It's getting really warm out." What a ridiculous thing to say. And he knew it.

"You want to tell me what's going on?"

Nope. That would mean admitting that having Winston back in her life affected more than her job. She was far from ready to claim that, so she started in on him instead. "You want to tell me who has you all riled up?"

He scowled as he opened the door to their lunch spot, Bea's Diner. She scooted into the cool interior and stopped the hostess before she could suggest patio seating. "We'll take a corner booth."

When they were settled into the padded black seats, leaning onto the cool white table, his lips twitched. A smile fought his frown, as though he couldn't quite decide if he were pleased or angry.

"Maybe you should tell me who's a 'conniving imbecile,'" Penelope said. "Which I feel it's my duty to point out is a bit of an oxymoron. I mean, you'd have to have at least a few wits about you to be conniving."

He drummed his fingers against the table and narrowed his eyes at her. "Fine then. He's a callous imbecile."

"Who's *he*?"

"Like you have to ask."

Buddy Jepson. Of course. She'd never doubted, but this strong of a reaction had to have come from somewhere. "What happened?"

"Well, I went to ask him about the letter." His voice rose, annoyance seeping from every syllable, then dropped as their waitress appeared—a college-age girl with pink hair that shone against the black-and-white tile décor of the throwback diner. She offered them both a smile, but there was a hesitancy in her motions, as though she wasn't quite sure what she'd walked into. Penelope gave her best grin and kicked Tucker's foot beneath the table. He smiled too, which seemed to put the waitress at ease.

They both ordered the usual. Biscuits and gravy and extra sausage for Tucker. She had the Cobb salad—extra dressing. When the waitress disappeared, he picked up like they'd never been interrupted—except for his much quieter tone.

"He says he didn't write the op-ed." Pressing his large hands flat against the table, he let out a long sigh. "He said he doesn't know anything about the letter, but of course he does. I mean, the guy could barely look me in the eye."

"You went to his office?" She couldn't keep the shock out of her voice. "I hope you took a witness."

Tucker's shoulders twitched. "I wouldn't assault him."

"I never thought you would. But I wouldn't put it past him to accuse you of it anyway."

Three small lines formed above the bridge of his nose, and she had the worst urge to use her thumb to smooth them out. Instead she grabbed her napkin and spread it across her lap.

"I guess his assistant was around. And I never closed the door behind me." He squeezed his hand into a fist and gave the table a soft thump. "I wanted to beat him before because of his bad policies. Now I want to beat him because of his arrogance and dirty politics." He stared toward the ceiling, his mouth tight and eyes unmoving for a long minute. "It's just not how I wanted this to go down. You know?"

She did know. But she didn't know how to fix the problem for him. No number of to-do lists could make Buddy Jepson play by the unwritten rules of courtesy. So they sat in silence.

It was one of her favorite things about her friendship with Tucker. He wasn't afraid of long pauses, extended moments of silence. And his comfort in the unspoken had rubbed off on her some time before she'd left for college. So she didn't push him to expound. She just watched the muscle in his jaw clench and relax as he worked through his thoughts.

As the waitress slid their plates in front of them ten minutes later, Penelope finally asked, "So how are we going to win the election?"

Tucker dipped his head and said a quick blessing before answering her question. "I don't know." He scooped a big bite onto his fork and shoveled it into his mouth. Gaze lost somewhere over her shoulder, he shook his head.

Her stomach sank to the floor, and she lowered the bite of her salad that was nearly to her lips. "I'm so sorry."

"It's not your fault."

"Well, I know that. But . . . but I sympathize with your plight."

His eyebrows rose in that way that said he thought she was ridiculous but loved her anyway.

"Did you hear back from your aunt Shirley?"

He shook his head. "She's been MIA for a few days now. I asked my dad where she was, and he said he didn't have a clue."

Penelope dropped another bite of bacon and lettuce back to her plate. "Are you worried?"

"Nah. She disappears like this every now and then. Probably on a sixty-somethings singles cruise or learning to surf in Australia."

That sounded about right for Shirley—single for as long as Penelope had known her. All fun and fire, Shirley had taken them camping as kids, taught them how to play pranks, and helped Penelope pick out a prom dress. But there were weeks when she up and disappeared.

"I do know someone with a key to her house."

She looked up quickly. "You think there's anything in the old house?" It had been in the family for at least four generations.

He shrugged. "It's worth a look. She's been after me and my parents to go through the junk in her attic for years, threatening to throw out whatever we don't want. She won't mind if you join me. You interested in digging through a century of history with me?"

"Of course."

"Thanks." Tucker smiled. "Now, you want to tell me why Winston gave me a death glare when he left your office today?"

Scooping up a dollop of gravy with the last of his biscuit, Tucker raised his eyebrows. He expected an answer to his question.

PJ's cheeks turned pink. Not quite as pink as their waitress's hair. But close. And it made Tucker smile harder.

He'd lived for two things for as long as he'd known her—to make her flash those dazzling dimples and turn as pink as possible every single day. So far today he was one for two. Given his morning, he'd call her rosy cheeks a win. The fire in her eyes was an added bonus.

"It's nothing."

"Try again," he said.

"It's not a big deal."

"Nope."

"Ugh." She rolled her eyes and crossed her arms. "I don't really want to talk about it."

"And yet, you will." He wasn't sure what he wanted more—to needle her or to find out what had made that jerk shoot sabers from his eyes. Probably the former. He couldn't care less about Winston, except that clearly something in PJ's office had upset him.

She slipped a bill from her purse and dropped it next to her half-eaten salad before sliding from the booth. "I have to get back to the office."

"Hey!"

She was halfway to the door before he even managed to get his wallet from his pocket, but he threw a couple bills on the table and chased her down. Three steps down the sidewalk, he snagged her elbow and gave her a soft tug, catching her other shoulder before she could stumble.

She kept her head bowed, so he ducked down to look right into her face. "Talk to me, PJ."

"I just . . . I said something really stupid, and I guess maybe he didn't like it. Well, I didn't really *say* anything. It was more like . . . um . . ." She didn't look up, couldn't meet his gaze.

He'd never seen her clam up so completely. He'd seen her with puffy red eyes after hours of crying. He'd seen her laughing so hard she couldn't get out a word. He'd seen her so lost in thought that the rest of the world had fully disappeared to her.

But this was new.

Maybe if he could get her feet moving, he'd get her mouth moving too. Looping her arm through his, he took a step toward her office. The click-clack of her heels followed along, slowly at first. He kept his pace unhurried to match hers until she finally picked up speed. But she still wasn't talking.

Fine. She wouldn't talk? He would. "You know Winston was always jealous of us."

That snapped her head up and got her heels clacking at twice the speed. "He was not."

As they reached River Street and its cobbled stones, they waited for a white tour bus to chug past before walking across the tracks and strolling along the river wall. It wasn't much taller than his waist—a little higher on PJ—but they'd been walking beside it since it reached his chin. PJ liked the water. She liked the wind. She liked the big hotel across the water on the South Carolina shore.

"He sure was, PJ." Winston had been jealous of it all. That Tucker called her PJ—and she'd never minded—and that he knew all those things about her. But how could he not know when she'd told him a million times, when she'd raced down to the wall and jumped up to see the hotel lit up in all its glory at night? "There's only one reason he tried so hard to compete with our history."

"Oh, dear."

He didn't even have to ask her to expound. One look in her direction was enough.

"Well, that makes everything worse." Her little button nose scrunched up, but she didn't break his gaze. "It also makes sense."

"Tell me what happened."

"Emmaline—she assumed that . . . well, I don't think she knows that Winston and I were engaged. And I let her assume something." She pulled her arm free and pressed her hands against the top of the wall, turning toward the hotel. The wind caught a few stray wisps of her dark hair and teased them about.

"What'd you let her assume? That you didn't know him?"

She shook her head softly. "I just wanted him to think I'm okay."

"You are okay."

Turning back to him, she shoved his arm. "Well, I know that. But the last time I saw him, I was"—she took a slow breath—"not quite as collected. I might have dissolved into tears and run off after throwing his ring at him." She grimaced. "It wasn't my finest moment."

"It was also three days after what should have been the happiest day of your life."

"Right?" She sighed. "But that's still the last memory he had of me."

Fair point. But that still didn't explain why Winston had

looked like he was ready to tape Tucker's picture on a dartboard.

PJ cleared her throat as she stepped onto the street, headed back to work, leaving him to chase after her or risk missing what he'd spent the last fifteen minutes trying to get out of her. "So, I might have . . . implied that I was seeing someone."

The words hit him like a strange punch to the chest. Not painful really, but unsettling, unwelcome. It wasn't like he didn't know that PJ would start dating again. Shoot, even he had been on a few dates in the past year. He'd just . . . well, he didn't like the idea of anyone having the power to break her heart like Winston had. That was all this was—a protective instinct.

But at about the moment he got that settled in his mind, he realized she hadn't offered one important piece of information. "You told him you were dating? Who?"

She halted mid-stride and pressed her fists to her hips. "I did not tell him I was dating." Biting her bottom lip and staring toward the too-blue sky, she took a quick breath. "I did not correct Emmaline's assumption that I was dating someone." She took off again like a sprinter and already had the old key in the lock by the time he caught up with her.

Clamping his hand over hers to still the movements, his arms nearly wrapped around her, he breathed into her ear, "Who?"

"You."

FOUR

Dear Lord above. Penelope prayed that she could get the door closed with Tucker on the other side of it, and he looked almost stunned enough for her to succeed.

Until he didn't.

His features turned sharp, resolute, in an instant. Putting his shoulder into the wooden frame around the glass window, he leaned against it, even as she pressed her back to the door. She could not very well face him now. Not after that. Not when she didn't have a clue what she was supposed to say.

They talked about everything. But this was so ridiculous it didn't fall into that category.

"Penelope Jean Hunter." He growled her name, and she prayed the floor of her office would open up and swallow her whole. Then she wouldn't have to worry about any of this. About Winston and Emmaline and not actually dating Tucker. About Mrs. Haywood and her not-so-veiled threats about moving her event. And about what that might mean for this job she loved.

Letting Emmaline believe she was dating Tucker didn't fit into any plan she'd ever made. It was more like a bomb set to destroy every single one of her lists.

This was not good. Neither was the way her shoes slid across the wood floor. She scrambled for traction, but the slick bottom of her pumps could find none with Tucker trying to bulldoze his way through the door.

She leaned all of her weight against the frame. She supposed she was going to have to face him at some point. She couldn't very well eliminate him from her life. Not after so many years.

She wouldn't mind a little reprieve though. A moment to collect her thoughts and fully identify why she'd done what she'd done. Only, she'd already told him the truth.

She wanted Winston to know she'd moved on. Maybe she hadn't romantically, but she had emotionally. She was certain of it. She had to be. After all, she'd made a plan to get over him, and she'd stuck to it.

1. Eat all the wedding cake. (Not productive, but still worth it.)
2. Remove every picture of him from her apartment.
3. Talk through the anger.
4. Stay busy. Join the women's Tuesday night Bible study at church, find the perfect job, and start volunteering.
5. Join a gym.
6. Delete all of his shows from her DVR. She'd never liked those insipid nature documentaries anyway.
7. Adopt a furry friend.
8. Forgive Winston.

Okay, so she hadn't so much talked through her anger toward Winston as she'd let Tucker strap unwieldy boxing gloves on her hands and punched a big blue bag until she couldn't lift her arms. After that she'd had no interest in going to a gym, but the puppy she'd adopted from the shelter did require her to walk every morning and evening. So that kind of balanced out. And she'd refrained from calling the zoo to see if they'd name a cockroach after Winston.

She'd worked through the plan—most of it anyway. So it did not explain why she was at all concerned about what Winston thought. And thus, why she'd let Winston and Emmaline believe this particular lie. And why she didn't want to talk with Tucker about it.

Easing off the door, she slid forward, and then Tucker was inside her office, the door slamming behind him.

Slowly she turned around. He wasn't so much a thundercloud as those gray clouds that twisted and stretched to let a glimpse of sunshine through the rain, unsure of his next move.

She tried for a soothing smile. That failed to make any dent in his expression.

And why should it? She was the one who had stepped over the line—the always understood, never spoken line. They were friends. Never more. Never less.

"I'm sorry. Please don't be mad."

The lines at the corners of his eyes said he was still trying to decide how he felt.

"Okay, I'm gonna fix this. I promise."

He let out a long sigh and ran a hand over his hair. It was too short to run his fingers through it, but it got his point across. "Didn't you tell me last week that I needed to find a proper date for these election events? What's Winston going to think when I'm photographed with someone else at the mayor's banquet next week?"

"I know. I know. I'm sorry." She gulped for a breath and tried for another smile, but something inside her clenched, stealing her breath. "Do you have one?"

"One what?"

"A date?"

He shook his head. "Not yet. I've been . . . distracted."

By the election and the letter and some missing treasure and a missing aunt. "Right. I'm sorry. It wasn't my idea, if that helps."

He raised an eyebrow, the lines of his forehead easing a fraction.

"Emmaline suggested it. She asked how long we'd been together. And I tried to correct her. But . . ."

"Let me guess. Winston whisked her out of there before you could."

She shrugged. It sounded terrible. But it was the truth. "Pretty much."

Pacing the short distance to the wall and back to the door, Tucker crossed one arm over his chest and tugged on the short hairs at his chin with the other hand. "Do you think this is going to stay under wraps?"

"Do you mean, has Anabelle Haywood gotten ahold of it yet? I don't know. I don't imagine Winston would be eager to tell the whole world about it. But Emmaline is the unknown here."

He nodded slowly, still strolling, still rubbing at his beard. He kept it trimmed—if a little patchy—and he still played with it most days. She'd thought about running her own fingers through it only a handful of times in the last few years. She would count that as a win.

"And you *want* Winston to think we're dating?"

"No." The word popped out before she could analyze it for its truth. When she paused for a single breath, she let it out on a sigh. "I don't know." She offered a shrug while trying to read the expression on his stone features. Nothing there. Nothing readable, anyway. "I just want him to know that I'm not pining after him, that he didn't ruin my life. I'm fine. I'm great. Really."

Tucker shot her a look like she was trying a little too hard, and she clamped her mouth shut. Crossing and uncrossing his arms a couple times, he finally nodded. "Well, then I think we should date."

She nearly swallowed her tongue, which led to a coughing fit that shook her to her very core and made the skin of her upper arms sting with its violent force.

Tucker ran to her side, held her elbow, and gave her back three solid thumps.

"Excuse me." She wheezed the words, not even sure if she was apologizing for the scene or asking him to clarify. Both, maybe.

"You okay?" He held her by the shoulders and looked into her face. At arm's length, she could clearly see his eyes. They were gray and wild like the sky over the ocean before a storm, and she'd have given anything for them to be the serene blue they normally were.

"You want to date? Me?" She swept a hand down her front, not quite sure what she was trying to point out. Maybe it was the extra pounds that she'd always carried in her hips. It could have been her age—she was almost a year older than him. Or perhaps it was just that *she* had never been for *him*.

He'd never once suggested that he wanted anything more than friendship. So she'd never let her mind linger on such thoughts. Aside from a handful of notable exceptions, she'd kept her interest in him purely platonic. It was safe that way. Better. If she didn't love him as more than a friend, he could never break her heart. He could never choose someone else and walk away. Like Winston. Like her dad.

And now this?

Before he responded to her last question, she tacked on another one. "What on earth is wrong with you? We can't date!"

"Not for real. For now. For you to get through Winston's wedding. And me . . ."

"To get through the election."

He shrugged. "Would it be so bad?"

Two possible outcomes played out in her mind's eye. One ended up with their friendship intact and their summer successful. The other ended up more like Chernobyl. Shaking her head quickly, she said, "Nope. No way. I'm not going to pretend to date you."

"You already are."

She grunted and stomped across the office to her desk, then perched on the edge and stared him down. He clearly hadn't thought about what this might do to their relationship. It was safe, and it was the most stable one in her life—save her mom. But she only saw her mom for Sunday lunch and special occasions. Tucker was part of every single one of her days.

"I am not pretending to date you. There was just a little

mix-up. I'll get it straightened out. And then it'll be like nothing happened."

He slipped across the floor without a sound, not even drowning out the tick of his watch, and lowered himself beside her. "Hear me out?"

"Fine."

He crossed his long legs at the ankles and stared somewhere near her red high heels. He smelled of biscuits and the river and the blue sky. He smelled of Savannah. "Here's the thing. If the gossip mill has already heard, then correcting this misunderstanding is going to make everything worse—your job, my election, both of our lives."

She could almost hear Mrs. Haywood's scathing retort to the whole debacle. *"What kind of nonsense is this? Is this how Penelope runs her events? The Ladies' League will never stand for such an association with a traitor."*

Her stomach took a nosedive, and she wrapped her arms across her middle. Mrs. Haywood was more than half her problem, but solving that particular dilemma would require more time with Tucker—no matter what they called it. "I don't want to lie."

"Me neither." He pulled on his beard a little longer. "What if we just don't make a big deal out of it? We neither confirm nor deny the status of our relationship. We attend events together."

"And you pick me up for lunches when Winston is here."

He nodded. "And we try to find the treasure—or some proof that my ancestors weren't Southern traitors. It won't really be all that different from our real life. I mean, we already spend more time together than the average dating couple."

She held up her hand to stop his rambling. "I absolutely will not lie to your parents."

"And I'm not going to mislead your mom."

"So we . . . what? Let them assume we're together?"

He shook his head. "Or we tell them that nothing's changed. That they shouldn't believe everything they hear."

She squinted at him, trying to read the thoughts behind his eyes. He couldn't possibly be serious about this whole thing. Not when all she could see was how this could go so terribly wrong. And then what? Was their entire friendship at risk?

"And after?" she asked. "After Winston's wedding? After the election? What then?"

His hand curled around the lip of the desk, his fingers drumming slowly. "We'll be friends again." He reached for her hand and gave it a quick squeeze. "This is a little outside our norm, huh? I'm sorry if I surprised you. But I trust you. Always. I know this is safe. With you."

It was like he could read her mind. Like he'd been reading it for years.

Bowing her head, she stared at the enormous paw encasing her hand. "I'm not sure it's safe." Lifting her gaze with a tentative smile, she nodded. "But I trust you too."

"I'm not sure it's safe."

Tucker had been trying to shake off PJ's words for more than twenty-four hours, but even through the night he'd heard them in his dreams. He wasn't quite sure what she'd meant by that, but they'd been interrupted by a call from her boss, and she'd sent him on his way, leaving him to wonder just how stupid he'd been.

He hadn't given much forethought to the idea before blurting out that they should date each other. But it had come so naturally. It had seemed expected. There wasn't another woman in Savannah he wanted by his side at these ridiculous election parties. Not that he'd been looking, exactly.

After his last deployment, he'd needed some time to readjust, to remember what normal was—who normal was. It had taken him all of three minutes back on American soil to realize it was Penelope Jean Hunter. She made everything recognizable. Putting together a business plan for Westbrook Security had been brand-new and seriously overwhelming, but laughing with her in a praline-induced sugar haze until two in the morning had made it seem like something he'd done a hundred times. Even the new things were familiar with her. Like the evening walks with her yappy little mutt, Ambrose, who was new since her failed wedding. Strolling the uneven sidewalks of historic Savannah with PJ made him feel like he'd never left her side.

Why should this election be any different? He and PJ. Taking on the world. Or at least Buddy Jepson.

Of course, that didn't explain why his steps had been slower than usual, his concentration shot over the last twenty-four hours.

He tried to shake the strange weight on his shoulders and stop the endless questions running through his mind, but he couldn't. So he trudged up the steps to the Westbrook family home, head bowed and heart in his throat. No matter what he and PJ had decided the day before, he still needed her help to find this treasure.

Lord, please let there be a treasure. And please let us find it.

When he reached the front door, he finally looked up to

take in the expanse. Shuttered windows on each side of the door matched others on every floor, their white paint pristine and vibrant in the evening's diminishing light. The three-story brick home had housed Westbrooks as far back as the turn of the twentieth century. Probably longer. He'd just failed to pay close attention to the home's history when Aunt Shirley had told him about it. In his defense, he'd been only seven and much more interested in climbing trees and swimming in creeks at the time.

When he was fifteen, he'd had a particularly bad blowup with his dad, and Aunt Shirley had told him he was welcome here. "Whether I'm here or not, this door is always open for you."

The house was also his best hope for some information about his Civil War–era ancestors. With a quick rap on the door, he inserted the key and turned the lock. As he pushed the door open, it creaked into the darkness, letting only a small patch of light in.

He didn't need more. He'd been treading these threadbare carpets long enough to know the corner of the end table that had taken out more than one Westbrook kneecap and the upholstery nail in the arm of the sofa that had snagged his mother's Christmas sweater the year before.

Dodging those and a few other potential land mines, he reached the far wall and flipped on the light. It was dim yellow, turning every knickknack and piece of furniture in the room sepia toned.

"Aunt Shirley? You home? It's Tucker." He expected his call to echo back to him. The house was full of belongings and packed with memories, but it felt empty. No one was home.

"I thought you said she was gone."

His heart slammed against his rib cage, and he gulped a breath. Spinning, he eyed PJ at the open door. She was wearing faded green shorts and a gray T-shirt with the words "But first we plan." Her standard high heels had been replaced by well-worn sneakers, which explained why she'd been able to sneak up on him.

When his heartbeat slowed, he finally responded to her. "She is gone—I think. I just wanted to make sure. I wouldn't put it past her to claim to be out of town but really be hiding out at home to avoid Sunday family brunch."

The corners of PJ's eyes crinkled, and he wondered if she would start using Aunt Shirley's tricks. A confirmed bachelorette, Aunt Shirley had bucked her generation's convention—and the title of old maid—and lived a full life of verve and joy. PJ might do the same. If she never married.

But that was ridiculous. Of course she'd marry.

Why was he thinking about PJ getting married? Again. He'd been thinking about her matrimonial state far too much recently. And it was none of his business.

Except that he was "dating" her until the end of the summer.

Taking a step toward her, he gave her his most dazzling grin. "Glad you could make it tonight, *hot stuff*."

She cringed. "What is wrong with you?"

Bumping her elbow with his, he gave her a sly wink. "You know. We're dating. *Together*."

Putting her hands on her hips, she looked him right in the eye and gave her head one solid shake. "Not if you keep talking like that. No boyfriend of mine is going to call me 'hot stuff.'"

"Baby?"

She shook her head.

"Honey?"

"No."

"Schmoopsie?"

"That's a hard pass."

The corners of his lips twitched as she crossed her arms, tilted her chin down, and glared at him like a librarian. Fighting to keep his smile from revealing how much fun he was having, he asked, "Well, what should I call you?"

"PJ is just fine." Her face was like stone, giving away nothing. But the tiniest flicker in her voice promised she wasn't mad. Promised he could go a few more rounds. Just not tonight. Tonight they had work to do.

After closing the front door behind her, he led the way up the stairs to the third floor and ducked into the room that had once been his father's. The walls were tight, almost hugging the sides of the full-size bed, and the sparse furnishings—a three-drawer dresser, small desk, and chair—were at least twice his dad's age. But they were dust-free, and the pillows on the bed looked freshly fluffed.

On the far wall, partially hidden by the wrought-iron bed frame, a white half-door broke the strands of ivy in the pale green wallpaper. He strode across the room and bent to open it. Tired hinges let out a terrible cry as a wave of heat from behind the door threatened to bowl him over.

"Ack!" PJ cried, clapping a hand over her nose and mouth. The heat carried the distinctly moldy smell of a shut-up attic, and she jumped back.

He didn't blame her. His mother would call the attic unpleasant. He called it an evening activity.

"Ready?"

She shook her head. "Do we have to?"

He raised his eyebrows. "Having second thoughts?"

"And third and fourth." She leaned to peer around him, her eyes focused on something deep in the darkness beyond, nose wrinkled and lips puckered. "Do you really think there's something in there that is going to help us?"

"Excuse me." He crossed his arms. "This was as much your idea as mine."

"Fine." She huffed out a breath of air and, if he wasn't mistaken, followed that with a quick gasp. She held her breath as she bent over and crawled through the portal into the darkness.

Flipping on the flashlight on his phone, he followed her in and swung the beam of light around the room. The steep ceiling slope made the room feel smaller than a bread box, the center aisle the only place he could stand without hunching. It was also the only space not piled with *something*. And, oh, there were so many somethings. Couches and chairs, fabric faded. Antique steamer trunks stacked upon more trunks. Metal dress forms, naked—except for the one wearing a women's suit with a rather well-endowed rear end. That must have been the style once upon a time. Now it just looked creepy.

The far back wall included several stacks of newspapers, but even in the dim light from his phone, the black-and-white pages looked frail, like a faint wind might sweep them away.

And over it all hung a thick layer of dust and strategically placed cobwebs.

PJ picked up a hatbox from the rolltop desk beside her,

dislodging a cloud of dust. She immediately coughed, then gagged.

"It's not so bad," Tucker said, trying to find something hopeful in the mess.

"I think we have differing opinions."

"Do you want to go?"

She rolled her eyes. "I want to complain."

"Fair enough." Sometimes a person just needed to grumble. PJ more than some. But it never lasted long. "Maybe if we hurry, we can make it to Leopold's for a scoop of ice cream before it closes."

She eyed him with a narrow gaze, then looked at her hands, which were already covered in dust. "You think they'd let us in without hosing us down first?"

"Only one way to find out."

They dug in, taking opposite sides of the attic, opening every box and weathered suitcase. He wasn't sure what they were looking for, only that he hoped they'd know it when they found it. It probably wouldn't have a giant sign on it saying EVIDENCE THAT REFUTES JEPSON'S LETTER. But that wasn't going to stop him from praying that it might be just as clear. *God, if you could see clear to showing us the way, I'd be grateful.*

A twist in his gut reminded him he hadn't bothered to pray about much bigger life decisions. Like entering the election. And he should have. He should have done a lot of things before marching down to the county election commission and adding his name to the ballot. He should have asked God for some wisdom—a lot of wisdom. He should have asked PJ what she thought—after all, she'd talked him out of many a stupid decision. He should have taken a deep breath, counted to ten, and walked away.

But he hadn't. Because he was impulsive and reckless. And now he had to win an election he wasn't entirely sure he wanted to.

Losing simply wasn't an option. For one specific reason.

The light on his phone shivered over a stack of photo albums before his hand registered the vibration of the incoming call. He glanced at the screen.

Perfect. That one specific reason chose this moment to call.

Glancing toward PJ, he shrugged. "I've got to take this. I'll be right back."

"Oh, sure." She mumbled something about how convenient it was, but she kept digging, her own flashlight illuminating her sorted piles.

The notable change in temperature and aroma in the bedroom didn't relieve the tension in his shoulders as he accepted the call and put the phone to his ear. "Hey, Dad."

FIVE

*Y*our mother tells me that you picked up the key to the old house today."

Tucker took a deep breath and tried not to dwell on his dad's curt tone. He dived in without preamble or pause, per usual. Doctors didn't have time to dawdle. At least that's what he'd always said while Tucker was growing up.

"Are you looking in on her place while she's gone?"

"Umm . . ." He was tempted to stretch the truth. What was the harm in agreeing with his dad? Except he'd find out. When Aunt Shirley returned, his dad would certainly ask her why she'd called on her nephew instead of her brother to care for the old place. And Tucker didn't need to give his father one more reason for disapproval.

"Not exactly. I was hoping to find out a little more about the Westbrook family history. I thought she might have something in the attic."

They were both silent for a very long moment. Then his dad spoke like his lip had curled. "Is this about that ridiculous letter in the paper?"

Maybe. Probably. None of your business.

He bit back each of those responses and tried for something a little more diplomatic. Wasn't that what politicians were supposed to do?

"I'm going to have to address it at some point. Might as well have the truth on my side."

His dad grunted. For a man with multiple advanced degrees, who had lectured eloquently for more than a dozen years, he should have been able to come up with something more. But where Tucker was concerned, he rarely had.

"I don't suppose you have any information about our family's history."

Another grunt. This one mostly disbelief. "Your aunt is the unofficial genealogist in the family. She has time to track that stuff down."

Tucker pinched the bridge of his nose and squeezed his eyes closed, trying not to let his old man's words get to him. Beneath the subtle comment about Aunt Shirley having time to track history down was a belief in a hierarchy of employment. And doctors were at the very top. Security experts, not so much.

"Thanks anyway. I'll talk with her as soon as she gets back."

His dad sighed, as though this conversation was almost more than he could bear. "Be careful with all that, with uncovering something we'd rather forget. If you don't leave well enough alone, you could affect more than your election."

What did the family wish would remain lost to history? He'd never heard his dad talk about anything like that, and something inside him latched on to the question. What would they rather keep hidden?

"Not that it's going to affect your election."

And there it was. The punch that always came. The left hook that always reminded him what his dad really thought.

"You don't really believe you can beat Buddy Jepson, do you?"

Oh, that was a twofer. First, he couldn't possibly win the election. Second, he was foolish for ever thinking he might.

The pressure behind his eyes slid to his temples, and he rubbed them in slow circles instead of looking for a response. There wasn't one when his dad got like this. But maybe that would change if his dad could see him as more than the scholastic failure he'd once been.

"I have a campaign dinner in a couple weeks." Tucker paused, hoping his dad would jump in. He didn't. "It's really more of a fundraising meet and greet, but PJ is planning it, so you know the food is going to be great and there'll be a local band. You and Mom should come."

"I'll talk with your mother."

Well, that went well. Shaking his head and glancing over his shoulder toward the partially open half door, he said, "I've got to go. PJ is waiting for me."

His dad made a noise, and Tucker was pretty sure it was because he thought Tucker wasn't good enough for her.

It wasn't true. And he'd cling to that like a life raft in the middle of the ocean.

He'd also wonder if there might be a shred of truth in his dad's implication, whether he wanted to or not.

Hanging up after a quick goodbye, Tucker reached for the door but paused before stooping to enter. His dad was worried there was something in the Westbrook past that should remain hidden, and only one person would know if it was connected to the letter Jepson had unearthed.

Pressing a button, he called his aunt. Again. Third try in as many days and third time he'd been sent straight to voicemail.

"Aunt Shirley, hey. It's Tucker. Listen, I had a strange conversation with my dad. He made it seem like there were some things in our family's past that he'd rather remain hidden. But I'm looking for some proof that the Civil War Westbrooks weren't Southern traitors. Or at least something to point us to a lost treasure. This all came out in a letter that Buddy Jepson found. Anyway, I know it's random, but if you know anything that might help . . . well, would you call me?"

He hung up and ducked back into the attic, the heat immediately making sweat break out across his neck and back. PJ stood on the far side of the room, reading something she was holding in one hand and wiping her forehead with the back of her other hand.

"How's your dad?" She didn't even look over at him.

"Same as always."

She nodded, her long ponytail bobbing in the light she'd leaned on a desk. "I'm sorry he's like that."

Tucker offered a half smile, even though she was still focused on the paper in her hand. Sometimes she knew him so well, it felt like she could read his mind. And that was usually a comforting thing, like in this moment.

It wasn't quite as comforting when his gaze dipped to her long legs. He could only pray she didn't read that part of his mind.

Shaking his head, he returned to the suitcases he'd been inspecting before the call. "So, my dad thinks there's something in our family past worth keeping hidden."

"Excuse me?" Her voice was sharp, and he could see her

snap to attention out of the corner of his eye. "And you didn't lead with that?"

He shrugged.

"What kind of something?"

He frowned. "I have no idea. Maybe it's connected with the treasure. Maybe not."

"But it was something you'd want to keep hidden? Something . . ." She paused, her face working as she fought to find the word. "Something disgraceful?"

"I would imagine."

She whirled, pouncing on a hatbox, and pulled out a folded sheet of yellow paper. The frayed corners and wrinkled edges were a dead giveaway that it had been in this box for decades.

"This letter. I didn't—I wasn't sure what it was about. It has no date or mention of a treasure, so I just glanced at it."

Sliding between a stack of boxes and one of the dress forms, he made his way toward her. "What's it say?"

She held it out to him in a gentle grip. But he shook his head, so she read it aloud.

Dear Papa,

I am so sorry. I never meant to go against your wishes. You must be furious with me. How could you not? Mama says you may never speak with me again. I know you believe I've disgraced you and our family name. I pray that someday you might forgive me for the shame I've caused you. I have no explanation for my choices, only the sure knowledge that I had no other option.

I pray that you may one day find it in your heart to forgive me. Until then, I remain ever your loving daughter,

Caroline

As she read it, his hands shook. Who was Caroline, and when had she written this? He tried to put together the family tree in his mind, but there were several missing branches and generations of missing names. He needed Aunt Shirley's help.

"I'm going to call my aunt again." He moved toward the door, and PJ followed him. He shot her a questioning glance.

"What? You're not the only one who can escape. I found the letter. I think that earns me a few minutes of fresh air."

True. She had found the only evidence so far. "Come on. I'll even get you a glass of water."

"Ooooh. Big spender." She laughed and shoved his shoulder from behind as they traipsed down the stairwell. At the bottom level, she ducked into the powder room, as Aunt Shirley called it, to wash her hands while Tucker took advantage of the lemon-scented soap in the kitchen. It smelled like freshness and sunshine. The opposite of the attic.

By the time she arrived, he'd poured them both tall glasses of water and pressed the button to call his aunt again.

PJ took a swig of her water as the phone on the other end rang once. *Thank you*, she mouthed.

He nodded as it rang again, fully expecting it to go to voicemail at the end of the second ring. It didn't. Instead, a cheery voice answered.

"Tucker? Is that you?"

He pressed the speaker button and laid his phone on the granite countertop between them. "Aunt Shirley! I didn't think I'd reach you. I've left a few messages."

"Oh, you know how spotty service is in Japan."

Actually, no, he didn't. He'd never been. His deployments had all been in the Middle East. "You're in Japan?"

"Of course. I had a hankerin' to see Mount Fuji."

Tucker's heart skipped a beat. "You're not *climbing* Mount Fuji, are you?"

"Don't be silly. I did that yesterday."

He caught PJ's eye, and they both stared in silent wonder. Shirley Westbrook was something else.

"So what can I do for you?"

"Well, PJ and I—"

"PJ's there? Peej! How are you, doll?"

"Hi, Shirley. I'm good."

Tucker smiled. Only Aunt Shirley had ever gotten away with calling PJ *Peej*. He'd tried it once or twice in their elementary school years and had gotten a few bruises for his trouble. That Penelope let him call her PJ was her concession to their friendship. No one else got to do that—not even Winston.

Not that he was comparing their relationships. Much.

"So, there's this letter," he said.

Aunt Shirley growled low in her throat. "Oh, I've heard about it. Anabelle Haywood couldn't wait . . ." Her voice trailed off. Or maybe the reception cut out for a moment. When she returned, there was a distinct bounce in her voice. "I suppose you're looking for something to help you find the treasure."

"Well, at least the truth," PJ said.

"Same. Same." Aunt Shirley chirped a giggle. "And you're at my house looking through the attic."

Maybe she had some serious mind-reading skills. Or maybe she'd listened to her voicemails after all.

"We found a letter from someone named Caroline. She said she'd disgraced her family."

"Uh-uh," Aunt Shirley said, and he could almost picture her shaking her head. "She said her father *believed* she'd disgraced their family name. Not the same thing."

It was semantics, but did it matter? He shot PJ a raised eyebrow, and she gave a silent shake of her head. He wasn't sure where to go with that. Thankfully she wasn't as tongue-tied.

"Is Caroline connected to the lost treasure?"

Aunt Shirley chuckled. "If you're looking for her story, you should have just asked."

"You can tell us more about her?" Tucker asked.

"Well, not right now. But I'll tell you where you can read it yourself."

PJ nearly glowed, eyes bright and smile spreading all the way across her face. He couldn't help but match her grin. Count on Aunt Shirley to come through in a pinch.

"Her diary is in my desk in the study." Aunt Shirley gave them a few more instructions before begging off for another travel adventure.

"Thank you," they called in unison before hanging up the phone and racing for the study.

Penelope had never once been grateful for Tucker's dyslexia. Except now. Just a little bit.

Watching him struggle through school had been nearly as hard on her as it had been on him. He was so smart, but he'd had to fight to read and understand every page, every line. In junior high, he'd gotten a special tutor who taught him some tools. But reading was never going to be a joy for him.

So he'd happily passed her Caroline's journal the night

before and asked her to read it. For them both. As if she had to be asked.

Penelope glanced at the tattered fabric cover of the journal in the top drawer of her desk. Still tucked in its clear plastic sleeve, it called to her. She hadn't had time to look at it since the night before, but one more appointment and she was free and clear to spend her evening with a cool glass of sweet tea and a good chunk of Savannah's past.

At the jangle of the bell on her door, she looked up. Her stomach sank beneath the floorboards. Winston. She stood quickly but immediately second-guessed her action.

He gave her a quick nod. "Emmaline asked me to drop off the deposit check."

"Right." She held out her hand as he shuffled across the room. She knew she was supposed to offer a thank-you, but her tongue refused to get on board with common courtesy.

Holding out the check a few inches shy of her reach, he paused. Face bunched up and eyes squinted toward a spot on the floor beside her shoe, he took a shallow breath. "I haven't told Emmaline that I was engaged."

His words struck her like a snowball, icy and unexpected. So clinical and completely devoid of any acknowledgment that *she* had been on the receiving end of his first proposal.

Tapping her shoe, she crossed her arms. "And?"

He looked up, one of his eyes closed. "Please don't say anything to her."

He was asking *her* for a favor? That took some gall. "I don't see why I should care what you want me to do."

"Please." He tugged on the cuffs of his blue-plaid sleeves, his deep brown eyes a little too similar to her puppy's. "Please, Penelope. I can't lose her."

He hadn't been worried about that three years before.

She took a deep breath and let it out through her nose. She was over him. She had a checked-off list to prove it.

Just then her door squeaked as it opened a crack. "Hello?" The voice was soft and delicate, just like the young woman who followed it into her office. "I'm Jordan Park. With Stepping Stones." Her gaze darted toward Winston. "Should I come back?"

Penelope quickly shook her head. "No. Come on in." She turned back to Winston, holding out her hand one more time. He paused, the check between them. "I won't tell her. But you should."

He offered a brief nod, passed her the deposit, and quickly excused himself.

Penelope tried for a cleansing breath, plastering a smile into place before turning to the young woman fidgeting with the strap of her purse standing just inside the door.

"I'm sorry I'm early," Jordan said.

The cadence of her voice was so inviting that Penelope walked across the room to shake her hand. "Welcome. Thank you for your call. Have a seat. How can I help?"

Jordan offered a shy smile and a loose handshake before tucking her long blonde hair behind her ears and sinking into one of the guest chairs. "I'm planning a fundraiser."

"Wonderful. What kind of event do you have in mind?"

Jordan's brown eyes—already large—nearly doubled in size, her hands twisting in her lap. Her right knee bobbed in time to a song no one else could hear, and she chewed on her bottom lip. "I'm not really sure."

Penelope nearly slipped out of her chair. This was a new one. Most people who walked through her door had a clear vision of what they wanted and when they wanted it. She'd never had a blank slate before. How exciting.

Leaning her forearms on her desk, she smiled. "Why don't you tell me a little about your organization and what you do?"

Jordan agreed with a quick nod but didn't say anything for a long second. Tugging at shorts that covered a good bit of her pale legs, she narrowed her gaze onto the front of the desk. "My nonprofit is pretty new. Less than a year old. But we want to help."

"Who are you helping?"

"Foster kids who are aging out of the system. We help them get job training, find a place to live. That kind of thing."

Penelope looked closer at the girl's porcelain skin and freckled cheeks. She herself couldn't be much older than the kids aging out of the system. But her eyes were wise beyond their years, filled with stories to share—some she'd probably rather forget.

"Jordan, may I ask you a personal question?"

With a hesitant nod, she agreed.

Penelope searched her words for the right ones. "Do you have some personal experience with the foster care system?"

Jordan ducked her head, her hands curling into the hem of her shirt. "That obvious?"

"Not at all," she rushed to reply. "I've just never met anyone so young doing something so big, so important." At Jordan's age, Penelope had probably still been in college, more worried about getting her next A than caring about anyone else. Not that getting good grades was bad. But they'd been such a focus that she wasn't entirely sure she'd treated her roommates and friends as she should have, often blowing off their calls and invitations for one more hour in the library.

Tucker had been off at Marine boot camp by then, and she'd been faithful to write him. But she'd walked away from college with good grades and very little else to remember it by. And with very little to make others remember her.

And here was Jordan, looking nervous and uncertain and doing something that helped people in real need. Something that would leave a legacy.

"How can I help?" Penelope walked around to the other side of her desk and sat next to the young woman.

"Um . . . I'm not . . . I don't even know where to start."

Penelope couldn't stop the smile that tugged across her face. "Oh, I do." Reaching for her legal pad and pen, she began asking all the questions. "What are your goals for this event? How much do you want to raise? Who are you going to invite?"

Jordan simply stared back like the proverbial deer in the headlights.

Okay. They were going to have to take this a lot slower.

After another hour and a half, Penelope had coaxed a bud of an idea out of Jordan. A special night specifically for local business owners—people of means who might donate to the cause or hire the young people looking to start their careers. They'd fleshed out ways for kids in the program to meet with business owners—a pre-interview of sorts. They'd identified a local band that might provide the music—they were playing at Tucker's upcoming event, and they owed her for getting them the gig.

All in all it was shaping up to be a great event. Just one more thing to consider.

"What's your budget?" Penelope asked.

Jordan cringed as though she knew it was going to hurt to say it. "Pretty small."

Penelope motioned for her to go on. Better to get it out in the open so they could figure out how much they could do.

"Twenty-five."

"Thousand?" Penelope couldn't hold in the sigh of relief. "We can work with that. We might have to cut back on a few things, but we can definitely put together a great event."

Jordan shook her head. "Hundred."

Twenty-five hundred. Two thousand, five hundred dollars.

She said the words over and over in her mind, but they never stopped feeling like a bad punch line.

Maybe Jordan didn't understand. "You know we're going to ask the attendees to donate, right? And they have deep pockets. So you'll make back everything you put into this event. And then some."

"I'd give you more if I had more. That's all I have in my account."

Why did it sound like she was prepared to spend every penny of her own money to make this work? "In your account or in the organization's account?"

Jordan shrugged. "Both."

"Oh, sweetie." Penelope pressed her palm to the girl's skinny knee and hung her head. "I don't think we can do—"

"Please. It doesn't have to be big. Could you give us a discount on the Hall? Or maybe let us pay after the event? I know the Ladies' League is going to hold their fundraiser here at the end of the summer. This is where all the nonprofits say you have to be to be seen. Please."

Penelope wanted to help. Everything inside her screamed

to let Jordan use the Hall at no fee, at a steep discount, on a payment plan. But that wasn't something she was free to offer.

"I'm so sorry. Maybe I can help you find . . ." But her voice trailed off because she knew the truth. Jordan was never going to be able to throw the kind of event she needed to earn back her investment on twenty-five hundred dollars. She needed more capital, and that wasn't Penelope's expertise.

Jordan pushed herself out of her chair and clutched the little cross-body strap purse that had been by her side like a shield. "It's okay. I understand." Her lip quivered like she definitely did not understand. "Thanks for your time." And then she was out the door.

Resting her arm on the desk and her forehead against her wrist, Penelope fought the burning sensation at the back of her eyes. She'd broken rule number one of event planning. She'd made a plan without knowing the budget. That was amateur. And she'd pulled that stunt on a young woman who couldn't afford to have hope ripped out from under her.

She couldn't ask herself what she'd been thinking. Because she hadn't been.

"Who was that?" The question arrived at the same time as the unmistakable staccato clip of heels.

Penelope righted herself, running knuckles under her eyes to make sure she hadn't loosened her mascara, and turned to look into the unforgiving gaze of Madeline Baxton. "A potential client. My last appointment of the day."

Madeline looked over her shoulder as though trying to imagine how a sprite of a girl like Jordan could afford to book the Savannah River Hall. Glancing at her watch, she said, "It's almost six."

Penelope knew the implication. Why had she wasted time on a client who was never going to rent the Hall?

Because Jordan needed her help. Because Penelope needed *to* help.

But Madeline would never understand that. She understood dollars and cents and bottom lines and red ink and black ink. She did not understand giving more than she got.

Penelope shrugged weary shoulders and said, "I thought we could make it work. I was wrong."

Madeline's gaze narrowed, her big blonde updo swaying as she surveyed the scene before her. Finally she brushed her hands together, careful not to clip her long pink nails against one another. "Well, you have more important things to worry about. Anabelle Haywood called me today."

Oh, Lord. It was her favorite two-word prayer, and at that moment it was on repeat deep in her soul. Her stomach sank, and she squeezed her hands into fists at her sides.

"She's concerned about this situation with your friend Tucker Westbrook."

She didn't need to spell out his name. Penelope knew about the concern and the problem. She just wasn't very close to solving it.

"We can't afford to lose the income from the Ladies' League event in August."

"Yes, ma'am." She sounded about ten years old, but there wasn't anything to be done except act contrite and be respectful.

Madeline smoothed her hands over her flowy floral skirt and nodded appreciatively. "Good. I thought it wise for us to offer a show of goodwill toward the Ladies' League. I've volunteered you to serve at the Fort Pulaski Picnic next week. You can pick up your costume tomorrow."

Biting her tongue so hard she could taste blood, she nodded, but in her mind she was already plotting revenge on the one and only Tucker Westbrook. She was going to have to don a hoop skirt and petticoats and cotton gloves. And it was almost entirely his fault.

Thursday, November 3, 1864

Papa has left again. 'Tis well after dark, and the streets below my room are silent, save for the occasional horse. I usually sleep through the sharp clap of horseshoes against the stone streets, but I have not slept these last several nights.

So I sit at my desk, a single candle burned nearly to a nub. The light is enough for me to see this page, but the rest of my room is only shadow.

I asked Papa to let me go with him, but he says it is far too dangerous. He thinks I do not know what he and the others are doing. He thinks I am unaware of the terrible cost they would face if discovered.

But I know. How could I not? The missives that arrive bear his name—Daniel W.—and Bradford is not as circumspect about the contents inside as he believes himself to be. I heard him speaking to Papa of the ship soon to arrive. I have no idea what they plan to do with the treasure they seem certain it will carry.

Of one thing I am sure. Papa knows. And he is involved. Bradford would not dare to defy Papa's wishes. Though nearly four and twenty, my brother has always done as our father asks. When he tried to enlist, Father took a hard look at his leg and told him he must not. Some call his limp an excuse, but it has saved his life. Papa nearly put down the ornery horse that threw him, but I am ever grateful for a broken leg that did not set right. Else I might be grieving my brother lost on a battlefield in the North rather than eavesdropping on his conversations.

I heard the kitchen door open and close nearly an hour ago, but through my window I could see only Papa's form sneak around the side of the building. Bradford was not with him, nor any of our people.

Surely he is not going to meet the ship alone. Yet I cannot help but wonder where he has gone alone so late at night.

Tuesday, November 8, 1864

I followed Papa last night. I knew I should not, but I had to be abreast of his comings and goings. Bradford watches me with a wary eye now, and I fear Father has warned him that I am not to be trusted with their secrets.

But I am. I need only to know the secrets to keep them safe.

Alas, I learned nothing of import. Dressed in the mourning clothes I wore when Grandmama was buried, I waited in the shadows outside the kitchen door. I did not have to wait long. With the moon covered by well-placed clouds, I heard the old hinges turn rather than saw the door open.

Two figures slipped through the door, silent and dressed to match the night. Papa's form was broad, his shoulders stretching his coat as always. Bradford was smaller but no less recognizable, his gait agitated, his walking stick abandoned for the night.

I waited until they turned at the back corner of our house before slipping after them. Only when they reached the stone street did they speak, but they were much too far away for me to hear their conversation. I only understood the intensity in their voices, the urgency. They picked up their pace, Bradford struggling to keep up yet somehow urging Papa on.

I was forced to run, and the heels of my boots clacked

against the ground. I feared they might hear me. But what if they were in trouble? What terrible fate might befall them? There is naught worse than living amid the unknown.

I have known little else for these past four years, since Josiah has been gone. He promised to write, but neither his mother nor I have received even a scrap of news. They say that his regiment fought bravely and suffered heavy losses. Whatever hope I have left has worn thin.

But I need to know that I will not lose more dear men. I could not sustain it.

So I struggled on after them, picking up my petticoats as I ran. They wove through the shadows, hiding from me as from the rest of the world. They must not have seen me. At least, they did not know who I was, or they would have demanded I return home, return to safety. Why do they not demand the same of themselves?

I was several seconds behind them as they turned from Price Street onto Bay Street, but as I tiptoed around the tree at the corner, I realized I was too far behind. They had vanished.

Bawdy music from a nearby tavern twirled around me, but my brother and father were nowhere to be seen. I glanced into a few windows, all covered with lace curtains, candles long since extinguished. Hurrying down the street, I hoped to see that they'd turned up another alley. They had not.

But the alleys were not deserted, and I suddenly realized my vulnerability. Alone on a dark night, the streets still alive with men reeling from liquor. The type of women on the streets at such an hour would make my mother blush.

Racing faster than Father's prized mare, I set out for home and arrived to a house as asleep as it had been when I'd left not an hour earlier. I removed my dress and stays, slipped into

my cotton nightgown, and slid between the sheets of my bed.
Then I waited.

Hours later Papa and Bradford returned home as quiet as
mice. Only then did I let myself close my eyes and fall asleep.

Thursday, November 17, 1864

General Sherman heads this way. The newspaper need not tout
it, as it seems to be the only news anyone can speak of. In the
churchyard even young Henry Billings pulled his slingshot from
his pocket and promised to defend this land.

But how can anyone? How can we remain safe and free
when General Sherman overwhelmed Atlanta so soundly?
They say he is burning the state in his march toward the
Atlantic. All who oppose him lose everything. Will he do the
same here? I know not how Savannah can survive such an
onslaught.

The air has begun to chill, autumn making way for winter,
but still Papa and Bradford disappear more nights than not.
I still lose them in the night when I attempt to follow them.
Papa's shoulders have begun to slump, and he is weary and
heavyhearted.

Something is nearly here. I know not what it is, but I know
that I must be vigilant. For when the Union army arrives, 'twill
be too late.

SIX

"Where are we going?"

Penelope tried to keep the evil from her smile as she strolled down the Savannah sidewalk beside Tucker the next day. "I told you. I have to run a quick errand. I thought you'd enjoy it too."

He shot her a sideways glance, his pace slowing down as though he already knew he wasn't going to enjoy this particular errand. But he didn't push the issue, instead changing the topic. "Have you read any of Caroline's diary yet?"

She opened her mouth to spout all of her thoughts on the handful of entries she'd read so far, and almost missed their turn down Abercorn Street. Smart man. He thought he could distract her. Nice try.

Tugging on his arm, she steered him around the corner but pulled up short as they nearly ran into a couple headed their direction.

"Excuse me."

The tenor voice made her cringe, and she wanted to duck behind Tucker and hide until the danger had passed. But that wasn't an option when a slender hand grasped her arm and pulled her closer.

"Penelope," Emmaline cried as though greeting an old friend who had been lost at sea. "Fancy running into you here."

"Emmaline. Winston." She nodded at each of them in greeting. "You remember my . . ." She'd been about to say *friend*, but the twinkle in Emmaline's eyes reminded her that he was more. At least for now. So she left the sentence unfinished. "Tucker, this is Emmaline and Winston."

"I remember." He didn't reach out to shake Winston's hand, and if the scowl on his face was any indication, Winston wasn't terribly upset to miss out on it.

Emmaline, her blonde hair swept back from her face, didn't notice or didn't care. "What are y'all doing today? We're going to the market. I still need to find something blue."

Tucker looked clueless, Winston a little bored. Which left Penelope to smile and nod her enthusiasm. "Sounds fun. We're just off—" Her voice disappeared as a very large, very strong hand swept across the small of her back. With a tug, she was pulled against Tucker's side. His fingers splayed at her waist kept her from being able to pull free. Not that she wanted to. Exactly.

Being held like this—by Tucker Westbrook—was just unusual. Strange. Mildly terrifying.

Tucker cut her off with his own version of the day's events. "I stole her from her office so we could spend a little extra time together."

Emmaline nearly glowed. "That's so romantic! Winston, isn't that the sweetest?" She hung on her fiancé's arm and snuggled up next to him.

Penelope didn't have to do that because Tucker had already brought them together. She risked a glance up at him, and he was looking down at her, smiling. And then he winked. It wasn't obvious or cheesy. It was sweet and playful.

This was one of a hundred reasons why she loved this man. But just now she wanted to ask him what on earth he was thinking.

"Well, we should get going. I don't want to miss a minute of time with this one." He squeezed her waist. "She's throwing me a campaign fundraiser in two weeks. The Barnett Brothers are playing, and the food will be amazing. Y'all should join us."

Winston looked ready to pass on the spot, but Emmaline's eyes lit up. "I saw the Barnett Brothers last year," she said. "They were so good. We'll be there for sure. Send us the details, Penelope?"

She nodded just in time as Tucker pulled her away, still holding her close. When she was sure they were clear of earshot, she whispered, "Genius."

"I do try." He let go of her to straighten an imaginary bow tie, and she tried not to miss the feel of his arm around her.

This was normal. But she might have to tell herself that a thousand times before it sank in.

"So, seriously. Where are we going?" he asked.

She looked up at the row of two-story historic buildings lining the Savannah street. Almost a block from the nearest square and across the street from the cathedral, she pointed to a sign hanging from the brick building: BROOKS AND BROOKS TAILORS.

"Shopping? You want to go shopping? Please tell me I don't need a new wardrobe."

"Not exactly." She smiled at the furrow in his brow. He would be worried about changing up his standard uniform. After his many years in the military, she couldn't blame him for embracing the soft, cool jersey knit polo shirts with his company logo on them.

Pushing open the door to the shop was like opening the door into history. Frilly dresses and full-skirted frocks lined the walls while mannequins in full Confederate uniforms filled the far corner. She couldn't help but wonder which of these dresses Caroline might have chosen. Or if she'd have snubbed all of them and chosen trousers instead.

Looking at the cinched waists on the dress forms, Penelope wouldn't blame Caroline for eschewing the accepted fashion and wearing pants instead. Penelope wasn't quite sure she'd fit any of her many curves into these dresses. She didn't know if she should pray for a corset tight enough to shoehorn her in or pray there wasn't a corset in the world that would squeeze her into one of these frilly costumes.

"Miss Hunter, welcome. Mrs. Baxton said I should expect you."

She didn't know the man who appeared from the back room, his back stiff and his black mustache perfectly coiffed, but she held out her hand. "Please, call me Penelope. And this is Tucker."

"Simon Brooks, at your service." He gave a quick bow, and Penelope had to stifle the giggle that threatened with his formal delivery.

Tucker drew all attention to himself when he sputtered, "What . . . what's going on here?"

Simon looked positively affronted, his hand coming to his throat and his eyes growing large. Even in the shadow where he stood, she could see the pinch around his mouth. Utter disapproval. Smoothing his slicked-back hair with one hand, he patted his paisley tie with the other. "The Ladies' League Fort Pulaski Remembrance Picnic is next week, and we're the exclusive tailor of period costumes for it."

Tucker narrowed his gaze on her, his arms crossing. "And why did we need to come here?"

"Well, to pick up your costume, of course. We don't have much time if you need alterations." Simon's gaze traveled from Penelope's head to the tips of her pumps, pausing at the places where she fully filled out her floral skirt. He frowned and leaned to the side, probably checking to see where they could tuck in some of her looseness. For a moment she felt like a beauty pageant contestant, certain she was going to have to spin for the judge and let him point out all of her flaws.

She shot a glance at Tucker. If he noticed her discomfort, he was doing a pretty good job of appearing otherwise engaged with analyzing a nearby green evening dress. Its capped sleeves were iced in the most intricate lace, and a row of silver buttons down its back dazzled in the overhead lights. The full skirt would cover any number of brownie-related sins, but the waist looked like it would barely fit someone half her size.

At least Tucker was distracted. He may have seen her in a two-piece once upon a time—and twenty pounds ago—but she certainly didn't need him witnessing a full dressing down.

But when she looked back at Simon, his eyes sparkled and a knowing smile had fallen into place, showing off a couple crooked teeth and a full measure of joy. "I have the perfect dress for you." He spun around and paused for a quick admonishment over his shoulder before disappearing into the back room. "Stay right there."

When they were alone, Tucker finally spoke without looking in her direction. "Are you really going to wear one of these things?" Rubbing a piece of lace between his thumb and forefinger, he chuckled. "This thing feels like it would fall apart under a stiff breeze."

"Maybe that's why they wore so many undergarments. To avoid any wardrobe malfunctions."

He snorted. "Sounds pretty awful to me. Those uniforms look even worse, like a sweat machine." He motioned toward his tan cargo shorts and polo. "I much prefer cool and comfortable."

"Oh, but I'm not the only one getting a costume today."

His jaw went slack for a long moment, his nostrils flaring. "No. Absolutely not going to happen." The muscles in his neck flexed, his shoulders shifting to make his stance even more formidable.

Well, two could play that game. Pressing her hands to her hips, she faced him down. "Don't try that with me, Westbrook. We're in this together, you and me. Remember?"

"Yes, but wearing a wool Confederate uniform in the middle of June was never on the table." The muscle in his jaw twitched, the rest of him as still as a statue for a long moment. "Besides, how is my playing Civil War soldier helping either of us?"

"Actually, it'll help both of us. So get ready to suit up."

Not. Going. To. Happen.

There was no way Tucker was going to put on that uniform. No words PJ could say would convince him to change his mind.

And then she smiled.

She had a plan, and he could read it on her face—if not quite the details. The only thing missing was her checklist. That was probably in her purse.

Staring at the ceiling for a long moment, he prepared his defense. This was a stupid idea. He was a grown man who did not play dress-up. Moreover, he was running for office, and this was bound to make him look a fool in the eyes of potential voters. His argument was solid. So why did PJ look like a cat that had just discovered a canary?

"No. I'm not—"

"I've got an ace." She spoke the words so softly that he nearly missed them, but they stopped him as soon as they registered.

He growled low in the back of his throat. He never should have taught her how to play poker. It had seemed like the smart thing to do when they were eighteen and about to go their separate ways. It had seemed like a skill she should have before trading their small Savannah life for the University of Georgia. He didn't know what the guys were like there, but he'd heard stories—or rather, seen movies—where college guys tried to take advantage of pretty girls. Tucker decided that if he couldn't be there to protect PJ from those frat boys, then he'd prepare her to take care of herself.

There had been a few self-defense lessons. A couple big-city-driving expeditions. And several sessions of teaching her how to win at poker, one in which he'd told her not to call. He had the ace she needed, and she wasn't going to win. "I've got an ace," he'd said.

She had called. And lost the hand.

Since then, "I've got an ace" had become their slang for "trust me" and "I know something you don't."

She tipped her head to the side, and he cringed. Trusting her would probably end up with him wearing one of those uniforms. But not trusting her wasn't an option.

"Fine." He whispered the word just as Simon Brooks reappeared, a billowing mass of sky blue draped over his arm.

"Shall we begin?" Simon nodded toward a black-curtained partition beyond a three-way mirror and riser.

PJ followed him, and they disappeared behind the closed drape. Simon's low voice pointed out the various pieces of her costume, but before he ducked out to let her get dressed, she asked, "Do you have a lieutenant's uniform for Tucker?"

"Another actor for the picnic?"

Tucker groaned. *Please don't have one in my size. Please don't have one in my size.*

Simon clearly didn't hear his silent plea. "I have just the thing."

Before Tucker knew it, he was in the room beside PJ's, listening to the rustle of her skirts as she grunted into the dress. He pulled on surprisingly soft wool pants and buttoned them. They fit well and even reached almost all the way to floor. Nothing a tall pair of boots wouldn't cover.

Rats.

He had his flowing white shirt tucked in and the suspenders over his shoulders when PJ waved her hand around the sheet that separated them. "Tucker." Her whisper was sharp, soft.

"What?"

"I need help."

Of course. She couldn't get herself into her own dress. And she was the one who'd thought this was a good idea. At least he could dress himself. "You decent?"

"Yes. I'm out here."

When he ducked out of his room and into the short hallway, he blinked. Hard. PJ was gone. Vanished. In her place was a Southern belle, the belle of any ball she attended. Rosy cheeks, full lips, and a soft smile. The blue silk made her eyes dance, full of joy.

"Stupid thing doesn't have a zipper, and I can't reach these buttons."

Ah, there she was. He smiled as she turned to show him her back. The buttons were half done, and the rest of her back was covered by a white piece of fabric with some rigid pieces stuck through it. It looked like rebar for women's clothes.

Poking one of the slats, he said, "Doesn't that hurt?"

"Well, it doesn't feel good." She giggled. "But look."

He looked up at her reflection in the mirror at the end of the hall, and his breath vanished. Forget belle of the ball, she was absolutely breathtaking. Literally.

She pressed her hands to her waist, which looked strangely narrow, her hips fuller than usual. But that wasn't what made her beautiful. It was all of her—the joy in her laugh, the sparkle in her eyes, and the dimple that seemed to be for him alone. She made his stomach swoop and his chest feel two sizes too tight.

Lord, what I have I gotten myself into?

He was dating her. He wasn't supposed to be *dating* her.

His heart seemed to be more than a little confused about the difference.

This was an analysis better saved for another day. Another time when she wasn't dressed up like a debutante being presented to the king. Or whatever debutantes did.

Fumbling with the buttons before him, he focused his attention on getting the little silver pieces through their holes. The silk was cool and slippery, and it took him more than one attempt on every button until finally he was done.

"Grab your jacket," she said, ducking into the main room. She floated to the riser, picked up her bell of a skirt, and stepped up. Then she stood there like she'd walked out of Caroline's journal and into his life.

He hustled to do her bidding, buttoning his jacket as he joined her in front of the mirror. She pulled on a pair of white gloves, and he held his elbow out for her. She rested her hand there, smiling up at him like she was going to her first ball.

"We look the part, don't we?" she said, staring at their reflection.

"Which part is that, Miss Hunter?"

"All of them." She swished her skirt. "Confederate royalty. Southern charmers. Savannah power couple. And it'll work."

"What'll work?"

She paused, smoothing her gloved hand over the glowing fabric. "Madeline told me last night that I have to volunteer for the Ladies' League picnic or my job is on the line."

"She can't—"

PJ lifted a quick hand to quiet his argument. She glanced over her shoulder too, presumably to check if Simon and his mustache had returned. They were alone.

"She didn't threaten me exactly, but it was definitely implied. You know I can't afford to lose the Ladies' League fundraiser later this summer, and if dressing up like a Southern belle and serving punch at a picnic keeps me in Anabelle Haywood's good graces, then I'll gladly do it."

With a quick motion toward his gray uniform, he flicked a brass button against the pale fabric. "So where do I fit into this charade?"

"Well, I figured having you there could work twice for us." She held up a slender finger. "First for your campaign. The people in attendance are likely the voters worried that your family were traitors. This might help remind them that Westbrooks wore gray too."

He nodded, not too fond of wearing any uniform other than that of United States Marine, but she had a point.

"Plus this is a great time to invite them all to your fundraiser. You'll come off smelling sweeter than azaleas. Your campaign fund should get a hefty boost too."

Okay, that was a really good idea. "And second?"

She shrugged, the creamy skin of her shoulders poking out from the swooping neckline of the dress. "Second, this is a chance for us to have a very public appearance—you know, you supporting me like I'll be supporting you the following week."

Her arguments made good sense, but he hadn't needed them to convince him. The truth was, if she asked him, he couldn't deny her. He'd never been able to.

She smiled. "Besides, you just got promoted to lieutenant."

He'd been happy as a sergeant when he left the Marines. But if he was being really honest with her, he was happiest anywhere she was.

And that realization wasn't going to do a thing to help his heart line up with his head.

Friday, November 25, 1864

Papa caught me eavesdropping. It was not intentional on
my part. But as I passed his study on my way to the library,
Bradford's voice carried into the foyer.

Tonight.

He said it will arrive tonight. It must arrive tonight, for
Sherman's men grow ever nearer. Confederate scouts leave
every morning and return days later with worrisome news.
They will arrive within the fortnight. Whatever this ship
brings, they must claim it tonight. But the ship is not arriving
in Savannah. It is bound for a hidden cove. Under the cover of
night, they will take it.

Then I heard a name that has not been uttered in these
walls since his regiment marched out of Savannah. Josiah
Hillman.

I must have gasped, for Father stormed from behind his
desk and marched me to my room, telling me I must stay there.
He has never hurt me before, but his grip was unforgiving as
my arm pulsed within his vise. When I was firmly sat on my
bed, he bent low over me until our eyes were even.

His lips seemed to be fighting a smile. Then he said the
strangest thing.

He told me that he knows I want to go with them, and he is
proud of me. But he loves me too dearly to see anything come
between me and a long life. There are others who need to be
protected too. He said I could not join them tonight, but soon.
He will let me venture out with them soon. And then he kissed
my cheek, marched from my room, and closed my door more
firmly than was necessary.

I heard him speaking to Mama, and after a brief, emphatic

encounter, Mama opened my door, eyes narrow, voice low. Papa is terrifying because of his size and strength. Mama is terrifying for every other reason. When her voice turns to iron, she expects to be obeyed.

I am forbidden from going with my brother and father. Ever.

Saturday, November 26, 1864

Mama is terribly cross with me. One can hardly blame her when one considers that I did the very thing she told me not to. But I had to know that they were safe. I had to see with my own eyes what could make them risk so much. With General Sherman's imminent arrival on the tip of every tongue in town, I could hardly wait. I will not deceive myself to believe that it will be safe for me to be about the city after dark upon his arrival.

I knew that I should stay home and obey my mother, but when I imagined that Josiah might be there, that I might be afforded even a glimpse of him or hear of his fate, I had no choice. Of course, I was curious about what treasure the ship might carry. I imagined diamonds dazzling even in the moonlight, and silks glimmering beneath the stars. Would there be champagne and spirits or gold and silver?

But more than any other thought, I dreamed of Josiah. Perhaps he was aboard this ship. But how could he be? The North's blockade has halted all but the most daring ships from reaching our ports. What would Josiah be doing on such a vessel?

I had too many questions and longed for any answers. I

prayed for forgiveness. I dared not pray for protection. Not when I was about to leave the security of my father's roof. He is a good man, respected among the men in town, and I prayed that I would not bring shame upon him. I knew I must stay hidden. For my protection and his.

Well after dark I dressed in Bradford's trousers and left the house, for the ship would not arrive unless under a black and moonless night. Sneaking to the stables, I was sure I must be alone. But when I reached Marigold's stall, I heard Sarah click her tongue at me. I turned in the direction of the familiar chastising, but her dark skin and even darker dress blended into the rest of the inky night.

She said I knew better, but she still called me Miss Caroline with the affection of a woman who had raised me. Sarah has been by my side since before I can remember.

But she was wrong. I did not know better. I knew only the opportunity to see if Josiah might be there, to discover where he has been. It mattered to me. And to his mother. Mrs. Hillman has grieved as though her son has been lost forever. She has clung to my hand as if it might keep her from drowning. I think she might be sinking below the waters now. Josiah's father has long been gone, and now she bears the broken heart of the loss of her only other love.

I told myself that I would do this for her. But my heart knew the truth. I went for myself. For some rag of hope, no matter how worn.

Despite Sarah's call, I pulled myself onto Marigold's back with a pleading cry that Sarah keep my secret. I prayed she would, though now I know she did not, which is why Mama is so cross.

I could not think of such things as I rode east toward Tybee.

I could hear the horses before I saw anything but the mere outline of trees along the road. The horses whinnied and champed at their bits, and Marigold fought me. She wanted to return home. For a moment I did as well.

But then I might never see what had finally arrived. I slipped from Marigold's back and tied her to a tree a hundred paces off the road. With fresh grass she was content as I snuck toward the coast. It felt so near, the wind blowing off the sea so I could almost feel the salt spray, the waves rolling into the shore. But the men were silent. I was not sure they were there until at last I saw them.

Lowering myself until my stomach pressed against the ground, I gazed out over the bluff, staring intently at the men milling about. There were at least a dozen, all in pale uniforms.

Strange. Bradford had tried to enlist at nineteen, Josiah only eighteen as he'd marched away. These men seemed older, grizzled. But their rifles were still at hand, their eyes alert. A large man with hands as big as hams ran them along the flank of a horse harnessed to a wagon. The big animal stamped its feet as though it didn't like being in the sand, and I nearly believed I heard him tell the horse it would be only a few more minutes.

My father and Bradford were nowhere among them, and I knew not what I had stumbled upon. Where were the men I knew, the ones from my community, the ones I trusted? These men waited for a ship, but what did they intend to do with it?

I had just pushed myself up when a black shadow slithered across the sand. One of the gray coats dropped, so silent that none of the other men noticed.

I let myself back down and held my breath, praying I could be silent, praying the thunder of my heartbeat did not carry from my perch at the top of the dune. I held my breath just as another black shadow swooped up to the man with the big hands. A muffled cry. A shot rang out.

A horse shrieked behind me. Marigold! I leapt to my feet, terrified I might be seen, too afraid to stay where I was.

Suddenly a hand clamped over my mouth and another arm snaked around my waist. I kicked and screamed and fought with every breath inside me. It wasn't much. It wasn't enough. I was being dragged toward the copse of trees where I'd left Marigold, but I could not twist my head around far enough to see her form. I prayed she was somewhere safe.

But I had no more room to consider her as I was dragged farther from the beach.

A deep voice in my ear demanded to know who I was. His breath on my ear sent shivers down my back, and gooseflesh burst out across my arms.

I bucked against him like I'd seen Marigold do, but he refused to release his hold. My heart raced as I tried to find a sustaining breath. The air had vanished. My knees began to give way, and I felt myself go faint. I did not fall. Instead, powerful arms scooped beneath mine.

And then that voice, so familiar, so foreign, whispered, Get his feet.

He thought I was a man. And there was at least one more who grabbed my ankles. I did not dare contemplate what would happen when they realized I was not a man. Nothing less than terror surged through me. I could not let them take me. I lashed out with every bit of strength left in me, whipping my head back and forth and connecting with a nose behind me. It made a satisfactory crunch even as pain shot through my head.

They dropped me, and what breath I had left disappeared upon impact. Still I forced myself to scramble away on my hands and knees. I was not fast enough.

A body landed on me, heavy and painful, pressing my face into the grass below. It smelled of salt and earth, and I wished to disappear into it. Every part of me ached, and I tried to hold back tears. They were too persistent. When he rolled me over, I met his gaze, though my vision was clouded.

His eyes grew large, and he reached a hand up. I prepared myself to be struck, but instead he pushed the cap from my head, letting my plait fall to the ground.

I could not be concerned with the revelation. I gasped, for I knew the eyes staring at me, just as green as my garden. The line of his lips had become sterner, and the dimples I remembered were hidden behind a young beard. His nose was red and blood trickled from it. Still, I knew this man.

Caroline?

He said my name as a question, but all my doubts vanished in an instant. Josiah Hillman had been returned to me.

I reached for his face, to touch him, to feel him, as though his weight upon me was not evidence enough that he had returned. Before I could even respond to his question, another familiar voice intruded. Bradford insisted that we move. If he was surprised by the return of his best friend, he did not show it. Instead he shuttled us toward the trees where Marigold had been tied up. She was gone, but I could not take my gaze from Josiah. He is not the same boy who left four years ago. Now he is older. Serious. Weary.

I wanted to take account of every single change in him, but there was not time. I was hardly standing before my father joined us, his scowl deep. He accused me of breaking Josiah's nose, but Josiah quickly amended the statement. Not broken, he insisted, even as he mopped the blood from his lip with the cuff of his shirt.

There was no time to apologize as my father ordered me to ride with him. He had no time to take me home, and no one could be spared to escort me. I would have to join them. Father boosted me onto the saddle and climbed up behind me. I thought I heard him whisper that he wished I had stayed at home.

I tried to wish the same. I could not.

We trotted down the road for a moment before coming upon the same wagon that had been on the beach. Gone were the uniforms, and only then did I realize that Josiah had not been wearing gray. I tried to twist toward him, but my father kept his arms tight at my sides so that I could see none of the faces of the men surrounding the wagon.

I settled on watching the wagon loaded with the ship's cargo. All that time I'd wondered what might be aboard, I had not taken into account the containers used to carry such a haul, so my first view of the smugglers' goods was nothing short of disappointing.

We then rode for nearly an hour, not toward Savannah but south toward the Carrey farm. I had visited the farm when Mrs. Carrey had her second, third, and fourth babies. Mama had said we had an obligation to help how we could. Their home is worn, but their barn looked nearly new.

When we arrived, Mr. Carrey came out of his house. The only evidence of Mrs. Carrey was her shadow in the front window. He helped the men unload the wagon into the barn. There were nearly a dozen men with my father, but as they carried the crates down a set of stairs beneath the wooden floors of the barn, it seemed to take them an eternity. My father insisted I stay on Thunder until they were done.

The night was well past half through by the time we set out for home. Only then did I realize that Josiah was no longer with our party. I asked my father where he had gone.

Back.

It was all he said, and it settled in my stomach as a brick. But I was weary. My head throbbed, and my eyes closed of their own volition. I leaned against my father and fell asleep until he carried me into the house, tucked me into bed, and kissed my forehead. I asked him about Marigold, and he assured me that she would find her way home.

God surely protected us tonight.

He whispered those words over me before returning to his own room and Mama's side. She woke me up this morning, her voice shaking the roof. My head pounded, and my whole body ached.

I cannot be made to care. Not when I know Josiah is back from the dead.

SEVEN

*I*t was the perfect day for a picnic, but Tucker would rather be just about anywhere else in the world. He pulled at the neck of his costume, running a finger beneath the stiff collar, and jerked his shoulders beneath the unfamiliar wool jacket as PJ's ride pulled up to the curb at the entrance to the fort.

He opened the back door, and a deluge of blue silk spilled out. Reaching for her, he helped her find her feet, then she shook out whatever wrinkles had dared to find a way onto her dress.

"Hurry up. We're late," PJ whispered as she slipped her white-gloved hand into the crook of his arm.

He glared down at her, but he could feel his lips twitching, refusing to hold the frown. Especially not when she swished her skirt like a bell ringing in the church steeple. "I'm not the one running behind."

"Come on, you lug. Let's go show off your uniform, my dress, and our *relationship*." She took a step from the paved parking lot to the green lawn, but he didn't move, so she paused. "Besides, there are some big-time potential donors about fifty yards that way."

The tilt of her head indicated the section of grass filled with colorful dresses and gray uniforms against the ruined red walls of Fort Pulaski. The Union's cannons had over-taken the fort early in the war—shortly after it had been completed—and what remained was a testament to the power of rifled cannon fire rather than a proud Southern bastion.

"Remind me again, why do they have this every year? I mean, we gave up the fort without much of a fight."

She tugged on his arm, marching them across the grass. "Yes, but there were no casualties."

"By that logic, Gettysburg would be the least important battle in the war, and that doesn't sound accurate to me. Even if I did almost fail American history."

She tripped, and he swung his arm around her waist to keep her upright. If she fell over in that skirt, they'd make some scene just getting her back on her feet. Not what he needed when he was about to ask donors to attend his fund-raiser.

Plus keeping his arm around her gave him the added benefit of being able to smell the honeysuckle on her skin. And re-minding Winston what he'd missed out on. Yes, that last one. There would be plenty of wagging tongues at the picnic all too eager to let Winston know PJ was just fine. That was the point here.

She swatted at his chest, but he noticed she didn't pull away. "You did not almost fail American history."

He shrugged. *Almost* was a loose term, and if she'd known how many times he had to read the assigned chapters and how he'd had to negotiate extra time to write the essays . . . well, it had been worth it in his favorite class.

He'd hated the way she looked at him with pity back then, and he wasn't about to invite that look again. "Fort Pulaski wasn't what I'd call a defining moment in the war."

"Fair enough. But it could be a defining moment in your campaign." Her smile was bright and wide as they approached the punch table. "That's Mrs. Catherine Saunders over there. Old money."

He risked a glance toward the regal woman, her pale purple dress shimmering in the sunlight. The whole city knew that she'd single-handedly financed the search for the *Catherine*—the ship that had been lost off the Georgia coast and found by Carter Hale and his now wife, Anne Norris.

There was no question about the depth of Mrs. Saunders's pockets. But old money generally meant loyalty to Savannah—to the South—above all. He doubted she'd be eager to reach into those pockets for someone whose family was accused of being traitors.

When they reached the punch table, the young woman standing beside Anabelle Haywood looked PJ up and down, a frown firmly in place. "Penelope. I wasn't sure you'd show."

"Ginny." PJ nodded her head in a warm greeting. "I wouldn't miss it."

Ginny had a face like she'd sucked too many lemons, pinched and sour, and her blonde hair was pulled sternly from her face.

"Good of you to bring extra help," Mrs. Haywood said, although her tone suggested otherwise. "You'll be at the punch table with Ginny. And Mr. Westbrook can help deliver the baskets."

PJ's eyes went wide. "Oh, I was hoping to work with—"

"Right this way." Mrs. Haywood escorted him away from the ornate punch bowl, and he let PJ go.

"I'll see you later," she said.

He nodded, allowing himself to be led away. More than two dozen round tables had been set up on the lawn, each covered in a red-and-white-checkered blanket. And, of course, the food was served family style. From a picnic basket.

Mrs. Haywood pointed him to a rack of wicker baskets, each with a handle and flaps covering the contents. "Each table gets one basket. You'll unpack it for them, set the food on the lazy Susan, and offer to refill their punch cups. Any questions?"

Tucker picked up a basket. "Any particular table I should start with?"

Mrs. Haywood pointed to the nearest one. "You'll take the even tables. Jethro will deliver to the odd ones. But wait until I give you the signal."

As she sashayed away in her hoop skirt, he swung his gaze toward Jethro Coleman. According to Carter, Jethro was one of the best local historians. But the way he patted the silver flask at his hip did not make Tucker inclined to trust him with family secrets. His Confederate uniform, faded and pulling at the seams, had seen better days. The jacket barely buttoned around his middle, and his silver hair stood mostly on end. His overgrown whiskers made him look almost authentic. He looked the same as he had at a reenactment the year before—rough and ready for a rumble.

"Westbrook," Jethro said, reaching out his hand.

Tucker shook it, giving a genuine smile. He was not going to use his political grin today. "Good to see you, Jethro. How are you and your family?" He couldn't exactly remember the last time they'd spoken, but his mother would think she'd raised a barn animal if he didn't show some social graces.

Jethro's smile was missing a tooth but none of the joy he usually displayed. "Mama 'n' them are good. You?"

"We're doing just fine. Thank you."

Jethro scooped up a basket but made no move to deliver it. "And the election?"

Tucker couldn't keep his eyebrows from jumping. He hadn't counted on Jethro being up on the local political landscape, but maybe he'd failed to consider who cared about the acting sheriff. With a nod and shrug, he said, "Fine. Still a little more than three weeks to go."

"Buddy is buying up most of the TV and radio spots. You going to counter?"

He knew that Jepson was buying up advertising space—whereas the "Tucker Westbrook for Sheriff" campaign fund had only a couple nickels to rub together. The surprise was that Jethro Coleman knew too.

Then again, the special election brought about by the previous sheriff's sudden passing had surprised everyone. Tucker had just had less time to put his campaign together since his accidental announcement. Buddy had been stirring up support for a run in the next regular election for almost a year. He was miles ahead.

After a long pause, Tucker said, "I'm working on a few things."

He glanced over the lawn as couples decked out in their finest antebellum attire began to find their seats, and his gut twisted. Did they all know? Did they think he was a joke like his dad did?

Sweat broke out across the back of his neck, and his palms itched to wipe it away. Only mustering every bit of training that he'd acquired in the Marines kept him from squirming under the sudden realization.

He caught a vision in blue in his peripheral vision, and his gaze locked on PJ as she ladled punch into a dainty cup.

PJ didn't think he was a joke or she wouldn't be wasting her time working on his campaign events. She thought he could win. Which meant he could win. And when he did, he'd show her she hadn't wasted her belief in him.

It also meant he should probably listen to her advice.

Surveying the tables, he found Mrs. Catherine Saunders, her fair skin protected by a frilly umbrella, which she twirled in a lazy fashion. She sat at table number three.

"Hey, would you mind swapping tables with me?" he asked Jethro. "I'll do the odds and you can do the evens."

Jethro shrugged. "Sure."

Tucker smiled and patted him on the back. "Thanks, man."

"Don't thank me yet. You're still looking for that treasure, ain't you?"

Tucker couldn't keep his jaw from dropping. Only a handful of people knew that he and PJ had started looking for a treasure. Carter, probably his wife, and Aunt Shirley. Besides, they'd barely started. "How'd you know?"

With a lazy wink, Jethro chuckled. "It's what I'd be doing if it was me in your boots."

"So . . ." Tucker had dismissed the idea of working with Jethro, but maybe he'd rushed judgment. "Do you know anything about it?"

Jethro shook his head. "Not much more than mosta the people who've looked fer it over the years."

His stomach hit the grass just as Mrs. Haywood waved for them to begin delivering baskets. Jethro was gone like a shot, his grin on full display as he schmoozed the first table to their left. Tucker stumbled toward table number one, but one phrase echoed in his mind. *People who've looked for it.*

There were others. Maybe many others. And none of them had been successful. Would he be any different? Could he find the only thing that might give him a chance of beating Buddy Jepson?

No sooner had the name come to mind than the person appeared at his table. Tucker bit his tongue and lamented his brilliant idea to change assignments with Jethro as he set the basket on the edge of the table.

"Well, well, if it isn't Tucker Westbrook." Buddy sing-songed the greeting, and a generally uncomfortable titter rose from the ladies on either side of him. "You look good in service. Maybe you should stick to it."

Tucker grimaced but forced that political smile he'd sworn not to use into place. "Thanks, Buddy." He nodded a greeting. "I figure elected officials are public servants, so I thought I'd get a head start on serving my community."

Buddy frowned, but Tucker pushed forward, refusing to give the other man a chance to insert himself. Pushing his political smile as far as it would go, he asked, "Is everyone having a good time?"

There were several nods and mumbled responses as he flipped open the basket lid. The scent of fried chicken and apple pie wafted out on a cloud of steam, and taking a deep breath of it replaced his tense smile with a genuine one.

"Looks like a good lunch today," he announced, setting a

bowl of potato salad next to the chicken on the lazy Susan. "Can I refresh anyone's drink?"

A girl on the far side of the table, no older than junior high, held up her glass. "Yes, please."

"My pleasure, miss." His wink made her giggle, and his bow had her leaning on her dad's shoulder. With a glance at her father, he asked, "Anything for you, sir?"

The man, not much older than Tucker himself, simply mouthed, *Thank you*.

His fake smile long gone, Tucker ambled across the grass toward the punch table. Ginny had abandoned PJ, who stood behind the crystal bowl with a sweet smile in place, her hands clasped in front of her.

"You sure like swishing that skirt," he said.

She treated him to a smile. "Truthfully? It keeps the air moving."

His laugh broke free, and he looked down at his own clothing devoid of any such cooling mechanisms. "Lucky." He didn't reveal that the wool was fairly cool, the loose weave allowing the summer breeze through to his damp skin.

"I saw you had a run-in with Buddy over there. Everything okay?" She took the glass he'd been carrying but didn't move to fill it.

"I think so. He took a stab, but I blocked it."

Dipping her ladle into the too-pink concoction, she said, "I can't wait to hear all about it."

"Well, that's not the most interesting thing that's happened so far."

The tip of her nose wrinkled. "How is that possible? We've only been here for fifteen minutes."

"I was talking to Jethro—turns out we're definitely not the first to look for the treasure."

"What?" She nearly dropped the cup he had to return. "I almost forgot. I have to—"

"I better get this punch back to its owner," he said at the same time.

Her face pinched like she was going to argue, but then it relaxed. "I saw the way she was looking at you. A little hero worship for the dashing lieutenant. Should I be jealous?"

He knew she was only teasing, but something in his chest gave a pleasant squeeze at the thought of her being jealous. As he took the cup from her, he let his thumb brush the tips of her fingers. It lasted only a moment, but her sharp breath and wide eyes were all he needed.

"I'll see you later, Penelope Jean."

After returning the cup with another grin and wink, he picked up his next basket and moved toward table three. Mrs. Catherine Saunders waved him over to stand between her and her granddaughter Minnie. He smiled and offered the same bow he'd given his young friend at the first table.

"You look very sharp in that uniform, Mr. Westbrook. But I think I prefer your Marine dress blues."

He couldn't help but chuckle. His parents went to church with Mrs. Saunders. Had his mother been passing around his picture?

"Me too, ma'am."

She patted his arm, her gloved hand a mere whisper. "Was that Buddy Jepson giving you a hard time?"

He reached into the basket and pulled out the plate of golden fried chicken, shaking his head. "No, ma'am."

"Good. Now why have I not been invited to a fundraiser for you? Buddy has sent me three requests."

He swallowed the question he wanted to ask—had she given to Buddy's campaign? Instead he did what he apparently should have done all along. "Now that you mention it, ma'am, I was hoping you'd join us for dinner on Friday night. It's at the VFW." As soon as he said it, he *heard* it. Mrs. Saunders, who lived in a three-million-dollar home and dined at The Olde Pink House and The Grey, did not have dinner at a VFW post. Even if renting the historic hall had nearly emptied his campaign coffers. But he had to spend money to make money—or so PJ assured him.

Now it was all sounding like a sad story. A guy without much money running for office on the proceeds from his profitable—but young—business.

"The VFW?" She narrowed her eyes, the wrinkles around her lips more pronounced as she puckered her displeasure.

He focused on unpacking the rest of the basket and prayed that no one else at the table was listening. Maybe he wasn't going to get their vote anyway, but he didn't need them to see her toss him to the side.

"Near Forsyth Park?"

He nodded quickly.

"Minnie, put it on my calendar. What time?"

He nearly dropped the whole apple pie. "Um . . . seven?"

"Are you asking me?" Her words were clipped but not unkind.

"No, ma'am. Seven. On Friday."

Mrs. Saunders looked at her granddaughter, who had pulled her phone out and was typing with her thumbs. "We'll be there." The breeze tugging at her umbrella was almost enough to knock him over, and he nearly went down when she spoke again. "Jerry, Meg, you'll attend too. Bring your checkbooks."

The couple on her other side nodded absently, too busy poking their forks into the crispy chicken.

"And bring your son too." She looked up at Tucker and stage-whispered behind her hand, "He's a wealth manager. Who knows what he really does, but he drives the same car as James Bond."

As she poured more Sprite into the punch bowl and the pink sherbet turned to foam, Penelope let herself imagine what an event this size might be like for Jordan and Stepping Stones. The only thing bigger than the backdrop of Fort Pulaski was the pocketbooks of the attendees.

Imagine if each of them were to offer a job to one of the kids in Jordan's program. Imagine if all of those kids had a safe place to live and reliable transportation and the support of adults who could help them find their way in the world. What a boost an event like this would be for each of those kids. Kids with faces and names and hopes and dreams.

And she'd let them all down.

She hadn't heard from Jordan since she'd slumped out of the office, shoulders hunched and head bowed. Her eyes suddenly started to water, and she blinked hard to keep a tear from escaping and dragging her mascara down her face. She couldn't very well wipe it away with the glove on her hand.

"You could use more punch." Ginny announced her arrival in what Penelope had quickly identified as her usual way. "I brought you more juice. Why didn't you use it?"

Penelope stared at her recently refreshed punch bowl three-quarters full. "I did, actually."

"Well, it's not enough." Ginny marched off, more likely looking for an excuse to escape the table than because she truly believed the punch was running low.

That worked for her. Penelope would much rather stand alone at the table than be stuck with Ginny for company. Dreaming about what an event for Jordan might look like was much more fun than grasping for any common ground with Mrs. Haywood's right-hand woman.

She was slowly stirring the punch, lost somewhere far away, when Jethro arrived at her table, holding out two empty punch glasses. "Hello, Miss Hunter."

"Oh, Penelope, please."

He nodded, his eyes direct, piercing into her. "You and Westbrook, then?"

"Ex-excuse me?" She wasn't sure what he was asking, and she sure wasn't certain how to respond. Did he think they were together? That was good. Right?

"You're helping him look for the treasure."

The statement had no question mark attached, and she gasped. Tucker had said Jethro knew things about the treasure. But he seemed to know things about her too. And it made her hands tremble so much, she struggled to fill the cups.

"How did—did Tucker say something?"

"Naw. But y'all's thicker'n thieves. Figured if he was goin' after it, you'd be there too."

But how did he know that about them? She'd never spoken a word to him before this moment, barely been in the same room.

"You'd better hurry if you want to get there in time for the election." He took his cups and disappeared between the tables.

Squinting in his wake, she jumped when a cool voice in her ear said, "It's going well, don't you think?"

Clutching at her charging heart, she nodded quickly in Mrs. Haywood's direction. "Yes, ma'am."

"Looks like you have plenty of punch."

Ha. Take that, Ginny.

"Yes, ma'am." Penelope followed the direction of Mrs. Haywood's gaze toward a table where Tucker was unpacking a basket. His deep chuckle carried across the expanse, and she could nearly see the twinkle in his eyes. "He looks good in the uniform, doesn't he?"

Mrs. Haywood clucked her tongue in what could only be resigned agreement. "I'm glad he hasn't spent the whole afternoon by your side."

"Of course not." She clamped her mouth closed and swallowed the truth that had made her voice jump an octave. The truth was she wanted to spend more time with Tucker, and she'd have been happy for an opportunity to tell him what she'd read in Caroline's diary the night before.

Taking a deep breath, she tried again. "We're here to support the League, to help out however you need us. It's really important to me—and to Tucker—to support our community."

"Hmmm." Mrs. Haywood made a low sound in the back of her throat. "You seem eager to speak for him. Are you . . . more than friends?"

Lord, save me.

There was no way to get around this without an outright

lie—or revealing that she'd let others believe something that wasn't quite accurate. She could say that they were dating. They were. Even if it was for show. But that was splitting an awfully fine hair.

"Well, we've known each other forever, and . . ." Her voice trailed off, words disappearing.

Mrs. Haywood tsked. "You do know if you're courting, do you not?"

"Of course I do." They were not *courting*.

The trouble was that the idea didn't sound entirely terrible. She'd let it enter her head a time or two—not to mention she'd jumped on Emmaline's implication without prodding. But dating him had its risks. The potential loss was too much to even consider. What if things went south? What if he saw the thing that was missing in her—the thing Winston had seen? Possibly the same thing her dad had seen?

What if Tucker decided she wasn't worthy of the rest of his life too? She wasn't sure she could endure that again. She wouldn't risk losing him.

Besides, this had all started because Winston had waltzed back into her life. She was not about to give him the power to speak into her relationship status. Not again.

Except you already have.

She gave the punch a vigorous stir. Whatever was going on between Tucker and her was not Winston's doing. Anyway, there wasn't anything going on. Winston did not have the power to conjure feelings where there had been none for twenty-five years. Neither did Anabelle Haywood.

With a glance down her nose, Mrs. Haywood gave a little cough. "You couldn't possibly be serious with such a man."

Penelope swung her haughtiest gaze onto the older woman,

glaring with everything inside her. "What do you mean by that? Tucker is a good man—a great man."

"But his family history speaks for itself. They were traitors to their homeland. Thieves and smugglers."

Penelope cringed but never let her gaze stray from the older woman's. True, the journal entries she'd read the night before revealed some . . . indiscretions on the part of the Westbrook family. But surely they weren't as terrible as Buddy Jepson and Anabelle Haywood made them out to be.

With a shake of her head, Penelope said, "You can't be sure of that. And even if the Westbrooks from a hundred years ago were as terrible as you say, does that mean Tucker is made from the same cloth? He served in the Marines for more than five years. You're not discounting his service, are you?"

Mrs. Haywood pressed a white-gloved hand to her throat, her mouth hanging open but silent for several long seconds. When she did finally regain the use of her tongue, her voice went up an octave. "Well, I certainly never meant to suggest any such thing."

Of course she had. Only Penelope wasn't free to tell her that she knew the truth.

"I only meant that you—a smart, educated"—her gaze dropped, a dissatisfied frown falling into place as she performed a quick survey—"nice-enough-looking girl—should be careful who you link your name to."

Penelope nearly snapped the metal ladle in her fist. *Nice-enough-looking girl? Nice.*

The mirror wasn't always as kind as she would like, but the backhanded compliment stung. Sure, she wasn't glossy-magazine pretty. Her wedding dress had had to be special ordered in a bigger size. Her corset was starting to dig into her ribs, and she doubted its worth, even if it did give her a slim waist. But she didn't need some old bat telling her she looked nice enough. And she sure didn't need her saying that Tucker was somehow unworthy. She wanted no part in this snooty society.

It doesn't matter. You need them to keep your job and to win Tucker's election.

Everything inside her wanted to silence the voice in her mind, but it made a good point. Rats.

Apparently taking her silence as agreement, Mrs. Haywood patted her arm gently. "We all want what's best. And you can do better."

Oh, that was taking it too far. It didn't matter if she needed to be in Mrs. Haywood's good graces.

Penelope took a deep breath and let it out slowly. Squaring her shoulders and turning to face Mrs. Haywood directly, she made her decision. "If he asked, I'd marry Tucker Westbrook tomorrow."

She enjoyed seeing Mrs. Haywood's trembling lips for a split second. Until a deep voice behind her said, "PJ?"

EIGHT

*P*enelope hugged the extra fabric of her dress to her chest as Tucker gave her one more glance before closing the passenger-side door of his truck. She grimaced as she watched him stop and talk with Jethro Coleman. Her discomfort had nothing to do with the sun beating into the car and everything to do with opening her big mouth.

Why did I say that? What was I thinking?

She hadn't been. It was that simple. She'd let Mrs. Haywood goad her into saying the absolute worst thing. At the worst possible time.

She and Tucker had had a plan, and she should have stuck to it. They were dating. Just without the feelings. And definitely without the future possibilities. They were spending a little extra time together, letting people see whatever they expected to see.

What they were not doing was implying a forever kind of commitment. To anyone. Least of all loose-tongued Anabelle Haywood.

She covered her face with her hands and managed a strangled breath. *God, my plan is falling apart.* Maybe it was bound to—a plan based on an untruth. And that ugly truth twisted in her stomach. *Lord, you're going to have to work a miracle to get me out of this.* But her prayer felt like it didn't even make it out of the cab of the truck, let alone to heaven.

The driver-side door opened, and Tucker slid behind the wheel. He glanced over his shoulder as though checking to make sure that her hoop was still tucked in the back of the cab, but he never looked at her. As soon as he turned the ignition, the air-conditioning blasted them.

He didn't reach for the gearshift, his hands resting on the steering wheel.

Her swallow was loud enough to echo in the cab, and she steeled herself against whatever he was going to say—probably that this had been the worst plan ever conceived. If she was honest with herself, it had all started because of her bad decision.

She was definitely in the market for a miracle. Sudden time travel would work. Or a sinkhole to devour her. She'd take mysterious amnesia on Tucker's part or just a rocket ship to the moon, where she could live out the rest of her life in relative peace, devoid of crippling embarrassment. That wasn't too much to ask, was it?

She looked toward the sky, but the happy clouds gave no indication of a pending miracle. Not that miracles came with a visible warning of their arrival.

"So, that was different," he said.

"I'm so sorry," she spoke over him.

She tried for a chuckle, but it didn't make it very far out of her throat.

He stared at her, his gaze digging into the deepest parts

of her, and she was tempted to jump out of his truck and walk home. But she'd never before run from telling him the truth. She wouldn't start today.

"Okay, so what happened was Mrs. Haywood started in on how much time we spend together and suggested you weren't worthy of my time. Even though we're not really dating . . . well, that doesn't mean I don't recognize what an amazing man you are."

The corners of his mouth crinkled into a smile that his beard couldn't hide. "You think I'm amazing?"

"Shut up." She shoved his arm. "If you were anything less, I wouldn't have put up with you for so many years."

He chuckled. "I get that, but it feels like quite a stretch to get to marriage. Tomorrow?"

"Well, what was I supposed to do? She kept pushing— she was so haughty. She thinks they're all so much better than . . ."

"Me."

"And me too." That felt like a weak addition. Penelope hated that she'd led him there in the first place. He didn't sound surprised, but she didn't want to rub it in. Because as she looked at him, at the strength in his posture and the determination in his eyes, she was reminded he was trustworthy and principled. A man of integrity and compassion.

She was the one who had dragged him down with this fabricated story that they were dating.

Pressing a fist to her stomach, she tried to dislodge the stone sitting there. It wasn't a result of her corset being too tight but a nagging reminder of her own sin.

"Tucker, when I asked you to pretend to date me, I opened

you up to wagging tongues and disparaging remarks." She shook her head. "I never should have done that. I'm sorry."

He narrowed his gaze at her, his eyes more intense than lasers. She could physically feel their touch, and she shivered in the cool air of the vent.

"You *asked* me?" His eyebrow hooked up. "That's not how I remember it."

"Well, you know how it was—I was the one who implied a relationship."

His lips twitched as he reached for her hand, swallowing it with his own. "PJ, as I recall, I was the one who suggested we give this thing a try. I thought it was worth it. I still do."

She memorized the feel of his hand on hers, his fingers rough and callused. The tips of his fingers were blunt but clean, his knuckles a little bit dry. Hardworking hands. But so gentle. He held her like she was worth more than any treasure Caroline's diary might reveal. It didn't remove the stone in her middle but sent butterflies to join it until she thought her corset might burst.

She took a deep breath and let it out in a slow puff. "I think this was a bad idea. Maybe we should just go back to being friends and remind people we're nothing more."

His eyes were so blue, like the sky. "Well, that's a fine how-do-you-do. You're breaking up with me before my fundraiser next week." He gave an exaggerated eye roll. "You just wanted to use me to fill out the uniform, and then you drop me like a football."

With a chuckle, she shook her head. "I don't think that's a saying."

"Oh, I've seen you play football, and you've never caught the ball once."

"Okay, fair. But that's not what I was doing. I just mean this could easily become complicated, and we don't have an exit strategy. And the next time I tell someone I'm going to get married, I'd like to actually be engaged."

His shoulders shook as he licked his lips. "You know, there's a really easy way to do that. You don't tell anyone you're going to marry me."

She slugged his arm again, and he gave an exaggerated slump against the driver-side door. "Stop it. I'm being serious. That was an accident, but I can't stand it when they talk about your family like that. I need a better plan if we're going to do this."

"Count on you to need a plan."

"Well, I had one." She smoothed her hands over her skirt. "By this point I was supposed to be married, expecting my first baby, and settling into our first home. And then . . ."

She didn't expound. Didn't need to.

He squeezed her hand again. "I know that plan didn't pan out, but it doesn't mean God doesn't have another one for you."

"I know. It's just that . . ." She rolled her eyes against a sudden burning there as Mrs. Haywood's words jumped back to her mind. She was barely nice enough looking.

Adjusting himself in his seat so he could look at her directly, he asked, "What?"

Letting out a shaking breath, she whispered, "Mrs. Haywood may have implied that I'll have to rely on my brains to attract a husband. Because . . ." She used her free hand to gesture to the rest of her.

His face turned red, and his lips disappeared in a thin line. "She said what?" His words came out on a growl, his eyes turning feral.

"It's stupid, I know."

"I'll . . ." He let her hand go and shook his fist between them. "Where is she? I'm going to—"

Penelope lunged for his arm and hugged him to her with a chuckle. "She's an old woman, Tucker. But I love that you're willing to defend my honor."

His scowl remained as he cleared his throat. "You know it's not true, right?"

"Why, Mr. Westbrook." She fanned her face and used her best Scarlett O'Hara impression. "Are you saying I'm pretty?"

He didn't say anything for a very long moment, and she could have bitten off her tongue. Too far. Why was she taking everything too far today?

Then his words came out on a breath. "Miss Hunter, you're lovely." They wrapped around her, warmer than an embrace, sweeter than a peanut butter cup.

If only his words didn't have so much power.

Tucker turned back to look out the rear window and shifted into gear. "Let's go home. I could use a change of clothes and a nap."

She nodded. "Okay, but I thought you might like to go to the Carrey farm today."

He dipped his chin as he pulled out of the almost empty parking lot. "The Carrey farm? I don't know where that is."

"I read about it in Caroline's diary last night."

"And you waited to tell me?"

"Honestly? I was afraid you'd decide the picnic wasn't worth it and steal away to the farm instead."

His laugh came from deep in his chest, and he nudged her with his elbow. "You know me well. But I'm glad we came to the picnic."

"You are? Even in that uniform?"

"Hey, Catherine Saunders is coming to my campaign dinner. And she's bringing friends."

"And you waited to tell me that? That's big news! Congratulations."

He laughed again. "All right. Tell me about the diary."

So she told him about the smuggled goods—whatever they were—and that Caroline's family had been caught up in something. She told him about the wagon carrying it out to the Carrey farm. She told him about all of it.

All except Caroline and Josiah. Because even through the page and 150 years, she knew true love. She'd overseen enough weddings, talked to enough brides-to-be, seen enough grooms. She knew what love sounded like. And Caroline was in love.

She didn't know yet if Caroline would find her happy ending, but for now it was her own private treasure hunt, a special story tucked beside her heart. She'd keep reading it until she knew the truth.

When she had laid out all the important pieces, Tucker tossed her his phone. "Let's figure out where the old Carrey farm is and if there's still a barn."

Tucker could kiss the county recorder. Even if Evelyn Butcher was twice his age and loosely related on his mom's side. He didn't care. She'd called him back on a Saturday to tell him she didn't even need to go into the office to find the answer to his question. The old Carrey farm had long been abandoned, its lands bought up by neighboring spreads.

The property's barn was still standing—barely—and

the small plot was currently owned by the county. Apparently none of the neighbors or developers wanted to buy the land—not when it would cost them a few nickels to raze the old barn.

"Which means it's okay for us to take a look around?" he asked.

"Suppose so. Just don't go trespassing on no one else's property. You do and we never spoke."

He snorted into his phone. "Fair 'nuf. Thank you, ma'am."

He hung up the hands-free call just as he pulled back up to the curb at PJ's apartment. He'd dropped her off more than an hour before and promised to come back for her after they'd both had a chance to change out of their picnic clothes.

But now that he was here—without the facade of his Confederate uniform—his stomach twisted tighter than a knot. In brown cargo shorts and a T-shirt, he was just Tucker. Tucker who everyone said wasn't good enough for PJ Hunter. Tucker whom PJ had said she'd marry.

When he'd overheard her, those words had felt like a left hook out of nowhere—but not because they were so awful. They were unexpected. Not entirely unpleasant.

More than 150 years before, they couldn't have been friends like they were now. If he'd wanted a few minutes alone with her, he would have had to marry her.

And he would have wanted to.

That hit his gut, and he squeezed the steering wheel until his knuckles turned white. He was not going to think about how much he liked talking with her or how she made him laugh. And he sure wasn't going to think about how pretty she was.

Thinking about those things could only distract him. Especially when he had an election to win—and a point to prove to his dad. He was good enough for any educated woman, even—maybe especially—PJ.

She bounded up the steps of her garden apartment as though on cue, brushing her fingers along a honeysuckle hedge. Maybe that's why she always smelled like the stuff.

Sure enough, the scent of the flowers followed her in as she launched herself up into his truck, her skirts replaced by green shorts and a multicolored tank top. She'd exchanged her boots for a pair of purple low-top Chuck Taylors.

"What did you find out?"

That my thoughts are wandering into dangerous territory. She probably meant besides that.

"The barn is still standing, and it's on county property."

With a clap of her hands, she said, "Well, what are you waiting for? Let's go."

Putting his truck into gear, he checked his blind spot and pulled away from the curb. They drove in silence for five minutes before the truth hit him. This should be awkward. It wasn't.

This was the reason they were best friends. No amount of ridiculousness stuck. Forgiveness came fast and certain. Or at least forgetfulness. Even if he had to actively choose to forget what she'd said.

He smiled as he caught her eye. "So, what do you think was in this lost treasure?"

The tip of her nose wrinkled, her lips working from side to side as she stared at the row of trees guarding the road before them. "I don't know. Caroline didn't sound sure either. Probably the same things everyone else was trying to smuggle in."

"Yeah, like what?"

She scowled at him. "Like smuggled stuff. Like stuff that would come over on a boat. Like . . . I can't even remember what Caroline said she thought would be in the crates."

He snorted.

"Why are you asking me anyway? You probably know."

True. He had some guesses. There were only a few things worth running the Union blockade—and they all equated to dollars and cents. Or weapons and ammunition.

"Do you think we're going to find it? These dazzling diamonds or whatever?"

His shoulders twitched. "I sure hope so." The money could make a world of difference for his campaign, and that truth came through his tone.

"You saw the new commercial." She didn't bother adding a question mark to the end of her words.

"Yes. I saw it." Or rather, he'd heard it, since he'd covered his eyes. It had been almost enough to make him sick.

She made a fist and slammed it into her other palm. "That Buddy Jepson—he can't be allowed to do this."

"What? Run a campaign?"

"Run a *dirty* campaign." She squeezed her fist, and her knuckles turned white until her whole arm shook.

He rested his hand on her knee. "It's okay, PJ."

"But he knows you don't have the money to run TV spots. So he ran that . . . that . . ." She waved her hand toward the window as though she could conjure the deplorable ad. And it had been awful.

He'd cringed through every single one of the fifteen seconds. *Barely graduated high school . . . the heir of traitors . . . Tucker Westbrook is the wrong choice for Chatham County.*

He'd memorized that last line real quick. And then he'd steeled himself for the call from his dad.

He didn't know which was worse—the tense waiting or the fact that the call never came. Was it better to be reprimanded or ignored? It was a question he couldn't answer, so he welcomed one from PJ that he could.

"How are you going to retaliate?"

He patted her leg before pulling his hand away as they left the city limits and most of the traffic behind them. "I'm not."

PJ let out a burst of air. "You're kidding. I've never known you to take a hit lying down."

"I'm not lying down. I'm just not going to hit back." He shrugged one shoulder, leaning into the steering wheel as he followed the route Evelyn had mapped out for him. "Besides, I don't have any money to fight dirt with dirt. My campaign fund is hemorrhaging at the moment." A fact that Beau Bailey, his campaign manager, had been quick to remind him of the day before.

"Then you need more donors. Like Mrs. Saunders. You said she's coming." Her words spilled out in fits and starts like overflowing popcorn.

"I'm still not going to dig up dirt on Jepson."

"You can do that?"

He gave another shrug. "My team monitors more than half the private security cameras in the city. I could do that."

"Well, why didn't you tell me that when Winston broke up with me? I could have used some ammo right about then."

His laugh filled the cab, bouncing off the ceiling and lifting an unnamed weight from his chest. He hadn't known he needed the release until that very moment, until he could breathe easily again.

"Thank you for that, PJ."

Bumping her forearm against his, she didn't even crack a grin. "I'm serious. I could have used that info."

"To do what?"

Now her smile slid into place, shy and thoughtful at first. "Oh, you know . . ."

"You didn't need it. You got over him on your own." He reached out to tug on her ponytail and immediately regretted letting his fingers wind into her silky hair. He did not need another reminder of how soft, how feminine she was. Of how he'd failed to notice for twenty-five years. Of how the knowledge seemed to be slapping him upside the head every other minute lately.

Clearing his throat, he pulled his hand free a little too quickly, catching a strand on his watch. She cringed, and he offered a quick apology, his mind racing for another topic. Anything. He came up blank just as his phone alerted them that they had almost reached the farm.

Allowing himself a quick sigh, he turned onto a dirt drive. The truck bumped over several holes and rounded a bend before the shabby wooden barn appeared before them. PJ gasped and leaned against the dashboard.

"Does it look like Caroline described it?" he asked as he pulled to a stop beside the lone structure.

"Well, she didn't really describe it. She was more . . . um . . . she was distracted by everything going on, I guess."

Well, this had to be the place—the only barn for miles. It had belonged to a Carrey family for a few generations. But the barn didn't look like it had been around for more than 150 years.

He cocked his head and shaded his eyes against the setting

sun as he got out of the truck. The structure was rough, to say the least. The angled roof sported large holes, and the red paint that had once adorned the exterior had long since been peeled off by wind and sand. The salt air—and probably a hurricane or two—had warped the boards, and the pair of doors on the front of the building hung on rusted hinges.

But the corners were stable, sharp ninety degrees each. A wooden building as old as the Civil War wouldn't have been standing so erect.

That weight fell back on his chest.

"Come on. What are you waiting for?" PJ was nearly halfway to the doors, but she paused to look over her shoulder at him.

He jogged to catch up, not sure if he should tell her the truth about the building or let her go in and explore. By the time he reached her, he remembered that he didn't *let* her do much of anything. She decided.

PJ had wrestled a big door open about six inches by the time Tucker reached her. He opened his mouth to tell her to stop, but suddenly the door buckled, splinters flying as the boards crumbled. If it made a noise, PJ's scream drowned it out. He scooped her out of the way, shielding her head with one arm and holding her against him with the other. The rotted wood slammed into his shoulder and nearly dissolved upon impact, coating him with a fine layer of dust. He smacked his tongue against the bitter taste covering his lips but didn't let go of PJ.

"You okay?" he asked, his heart hammering so hard it filled his ears with the steady rhythm.

"Fine. Feeling stupid." She spoke directly into his T-shirt, leaving a warm patch in the center of his chest.

Loosening his arms, he let her step back, and she swiped at his shoulders and arms.

"You're covered in this stuff."

He shrugged. "I've been covered in worse."

Her eyes filled with something too tender, and he steeled himself against sinking into her compassion. His memories from his tours were vivid, but she didn't need to be reminded that he was used to being covered in a permanent layer of Iraqi dust. She certainly didn't need to know that once he'd been covered like this in blood as he'd put pressure on a bullet hole in his friend's leg until the medics carried him off.

PJ's life had been—for the most part—sweet. Safe. He wasn't about to fill her head with images she didn't need.

A lot of his buddies had returned home living and dreaming those nightmares. Those experiences had lodged deep inside them and refused to let them find peace. Tucker knew that but for the grace of God—and PJ Hunter—he could have suffered the same. But PJ, in all her innocence, joy, and vigor, had pushed those nightmares away. He remembered the hard experiences, but they never consumed him. So PJ never had to know them.

Forcing a smile, he said, "Better this kind of dirty than Jepson's." With a tug on her hand, he led her into the relative darkness of the barn, using the light from his phone to guide them. "Come on."

She followed, letting out a little squeal when the beam of light captured the tail of a creature scurrying into a darker corner. "Gross." He didn't need to see her face to know the tip of her nose had wrinkled. "Do you think there are more?"

"Probably bats too."

"Ew." She didn't touch him, but he could feel her presence close in on his six. "Do you see anything?"

"I see a family of rats."

"Not that. Something good. Something useful."

He shook his head, his light sweeping across broken beams and buckled stalls. Then his beam disappeared into the floor. It swept across the cement to the right of the door but didn't reach the far wall. His stomach dropped into the floor too.

"What's that?" She'd stepped around him, her feet following his gaze.

Ignoring the layer of debris covering the ground, they both scrambled toward the hole, falling to all fours before the opening. His light filled the dark space, revealing what appeared to be a lower rung of a ladder, the rest of the steps crumbled around it. Approximately a six-foot cube, the dirt-walled storage space would have been perfect for hiding a treasure.

PJ looked up at him, a silly grin in place. "I guess Caroline was right."

"There's no treasure here."

"But there was. So all we have to do is follow her clues," she said.

The weight on his chest doubled down. "Before Jepson buries me in this election."

Sunday, November 27, 1864

I fear that my mind is failing me. I have heard stories of those sent to the asylum. I may be among them soon if something does not change.

I know it to be true in my soul. I am certain that the man I saw only two nights ago was Josiah Hillman. But Bradford swears that it cannot be true. I cornered him this morning to beg him to tell me where I might find Josiah, and he said he did not know what I meant. I made certain that not even the servants were nearby, then whispered that he must have seen our old friend that night. Surely they had spoken before coming upon me. For heaven's sake, Bradford helped Josiah carry me away.

Yet Bradford says it was not so. He shrugged so casually when he suggested that the man perhaps had a passing resemblance to Josiah. But 'twas not him. It could not be him, for Josiah has been dead these many years.

I felt as though someone had pulled on the laces of my stays. I could no longer breathe. I wished to lash out at him, to strike him with my fists as his words had assaulted me. But how could I do that without drawing undue attention upon us? Mother would insist on knowing the cause, and Father would never let me join them again. Though 'tis unlikely he shall relent after the last excursion.

It no longer seems to matter. Not when Bradford was so cavalier about Josiah's death. Not when I am so fully convinced that it was not a ghost I have seen.

Mary once told me after Sunday services that she had seen a ghost in the graveyard across from her bedroom window. I do not believe in such things, and I think she was only attempting to scare the children among us. Nonetheless, she described him as a willowy figure, white as light, strolling among the headstones. He was neither fully flesh nor air. He was a strange combination of both.

Josiah was not that at all. His form had enough weight to press me into the grass. He did not shine. In fact, his face was rather darker than I remembered. And his eyes. I would know those eyes by any light, the touch of his hand upon my person in any way.

I know Mother would not approve, but I let him hold my hand before he left. With no gloves between us, skin to skin, his warmth surrounded me. I can never forget the way he stirred something deep in my chest. It is why I have waited these many years. I need no other suit. I need only Josiah to return to me.

I cannot believe the man I saw was anything other than flesh and blood. But perhaps I have imagined the face of the one I care for so deeply on another.

I have yearned for him for too long. Perhaps my hope has been foolish and my brother is right. Perhaps it has addled my brain. I dare not ask Father if he knew it was Josiah, for it would require me to remind him of my transgressions. Nay, I will not do that. I will spend my afternoon with Marigold, who returned home this morning, eager for her oats and a good brushing.

She cares not if my brain has turned.

Friday, December 2, 1864

They are moving the goods once again. I did not mean to eavesdrop again, but they should know better than to whisper such things in the carriage house. I was merely brushing Marigold down when I heard Bradford whispering. I am not sure who he spoke to, only that he confirmed that our wagon would be ready at the agreed-upon time.

When I heard him speaking, I pressed myself against the wall of the stall, wishing not for the first time that I was tall enough to see over the barricade. I pressed my ear to the cracks in the wood, praying to hear Josiah's voice. I heard nothing.

And now I must decide my course. Shall I follow Father and Bradford once again, hoping to prove the man I saw was Josiah? Or shall I do as Mother has bade and remain tucked in bed? Truly, there is no question in my mind.

Saturday, December 3, 1864

I did not get but a few feet from home before my plan to follow Father was thwarted. I cannot find it inside myself to be upset.

I had decided it would be quieter to lead Marigold from her stall than to ride her. I could mount when we reached the square. But I did not reach it. As soon as I stepped into the alley, a hand grabbed me, spinning me against the oak in the corner of our yard. I meant to scream but could find no breath from the shock of the moment.

Marigold had no such misgivings, letting out a bray like a donkey as she reared back on her hind legs, her reins dragging upon the ground. Then a soft voice cooed at her, telling her all was well, soothing her fear.

He may as well have been speaking to me, for the sound of

his voice erased every ounce of fear within me. I sagged against the tree as Marigold nibbled on the grass around us, always on the lookout for a meal.

I was merely looking for the man I had loved and feared lost. I told myself that my addled brain was at work again, fooling me into believing such nonsense.

Then he turned to me, his hand finding mine in the darkness, and every doubt disappeared. He said he had not intended to frighten me, but he knew what I was about, and he could not allow me to stumble upon the night's activities.

I failed to ask what those activities were, instead clinging to his hand and staring hard into his face. The light of the moon dancing through the branches above drifted over his features, his dear features. I saw what I knew to be true. This was Josiah Hillman. But could I trust my own eyes when Bradford had questioned them so soundly?

I begged him to confirm that it was him and not a figment of my imagination.

Aye. 'Tis me.

He lifted my hand to his lips and pressed them so gently there, only enough that I could sense the smile upon them. Then he said that he nearly did not recognize me in my attire, my brother's trousers. He had not known me in our previous encounter until he was upon me.

I assured him that I am the same Caroline Westbrook he knew all those many years ago.

He shook his head, his curly hair bouncing as it had when he was young. He swore that I am not the same girl he knew. I have grown into a woman.

I have never been so grateful for the covering of night, lest he should see the pink in my cheeks. I am inordinately grateful he has recognized me as a woman, but I fear it may not be enough. For he made no promises.

After I asked him to tell me why he has not written, he could only bow his head and beg my forgiveness. He said he cannot tell me the truth, and even now he fears for my safety. We must never be seen together, and he made me promise I will not tell a soul that I have seen him.

I had so many more questions to ask him, but he answered none of them. He only leaned in, and I thought for a moment that he might kiss me. But he pressed his lips to my forehead and squeezed my fingers one more time. Then he disappeared, leaving my hands empty and my soul downturned.

My questions are endless. Whatever has he been caught up in? What danger lurks that he was so concerned we might be seen together? I long to ask Father, but he is forever consumed with the imminent arrival of Sherman's army. It shall be soon, I am sure.

I nearly asked Bradford yesterday, for he must know something. But I have promised my secrecy. I must tell someone or I shall burst. So I have told you, dear diary. May you keep my secrets and Josiah's too. Whatever they may be.

NINE

*P*enelope squeezed Tucker's hand as they stepped up to the nondescript double doors of the VFW hall. "Are you ready?"

He nodded.

He was lying.

She would have recognized the nerves of his stiff shoulders and the tense line of his jaw anywhere, so she squeezed his hand again, pressing his fingers against her hip. "Deep breath." She modeled inhaling through her nose and letting it out through her mouth.

Tucker scowled at her. "I'm not nervous. This is nothing compared to what I did in the Marines."

"Uh-huh." With a tug on his hand, she turned him to face her. Releasing her grip, she let her gaze sweep from the top of his head to the toes of his freshly polished shoes. His gunmetal suit was sharp, tailored, hugging his broad shoulders and cutting in at his narrow waist.

He stuck a finger into his collar and pulled at the edge of his deep-blue tie. "It's too tight."

"It is not." She'd sent him to the same tailor who had fitted them for the picnic, and there was no arguing that this suit fit him like the ocean to the shore. "Stop fidgeting." She pulled his arms back down to his sides and brushed an imaginary piece of lint from his shoulders. "You look great."

His eyes shot toward the door, and she could almost hear the question he didn't ask.

"Tucker Westbrook, this county would be lucky to have you as its sheriff. The people who are here tonight know that, or they wouldn't have come up with a small fortune just for the joy of eating with you." She shrugged. "And giving you even more money."

He chuckled at that but didn't say anything.

"It's not just that you're capable, which we all know you are. You're smart and—"

He cut her off before she could continue. "So was the last sheriff, and look what happened to him."

She slammed her hands on her hips and glared at him. "You think you're going to have a massive heart attack in office? Unlikely. Longborne was a good sheriff, and you have a few of the same qualities that made him a good public servant." She held up her fingers as she ticked them off. "Decency. Sympathy. Integrity."

"You are good for a man's ego," Tucker said, pulling her into a hug. "Maybe I should put you on staff just for that."

She leaned into his embrace, wrapping her arms around his back and breathing in the faint scent of wood and wool. "You couldn't afford me, Westbrook."

His shoulders shook with mirth as he pressed a kiss to her cheek.

She wanted to spend a second enjoying the sweet moment, the feeling of his lips against her skin, his beard brushing her cheek. She could have spent hours pondering the shivers that ran down her arms and made her fingers tingle.

This was everything right and wrong with their charade. These moments, these glimpses into what could be. These reminders that she could not afford to risk their friendship. The plan had always been for them to be best friends forever. And she knew that romantic entanglements didn't always live up to the promises.

It was better to stick to the plan. What might be simply wasn't worth it.

So she enjoyed the moment in its brevity just as the double doors slammed open with a sharp crack. Everything inside her screamed that she should pull back, but even as she moved, she noticed three things. A hush had fallen over the tables closest to the door. At least a couple dozen pairs of eyes stared at them. And one of those pairs belonged to Winston St. Cloud.

His gaze was narrow, and the muscle in his jaw worked overtime. At his side, Emmaline Adams was nearly bouncing with excitement.

Penelope wasn't even sure if Tucker had noticed they suddenly had an audience.

Insides a spaghetti mess of emotions, Penelope cleared her throat as Tucker whispered, "I guess we're on. Thank you." He took control, leaning back and arranging her hand into the crook of his elbow as he plastered a smile into place and stepped forward.

Smoothing a hand down the front of her blue dress, she stumbled after him, forcing a toothy smile as she nodded at several familiar faces. Her mom was seated off to the left with several of her church friends, and the mess in Penelope's stomach turned into a knot. If the wrinkles in her mom's forehead could be believed, she'd seen Tucker's kiss. Even a kiss on the cheek was new for them. She'd told her mom not to worry if things began to look different. But she hadn't quite prepared her for a public display of affection.

Penelope couldn't hold her mom's gaze without confessing the truth—even from across the room—so she looked at the floor, watching her red shoes stumble across the wood as Tucker led her to their table at the front of the room. He pulled out her chair and scooted it in as she sat down. Then he strolled up to the dais at the front of the room. Resting his hands on the podium, he took a deep breath. He caught her eye and gave her a quick smile. As he spoke, his words rippled over the crowd, every eye on him.

All at once the knot in her stomach released, and she sat back and just let herself enjoy his voice, deep and rich and warm as his embrace. There wasn't a note in sight or a teleprompter to be found. He spoke from his heart. And his memory. He'd told her early on that he wasn't going to risk having to read in public. It was so much better this way anyway.

After fifteen minutes, he nodded and stepped away from the microphone. The audience stood and clapped, and it was time to mingle. She'd thought she would stay by his side, but as soon as he returned to their table, a white-haired man in a blue blazer stole him away.

"I'll be back," Tucker whispered as he moved to the other table. That seemed to be the cue for the whole room to relax. Voices raised in conversation, and people began milling about, some waiting to speak with Tucker and others crossing the room to speak to friends at other tables.

Beau Bailey, Tucker's campaign manager, stood and strolled across the room to chat up some other potential donors. She should be doing the same. Running her hands down the skirt of her dress, she squared her shoulders and stood, ready to find some deep pockets.

As she scanned the room, she cringed at how empty it felt. The stage with its blue backing sat in the middle of the room instead of against the far wall, effectively cutting the room in half. There were a dozen tables—almost a hundred people. But she'd heard rumors that Buddy Jepson's recent fundraising dinner had brought in three times as many. That had been three hundred deep pockets that were funding derogatory television ads. Three hundred people who would not only vote for Buddy Jepson but also convince their friends to do so.

Tucker needed a miracle.

"*That* man is a snack."

Penelope jumped at the voice in her ear, turning just enough to see Emmaline next to her, her gaze following the same line across the room to the spot where Tucker was speaking with a handful of potential donors.

"A snack?" She tried not to sound as outdated as she felt.

In her office, Emmaline hadn't seemed that much younger. But here and now, Emmaline parading around in a little romper and flawless long legs, Penelope felt every minute of her old maid status.

Emmaline giggled, looping their arms together. "You're so cute. As though you wouldn't know. I mean, I love Winston with all of my heart, but Tucker Westbrook is extra."

With a choked chortle of her own, Penelope nodded. "Of course." She was smart. It wasn't hard to figure out the slang.

Tucker was a *snack*. Thinking about him was like remembering she'd stashed Reese's peanut butter cups in her top desk drawer.

"And that voice, so deep and smooth. I could listen to him speak for hours, couldn't you?" Emmaline leaned in, her floral perfume drifting along with her.

Penelope tried to laugh, but the sound caught in her throat. Yes, she could listen to him speak for hours. She had listened to him practice that speech three times, in fact.

Emmaline didn't seem to mind that Penelope hadn't answered her question. "Wouldn't it be nice to have such a handsome sheriff? Imagine his press briefings." She pressed the back of her hand to her forehead and pretended to swoon. "Oh my! I'd evacuate for a hurricane if he told me to, for sure."

"It would be nice." Penelope nodded, her smile trying and failing to hold its place.

"So, when will you get married?"

Penelope nearly swallowed her tongue. Twice in as many weeks their marital status was the topic of conversation, and she was determined not to screw it up like last time. "Oh, we're not engaged."

Playfully swatting at her arm, Emmaline giggled. "Well, that's just a matter of time. You're the perfect couple. Have you been together forever?"

Shaking her head slowly, eyes still trained on Tucker, Penelope said, "No. I was engaged to someone else a few years ago." As the words slipped out, she nearly bit her tongue off.

Emmaline's eyes grew wide. "What? You broke some guy's heart to be with Tucker? Tell me everything."

"No, it wasn't like that." Penelope scrambled for words, but what could she say? She'd promised Winston she wouldn't tell Emmaline about their engagement, about being jilted at the altar. But now she'd opened a can of worms. It would be so easy to blurt out the whole truth about her ruined wedding.

She didn't owe Winston anything. But neither did she want to see the light in Emmaline's eyes dim when she learned the truth. Despite the awkward circumstances that had brought them together, Emmaline was a sweet, kind woman, and Penelope didn't want to see her hurt. Inevitably she would be when she discovered Winston's previous actions.

But that's Winston's problem.

The voice in her head made a good point. It had been up to Winston to reveal their history since the beginning. Maybe she could nudge him again to be honest with Emmaline.

Emmaline squeezed her arm. "Well, you and Tucker are meant to be. It's obvious."

It might be obvious, but it wasn't true. And the charade was starting to sit badly with her. They'd said they weren't going to lie. They would date—only without the feelings. They'd just let others believe what they would.

But as her mom began a quick march across the room, Penelope realized the truth. It wasn't just the Emmalines and Mrs. Haywoods of the world who would question what was happening. Her mom would want answers. And she deserved them. Penelope just didn't have any to offer.

"Would you excuse me?" she said, pointing toward the four musicians at the side of the dance floor. "I want to make sure the band is all set up. You should go find Winston and put those dance lessons to use."

Emmaline squealed and pranced off to find her fiancé, while Penelope practically ran from her mother.

"You should ask her to dance."

Tucker looked up at the voice beside him, the woman thin and frail, her voice anything but. Mrs. Saunders's skin was so thin it barely covered the veins on the backs of her hands, and the wrinkles on her face had not been fixed by Botox or whatever the plastic surgeons used to make women pretend they looked a decade younger. She had chosen to age naturally, her white hair styled into perfect curls and her lipstick giving a bit of color to her face. Her mind was as sharp as ever.

"Excuse me?" he said, more to have something to fill the silence than because he didn't understand her implication. She had clearly been referring to PJ. And he'd obviously been staring at her.

"Oh, don't play coy with me, Mr. Westbrook. The two of you have been thicker than thieves the last few weeks. Did you think we wouldn't notice?" Her Southern drawl was strong, drawing out the vowels and sliding like melted butter. But her words were sharp.

"Ma'am?" Again, he'd rather play the fool than admit that the idea of holding Penelope close on that dance floor had crossed his mind long before Mrs. Saunders had suggested it.

"You're not fooling anyone." She raised her eyebrows and looked down her steep nose at him.

The words hit him like a gut punch. Did she know they'd been pretending all along? He'd never been much of an actor, and maybe the truth was clear.

Or maybe you haven't been doing much acting?

He wanted to strangle that little voice in his head. It had no business popping up on a night like this and making him wonder if he'd been an idiot for the last twenty-five years.

"You're going to marry that girl. Mark my words." Mrs. Saunders tapped him on the arm with each of her last three words, a grin playing across her normally severe lips. "And you'll be lucky to have her."

Tucker cleared his throat and tried to take a steady breath. The air caught in his chest on a brief stutter, and he prayed she hadn't heard it. He dived in just in case she had. "Oh, we're not quite there yet, ma'am."

Her eyes were almost transparent, her gaze sweeping over him in a single pass. "I never took you for a coward, Mr. Westbrook. Or a fool. And only a fool would let a woman like Penelope Hunter get away."

He couldn't help it. His gaze flew to where Winston stood on the far side of the room. Yes, that man was definitely a fool, and Tucker had always thought so. He'd never been good enough for PJ.

Then again, Tucker hadn't been either.

The thought slipped into his mind, unbidden and thoroughly unsettling. He didn't think about that. He refused to. Even as he remembered her squeal of joy when she'd found out she was valedictorian of their graduating class and the jig she'd performed when she got into the MBA program at Georgia. And he'd never forget the way she'd rather bury her nose in a book than go to their prom. She must have turned down several invitations, and the night just hadn't been the same.

She was more than smart. She was educated and driven. She worked hard and followed her dreams.

If he was honest with himself, he'd admit that he'd never felt good enough for her. There'd always been at least one voice in his life reminding him of that.

If Mrs. Saunders noticed the scowl he couldn't contain, she didn't mention it. "I like Miss Hunter. She's sweet and funny, and her peach tarts always sell out at the church bazaar."

Tucker laughed. "Yes, ma'am. They do." Not that he'd ever had to buy one. He got to sample the "misfits." The misshapen, overdone, slightly crispy ones that didn't make the cut. But they tasted just as good to him.

They were also the only thing PJ had mastered in the kitchen. Not that he was going to reveal that little secret to the woman singing her praises.

"Last fall I was in the hospital. Did you know that?"

"No, ma'am." He shook his head slowly, not sure where this was leading but certain he wanted to see it through.

"Pneumonia. Terrible thing. And my granddaughter Minnie stayed with me for nearly a week. Until Penelope showed up."

PJ? *His* Penelope?

"She stayed with me so Minnie could get some rest. I never sleep well in a hospital, and I don't mind saying, I don't like being there alone. Penelope sat by my bed and read to me. Jane Austen and Agatha Christie. And often from the Scriptures. She told me stories and even snuck in my favorite cinnamon rolls. My doctor was none too happy, but I'm certain they were part of what cured me."

"Huh." He crossed his arms and rocked back on his heels. That sounded like PJ.

"I like investing in smart people, especially ones smart

enough to recognize Miss Hunter's worth." Mrs. Saunders tapped him on the arm again, but this time a blue check was tucked between her fingers. "Do you understand?"

"Yes, ma'am." He took the check and tucked it into the inside pocket of his jacket. With a smile he nodded at her. "I suppose I should go ask Penelope to dance."

Her grin barely lifted the corners of her mouth, but her eyes twinkled. "That's a very wise move, young man."

TEN

*P*enelope had done everything but handcuff herself to another person to keep from being alone with her mom. Tucker's fundraiser was only half over, and her mom had hounded her every step. She was ready to throw herself at the mercy of Winston, who was marching her direction, just to keep her mother at bay.

Except Winston was alone, Emmaline having ducked out of the room.

And she would much rather admit the whole farce to her mother than have a conversation with Winston.

Penelope whipped her head around to look for some help, but the already scant crowd was thinning even more. Tucker was fully engaged in conversation with Mrs. Saunders, so she didn't dare interrupt that—no matter how much she liked the old woman. She wouldn't risk a donation to Tucker's campaign.

Where was her mother when she needed her?

She spied her mom's sleek brown bob across the room. She was deep in conversation with a couple Penelope didn't know.

She glanced back just in time to see Winston's long strides eat up the last few yards between them. Then he was in her face. Not literally. To an observer, he was probably standing a very respectable three feet away. But when he spoke, his voice hissed an accusation.

"What are you doing, Pen?"

She cringed. Why did he insist on calling her that? She'd hated it when they were together, and that hadn't changed in the years since. But she managed to plaster a smile into place. "I have no idea what you mean."

"You know exactly what I mean. Parading around with that guy like I'm not even in the room."

The truth of his words slid down her neck, making her hair stand on end. She'd missed this selfish streak in him before. She hadn't seen it when she'd been too busy making plans for the rest of their lives. But now . . . well, it was too blatant to ignore. And it lit a fire somewhere deep inside her.

Glaring at him, she squared her shoulders and clasped her hands in front of her. "What on earth makes you think that anything I do has anything to do with you?"

He opened his mouth, a retort certainly on the tip of his tongue. But she didn't give him a chance.

"You walked out on that right the same day you failed to show up at our wedding." It took everything inside her to keep the words soft, but her mama hadn't raised a fool. This night was not about making a scene. Neither was it about putting Winston in his place. That was just an added benefit.

"I will spend time with whomever I choose. And right now, I choose Tucker Westbrook. If you had even a lick of sense, you'd spend time thinking about how to make Emmaline happy and how to tell her about our past. And you'd spend a whole lot less time thinking about me. Because I assure you, I don't waste my time thinking about you."

Dear Lord in heaven, had that really come out of her mouth? It most certainly had, but it had originated somewhere much deeper. She'd been carrying that around for a while, for at least as long as she'd wanted Winston to know that she was just fine.

She couldn't move. Neither, apparently, could Winston. He stood before her unblinking, motionless. Something flickered in his eyes. Anger, maybe. Hurt, definitely.

She should apologize. But she meant what she'd said. She just hadn't meant for it to come out quite so harshly.

Before she could even begin to form the words to backpedal, a hand slipped around her waist, an arm across her back. Then his lips were at her ear. "Have I told you how beautiful you look tonight?"

Like she'd been doing it for ages, Penelope sank into Tucker's embrace. "Hi."

His smile was just for her, and as his gaze swept to Winston, a sour expression settled onto his lips. "St. Cloud."

There was no "glad you could make it" or "good to see you." Tucker wasn't playing around with niceties. He knew how to be diplomatic, but he didn't seem particularly inclined to be where Winston was concerned.

Turning his smile back on her, Tucker said, "I believe I owe you a dance."

She laughed. "*You* want to dance?"

Tucker shrugged. "With you, I do."

She didn't spare Winston another look and only the briefest of thoughts—the tiniest moment of regret for letting three years of pent-up anger break free all at once.

Then they were on the dance floor, the slick faux-wooden surface set up near the dais and lined by four musicians zeeb-zoop-dooping up the register and back down with a rat-a-tat-a-tat. The trumpet player wailed a high note just as Tucker held one of her hands in his and pulled her all the way against him with the other.

She lost her breath for a moment and stared down at his shining black shoes until she could regain her composure.

"Are you having a good time tonight?"

"I was."

He squeezed her hand. "Until Winston?"

She wanted to agree, but that wasn't quite true. "Until I realized I was going to have to avoid my mom all night. And until I thought about how much good an event like this could do for Jordan and her group—I told you about them."

He nodded, then stopped as his eyebrows met in the middle. "Why are you avoiding your mom?"

"Probably the same reason you haven't spoken to your parents tonight."

He glanced over his shoulder before pulling her into a quick spin, his feet following the music. "They're going to have some questions, aren't they?"

"Yep."

His Adam's apple bobbed, his swallow audible. "And what about Jordan? She's the one who wanted to do a fundraiser for her nonprofit that helps kids coming out of the foster care system, right?"

That was harder to explain, and she tried to get her list together before unrolling it. "If these people knew—if they *really* knew how hard it is for kids aging out of the system, if they knew how much potential these kids have . . . I mean, look at Jordan. She has almost nothing—I don't even know if she has a place to live. But you know what? She's amazing. And if she's any indication of how far these kids would go—if only someone would believe in them—don't we owe it to them to try to help?"

He brushed a strand of hair that had escaped from her French twist off her cheek, tucking it behind her ear and pausing there for longer than a breath. His fingertip flirted with the top of her ear, a whisper of fire as it traced its way down to her silver earring.

Suddenly the whole room stood still. The band stopped playing. Everyone else disappeared. And she forgot to breathe.

He was staring at her like she was the only thing in the world that mattered, and a swarm of butterflies released in her middle. Her limbs went limp and her chest seized.

Just before she thought she'd sink straight to the ground, he broke the silence. "Are you suggesting these people should be giving to another cause?"

She laughed and the whole room came back to life, every chattering conversation and zippity-doo-wop. "Well, I do believe I might have lost you a donor tonight."

He smiled, his arm pulling her tight against him. "How's that? Your conversation with Winston not go so well? Color me surprised." His tone said he was anything but. She pressed her face into his shoulder to suppress the laugh attempting to escape.

He spun them in a slow circle to the syncopated rhythms of the Barnett Brothers, dodging a few other couples, his hand still pressed to the small of her back. It was absolutely in an acceptable range, but that didn't mean she wasn't hyperaware that it was simply *there*. Its shape was branded against her back, so warm, so close.

With that awareness came another certainty. He could feel the extra serving of curve at her hip, the extra on her back. Things Winston's new bride-to-be certainly didn't have.

But when Tucker whispered in her ear, she almost forgot. Almost.

"I'd rather not owe St. Cloud a penny. Besides, Mrs. Saunders gave me a check."

She leaned back just far enough to look into his face. "She did?"

"She's a big fan of yours."

Her cheeks flamed. "She's very kind."

He pushed her away, still holding on to her hands, and then spun her back into his arms. "The way she talks, it sounds like you were the kind one."

"Oh, that." Penelope took a step and landed right on Tucker's toe. "Ack! I'm sorry." She laughed as she dipped her head to make sure she hadn't done any permanent damage. "Maybe we should sit down."

He nodded, leading her through the twirling couples and pausing by their now empty table. "I suppose I should go say hello to my parents. Are you going to talk to your mom?"

"When Mrs. Saunders is here?" She wrinkled her nose and gave a small shake of her head. "I'll go thank her for her donation."

Tucker nodded but paused halfway through the motion. "You know, she said . . ."

Penelope waited, but he didn't continue. "What?"

He shook his head, a strange distance settling into his

gaze. She tried to follow it but couldn't see whatever had caught his attention.

"Tucker? What did Mrs. Saunders say?"

He shook off the faraway look. "Oh, nothing. Just . . . that apparently you broke the doctor's orders and brought her a cinnamon roll. Shameful."

"Don't believe everything she says. She's the one who asked for it." After giving his arm a quick squeeze, she strolled across the room in search of his newest supporter. Maybe Mrs. Saunders could explain why Tucker looked like he wasn't telling her the whole truth.

After visiting every table and shaking every other hand in the room, Tucker was left with no choice but to visit his dad's table. He clapped his dad on the shoulder and fell into the seat beside him. "How was your chicken?"

"Dry."

Of course. Count on his dad to find the fly in the ice cream. At least *he* had gotten to eat. Tucker had barely had time to stuff a roll in his mouth. Good thing PJ had reminded him to eat before he put his suit on.

He swallowed the retort on the end of his tongue. "I'm sorry to hear that. Did you get to dance with Mom?" He looked around for her but didn't see her petite frame among the others hanging on.

"She doesn't like this kind of music."

Tucker bit his tongue again and forced his gaze to stay on the floral burst in the center of the table. He didn't remember ordering those, which meant they were a PJ special. A reminder of the deep dive she'd gone into to make this night perfect.

As though his dad could sense what Tucker was thinking, he said, "You've sure been spending a lot of time with Penelope Jean lately."

Tucker nodded, rubbing the spot on the back of his neck that always itched when his dad took an interest in his personal life. "Not much more than usual, I guess."

"You guess." His dad nearly guffawed. "Your mom couldn't stop talking about how close the two of you looked at the picnic last week. And we all saw you dancing up there. You better be careful, son, or she'll blame you for scaring off her chance at getting married—I mean, she's not as young as she was the first time she almost walked down the aisle."

Tucker nearly swallowed his tongue. The man had some gall talking that way about a woman who had practically grown up in his house.

"She'll be just fine, Dad." And she would. Because she was smart and kind and funny, and sometimes her smile absolutely stole his breath. He couldn't stop someone else from realizing that too.

"Yeah, but she won't want the whole town thinking she's dating you." His dad shot him a quick look, a brief survey that said what it always did. Tucker had been measured and found wanting.

His face flushed hot, and he tasted blood as he bit his tongue, trying to remember the Bible verse about children honoring their father and mother. Wasn't there also one about fathers not provoking their children to anger? But at the moment, with his dad's eyes roaming the room, there was no way Tucker could remind his dad of the second verse without wholly disobeying the first. So he tightened his jaw, fisted his hands on his knees, and counted to ten.

Make that twenty. Maybe he'd just keep going until he was under control.

"What about Flynn Rutledge? He's a lawyer, you know." His dad's question sounded like it should have come from the busybodies in the church foyer rather than a retired physician. "Your mom mentioned him."

There it was.

"She wondered if PJ might need some help moving on," his dad said. "You know, since Winston's engagement announcement was in the paper. Your mom thought maybe you could help PJ out. You're friends with Flynn, right?"

"No. I'm not friends with him."

He had helped the guy win a case by providing him hours of recordings from Westbrook Security surveillance cameras at his client's request. But he was not friends with the guy, and he most certainly wasn't going to suggest he date PJ. Not with his slicked-back hair and tailored suit and too-white smile.

His dad pressed his hands on the table. "Well, do something so the town knows she's free. I mean, look at her."

Tucker did not need another invitation. He'd been looking at her way too often lately. Appreciating the way her hair fell over her shoulder or how it shined in the moonlight. Or allowing himself to get swept away in the current of her eyes.

Of course, he took the opportunity anyway. She was across the room, standing beside an empty table, holding one of those little china plates with most of a piece of cake left on it. Her other hand held a silver fork—bite still on it—poised halfway to her mouth. But her gaze was only for the woman across from her, her chin bobbing in agreement every few seconds. Whatever they were discussing, PJ was enraptured.

Tucker could relate.

"She needs someone sharp. Serious. Well suited for her. Winston wasn't a bad choice. Too bad that didn't work out."

Tucker could have put his fist through a cement wall. Everything inside him shook in an effort to control the urge to tell his dad what to do with his opinion on who was or was not good enough for Penelope Jean Hunter.

He ground his teeth together, his jaw working back and forth as he took a deep breath through his nose and let it out through tight lips. Crossing and uncrossing his arms didn't release any of the tension churning deep in his gut. His dad kept looking around the room, as though he was sure to find PJ a suitable suitor among the many men in attendance—most of whom they'd known since grade school.

And then his dad decided to offer one more jab. "I mean, she's got a master's degree—with honors. She's a smart cookie. She'll end up with someone else like that."

Something inside him snapped, and he slammed his palm on the table, shaking several plates and nearly overturning a glass of tea.

His dad's blue eyes, so much like his own, narrowed in on him. "What's gotten into you, Tucker?"

"I wish you wouldn't talk about PJ like that. She's a person with feelings, and she's my best friend. And I'd rather you and Mom not speculate about who she's going to marry or when. Because you know what? It's not your business."

"I was only giving her a compliment. She can do better than . . ." His voice trailed off, but Tucker felt every pound of the unspoken word.

Shoving himself to his feet, Tucker caught his dad's gaze. Two elks, antlers locked. "Would that be the worst thing? If people thought she was dating me? If she *was* dating me?"

His dad's mouth hung open, his eyes wide.

Tucker marched away, his movements stiff, single-minded. He wasn't entirely sure what he was doing, only that he knew he needed to do *something*. He needed to prove to his dad that he was worthy. He was enough. And there only seemed to be one way to do that.

As he neared PJ, she put down her plate and smiled up at him, soft and warm. "Hi, Tuck—"

But she didn't finish his name. He didn't let her.

She stopped the moment his hand reached her waist. It slid over the silky fabric of her slate-blue dress, and his arm wrapped all the way around her before he even knew it. Her eyes went wide, and his other arm shot around her back to keep her from escaping—er, to hold her close. That was better.

He leaned down, closed his eyes, and took a quick breath. And then he did something he'd never even let himself think about. He pressed his lips to hers.

She froze. He could feel every single muscle in her arms, back, and shoulders stiffen. Even her breathing stopped, which he had a front-row seat to, their mouths still locked.

And then he froze. Because the only correct response to being attacked without warning was a punch to the gut. In PJ's case, he fully deserved a slap in the face.

Oh, Lord. He prayed the words while silently berating himself. What was he doing? He had no business—zero, none—kissing PJ in private, let alone in front of a roomful of potential campaign donors, not to mention his parents

159

and her mom. And yet here he was, mauling his best friend in front of half the city, all to make a point to his dad.

A point that did not need to be made.

He should pull back. Step away and thank her for doing such a great job on the event. He should pat her back awkwardly and pretend like this had never happened.

Except she was just so decadently soft. Everything about her was warm and comforting, and for a moment he forgot how he'd even ended up in this place. Her dress felt like cool silk—it probably was—and he slid his hand down her back, stopping at the hollow above her waist. Then he let his fingers sink into her.

She let out a small peep, the tiniest sound, but it seemed to be the only one around them. The rest of the room had disappeared. They were all that remained. All that mattered.

Her hands found their way to the front of his shirt, fingers flat against his chest. He'd bet the election that she could feel his pounding heart beneath her palms, and he expected her to push him away. She didn't. Her fingers curled into the starched cotton of his shirt and tugged him one step closer.

It was all the invitation he needed, so he added an extra measure of pressure to his lips against hers and held on for all he was worth.

With a soft sigh, she melted against him, and he was lost.

Penelope couldn't be bothered by the question of the moment—*why?* Not with Tucker's arms around her and his lips still pressed to hers.

This was not what she'd anticipated. Not that she'd been

anticipating this moment. Because it was never going to happen.

Only it was happening. Right. Now.

Unexpected. Surprising.

His lips were firm but not demanding, insistent yet gentle. He invited her into his embrace like her favorite sweater on a cold winter day.

She thought she'd known everything about him—everything that mattered. But she hadn't known how he kissed.

And he was good—really, really good.

So she was going to enjoy every bit of it. She focused on the brush of his fingers across her back, barely skimming the fabric of her dress yet reaching somewhere deep in her chest and making her heart trip over its rhythm. Suddenly one of his hands disappeared, and she tried to lean toward where it had been, only to have him catch her cheek in his palm, his thumb brushing over the apple of her cheek. His fingers were callused, hardworking. But his brief touch against her skin had her insides swarming and her head spinning.

She'd seen older ladies of the town succumb to the vapors— swoon under the weight of some unseen force. And she'd always thought them rather silly. Of course, she'd offered a "bless her heart" and moved along.

But now she knew. She *knew*.

There was nothing silly about the force buckling her knees. Then again, he wasn't unseen either. Thank goodness he was stable. The only thing keeping her standing was the steel of his arms. His strength radiated through her, lighting a fire somewhere deep in her chest.

This wasn't supposed to be happening. She knew that somewhere deep inside. But how could she be expected to care when he tasted like rich buttercream frosting? Or maybe that was from the cake she'd been eating. Either way, he was sweeter than any snack she'd ever tried.

One taste might not be enough.

Oh dear. That was not the plan.

Well, they hadn't put together a plan. Rookie mistake. But if there had been a plan, it would not have included her wanting a repeat of tonight's performance.

She knew she should let him go. She should step back. She should recognize they were still in a half-full room. But if she let him go, she might never get to do this again.

Unacceptable.

Someone behind her cleared his throat, and Penelope stepped back, her gaze locked somewhere in the vicinity of Tucker's knees. She couldn't blink, and she sure couldn't meet his gaze. Not until she'd managed to get her goose bumps under control at least.

It took everything inside her not to press her fingertips to her mouth, to relive the memory of his lips on hers. Instead she brushed her hand against her cheek and flinched at even the brief contact. The skin around her mouth felt like it was on fire. She'd thought it was from his touch, but the truth made a terrifying case. His beard had left its mark.

And then the truth of it all—of what they'd done—crashed into her, stealing her breath. Without a glance up, she whispered, "Good night, Tucker," and made her escape.

Tuesday, December 13, 1864

I was not sleeping last night when Bradford burst into my room. Not even the moon shone through my window, and I saw only his shape, but I know his voice. His words were somehow both hushed and loud. They filled my room as I sat up in bed, my covers clutched to my chin and covering my night rail.

He whispered that we must move tonight. He said the soldiers are close, the Yankees are but mere miles away. We cannot afford for the goods to find their way into the wrong hands. He told me that I must dress as a woman, that I must not hide my identity.

I still do not know what the goods are, but I could not mistake the urgency in his voice, so I quickly jumped from my bed and ushered him from the room. I pulled on a simple dress, one I could fasten on my own, for I could not afford to call Sarah or any other servant. My fingers were trembling, and I could hardly button my boots or braid my hair.

A knot deep in my stomach told me I might see Josiah, and I prayed it would be true. However, another glimpse of him could do naught but make me long to see him yet again. I have thought of little else but him in these days since last he appeared and confirmed he is alive.

Finally I managed to make it to the kitchen, where Bradford waited for me by the back door, a heavy coat in his hands. He had wrapped a scarf around his neck and the lower half of his face. I assumed it was to conceal his identity, but as we stepped into the night, the cold stole my breath. I am not accustomed to leaving the warmth of the fire in the hearth after the sun has set, and I did not know that Savannah's winds could carry such a chill.

Bradford held me to his side as we scurried down the barely lit streets, and I tried to claim what warmth from him I could. Some of the streetlights had gone out, certainly a result of the wind. We kept to the shadows, our steps hurried. I could feel Bradford's discouragement at his own limitations, but I was ever so grateful for his lame leg that kept him from leaving us. Still, I know his heart is for our home, for our friends. Like Josiah.

As we turned onto Bay Street, I saw what at first looked like a mob. No, not quite a mob. But there was certainly a restless spirit among the five or six men spread out along the street. Three men stood along a storefront. It was Mrs. Fitterling's Dress Shop, no less. Once, directly before the war, Mama bought me a special frock from Mrs. Fitterling for a Christmas ball. Lace and silk are not so readily available any longer, so after I stretched its seams as far as they would allow, I made the fine fabric into two pretty dresses for Henrietta and Margarita next door. Their papa had been lost at Manassas, and I could not bear to see them sew another patch onto their dresses.

On Bay Street, I demanded that Bradford tell me what was going on. I had asked no questions before this, but I insisted then.

He told me only that they needed my help. Could I please reason with Mrs. Fitterling?

Reason how? I had never known the seamstress to be anything other than reasonable. But not even the most reasonable woman would allow a mob of men into her store at such an hour.

That's when I put my foot down and refused to go even a step further until he explained what was going on.

It was not Bradford who answered me. Instead Josiah whispered into my ear. He said they very much needed to store something within her shop. But they could not convince her to allow such a thing. Not without my help.

I spun around and glared into his shining eyes. I had to crick my neck just to look at him. My, but he has grown over the years. And the growth of whiskers along his jaw is anything but boyish. He is a man now, but I refused to succumb to the swirling in my middle at his appearance or his breath against my ear.

I told him I would do no such thing. He must let the poor woman be.

I could not tell if Josiah was battling a smile or a frown, but his lips twitched, and I could barely keep my gaze from them. Finally I managed to look toward my boots, my breath coming out as a cloud between us.

He might have ignored me or forced me. Instead he cupped my shoulders in his hands and leaned in close. He said he should have expected nothing less from me. I would not be intimidated. I stood taller, stretching my neck and straightening my shoulders.

And then he whispered the truth. I know it can be nothing less, for it is too much to be fabricated. I daren't even record it here, lest anyone else discover the truth among these pages.

But I did just as he asked. I marched to the front door of Mrs. Fitterling's shop and knocked softly. I called to her through the glass and begged her to trust me.

She squinted at me, and I pleaded with her to open the door. When she finally did, she peered through a mere crack, a wool shawl pulled tightly over her nightgown. She held a candle up to my face, her eyes pale and short-sighted from years of intricate work. But when she knew me for who I am, she relaxed her hold on the door and asked what I was doing about at such a time.

I told her that Savannah needed her help. Could she spare

a small intrusion so that hope might be stored among her goods? She said nothing but looked between me and the faces of the men behind me. The standoff seemed to last an age, my hands growing so cold that I could barely move my fingers.

I asked if we could come in to discuss it out of the chill. We all wanted to be in our own beds on such a cold night.

Mrs. Fitterling seemed disinclined to allow this disturbance to last any longer, so she asked if I vouched for these ruffians. I said that I did, and she held open the door with the warning not to disrupt her fabrics or there would be a price to pay.

I looked over my shoulder at the ragged faces of these men, not one of them in uniform, and knew that none of them could afford to replace her cherished sewing materials. So I told them to be careful as they tiptoed past me.

I waited with Mrs. Fitterling in her front parlor, huddled together against the biting wind as the men carried in a dozen boxes, some small, some half the size of the square piano at the church. They disappeared into her dressing and storage rooms down the hall, their movements like that of a ghost.

When they were done, they disappeared just as quickly, dispersing into the night. I hugged Mrs. Fitterling and thanked her for her kindness. She looked uncertain and asked if she had done the right thing.

I could only nod, and now I pray that she has. I pray that Josiah has a plan that might save Savannah. Our own General Hardee waits for Sherman's men. And what will happen when they arrive? Will they clash in our very streets?

I wished I could have asked Josiah what lies ahead, but he had dissolved into the ether once again, leaving me to walk home with my brother, cold and uncertain.

Wednesday, December 14, 1864

Fort McAllister has fallen to the Yankees. There is nothing left between us and Sherman's army. Talk among the men in Father's study this morning was not hopeful. I was not truly eavesdropping, but I could not very well sit in the parlor with my stitching and not hear their agitated voices.

General Hardee's men are here in our city, but I fear they may not be able to stop Sherman's army. They seem insistent upon overtaking us. I pray that this war will end soon.

Melody Singletary's family has left the city, setting out for where, I do not know. Is there any place safe, save Richmond? Between the blockades and the infantry overtaking the rail lines, how could they even travel? I dare not even consider what might become of them.

Selfishly, I pray that Josiah might be returned to me, whole and safe and no longer a man hidden among the shadows, a man I am not to know is even alive.

I cannot help but speculate that Sherman's arrival might force Josiah back into the light, back among the living. Is it right to pray for such things? Can I pray such things and still wish for my precious city to be spared further loss?

Monday, December 19, 1864

The city is preparing to be overtaken. And we have one less protector.

Papa barely spoke at lunch yesterday. He said he was pondering the sermon, but I do not see how anyone could have listened to the preacher. I believe he spoke from Jeremiah about a future. This city seems to have lost its hope, for what lies ahead is uncertain and terrifying.

I could think of little else as I lay in my bed last night, my gaze fixed on naught but the ceiling. That's when Bradford snuck into my room. I thought he needed my assistance once again, so I sat up swiftly, my head spinning.

He held up his hand to still my movements. His voice but a whisper, he informed me that I had a visitor, if I wished to see him. It could be no one but Josiah, so I pushed my brother from my room, pulled my wrap about me, and slid my feet into slippers. Bradford had not told me where I would find Josiah, but I knew to run for the kitchen.

I stopped at the doorway, my breath catching in my throat and my eyes filling with tears. He looked somehow terribly lovely and awfully ragged in the same moment. His beard was overgrown, and his cheeks were hollow. He was haggard and weary.

I had never seen anything so beautiful.

Rushing to him, I held out my hands, making him take them. He smiled and looked down at them, at my hands in his larger ones.

I have missed you, he said.

I told him that I had seen him only a few days ago, and he laughed. The fire in the hearth made shadows dance across his face, falling into the dips and valleys. He said that four years was far too long a drought for a man.

His words, the wistfulness of his tone, gave me a shimmer of hope that perhaps he felt for me as I had for him. All these years of waiting. He'd said nothing before he left, yet I had hoped. I had dreamed.

I stared into his dark brown eyes, praying he would tell me the words I had so longed to hear. For my drought had been just as long as his. But he did not speak them. Instead, he told me to be careful. He told me to take care. He said the Yankees would be there soon, and I must guard my tongue. They could not know all I have seen.

Of course, I promised him I would keep it a secret. But then he said I must keep him a secret. I must never reveal that he has been here. I asked when he would be back, and his smile dimmed. I leaned into him, wishing I could make it return. Wishing I could make the old Josiah return.

He told me he doubts he will ever return to Savannah. I fear there is more to his story than he has revealed, more danger than I had imagined.

I wanted to ask him if I was not worth returning for. I wanted to ask if he did not see a future for us. Mostly, more than anything, I wanted him to kiss me there in the glow of the fire. But I feared his answers to my questions. I feared they would break my heart, so I asked of his cargo.

He offered me a dip of his chin and squeezed my hand. Then he said it is safe enough. For now.

What does that mean? I still do not know what treasures it holds. Might there be jewels and precious metals? Or is it rifles and powder and shot? Whatever it is, Josiah has put his life on the line for it, and I must do everything I can to protect it. Perhaps I shall stop by Mrs. Fitterling's shop this week. Mama might like some new ribbons for Christmas.

Before Josiah left, I leaned into him and tilted my head back so that he might give me a proper farewell, but he did not. He pressed the back of my hand to his lips and then disappeared through the kitchen door. The night air came in like a flood, and I was left cold and alone and determined to do my part.

Whether Papa and Bradford like it or not, I am part of their scheme now.

ELEVEN

*P*enelope Jean." On the other side of the phone, her mom made her name sound like it tasted too salty. "What on earth is going on?"

"Hi, Mom."

"I'm serious, young woman."

That *young woman* hadn't been used in about fifteen years, not since Penelope had lived under her mom's roof. It gave her the same goose bumps it had back then.

"It's okay, Mom. I'm okay. Tucker is okay." And his kiss was more than okay. Which made her first three assertions a little less certain. But she'd keep telling herself it was all going to be all right until it was. She didn't really have another option.

"But, honey." Her mom's voice dripped like the South's sweetest nectar. "You've known Tucker a really long time, and you've never . . . well . . . it's never been like that between you two." She took a quick breath and then tagged on a question. "Has it?"

Penelope sighed and lowered herself onto her sofa, welcoming Ambrose as he trotted to her side and put his head on her lap. Scratching behind his ears, she tried to formulate a response that was both true and wouldn't hurt her mother's feelings.

I made it up to make Winston jealous.

Yeah, that didn't quite have the right ring to it. Her mom would be less hurt and more furious at that revelation. Besides, she hadn't wanted to make Winston jealous. Not really.

"We . . . um . . . it's kind of a new thing. I mean, it's not even really a thing. We haven't even talked about it." There. That was true. Every word of it.

"You haven't talked to Tucker?" Her mom sounded like Penelope had just announced plans to climb Everest.

"No." She straightened up, and Ambrose lifted his furry little head to stare at her. Maybe that had come out a little too forceful. "I wasn't feeling very well yesterday, so I didn't go to church, and I . . . I haven't called him." Not that he'd called her either.

"Penny, honey, what's going on?"

The backs of her eyes burned, and she blinked them rapidly as Ambrose jumped to the ground, his body going blurry as her eyes filled with tears.

Perfect. Now she was crying over someone she wasn't truly dating.

She wasn't crying over the guy. She was crying over the situation.

Okay, that was a little better. Sort of. But this wasn't ever supposed to be emotional. It was two friends helping each other out. Two friends searching for a lost treasure. Two friends working to get one elected. Two friends proving that one was over her ex.

"Nothing, Mom. Nothing's going o-on." But the crack in her voice told a vastly different story.

That kiss three days before was not nothing. And it was a whole lot more than two friends doing anything.

"Oh, sweetheart. I'm so sorry."

"Everything's fine." She gritted her teeth against the white lie.

Her mom cleared her throat. "Can I tell you what I think?"

Penelope already knew what was on her mind. Her mom knew the heartbreak of watching the man she loved walk out of her life. Penelope knew she expected Tucker to do exactly the same thing. But she gave a mumbled "go ahead" anyway.

"Watching Winston break your heart was almost as hard on me as it was on you. I love you so much, and I never want you to hurt that way again. And if you and Tucker are dipping your toes into whatever you're doing, thinking you can't get hurt, well, you're wrong. A man can only hurt you as much as you care about him. And you care about Tucker like a drought cares about rain."

A tear spilled over her eyelid, and her bottom lip shook. She could only manage a murmur in response, even though she knew all of it was true.

She'd loved Winston, and that had given him the power to break her heart. But losing Tucker? That would be infinitely worse. Her heart might never recover from such a blow.

She did not need a man in her life. She had plans and a purpose, and she was ready to check off the boxes of her future. But all of that would be dimmed without Tucker in her life.

"I'm worried about you," her mom said. "I just want you to be wise. Whatever is happening with Tucker, it sounds like it's not too late to save your friendship."

She didn't have to dive very deep into her heart to know that her mom was right. If she didn't end this charade, she would lose a lot more than she had when Winston walked out on her. She couldn't—wouldn't—let that happen again. And to make sure, she'd make a plan.

Ambrose pranced up to her, leash in his little mouth.

"Mom, I've got to go walk Ambrose. But . . . thank you."

"Love you, sweetie."

She hung up, the column of checkboxes already forming in her mind. First: Take Ambrose for a walk. Second: Make sure she never ever kissed Tucker Westbrook again. Third: Try to forget how good it had been the first time.

Tucker wiped his sweating palms down the front of his cargo shorts and shot a silent prayer toward heaven. He wasn't entirely sure what he was asking for, but words would be a good place to start. At the moment he had none.

As he drew even with the steps down to PJ's apartment, he paused and then kept right on walking. When he reached the end of the block, he turned around and walked back, his hands still damp, his mind still blank.

He hadn't been this nervous in a Humvee in Fallujah. But the United States government had trained him how to be a Marine. No one had trained him how to smooth things over with his best friend after he kissed her in public. And he was almost certain there would be some smoothing required. She hadn't talked to him all weekend. She hadn't sat with him at church or even texted him after the latest episode of *American Ninja Warrior*.

Running his fingers over his hair, he shot a glance toward her apartment but didn't stop.

He was being ridiculous and cowardly. Just because the kiss had been good—

Better than good.

Okay, just because they had some chemistry, it didn't mean the foundation of their relationship had to change. She was still PJ. Only now he knew that her lips were smoother than cream, and she tasted like raspberries and frosting. And she smelled like honeysuckle on the vine, her skin porcelain.

Those were normal things for a man to know about his friends.

Yeah, not even he was buying that. But he'd opened this can of worms, and he was going to figure out how to put them all back.

Except maybe he didn't want to put them back.

He scrubbed a hand over his hair again and stopped in the middle of his stride. None of this made sense. He'd never wanted more with PJ. Their friendship had always been enough.

So why had that changed?

Because now you know what could be.

And it could be good, something special with Penelope. He just wasn't sure where she stood on that subject.

Argh. He reached for his beard to tug on it, but it wasn't there. Running his fingers across his bare jaw, he scowled. It was too late to take back the kiss. And the beard too. Time to face up to what he'd done and figure out how to move forward.

Preferably forward with kissing.

Spinning around, he took half a step toward PJ's door before realizing she was right in front of him. She wore shorts, a baggy T-shirt, and a confused expression.

"Tucker? You okay?" The beagle-ish mutt on the end of the blue leash in her hand yipped as though asking the same question.

He squatted down in front of the dog, scratching behind his floppy left ear. "Hey, Ambrose. Decided to take PJ out for a stroll?"

Ambrose Bierce—named for an author Tucker had muddled through in high school and PJ had adored—yipped again, adding a high-step dance across the pavement tented over a tree root.

Tucker gave the dog one more scratch before standing and finally meeting PJ's gaze. "Mind if I join you?"

She took a deep breath, bit her bottom lip, and shook her head. "I doubt you'd let me refuse."

"Do you want to?" The question escaped before he could decide if he wanted to know the answer.

Ambrose tugged on his leash, and PJ followed after him, setting a slow pace toward Forsyth Park. She didn't say anything for long enough that Tucker wished he'd gone straight home after work instead of stopping by her place.

She'd been studying the sidewalk before them as they crossed through the square, but finally she looked up at him. Her eyes squinted, and her head cocked to the side. "You shaved."

He shrugged, rubbing his fingers along his jawline again. "I did."

"Um . . . why?" More importantly, why was her voice quivering?

Tucker shrugged again. "You know."

She shook her head quickly. "I don't."

He hadn't exactly planned it, but suddenly his knuckle was tracing the line between her lower lip and her chin. "I just wanted to be ready for next time."

Her jaw dropped open. "Next time?" Her words weren't more than a breath, but he heard them loud and clear. She hadn't been thinking about a next time or planning for a future.

"You looked a little red after our first go. I didn't want to rough you up again."

She stared at him unblinking for a long second before Ambrose jerked on his leash and tugged her arm toward the base of the tree in the corner of the square. She ran after him, her feet slipping along the pavement, and Tucker followed behind her. If only he could somehow give her the time and space to process the idea without having to leave her side.

As Ambrose dug his nose into a bed of pink flowers, PJ kept her gaze on her dog. "I'm glad you came by."

Clapping a hand over the back of his neck, he sighed. "Listen, PJ, I'm really sorry . . ." Not for the kiss. He wasn't the least bit sorry it had happened. Just for how it happened. "I'm sorry I surprised you the other night. I let my dad rile me up, and in the moment it seemed like the best way to deal with him."

Her nose scrunched up, lips pursed, she turned to look at him. "Kissing me was the way to deal with your dad?"

"Yeah, he was going on about you and Winston and Flynn Rutledge, and I was fixin' to punch a wall."

She paused to let Ambrose investigate a crack in the bricked path. "So, kissing me was like punching a wall?"

"No!" He shook his head hard. "It was . . . When we

agreed to date, we never talked about it, and I shouldn't have grabbed you like that." Even though it took everything inside him not to do it right this minute. Now that he knew the softness of her skin, the silkiness of her hair, he wanted to drown in them.

Her hand drifted to her waist, her gaze lost somewhere in the past. His palm tingled, the memory of her shimmering dress against his skin still fresh. Did she remember his touch too?

With a jerk on the leash, Ambrose broke her trance, and she smiled at him. "It's okay. You're right. We didn't talk about it, but—"

"Winston sure saw it."

"He did?" A smile played with the corners of her lips, thoughtful at first and then radiant.

Tucker chuckled. "He looked ready to spit fire when I walked past him. He's jealous for sure."

Her smile dimmed. "I don't want him to be jealous. I just want him to know that—"

"You're okay."

She nodded.

"I think he's getting that message loud and clear." Winston wasn't stupid—except for that whole leaving her at the altar thing. But the man had done the rest of Savannah's single male population a big favor. And his dad was right. Someone like Flynn Rutledge was going to notice.

But at least for now they all thought Tucker had staked his claim. And if he had any say in it, he wasn't going to give that up anytime soon.

"Then, thank you." She beamed up at him for a moment, then her gaze dropped to the big white fountain at the center of Forsyth Park, the rush of its water drowning out the sound of traffic on the nearby streets. It held her attention for several long seconds, and even Ambrose was still before the wonder.

"Thank you," she said again. "But I don't think we should do that anymore."

His mouth went dry, and he squeezed his hands together to keep from swinging her into his arms and reminding her just how great their kiss had been—how great it could be again. Instead he took a deep breath and steeled his features against any reckless reaction. He couldn't afford to scare her off.

"Oh, really?"

She ducked her head but didn't watch Ambrose trot off to the length of his leash in pursuit of a butterfly. "I just think maybe we took things too far. Maybe pretending we're dating isn't . . . I'm not sure it's fooling anyone."

"Yeah, right. We've convinced everyone. I mean, Winston certainly thinks so."

"Well, my mom isn't fooled." She whipped her head back, her eyes gray like the clouds before a tornado. "And . . . and I don't want to lie to her. I told you I wouldn't. And if my mom is asking questions, then your mom sure is."

He lifted a shoulder. "Maybe."

Her glare told him he better be fully honest.

"Okay, probably. But she hasn't asked me. She's just been talking with my dad." And deciding that Tucker was wholly unfit for their favorite Southern belle. He tried to ignore the tightening in his chest that accompanied that truth.

"See? Wouldn't it be better for everyone if we just ended this? Well, there's not really a 'this' to end, but you know what I mean."

Actually, no, he did not know what she meant. "So how does that look different than how we normally interact?"

Leaning into him, she whispered, "We end the charade. We just go back to hanging out as friends. Just like it used to be."

"You think anyone will believe that there's really nothing but friendship between us after what happened on Friday night?" He sure didn't believe that.

She opened her mouth to speak and then pursed her lips as though she needed to think through her response.

Please, let her say no. Let her say no.

Just as she looked ready to speak, he grabbed her hand, lightning shooting up his arm—hers too if the flash in her eyes was any indication. This was too much to ignore. But declaring that they should give dating a real chance was too risky. Not when she wasn't fully on board yet. Not when she might decide she agreed with his parents on his worth. He had to prove he was worthy.

He squeezed his eyes closed and prayed the only words he could think. *Oh, Lord. What am I going to do? Give me the words to convince her.*

"I've got an ace." He didn't really, but they were the only words he could come up with at the moment, and she seemed to know it.

Her eyebrows furrowed. "I hardly see what that—"

"I won't kiss you again." Those were not the words he wanted to say either. He wanted to backpedal, rewind, and try again. What an awful promise to make to the woman he already cared about more than any other human on the planet.

Except his words made her visibly relax. The lines in her forehead eased, and her features softened. "I hope I'd have some say in that."

He laughed, and Ambrose ran toward him, dancing around his ankles until he scooped the dog into his arms. "Of course you do. I just meant that I won't surprise you again."

"Thank you."

"But we started this whole thing for two specific reasons—my election and your . . . Winston."

"He's not mine." She spoke the words solemnly, and he prayed he hadn't opened that wound again. He knew he was free and clear when she smiled brightly. "He's Emmaline's problem now."

He laughed out loud at that. "Yes, he is. But are you going to be okay working with him for the rest of the summer?"

She stared toward the clear blue sky and scratched Ambrose behind his ears. "I am. He . . . well, let's just say he reminded me at the party what I'm not missing."

"So, you have nothing left to prove to him?" He'd never thought she did, but now he wasn't sure he wanted her to agree on that point.

PJ shrugged and pulled Ambrose out of his arms, hugging her dog beneath her chin, a thoughtful frown in place. "How about this? I'm thinking about other things a lot more than I am Winston St. Cloud these days." Her smile fell onto him. "The election is coming up soon, and then we won't have to worry about any of this anymore."

"So we'll stay together until then?"

She nodded. "I think I can handle another couple weeks. After that, we're right back to normal. No explaining our relationship. Nothing but friends."

Two weeks until the election. Two weeks to make her see how good they could be together. Two weeks to convince her to try.

And less time than that to find the treasure that would help him win the election and prove once and for all that he was worthy of her.

PJ began to stroll back toward her home but stopped and gave him a Cheshire grin. "You're never going to believe what I read in Caroline's diary last night."

TWELVE

*P*enelope sat down at her desk, propped her elbows in front of her keyboard, and rested her chin on her folded hands as the speaker on her phone announced the voicemail from Mrs. Haywood. Her voice was shrill, almost disbelieving.

"I thought we were clear that you were going to fix this nonsense with Westbrook or remove yourself from the situation entirely."

On a sigh Penelope closed her eyes but could still see the light shining through the big plate windows of her office. She could still hear Mrs. Haywood's admonition as well.

"After what I heard happened on Friday night at that dinner, well, I just don't see how the Ladies' League can be associated with you or your venue. We'll be moving our event to another location."

The call ended with a decisive click.

"A handshake is good enough, they said. We've been holding this event here for years, they said." She grumbled to herself as she stared out the windows. A few pedestrians strolled by, probably tourists looking for the candy shop or the best place to buy a souvenir on River Street. But all Penelope could think about was the conversation she would have to have with her boss.

Of course, Madeline had been the one who insisted there was no need for a formal contract to reserve the Hall. They'd worry about contracts when it got closer to the event and food and drinks were being ordered. The Ladies' League always held their summer fundraiser at the Hall.

Until this year, apparently.

Penelope dropped her face into her palms and took a deep breath. In. Out.

Would Winston and Emmaline's wedding be enough to save her job? Maybe she could talk them into having their rehearsal dinner at the Hall too. That would . . . She tried to crunch the numbers in her head. It wouldn't even begin to make up for losing the Ladies' League.

Madeline would have no choice.

Her stomach suddenly felt sick, a sour taste rising in the back of her throat.

She, Penelope Jean Hunter, was going to lose her job.

That's when the tears came.

Suddenly the door to her office from the street opened, its loud rattle and jingling bell making her jump to attention in her chair. With a quick swipe of her fingers under her eyes, she made sure that her mascara hadn't smudged.

As the door swung all the way in, Jordan Park stepped inside, her sunny yellow dress as fresh as a day at the beach. She offered a timid smile, her hands clasped behind her back. "Hello, Miss Hunter. Do you have a second?"

"Of course. Come in. Have a seat." She jumped to her feet and pointed at the empty chairs in front of her desk—at least, it would be her desk until Madeline called. "Please, call me Penelope."

Jordan shook her head. "Oh, I can't stay long. I just wanted to . . ." Her voice trailed off, her hips moving the flowing skirt like a bell. "Well, I wanted to say thanks for meeting with me. It was real kind of you, and I'm sorry if I wasted your time."

"My time?" The tears that she'd blinked back a moment before threatened to spill again, and she bit her bottom lip to keep it from trembling. Suddenly she charged forward and pulled Jordan into a tight hug, the girl's skinny shoulders twitching under the weight of the embrace. "I wish I could do more."

The faces of all of the well-to-do men and women at Tucker's dinner flashed before her eyes, and she tried not to think about how much their money could have helped Jordan and her friends. There were always good causes to support, people in need. So why did Jordan's tug so at her heart?

Forcing herself to let go, Penelope took a step back. "How are you doing? How's Stepping Stones?"

Jordan brushed her dark curls out of her face before reaching into her bag. "I wanted to bring you something. When someone donates to Stepping Stones, we like to give them something to remember us by. Maybe it'll remind you to pray for us." When she pulled her hand free, she held a smooth, flat rock. It was sandy in color and would easily disappear into the beaches of Tybee Island, except for the bright pink block letters painted on top.

Savannah Stepping Stones
Joshua 4

Penelope accepted the stone like it was a child, cradling it in her palm and pressing it to her chest. "What a lovely gift. Thank you."

"It's not much—"

With a wave of her hand, she cut Jordan off. "It means the world to me that you thought of me and wanted to bring me a gift. I wish I could do more."

"No, ma'am. You were honest with me, and I needed that."

Penelope pulled her into another hug—this one more gentle than the last—just as the door to her office opened again, letting a blast of Savannah summer heat into the room. She looked right into Tucker's eyes. His eyebrows pinched, the nod of his chin seeming to ask who she was hugging. And somewhere deep in his eyes was a question—why was she upset?

Or maybe she was just self-conscious.

With one last squeeze, she released Jordan and turned to make introductions. Jordan's smile became smaller and her eyes grew larger. "I've seen you on those ads."

His flat chuckle seemed to come from deep in his throat. "Don't believe everything you see on TV."

She quickly shook her head and ducked toward the door. "I should be going."

Penelope nodded, waved, and thanked her for the gift before closing the door on Jordan's rapidly retreating form. "I think you might intimidate her."

"That's the girl with the kids aging out of the foster care system?" He tromped across the room and fell into one of her chairs.

Penelope nodded.

"She barely looks old enough to be out of the system herself."

It was true. But somehow the girl had more determination, direction, and pluck than most women twice her age. How else could she explain starting a nonprofit to help the people in her very own situation?

"Well, she's pretty impressive, if you ask me. But somehow I don't think you stopped by to talk to me about Jordan. What's up?" Penelope shuffled back toward her desk, setting her new stepping stone beside her monitor. It might be a good reminder when she had to start a new job.

"Well, I figured out . . ."

When he paused, she glanced up at him in time to see his frown.

"What's wrong?" he asked, standing and invading her space.

"Nothing." At least nothing she wanted to share at the moment. Nothing that wouldn't make her dissolve into a pool of ridiculousness.

"Not nothing." He motioned to his forehead, moving his finger right between his eyebrows. "You always get scrunched up right here when something's wrong. And you've got four lines there right now."

"I do not," she said. But her hand automatically moved to cover the spot, smoothing the skin there with her thumb and forefinger.

He pulled her hand away and ran his thumb up the middle of her forehead.

If he was hoping to relax her, he was epically failing. Every nerve inside her was strung about as tight as it had ever been, so she jerked away from his touch, ignoring the confusion written across his face.

"PJ, you can talk to me about anything. You know you're going to tell me eventually anyway."

She scowled at him, a low growl finding its way up from the back of her throat. She wasn't angry with him. Probably. She just couldn't name whatever was stirring in her gut. Whatever it was, it was almost definitely his fault.

The problem was that he was right. She would tell him eventually. They talked about everything—including that hold-up-traffic kiss. Somehow she'd let him talk her into continuing this charade. Sort of. But no more kissing.

Except kissing Tucker had been an unexpected—but decided—perk of dating him. The feelings that had joined in were not. Cutting out the kissing was supposed to eliminate those feelings. But whatever was stirring in her middle sure felt like feelings.

Ugh.

Leaning her hip against her desk and crossing her arms over her chest, she stared at the floor. Tucker joined her, pressing his palms against the wooden corner, his hand a little too close for comfort.

They stood in silence for what felt like an hour but was probably thirty seconds. Finally, her nerves couldn't take any more. "I'm going to lose my job today."

His head snapped up, his mouth open and moving but not making a sound.

"Mrs. Haywood heard about our shenanigans at your party, and she's . . . displeased."

Tucker pushed himself off the desk, marching to the wall and back, his jaw working back and forth. His cleanly shaven jaw. Even after she'd told him there would be no more kissing.

Her insides rioted, and she pressed a palm to her stomach, which did precisely nothing.

"She can't do that. It was my fault. Didn't you tell her that? I mean, I practically attacked you. You had no idea. I'll tell her you didn't even like it." He stopped pacing then, looking at her from under arched brows.

If he was looking for confirmation that she had indeed liked the kiss, he was going to be waiting a long time. "She left a voicemail, so I didn't get to explain."

Settling back in beside her, he asked, "What does she have against public displays of affection?"

Penelope cringed. "I don't think it's so much the display as the partner."

"Right." He hung his head, shaking it slowly. Even his shoulders drooped under a weight she couldn't see. She'd expected him to be angry on her behalf, but this solemn acceptance made her heart twist. She wasn't going to let him lose his fight.

"We haven't figured out your 'nonsense' yet," she said, forcing a smile and adding air quotes to the key word. When he didn't look up, she brushed her foot against his. "But we can."

He nodded. "I might have a lead in that direction."

"And you didn't start with that?" That deserved a shove with her elbow.

He gave an exaggerated sway to her push. "I'm just—I'm really sorry, PJ. It's my fault."

"Hey. If it's between you and this job, you know what I'd pick. Every day of the week."

"And twice on Sundays?" he asked with a wry grin.

"Don't push your luck, mister. Now tell me about this lead. Did you find something out about Mrs. Fitterling?"

Jumping to his feet, he held out his hands to pull her up too. "I did one better. Feel like going on a field trip?"

"I'm supposed to . . ." She glanced at her desk and the phone that hadn't rung yet. But when Madeline was ready to sack her, she could call her cell. "Okay. Where are we going?"

He opened the door for her, waited for her to walk through and lock it behind them, and pointed away from the water. River Street was filled with tourists sweating their way between tourist shops, fanning themselves with brochures for ghost tours and the like.

She felt strangely like a tourist, searching for a piece of Savannah that she didn't know, a piece of her hometown she'd never seen before. Before she realized what she was doing, she'd reached for his hand, stopping just before her fingers brushed against his. She forced her hand to her side and focused on navigating the cobblestone alley that led away from the river and toward the rest of the historical downtown. When her heel got stuck in a crack, she questioned the wisdom of wearing these particular shoes to work. Then again, she hadn't known that Tucker was going to show up with a clue to the treasure.

"So, what exactly did you find?"

He was a step in front of her but looked back with a grin at her question. "I found Mrs. Fitterling's."

"What?" He had to be mistaken. She knew Bay Street like the back of her hand, and there was no way there was a dress shop hidden among the hotels, coffee shops, and bistros.

He shrugged as they reached a steep staircase, then paused, a glint of mischief in his eye. "Well, it's not Mrs. Fitterling's anymore."

When he held out his hand to help her up the steps, she accepted.

"I dug into the county records, and sure enough, Caroline was right. There was a dress shop on Bay Street. It closed in 1877, but it turns out Mrs. Fitterling never owned the building."

Penelope was nearly out of breath by the time they reached the top of the steep cement stairs, her palm caked in dirt from the metal handrail. She brushed it against her skirt and refused to look down to see if she'd left a stain. She managed a gulp of air as they waited for a streetlight to turn green. "Does it matter?"

"Only in that a Mr. Owen Bennett owned it up until the 1920s. Then it was bought by Jackson Holt, whose son inherited it and still owns it. His family still runs a bar in the same location."

"You're kidding me."

His somber expression gone, Tucker winked at her as they turned onto Bay Street. "Nope. Jackson's Hole."

She laughed, immediately envisioning the neon lights of the bar that she'd passed a hundred times. "Mrs. Fitterling would be scandalized. Her poor little dress shop overrun by karaoke-singing college students a few drinks in."

He nodded as the bar appeared at the end of the block, a chalkboard sign on the sidewalk announcing the happy hour specials. "Probably no more than she was the night that Caroline and Josiah showed up."

They stopped outside the bar, its sign clearly announcing they wouldn't open for a few more hours. "What are we doing here?"

"Jackson Holt Jr. said he'd meet with us. And he said he might have something of interest to our search."

Her breath caught. "Something . . . from that night?"

Pushing the door open, he said, "Let's find out."

Tucker stepped into the dim light of Jackson's Hole, his eyes straining to see after the bright sunlight outside. He knew PJ was having the same problem when her outstretched hands landed on his back, feeling her way into a new environment.

"Mr. Holt," he called. Silence was the only response, so he tried again, louder.

"Don't light your breeches on fire. I'll be right there."

Tucker turned to PJ, her face still in the shadows, her shoulders shaking lightly. He clapped a hand over his own mouth to cover the laugh that threatened to escape.

"Why didn't you turn a light on?" came the same voice a couple seconds later. "It's darker'n midnight out here."

Overhead lights suddenly flicked on, and Tucker moved his hand from his mouth to his eyes, shielding them from the blinding light. "Mr. Holt?"

"Who's asking?"

Tucker dropped his hand enough to get a good look at the man. His whiskers were white, his eyebrows sprouting like an overgrown plant. The lines on his face made him look old enough to have owned the building when Mrs. Fitterling was still a tenant, but his eyes were sharp, knowing.

"I'm Tucker Westbrook. We spoke on the phone."

The man's squint eased up a bit until his gaze landed on PJ. Suddenly Holt ran a hand over his mop of silver hair and down his wrinkled button-up. "Weren't expecting a lady here today. Ma'am." Holt nodded toward her and then scowled at him. "You should give a man some warning."

Tucker quickly nodded, sweeping his arm around PJ's back and holding her to his side. "I'm sorry, Mr. Holt. This is Penelope Hunter. She's helping me search for that cargo that went missing during the war."

"Ma'am." Holt gave a quick bow, then slid across the floor until he could scoop up her hand and press it to his lips. "It's a pleasure."

"Oh—" PJ let out a small squeak, her shoulders shaking again. "The pleasure is all mine."

Mr. Holt ushered them to the bar, swiping his sleeve over a stool seat before holding it out for PJ. "I guess you want to see what we found, huh?"

Tucker nodded, but Holt didn't even pretend to look in his direction. PJ's sweet smile held him captive. Tucker knew the feeling.

"That would be lovely, Mr. Holt," she said.

"Oh, oh, Jackson, please." He skittered behind the bar, ducked beneath the wooden countertop, and reappeared with a small leather pouch in his hand. "I pulled this outta my safe soon as I knew you were comin'." The fabric itself was less than impressive—nondescript and worn by the years—but it was still solid. And when Holt blew on it, a layer of dust made a cloud over the counter.

"What is it?" PJ leaned forward on her elbows, eyes wide.

Tucker could see her reflection in the mirror behind the bar, such sweetness between the bottles of bitter amber liquid lining shelf after shelf.

"My dad, he came into some money and decided to buy this old place. It was a restaurant and then a food kitchen before the Depression. And then after Prohibition ended, well, he added a bar. About that time, food and drink were in high demand. But he never made much money from it, only enough to keep it up to code." His gaze drifted over PJ's shoulder and was lost to history. "I took it over right 'round '65. And when he passed in '72, he left me enough money to renovate. The pipes and wiring were out of date, so they had to tear out all of these walls. First day of demo, they found this." He held up his pouch, clearly his prized possession.

"What is it?" PJ asked again.

"Minié balls."

Tucker's stomach took a hard dive even as PJ shook her head. "Miniature balls?"

"Ammunition. Civil War era."

Suddenly her face reflected the hope in his chest. "And it was just . . . what? In the wall?"

Holt nodded. "And that's French." He pointed to the single word printed across the pale leather.

Tucker couldn't read it—he had a hard enough time with English—but he knew that it meant this particular bag of ammunition had come from France. Probably on a boat that had run the blockade. And if PJ's expression was any indication, she knew it too.

Holt leaned in a little more, his eyes moving back and forth, telling a story that he seemed to have been waiting years to tell. "The contractor, he said there was a hole back there he had to close up. Said it was dangerous. Said it wasn't safe."

"Do you have any blueprints from before the renovation?" PJ asked.

Holt shook his head. "Naw. I don't, but my contractor might."

Tucker bit his tongue to keep from asking if it was possible the man was still alive. PJ had the tact to ask the question in a softer way. "Could we get in touch with him?"

Holt shrugged. "His kid owns the company now, but I got a card somewhere." He ducked into the hallway in the back, leaving Tucker and PJ in stunned silence for a long second.

"What are you thinking?" he asked.

Her gaze swept over the open room, over a pool table and past a dartboard. "Just wondering what this place looked like when Mrs. Fitterling was here. And wondering when they moved the cargo."

His eyebrows rose.

"If this is all that was left behind, someone moved Caroline's treasure. I've skimmed the rest of the diary, but I haven't seen anything else about it."

"What's in the rest of it?"

"Sherman's arrival."

Right. The Christmas of 1864 had been anything but joyful for the residents of Savannah. But that didn't explain what had happened to the treasure.

When Holt returned, he handed PJ a business card. "Thank you," she said.

"Anything for the prettiest treasure hunter to come through here."

She began to smile but stopped short. "The prettiest? You mean there have been others?"

"Sure." He nodded solemnly. "It's been a few years"—he paused—"maybe a few decades, but there was a time when I had several visitors in the same year."

Tucker's throat went dry. Jethro Coleman hadn't been lying. There had been others looking, and they'd gotten at least this far, figured out at least as much as he and PJ had. So what had kept them from finding the treasure?

"What'd you tell them?" PJ asked.

Holt winked at her. "That Savannah is full of lost treasure."

They thanked Holt for his help and left. As they stepped onto the sidewalk, the sun felt like it had been turned up a few degrees, and Tucker blinked hard against it, still able to see PJ's silhouette against the backs of his eyes.

When he could finally see again, he turned to face her. Crossing his arms, he frowned. "What do you think?"

"Well, I guess we better meet with a contractor."

He nodded.

"You want to go now?"

"Tomorrow?"

Because first he needed to do something he should have done weeks ago.

Thursday, December 22, 1864

Christmas shall be a drab affair this year. I had so hoped that it might be filled with joy and reunion, but there is nothing left to celebrate. General Hardee and his men abandoned our precious city and have left it open to Sherman's troops, who have filled the city to bursting. There are bluecoats everywhere I look. Even now officers meet with Papa to arrange for their men to sleep under this very roof.

I can hardly imagine, but there are so many of them and not nearly enough beds in which they might sleep. I daren't think where they will all find housing.

Mama refused to let Sarah go to the market by herself, so Bradford escorted her this morning. Desperate to see beyond the view of my windows, I begged to join them. Clinging to Bradford's arm as we left the house, I could not believe my eyes. Even the cemetery has been consumed by them. They have made little camps among the headstones, the fires burning all through the day not enough to warm them.

The air is sharp, the wind chafing. These men look ragged. Their hair is uncombed, their beards rough, their uniforms even more so. I pulled my cloak tighter about me, but I could not help but shiver in the cold, as they must.

They glared at me as we walked past, and I moved even closer to my brother. Their words, though likely foul, did not reach me. Still, everything in me shudders to think what they will do to our city.

Yet, there was one man. No, he was but a boy too young yet for whiskers, his eyes haunted. Oh, the things he must have seen. And his mama without him for Christmas.

This war is unfair to all. It has taken so many sons and brothers and fathers. My heart aches for these men.

As we walked toward Bay Street, I could not help but wonder if our activities have done anything to help bring it all to an end or if we are merely delaying the inevitable.

Friday, December 23, 1864

Bradford has moved into my room, sleeping on a pallet at the foot of my bed. Every other room, save my parents', has been taken over by officers. They dine with us and meet in Papa's study and discuss things in softer tones. Despite my tendencies toward eavesdropping, I have heard nothing of interest.

But last night something most interesting happened. I could not very well have the candle burning in my room with Bradford asleep, so I tiptoed to the library so I might have a few moments to write down the day's events.

I had barely finished writing the entry when I heard a noise in the hallway. I slammed my book closed and stowed my pencil, ducking into the corner behind the door. I leaned toward the seam around the door frame, praying I might hear a voice, hear something that would help our home feel like it belongs to our family once again.

There was no voice, only footsteps upon the carpet. They moved slowly as though uncertain of the way. Surely it could not be Mama or Papa. And Bradford's gait was far too distinctive to be mistaken for anyone else.

The door opened slowly, creaking softly in the dim light. I

swallowed a gasp, only then realizing that I had left the candle on the table where I had sat. The house was not as safe as it had once been, and I knew that not even Sarah would be out of bed at such a time. Whoever this was, he was not a friend.

I could have run for the candle, but I feared any movement might alert the intruder that he was not alone. Then the door stopped. My heart did as well. I am sure of it. There was not a sound or a breath as I waited. The waiting seemed unending. I stared at the wall behind the door, lined with my father's leather tomes, for hours. Perhaps it was only minutes.

Then a voice called out a questioning hello. It was deep but gentle, though the image it conjured in my mind was of the giant Goliath in the paintings I have seen in churches. Could I be David? Was I placed in that very location so I might fight off the great monster?

I prayed that it would not be so, for my knees trembled and my eyes burned. I remained silent.

Again the man called out.

Is someone here?

I wanted to jump out and scare him. Perhaps he would believe me to be a ghost and tell his men, and they would all flee Savannah's streets and leave my family alone. But I could not muster the courage to face him. I wished to disappear into the floor, to become one with the books and blend into my surroundings. But my floral dressing gown could hardly be missed against the royal colors of the books adorning the white shelves.

Oh! Excuse me, miss.

His words sounded nearly as surprised as I was. I had been spotted, and there was nothing for it but to face my would-be attacker. As I looked over my shoulder, I found not a feral giant but a humble man, head bowed and waist bent. He offered profuse apologies for interrupting me and backed away slowly.

I think he might have left had he not looked up in time to see me watching him. When our gazes met, he offered a slow smile, asking if I was the Miss Westbrook he had heard so much about. Of course, I did not know who he had heard about or what things had been said. I managed a nod of agreement nonetheless.

He asked if I'd like him to leave, and I shook my head. Why ever did I refuse? What foolishness had overtaken me? I did not know.

After looking over his shoulder as though to confirm that we would not be interrupted, he gave me another smile. My, but it was handsome. His teeth are white and evenly spaced, and his entire face lit like a lantern from within.

He asked if I could not sleep, and I shook my head. He frowned then and suggested it might be because my home was filled with strangers. I offered only a shrug, just then realizing that I was wearing naught but a dressing gown over my thin cotton nightgown. I tugged the collar closed beneath my chin, clutching my book to my side with my elbow. I should have left him then. But every time he opened his mouth the most fascinating things escaped.

He told me a most diverting anecdote about the other officer sharing his room, a Lieutenant Carruthers, who apparently has some sort of nasal blockage that prevents him from sleeping silently. I nearly burst for holding in my laughter, for he was quite amusing as he demonstrated the terrible sound.

A strange silence settled upon us then. It was not uncomfortable, yet I felt my skin tremble beneath his inspection. I could not meet his gaze, but I knew he was looking at me. Me with my hair in a plait and my figure concealed beneath the billowing fabric of my robe. His survey was not unkind, but there was an intensity there I had never experienced.

Finally I thought he might devour me with his gaze if not distracted, and I blurted out the first thing I could think of. I asked him his name.

His laugh was deep and joyful, and it bellowed from low in his belly until I joined him. Then his gaze turned serious. His name is Lieutenant Haulder, and he is from Pennsylvania.

I nearly blurted out another question. I wondered if he was married with a family at home waiting for him. But why should that matter to me? No matter how handsome or charming, he has invaded my city and my home. I have no right or need to ask such a thing.

I excused myself then, racing for my bedroom, lest I meet another of our guests less inclined toward civility. But I could not seem to remove him from my mind. I lay in bed listening to Bradford's deep breaths, thinking over and over about my exchange with Lieutenant Haulder. My eyes finally drifted closed as the sun rose.

From the moment I dragged myself from bed today, I have thought of nothing but the tall lieutenant. He was civil and respectful, yet when he looked at me, I was sure he saw a woman. I was almost sure he looked at me with interest, as a man looks at a woman he finds beautiful. I know I should not care for his attentions, yet how could any woman deny such a feeling?

It was almost as thrilling as our trip to Mrs. Fitterling's last week. Yet I feel a small portion of guilt to have shared it with anyone other than Josiah.

Saturday, December 24, 1864

I can hardly believe that Christmas is but a day away. The air carries a promise of snow, and I cannot help but consider the men sleeping upon the ground. Lieutenant Haulder returned to the house from a walk yesterday afternoon, his face containing none of the humor it had held the evening before. I knew I was not free to ask him what has caused him distress. Not with Mama watching so closely, insisting that I work on my stitching in the parlor by her side.

It took some great maneuvering for me to extricate my person from her side, but as soon as I did, I hurried toward the kitchen, for Sarah knows everything that goes on in this house. Even with the extra residents.

Sarah was not to be found. Instead I found Lieutenant Haulder helping himself to a cup of coffee—or the version we have settled for for so many years. I must have looked surprised, for he begged my pardon for helping himself. How kind of him, even though his fellow officers have no such manners. I have seen them digging through the cupboards and even trying to pry open the sugar chest. I'm glad I came upon that awful man before he could discover that we have no sugar to steal. There has been none for almost a year.

For the second time in as many days, I was alone with the dashing Lieutenant Haulder, and I knew this would be my only chance to speak freely with him. I asked him what sadness had come over him, and he told me of his men freezing in the cold, without cover or protection. The corners of his mouth dipped under his fair whiskers, but his gaze never left mine. His eyes are so green, like the church lawn before a picnic.

I was too taken with his eyes to realize when he reached

for my hand. But suddenly he was holding it, his fingers warm about mine. He said that he hoped I did not think him impertinent, but he must speak or burst. That is when he said I am the most beautiful woman he has ever seen.

I did not know how much I had longed to hear those words until they were there before me, warming me more than the fire in the grate. He leaned forward, near enough for me to feel his breath upon my face. I do believe he might have kissed me then, but for Sarah's return. Instead he tipped his head toward me and slipped away before we could be caught in a compromising situation.

A man this kind could not be as terrible as they say. He has a good heart, a gentleness to him. Yet it feels wrong to even think of such a man when I hold another's secret.

THIRTEEN

The Ladies' League headquarters were housed in an expectedly historical home turned office. What Tucker did not expect as he stepped into the cool foyer was the decidedly modern finishes. The wall behind the receptionist was shiplap, the Ladies' League logo etched in metal over it. It looked like it had been designed by one of those shows on HGTV.

Then there was the woman sitting behind the front desk in a state-of-the-art office chair that provided lumbar, neck, and arm support. The only thing it didn't offer was financial support after you paid for the thing.

She swung toward him, acknowledging him but tapping on the ear of her headset and holding up a finger to let him know he'd have to wait his turn.

Tucker nodded, literally ducking into the waiting area so he didn't hit his head on the ceiling beam. All three of the high-back chairs were pristine white, with colorful pillows taking up the functional parts of the seats. The chairs were designed to look inviting but didn't actually invite anyone to sit down. At least that was what he concluded.

Several framed images hung above the chairs, and he

leaned closer to see what they were. One held the front page of a yellowed newspaper, but the words were long gone, the small headlines of the day marred by age and air. Another frame held a penciled sketch of the three-story Cotton Exchange just a few blocks north. The final frame contained a picture he'd never seen before—a black-and-white image of the Colonial Park Cemetery.

The cemetery in the heart of the city was the final resting place of many of Savannah's earliest citizens. Most of the victims of the yellow fever epidemic had ended up there—many buried below ground but some in family crypts. The red-brick structures were unmistakable.

He'd walked by the cemetery a million times, so he recognized it in an instant. But he didn't recognize the faces staring back at him. All of them were haggard and rough. And all of them were wearing Union uniforms.

His stomach pitched. He knew what had happened there. How Sherman's army, more than sixty thousand and weary, cold, and starving, had entered Savannah, not even half that large. And how the city hadn't had enough roofs to house them, enough hearths to keep them warm. So they'd filled every vacant patch of earth. Including the cemeteries.

Headstones had been smashed, crypts robbed, and someone had captured it all.

His ancestors had been there. Caroline had seen it and known one of these men. And fallen in love with him.

Was she the real traitor in the family? He couldn't help but wonder if she had decided Lieutenant Haulder was worthy of knowing the secret. If she had told him where the treasure was hidden, they could be looking for something that had been gone for a century and a half.

It certainly would have brought shame on the Westbrook name, as Caroline had said in that first letter PJ had found.

"Can I help you?" The receptionist's tone was clipped and efficient, and he spun around to face her, forcing his thoughts to the present.

"Yes. I'd like to see Mrs. Haywood, please."

"Do you have an appointment?" She squinted at him. "Oh, Mr. Westbrook."

Well, his reputation preceded him. Maybe not a great sign in this building. But at the very least, he wasn't forgettable.

"I'm sorry. We don't endorse candidates. It's a League policy."

He strolled up to the desk, feeling like a giant as he ducked once again under the beam in the ceiling. "I'm not looking for an endorsement. I'd like to speak to Mrs. Haywood about something else entirely."

The woman gave him an unsteady smile. "Well, I'm sure she'd be happy to speak with you. If you'll make an appointment."

"But she called first."

"Oh. Let me just . . ." She punched a number into her phone, and he waited, smile frozen in place.

Mrs. Haywood hadn't exactly called *him*, but certainly her voicemail to PJ constituted a first move. Maybe PJ had more grace than to return the call. Tucker did not.

Everything inside him wanted to tell the old bat just what he thought of her using her influence to get PJ canned. All because she didn't like some old letter that besmirched his family's good name.

Well, he didn't need their help tearing down the family name. All he needed was to get good and riled up at his dad and seek out the only bit of comfort in a cold VFW community room. Then again, PJ was pretty much the best bit of comfort anywhere in his life.

"There's a Mr. Westbrook here to see you." The receptionist paused, listening to the voice on the other end of the line. "Yes. *That* Westbrook. He said you called."

He squared his shoulders and shot her a partial grin. Not that that was going to help.

She hung up the phone. "She'll be right—"

She didn't even have time to finish as a door down the hall flew open, and the sharp report of high heels on the hardwood floor announced the impending arrival.

"Mis-ter Westbrook." Mrs. Haywood's greeting was not what he would classify as warm. All traces of Southern hospitality were conspicuously absent, and her glare could have sliced through cement.

"Mrs. Haywood." He nodded. "Thank you—"

"Oh, do not thank me yet, young man. We do not have an appointment, and I certainly did not telephone you first."

"No, you did not. But you did call Penelope Hunter."

Her lips twisted into what had to be a painful grimace. "That girl has a lot of nerve sending you here. Especially when I'm so busy looking for a new venue to hold our guests."

Everything inside him wanted to stand even straighter, stare her down, and defend PJ. He wanted to put Anabelle Haywood in her place, show her that he wasn't afraid of her or her threats. But he knew that look in her eyes. He'd seen it before from men in power, men too proud to back down.

So he bit his tongue, snuck a breath, and bowed his head. "No, ma'am. She doesn't even know I'm here."

The lines around her mouth relaxed slightly, and he leaned in, meeting her gaze.

"Penelope would never ask it of you, but I have to. Would you reconsider holding your event at the Savannah River Hall? You know she'll do an amazing job. She always has."

The receptionist watched them like a tennis match, her eyes bouncing back and forth, her jaw hanging open just a bit.

Tucker did his best to ignore her, keeping his focus on Mrs. Haywood. "I can explain." At least, he could try.

Mrs. Haywood crossed her arms over her yellow silk shirt, bouncing her string of pearls. After a long pause, she said, "You may have ten minutes." With that invitation, she spun and marched back in the direction of her office.

He followed her, hustling into the room painted in pale blue and white trim. Large and spacious, it had probably been the master bedroom of the old home. Matching windows on the far wall bathed the room in natural light. Her antique wood desk filled as much space as a queen-size bed. The leather chair behind it looked comfortable, but she didn't sit. She didn't invite him to sit in one of the guest chairs either—mirrors of the ones in the waiting room.

Facing him, arms still crossed, she nodded. "Very well. What is it you want to say?"

He hadn't prepared a speech because he hadn't really thought he'd get this far. Now that he was here, he had to say something. But his mind was blank, save one image: PJ's stooped shoulders and sad eyes.

"When PJ—I mean, Penelope—and I were in grade school, I complained about having to learn history." He shrugged and let out a laugh. "And our teacher told me that those who don't learn history are bound to repeat it. Do you think that's true?"

She nodded. "I suppose."

"You must have seen it as you've explored Savannah's history." He pointed to a framed portrait on the wall. "You see the choices that were made and how we can make better ones now. Our history doesn't define us. It just presents a choice."

"I hardly see how that's relevant to our situation." With a glance at her gold watch, she added, "You have five minutes."

Giving her a quick nod of understanding, he said, "I guess all I want to say is that Penelope has always been the person in my life willing to help me figure out my family's history but never willing to let me settle for it."

Mrs. Haywood's eyebrows rose into her wrinkled forehead, but she couldn't be any more surprised than he was. He hadn't planned to say it. In fact, he couldn't remember ever thinking it before. But just because he hadn't put it into words until now didn't make it any less true.

A slow smile fell into place as he remembered how she'd grumbled about crawling into an old attic but did it anyway to help him. How she'd straightened his tie and smoothed out his suit so he made a good impression. How she'd brought him soup when he was so sick that he refused to see anyone else.

She knew how to take care of him, and this was his chance to return the favor.

"Mrs. Haywood, I know you don't know me, except for maybe what you've read in the newspaper or heard in a disparaging television commercial."

She pursed her lips, which was about as much agreement as he was likely to get.

"But I know you. I know that you're a respected community leader. I know that people are following your lead.

And I'm asking you to give Penelope and the Hall another chance. I know you think her association with me is dragging her down, but the truth is that she brings out the best version of me. She's not willing to let me settle for who I might have been—for who my family might have been. Traitors or tricksters, smugglers or thieves. She would never let me live down to that."

"She must really want to keep her job," Mrs. Haywood said under her breath.

"No, ma'am. Er—I mean, she does. She loves that job. But again, she doesn't even know I'm here. I came to see you because my best friend's heart is breaking at just the thought of losing her job. One she's wildly fantastic at, I might add."

The lines around Mrs. Haywood's eyes deepened.

It was now or never, so he laid it on thick. "You've seen her do her job. Go ahead and tell me that your last two events at the Hall haven't been the best you've ever had and I'll walk right out of here." He turned toward the door but paused to look her square in the eyes one more time. "You know I'm right. You know she does great work."

The room seemed at odds with the fizzling tension inside him, the lazy sunshine floating across the floor. Clasping his hands together, he forced himself to wait for her to respond. After several long silent seconds, he feared she wouldn't. His stomach twisted, and he reached for more words. But he'd used them all.

Then she gave a barely perceptible nod. "I'll concede that point."

She could have pushed him over with a feather. She'd agreed. Now what? Fighting the too-wide grin that threatened, he said, "Well, do you want to risk doing this year's benefit with someone less talented? Your guests have come to expect a certain standard from your fundraiser."

Mrs. Haywood did not have what one would consider a colorful complexion. But apparently her pale features could turn ghostly. And they did.

"My family's past may be colorful and questionable, but I promise you it's not a reflection of Penelope Hunter."

She smacked her tongue like she'd swallowed something sour. "You speak pretty openly for someone running for public office."

"Yes, ma'am." He shrugged. "I've got nothing to hide."

"Not even Daniel Westbrook and that incendiary letter?"

With a shake of his head and a laugh, he said, "That's already out there. Why would I try to cover it up or ignore it? It may be part of my history, but it doesn't define me or my future."

She squinted at him, leaning forward on her toes. "Well said, young man, but I've already turned the matter over to our board of directors." With a pat on his cheek, she continued. "You may tell your friend that I'll speak with my board at our meeting next week. They'll have the final say. So it would behoove you to clear up that letter's nonsense by next Friday."

Tucker had no idea what swept over him, but he grabbed her and pulled her into a warm hug. Over her sputtering gasps, he whispered, "Thank you very much," before releasing her and booking it toward the door.

Penelope had spent far too many hours staring at her phone, waiting for it to ring and the other shoe to drop, when she should have been putting together package ideas for Emmaline and Winston. That was why she was wholly unprepared for their arrival.

She tried to give them a bright smile, pushing herself up from her chair and dropping the stepping stone she'd been rubbing to wave them in. "What a surprise to see you."

Her stomach dropped to the floor for an instant. What if they had an appointment? Had she completely forgotten about it?

"Oh, we just couldn't stay away," Emmaline cooed, snuggling into Winston's arm.

Penelope let out a tight breath. Well, at least she hadn't dropped a ball and given Madeline a real reason to fire her. Not that Anabelle Haywood pulling the Ladies' League event wasn't reason enough.

She felt queasy all over again, and she was pretty sure her face showed it. Swallowing the acid at the back of her throat, she managed an uneven grin. "Oh?"

Emmaline's eyes sparkled with some mysterious knowledge. "I think you know why."

Penelope shook her head numbly. "Did you want to talk about the wedding?"

"No, silly! The *kiss*!"

She had no idea what expression her face showed, but she had a feeling it was pretty close to the one on Winston's. The one that said he'd rather have a chat with a shark than talk about her kiss with Tucker. Especially after what Winston had said to her that night.

Right, well, that wasn't any of his business. Smoothing

her palms down the sides of her flowing skirt, she searched for the right words, but they stayed hidden while Emmaline dived right into the deep end.

"Did he propose yet?"

Winston gulped and then coughed loudly.

Emmaline was not dissuaded from her course. "I mean, how could he not after that kiss?"

"Oh, no." Penelope waved around her naked left hand. "We're not—that is, we're going to try—" To what? To be better? To not make out in public anymore? Ever again, actually. No more kissing. Keep it simple. Just friends hanging out. Quasi-dating. No attraction.

Liar.

Ugh.

Emmaline's smile dipped, but Winston's ears remained red, his cheeks flushed. "Oh. But I saw him today, and he looked so happy," she said.

Who could have made him visibly happy?

It couldn't be the contractor from Jackson's Hole. They were scheduled to meet him the next day. And it wasn't the diary. They'd gotten no good news from that since the Fitterling revelation. And it probably wasn't his parents. Talking with his dad wasn't high on Tucker's list of favorite things. Something else had made him happy.

It wasn't her. And that shouldn't matter. There was no reason why she should care if she was the one making him smile. But she did.

Her face suddenly burned and her throat became full. Standing in front of a sober Winston and his bubbly bride was not the place to ask herself these questions. So she swallowed the lump in her throat and tried for a smile.

"You saw him?" Penelope tried to cover the insecurity in her tone with a quick follow-up. "Where was that?"

"He was walking out of the Ladies' League this afternoon. I just assumed he was asking about a wedding venue." Emmaline shrugged. "We went there first too."

"Oh, well, I'm sure he was . . ." Actually, she had absolutely no idea what he was up to. There was no plausible reason Tucker Westbrook would venture into Anabelle Haywood's territory. Not when he knew how strongly she felt about his "nonsense." She shrugged. "I'm sure I'll hear about it later."

"Of course you will. I bet he's your last call of the day." Emmaline's eyebrows wiggled.

Winston looked like he was about to lose his lunch.

Emmaline hugged his side, forcing him to put his arm around her. "I call Winston every night at eleven. I can't fall asleep if I don't hear his voice first."

Ha. Yeah, right.

Except she was right. Penelope talked to Tucker every night. His *was* the last voice she wanted to hear before falling asleep. And when they'd had their tiff about the kiss, she had lain awake for hours, tossing and turning and refusing to admit how much she missed her best friend. Every night that he'd been deployed, she'd reached for her phone, wishing she could hear him say three little words. *I'm all right.*

"Don't you just love being in love?" Emmaline's heart shone through her eyes.

"Yep. It's the best." Penelope couldn't contain the sarcasm. Being in love with her best friend—the one who'd said he wouldn't kiss her again—might actually be the worst. And she was afraid she might be halfway there already. Dangerous territory for sure.

As though speaking of him conjured him, the bell on her door rang, and all six feet two inches of Tucker Westbrook filled the entrance. "Excuse me. Am I interrupting again?"

"We were just leaving," Winston said, towing Emmaline from the room and closing the door behind him with a solid thwack.

Tucker raised his eyebrows. "So, good meeting?"

"They stopped in to see if we're engaged."

"What? Them too?" He let out a full-bellied laugh. "What is it with this town? We're friends for twenty-five years, and then the minute they think we're dating, we *must* be getting married."

"I know, right? It's like they think they know something we don't." She gave a half-hearted giggle, but she couldn't help but wonder. What if they *did* know something she and Tucker didn't? Or what if they *saw* something?

What if she'd done a terrible job of hiding those errant feelings that had exploded when he kissed her? No matter how many times she talked with her mom and reminded herself that she could never risk losing Tucker or having him turn his back on her, those feelings—the ones that made her wish she was the one making him smile—refused to stay away.

She glanced up at him, his face still softened by a grin. No, it wasn't soft. Without his beard, the lines of his jaw were sharp and hard as granite. The straight line of his nose and smooth outline of his lips were strong and firm.

Now she couldn't help but remember what it had felt like for those lips to be pressed to hers. They'd agreed not to do that again. It was a bad idea. The worst.

So why did it take everything inside her to keep from throwing herself at him?

Wrapping her arms across her stomach, she nodded toward the door through which Emmaline and Winston had exited. "Emmaline said she'd seen you coming out of the Ladies' League office. Isn't that kind of like going into the lions' den?"

He took a step toward her before sitting on the edge of her desk and crossing his long legs. "I thought it was enemy territory, but now I'm not so sure."

"Ooh." She plopped down on the spot beside him, matching his posture. "Do tell."

"I went to see Anabelle Haywood."

"And you made it out alive?" she asked.

Tucker scratched at his jaw for a long second. "I know. It's kind of a miracle. She even let me hug her."

Penelope worked her jaw, hoping to find a word or two, but her brain couldn't comprehend the idea of Tucker wrapping his arms around Mrs. Haywood. Or her letting him.

"I mean, it was more of a stealth attack. I got in and out fast. But she didn't send her attack dogs after me."

He seemed lost in thought, so she nudged him. "So . . ."

"She's going to talk to her board about not pulling the event."

"What?" She jumped to her feet and spun to face him.

He rubbed the back of his neck, bowing his head for a short moment before meeting her gaze again. "I asked her to reconsider having her event here. I told her how my history may be a mess, but you've been loyal and faithful even then. I told her how I couldn't make it without you, and that you refuse to leave me where I am. I'm a better man because of you."

The backs of her eyes burned, and she shook her head. "But she doesn't like you."

He lifted one shoulder, his black knit polo shirt molding to the muscles there. "I think she likes me a little more because of you."

"Me?"

He nodded. "Of course. Don't you know how much everyone around here loves you? I mean, Catherine Saunders couldn't stop gushing about how fantastic you are." He paused, but his eyes never left hers. "Mrs. Haywood still has to check with the board next week—and she said it would be good if we could clear up that letter before then—but there's hope."

"Why did you do that?" She didn't know why the words popped out of her mouth, but there they were, flapping like sheets in the wind.

Tucker stood slowly, his movements smooth and measured, his gaze never wavering. There was heat and life in his eyes, and she could feel the warmth across every inch of her skin. He reached out like he was going to touch her face, and she could already feel his embrace, sweeter than honey on her mama's biscuits.

Everything inside her thrummed with life and hope and wishes for what might be. Now that she knew how it could be between them, it was so much harder to deny it, to convince herself that it was fire guaranteed to burn her. That she should keep her distance. There were no number of to-do lists that would help her recover when it all fell apart.

And it would fall apart. It always did. Her dad had walked out on her mom. Winston had left her. Tucker would choose someone else too. When he did, she'd be left to pick up whatever shards were left of her heart.

But maybe—just maybe—it would be worth it to really love him for as long as it lasted.

She gasped as his hand cupped her cheek, his thumb brushing below her eye, his gaze focused on the southern half of her face.

"Don't you know I'd do anything for you?" His words sounded like they'd been dragged over a dirt road, and she couldn't think what had prompted them. Had she asked him a question? Oh, right. She'd asked him why he'd gone to see Mrs. Haywood. Why he'd risked Anabelle's wrath for her.

"You would?" Her throat went dry, and more words failed her.

His hand dropped to her jaw before he slipped his fingers into her hair and cradled the back of her neck. He was so close now that she could nearly feel the beat of his heart, or perhaps that was her own, drowning out every other sound. His other arm slipped around her back, inching her closer as she breathed him in—all clean and natural. He smelled like the sea after a rain.

"Always." His rasped reply came as he leaned in, closing the distance between them until he was only a breath away.

Suddenly his features pinched. He dropped his arms and hesitated. She remembered. He'd said he wouldn't kiss her again.

No. No. No. This was not happening. Not when she'd finally decided to just let it happen, to stop denying what they'd finally discovered. He wasn't the only one with a say in this.

Lunging for him before he could pull away, she wrapped her hands into the soft fabric of his shirt, stood up on her tiptoes, and leaned in. The last thing she saw before closing her eyes was his half grin. She pressed her lips to his and the world exploded. Her office disappeared, and her whole world consisted of Tucker.

He turned them so that she backed into her desk, which grazed her hip. She gave an involuntary squeak, and he immediately spun them again, protecting her from the sharp corner. She squeezed his shirt in her fists and tried to get closer to him as he kissed a trail from the corner of her mouth to her ear and back.

Her lungs ceased to work, and she threw her arms around his neck, hanging on as his hands swept up and down her back. He seemed to be trying to soothe her, but his hands were so strong and big and male and . . . well, Tucker's, that she couldn't catch her breath. It seemed a small price to pay for sharing this moment.

Finally, when she thought she must have oxygen again or swoon, he leaned back just far enough to look into her eyes. His smile made his whole face glow. "I guess my beard won't be coming back."

She ran a finger across the smooth skin from his cheek to the tiny cleft in his chin. He'd had a beard since he'd been discharged, and she still wasn't sure she was used to this version of his face. "I usually like your beard. Just not when we're making out."

He chuckled. "Like I said. It's gone for good."

Her stomach pitched and her breath caught. It sounded like they had a lot more of this in their future. Oh dear. How could she ever concentrate on anything else when kissing Tucker was an option? Work, the election, and the rest of her life were going to suffer.

Being in love with Tucker Westbrook might just be the worst. But she was all in. No halfway about it.

December 24, 1864

I hardly know what to believe any longer, for Lieutenant Haulder has kissed me. Mistletoe had seemed such a silly decoration this year, and we have no time for silliness.

This evening I was in the library once again. If I am to be completely honest, I may have been there hoping the lieutenant would once again visit, though I had a pretext of reading another of Miss Austen's novels. I could not tell you its title, for I was far too distracted, listening to every creak and groan in the house. I thought I heard a door open and close, and I held my breath waiting for him to arrive. He did not.

I had all but given up on his appearance, closing my book and sliding my feet back into my slippers, when I heard him. He called my name ever so softly. It was deep but restrained so as not to wake anyone else in the house. He stepped into the room, linen shirtsleeves rolled up to his elbows, one thumb tucked into his suspender at his shoulder.

I could not contain my smile, for he is even more handsome by the glowing embers in the hearth, and I fell back into my seat, tucking my feet beneath me. He asked if he might join me, and I agreed immediately. Perhaps too quickly, but he did not seem to mind. I hardly feel worthy, but when he looks at me with such intensity, I am lost. He sat on the couch opposite me and asked about the book still in my hands. I had to laugh. I truly had no idea, for I had not been reading. This made him smile too.

I had once pictured Yankees like feral dogs, their teeth sharp as razors, their smiles filled with malice. Lieutenant Haulder is not like that at all. There is a warmth in his eyes, a humor in the way he tells stories of his men. When he speaks, I completely forget that he has been part of a campaign that has burned homes and farms in my state to the ground. It is a product of the war, for he would never do such things if not ordered to. I am certain of it.

We talked for hours about his home and mine, what we enjoy reading, the places we have traveled. Before the war, he had begun his education at the University of Pennsylvania, and he hopes to complete it so he may become a doctor.

I asked him if the army would not have waited for him. Would he not be of more use as a field surgeon than a foot soldier? Even as my question left my lips, I could see a sadness fall over him, his shoulders carrying the weight of the world. His posture stooped, the line of his mouth growing tight. I thought he would not answer me and I had brought an end to our conversation.

After a long silence, he sighed. He said that he could have waited to join, but his younger brother, Frank, had been eager to be part of the fray. Frank, afraid he would miss the fighting, could not be dissuaded from enlisting, and the lieutenant, feeling it was his duty to protect his brother, joined up as well.

I asked if Frank was here in Savannah. He only shook his head. And I knew. He'd joined the war to keep his brother safe but had been unable to.

I did not mean to touch him, but I reached for his hand and squeezed it, wishing him all my sympathy. He held on to it as though it were a raft in the middle of a stormy sea.

We sat in silence like that for several more minutes, his gaze never leaving the embers as they popped and fizzled their way out. The room had grown cool, and I could hear the wind howling beyond the windows. That is not why I shivered. I shivered at his nearness, at the way his thumb stroked the back of my hand.

When he stood, he pulled me with him, never releasing my

LIZ JOHNSON

hand. We walked toward the door, and he paused beneath the door frame. He looked up, and I did also. When I realized what he was looking at, my stomach dropped to my knees. Sarah had laughed as she'd hung the ball of mistletoe weeks ago. It was one of only a few decorative concessions to the season, but she said when a young woman lived in the house, she ought to have some excuse for a kiss.

The lieutenant looked at me, and I could see the desire in his eyes. His voice was rough and cracked as he asked if he could kiss me. It is tradition, after all. I giggled, for I did not even know his given name. When I asked, he laughed as well. William Haulder. He said his mother calls him Will, but he prefers William. I rather prefer the way it rolls off my tongue as well.

With the formalities out of the way, I agreed to a small kiss, but there is nothing small about him. I felt his presence surround me, and his hands on my arms were warm and gentle. I had only dreamed to someday know such a kiss. But I had always thought it would come from another, and I felt a surge of regret through my middle even as I allowed him such liberties.

He released me, and I rushed to my room. I did not even try to stay quiet, for Bradford sleeps like the dead. I have risked a candle to write, for sleep eludes me.

I cannot rest for feeling as though I have betrayed Josiah. I have waited four long years for him to return, for him to do more than kiss my forehead in the dark. I have prayed for his protection and longed for a single letter. Even now, I worry for his safety and his secrets.

I have loved him since I was a child, and I have promised myself that I would do anything for him. But I did not save my first kiss for him. What will he say if he finds out? Will it break his heart? Does he care for me enough for his heart to break?

221

All the worse, I wonder if I have betrayed my family and my homeland. I pray that the Almighty will forgive my sins if I break Papa's heart.

Sunday, December 25, 1864

'Tis late on this Christmas day, and I am most conflicted. On this day of peace, in this season of supposed joy, I am in utter turmoil. Oh, what have I done? Can he ever forgive me? Can I forgive myself?

We shared a simple fare with the soldiers in our home at noon. It was no more than our usual meal, but Sarah had run a length of garland down the center of the table, and our napkins were red, the only hint at festivities. There seemed to be an agreed-upon truce between the Yankees and ourselves.

Lieutenant Haulder found his way to the seat next to mine, and amid the twelve others at the table, I think no one noticed anything unusual. Above the table, he was all things gentlemanly and good-natured. Below the table, he let his knee brush against mine. At first I thought it an accident, but when he let it rest there, I knew it was not. And heaven forbid, I liked it. I liked it very much. Is it such a terrible thing to want to be appreciated, to want to be admired? He told me last evening that he thinks I am beautiful, that my hair is as soft as silk, that I am the very reason for the term Southern belle. And when he holds me in his arms, I am undone. His kiss is sweeter than I could ever imagine.

Still, I know guilt as I have never known. Mama and Papa would surely disapprove. And if I care for him, why must I lie about the treasure? I don't even know what it is intended for. Only that it sits there, stored away. And that Josiah has disappeared once again.

I barely made it through the table games and the carol singing this afternoon before feigning a headache and rushing to my room. But I had forgotten that it is no longer my room, for it belongs to Bradford equally now. The sun had begun to set, the room turning to long shadows as I lay in my bed, when my brother entered. He had a simple scrap of paper in his hand, and he said nothing as he slipped it to me. It said only: I am in the carriage house.

For a moment I wondered if it was from the lieutenant. But he would never use Bradford for such an errand. Which could only mean one thing.

I rushed from my room, nearly knocking over Sarah in my haste, but she did not seem surprised.

When I arrived in the carriage house, I did not dare to even whisper his name, though my heart beat in time to the rhythm of his name in my mind. The carriage house was cold and dark, the sun nearly gone. It smelled of horse and hay and the cold Savannah wind. A single lantern hung at the edge of the stall, and I peered into it. But it was empty save Marigold swatting her tail.

Then a low whisper in my ear. I cried out, and a firm hand covered my mouth and ended my scream. But as I turned, I knew I did not need to be afraid.

Josiah. I sank into him, and he held me as a precious stone. We stood there for many minutes, simply staring at each other, until I finally whispered that I thought I would never see him again. I thought he had gone for good.

He confessed that he soon would be leaving, and he did not think he should return—even after the war. For he says he has done what he thought to be right, but he fears it has only put him in danger.

I asked if we could not just return the cargo, and his face became very sad. He says they wish for his head, and they are searching for him even now.

My heart cried out when he said such things, and I buried my face against his chest.

Suddenly the door to the carriage house creaked, and he pulled me into the shadows, holding me against his chest. I barely breathed, only inhaling the wool of his coat. Only then did I realize I had left the house without a wrap, and I shivered, though I know not if it was from the cold or his embrace.

His arms were strong and still about me, but my heart raced. He did not move as we waited for someone to see us, to see him.

Then Marigold's nicker and Sarah's familiar voice split the silence. She told us we best hurry up, for the soldiers in the house had been drinking. There was no telling what they might do.

I squeezed my eyes closed and clung to him, praying that the Good Lord might see fit to spare his life, to protect him, even if he did not want to stay with me.

He pressed one finger beneath my chin, tilting my head up. In the darkness I could not see his face, but I knew his features, and I knew him. He said he wished he could have written me all that was on his heart. He wished he had not left all those years ago without telling me how he felt.

How did he feel? I begged him to tell me.

But he said only that he could not make me promises. He could not give me hope or ask me to wait, for his future is uncertain, his life in jeopardy. And he will not put me in such danger.

Perhaps it was my small sob that gave away my tears, for he

brushed a finger across my cheek, wiping them away. Then he told me he had always cared for me. Even while he was a boy, he had hoped to make me his bride. But he could not bear to promise me a future he might not be able to fulfill, so he had said nothing. He begged my forgiveness that he yet could make no promises.

Then he kissed me. My body was aflame, my soul seared by his touch. Oh, his touch. So gentle yet powerful. It was all that I had waited these years for. Yet I know the terrible truth. How could I kiss one man when I am so much in love with another?

Josiah left then. Disappearing into the early night, slipping between trees and buildings until I could not see him from my place in the carriage house doorway. I could not help but compare William, who has sworn no devotion yet eagerly shown me his affection, and Josiah, who has withheld his affection but shown his trust. Who truly cares for me?

I am left unsettled and uncertain. And I still carry the secrets of the ship's cargo. It has brought nothing but pain. How could it possibly be used for good?

FOURTEEN

Tucker walked across his office and closed the door. Betty Sue did not need to hear this conversation. Nor did he need her sharing the news with anyone else in town. He'd always thought of Savannah as a good-sized city. But the minute gossip got started, it suddenly turned into Mayberry with porches full of wagging tongues.

"You were saying?" He spoke into his phone's speaker as he slid back into the oversized office chair behind his desk.

On the other end of the line his campaign manager, Beau, cleared his throat. "Listen, Tuck."

Tucker cringed. Not even PJ got away with calling him that, but Beau had decided it made him sound tough. They were going to need tough to win the election, so he didn't complain. Much.

"Things aren't going as well as they could be."

He shoved his fingers through his hair and pulled on his absent beard. "If we're not winning with a hundred percent of the vote, it's not going as well as it could. But somehow I don't think you're calling to tell me we're polling at ninety-nine." He couldn't keep the sarcasm from his voice. He'd spent almost a decade as a Marine, and if he'd learned any-thing, it was that knowing was better than not. "Don't skirt around the problem. How bad is it?"

"Our polls have you at forty percent of the vote."

He sighed, crossing his arms over his chest. "How many undecideds?"

"Um . . . it's not exactly . . . we don't . . ."

"Spit it out."

"Fifteen."

He put his elbows on his desk and leaned his forehead against his fists. "So you're telling me that I'd have to win more than two-thirds of the undecideds to beat Jepson."

"That's if everyone shows up to vote."

Of course Beau would be practical about it. "So what do we need to do in the next two weeks?"

"Have you had any luck discounting that letter?"

Tucker scrubbed a hand over his face. "Would that be enough?"

"It wouldn't hurt, that's for sure."

"Seriously, Bailey. What's it going to take to win this thing?"

Beau hemmed and hawed for several seconds, each hesi-tant grunt twisting a vise in Tucker's gut. Finally Beau said, "There's no guarantee in elections. But we need at least two things—soon. Proof that the letter is a fake."

With a humorless chuckle, Tucker said, "Unlikely. I'm pretty sure the letter is real."

Beau groaned. "Then proof that its author was wrong, at least."

That was possible, but their best hope for that was still an elusive treasure. "And the second thing?"

"About forty thousand dollars for TV spots."

"We made about that much at the dinner."

"And we need that much more again. Buddy is eating you alive in those TV ads. They're on every day. You've seen them."

Not since he'd stopped watching television, which had been about the time the first defamatory spots started running. He'd heard the newest one laid into his lack of higher education, which wasn't new to him.

"I'm not going to go low."

"You don't have to," Beau said. "Your platform is strong. You just have to get it in front of more people. Are there any other donors you can hit up? Should we comb through the list from the fundraiser?"

The treasure felt like his only chance. If he found it, he could prove the Westbrooks weren't everything Buddy had claimed. And he'd have enough to get his name in front of that fifteen percent and then some.

"I have an idea. Give me a few days."

"A few is all you've got."

Yeah, he didn't need the reminder. He already had the president of the Ladies' League breathing down his neck. He hung up and stared at the stack of files waiting for him to look through. Betty Sue had kept the office running, but he was behind. If he'd been smart, he'd have waited to make his bid for sheriff, waited until he had a COO in place to handle it all.

"You probably don't want to go in there," he heard Betty Sue announce. "He's talking to Beau."

A quick knock followed. "It'll be okay."

By the time the door opened, he was halfway there. He

scooped PJ into a hug and kissed her full on the mouth. "I'm glad you're here," he said as Betty Sue clucked at them.

"You'd think they were teenagers the way they're carrying on," she mumbled.

PJ giggled against him, tucking her face into the hollow at his neck. "I feel kind of like a teenager."

Cupping her cheeks with his hands, he said, "Me too. Now, what brings you down here?"

The tip of her nose wrinkled. "Did you forget? We're meeting with the contractor today."

"Oh." He glanced at the folders on his desk. They would wait. If Beau was right, finding the treasure would not. "I did. But let's go."

Slipping her hand into his, she led him through the office. "You can tell me what Beau said on the way there."

By the time they reached the offices of Marvin Ernest, licensed contractor, Penelope felt more than a little sick. She wanted to blame it on the heat, but an unseasonal breeze had picked up, making her skirt dance about her knees. And fluffy white clouds bounced across the sky, keeping the sun from being its most brutal.

Which only left one reason for the boulder in her stomach. If true, what Beau had said was painful at best. "I'm so sorry, Tucker. What can I do to help?"

He swung their linked hands up to eye level, squeezing her fingers between his. "You're already doing it."

But it didn't feel like enough. All of the extras—the benefits after so many years of just being friends—felt too easy to be helpful.

She wasn't going to complain though. Holding his hand, stealing kisses behind closed doors—and sometimes in front of open doors, with her apologies to Betty Sue—was nice. Actually, it was much better than nice. Doing more than quasi-dating was better than even her high school self could have dreamed.

But it didn't feel like she was helping him much. Especially when her part of finding the treasure had hit a dead end. A precarious one at that. "I finished the diary last night."

"You did? What happened?"

"Well . . . um . . . Caroline stopped writing on Christmas Day. I mean, it was the end of the book, so maybe she started the new year with another journal. But she was definitely involved with two men. She was torn between her loyalties to the South and this lieutenant from Pennsylvania."

He nodded, looking not at all surprised. "I've been thinking about that letter we found at Aunt Shirley's. The one from Caroline apologizing for bringing shame on her family. Do you think she ran off with the lieutenant? Was that why her father would be angry? Or did she tell him where the treasure was hidden?"

"I don't know. I mean, she seemed uncertain—like she still loved Josiah. She did kiss him. But whatever he was involved in was awfully shady." She finally spoke the words she'd wondered late the night before while reading Caroline's last lines. "Do you think there's another diary?"

"I have no idea. Aunt Shirley would have told us, wouldn't she?"

She twisted her face into an expression that she hoped showed just how much she loved his quirky aunt—and just how much it wouldn't surprise her if Shirley was holding out on them.

He pulled out his phone and pressed a button to connect them before turning on the speaker. "You've reached Shirley. I'm in Prague."

"I thought she was in Japan," Penelope whispered. Tucker shrugged.

"Leave a message, and if it's more interesting than the castle up the hill, I might call you back."

"Hey, Aunt Shirley, it's Tucker."

"And Penelope."

He licked his lip, a wicked gleam in his eye. "Is there another diary from Caroline? The one you pointed us to ends in the middle of the story. We've got to find the treasure this week, so call me back if you can. Also, PJ and I are dating now. So, just thought you'd like to know." He hung up, and she swatted his arm.

"Why'd you tell her that?"

"She'll find it more interesting than a castle."

That was probably accurate. But it didn't give them any new direction at the moment.

Tucker chewed on his bottom lip for a beat before lifting his gaze toward the heavens. "Lord, we could sure use a lead."

She squeezed his hand, echoing that prayer deep in her heart. She couldn't let Tucker fail. She wasn't oblivious to his dad's words and the weight they put on him, and she refused to be responsible for allowing even one more harsh comment to be added.

And if he didn't win the election, there would be so many.

Pulling him toward the blue door under the contractor's

shingle, she pasted a broad smile into place. "Maybe God will use Mr. Ernest."

Then again, maybe not. As soon as they stepped into the contractor's chaotic office, Penelope realized God alone could find anything among the piles of loose papers and hoards of blue folders. She'd thought that Tucker's office with its neat stacks of files was out of shape. Mr. Ernest seemed to be unaware of the purpose of the three metal filing cabinets lining the adjacent wall. The office consisted of exactly one room with one entrance, and if there was another door, the hodgepodge of furniture had blocked it. The place smelled of old paper, stale and damp and not nearly as pleasant as an old book.

She could just make out a mop of gray hair beyond two more stacks of paper at the desk in the far corner.

"Mr. Ernest?" she called, feeling like she had to yell to reach him, although he was no more than fifteen feet away.

"It's Marv. Be right with you." His voice was low and gravelly and altogether quite pleasant.

Tucker shrugged a shoulder but remained silent as they waited. Marv was mostly silent himself. There were no telltale keyboard sounds or even the scratch of a pen on paper. She half expected a snore to break the stillness.

Suddenly Marv bounced up, his head and shoulders just clearing the stacks on his desk. His hair was in wild disarray, and he shoved his hand through it, only exacerbating the problem. "Who are you?"

"I'm Penelope Hunter. This is Tucker Westbrook. We made an appointment."

"With me?" He sounded legitimately befuddled but not entirely unhappy with their interruption.

Tucker pressed a single finger to his lip, presumably reining in his mirth. Penelope, however, couldn't hold back the snort of laughter that fought its way free.

Marv didn't seem to notice, marching forward, his hand outstretched. "Good to meet you. What can I do you for?"

"We called about the blueprints for Jackson's Hole," Tucker said. "Jackson said your dad did the renovation on his property about fifty years ago."

"Sure did." He looked around like he might invite them to sit, but every chair in the room was already occupied. With a shrug he turned his gaze back to them. "Old building. Way out of code. Took a lot of updating. Could probably use it again, but Jackson Holt isn't interested in investing that kind of money again. Rather give it to me at the poker table." His laugh was dry, but at least his memory was sharp.

"Do you remember your dad saying anything unusual about that renovation?" Tucker asked.

"Like what? That bag of ammunition? It was the derndest thing. I never heard nothing like it in all the places I've worked."

Penelope crossed her arms. "You've never seen anything that old, you mean?"

Now it was Marv's turn to snort. "'Course I have. This city is older'n dirt, and I've worked on a dozen buildings they decided to call historical. I've seen all sorts of things hidden in walls. Found five thousand dollars once. Found a fair bit of Confederate dollars under the floorboards of a house one time. Guess when Sherman's boys arrived, some of the residents got a little nervous."

Caroline and Josiah hadn't been the only ones looking to hide things from the Union troops. But if not in the walls, where had they stashed it?

"Then what made this find so different?" Penelope asked.

"It was intact. The bag still sewed shut. Even the bag was in pretty good shape. No mice gnawing on it. It looked pretty well protected."

She didn't have a clue what that meant for the rest of what had been hidden at Mrs. Fitterling's, and she wished the seamstress still had an heir living in that building. She'd even settle for an heir living in Savannah. A story of a midnight knock on the door. A troop of smugglers stomping through her home. That was a story that could last generations. But it had disappeared somewhere in time. Only Caroline's handwritten pages seemed to remember the event.

Tucker leaned in. "Were there any walls that your dad didn't replace at Jackson's?"

Marv scratched his chin, his eyes focused on the ceiling. "Far as I remember—and I was only a boy back then—my dad tore every single one of them down to the bones and built 'em back up again. Weren't nothing out of the ordinary there."

Tucker nodded, scratching at his chin and looking in her direction. He lifted a shoulder, and she mirrored his movement. She didn't know where to go from here either, but she grasped for anything. "I don't suppose you still have the blueprints for the old building?"

Marv laughed, spreading his arms wide to encompass the whole room and all its stacks and stores. "Do I look like I throw anything away? Having them isn't the question. Finding them would be the problem."

Her face fell, all hope tumbling with it.

He must have taken pity on her, since he offered an alternative. "You might try the county clerk's office. The zoning commission may have the blueprints on file."

"Thank you for your time," she said as Tucker nodded toward the door. She turned to follow him but stopped short. "One more question. Do you remember if your dad closed up a hole at Jackson's?"

"A hole?" He fluffed his hair again, staring off toward the bar. "Where at?"

"I'm not sure. Maybe in the back of the building? Jackson mentioned it."

He shook his head. "I don't remember anything about that. But it's been a few years, and I've spent a lot of time in places like Jackson's since then. My dad only ever talked about finding those minié balls."

As they stepped outside, Penelope began a slow pace down the sidewalk. Evenly spaced trees kept the sun at bay most of the time, but she still dug into her purse for her sunglasses. "You think one of them is lying?"

"Or forgetful." He shook his head. "They're not young men. Neither of them."

As they rounded a corner and stepped into another of Savannah's precious squares, she asked, "What if Jackson was right? Let's say Marv's dad did patch up a hole. What could it have been to? A basement?"

"Or a cellar?"

She stopped suddenly, and he blew right by her. "Or a hidden room?"

Tucker strode back to her and tucked his hands in his pockets, a light in his eyes. "You thinking what I'm thinking?"

"Why store a treasure in a building that might be searched? We already know they were partial to that barn with the underground room. Maybe they did the same thing at Mrs. Fitterling's."

His phone rang, and he pulled it from his pocket. When he saw the name on the screen, he held it up to her. Aunt Shirley. Putting the phone on speaker, he greeted his aunt. "Well, that was fast. What time is it in Prague right now?"

"I have no idea. I'm in London."

"I thought . . ." He shrugged it off just as Shirley piped up.

"I'm on my way home. What are you doing calling me in the middle of the day? Don't you have a job and an election?"

"We're working on something."

"We?" Shirley's tone added a heavy implication to the word.

"Hi, Shirley," Penelope announced herself.

"Oh, you kids. It's about time, you know?"

Penelope met Tucker's bright gaze. His eyes were filled with joy and hope and something that looked a lot like love. Her stomach took a barrel roll. Could it be true? Did he really love her? Beyond friendship and companionship and so many years of history, had he come to see her as not just something more—but *the one*? His one?

Heat flamed at her throat, and she pressed a hand to it, suddenly looking for more shade.

"I know," Tucker said. "You can tell us all about how you knew we'd end up together since we were kids when you get back."

But would they end up together? This wasn't the end, and together wasn't a guarantee. She knew that better than anyone. Penelope swallowed, her throat suddenly full.

"I'll save my 'I told you so' for the wedding day."

Tucker looked up from his phone, but she couldn't quite meet his gaze this time.

"But that's not why I called," Shirley said, her voice filled with a smile. "At least it's not the only reason I called. About Caroline's diary—there's not another one, far as I know. But you got the letters, right?"

Tucker's hand trembled slightly. "Letter. We just found the one in the attic."

"Oh, there are more. But I might have moved them." A muffled voice called from beyond Shirley. "They're boarding my flight. I'll call you when I'm home."

FIFTEEN

ow that Mrs. Haywood had agreed not to press to move the Ladies' League fundraiser, Penelope spent a lot less time staring at her phone and a lot more getting things done. She was well into an event proposal, manipulating the numbers to meet the budget, when the bell on her door rang. Without looking up, she invited her visitor in. "I'll be with you in a moment."

"Oh!"

She didn't need more than that to recognize the voice. Glancing over her computer screen, she forced a smile. "Hi, Winston."

He nodded. His button-up shirt looked like it was fresh from the laundry, free of wrinkles, free of life. "I thought Emmaline would be here. We were supposed to . . ." With a quick turn toward the door, he said, "I can wait outside for her."

"Don't be ridiculous." Standing, she tried to sound flippant but failed. She should be used to this by now. Interacting with Winston shouldn't be so hard after half a dozen meetings. Except the only times they'd spoken alone had ended with raised voices or with her escaping to the dance floor and Tucker kissing her silly in front of a roomful of guests.

And if his current scowl was any indication, he seemed to recall that ordeal.

Clearing her throat, she tried again. "Want to sit down? I can show you the pictures of your reception setup."

"We can wait for Emmaline."

"Of course." Except that left them standing awkwardly in the middle of her office, which didn't work for her. "Can I get you something to drink?"

"No. I'm fine."

Okay. So they'd just be awkward. She swayed, letting her skirt twist about her legs. "So just another month to go?" Apparently she couldn't handle the silence.

"Excuse me?" His dark eyebrows dipped low.

"To the wedding?"

His brows danced up his forehead like he was surprised she remembered. Except that was her job. Just because he'd forgotten *their* wedding . . .

Wait. That wasn't fair. He hadn't forgotten. He'd chosen not to attend. Big difference. Thankfully she was over it.

"Listen, Pen. I'm—"

"It's Penelope."

He stumbled back. "But I always called you—"

"Yes, well, we're not engaged anymore. And I prefer Penelope."

"Why didn't you ever . . ." Tucking his hands into his pockets, he shrugged. "Why didn't you tell me back then?"

"I don't . . . I'm not sure." She wasn't sure of much except that she needed to stand up for herself with him. She wasn't the same woman who had been engaged to him. The one who had been so afraid to rock the boat of their relationship that she hadn't told him she didn't like his nickname for her.

"Well then, *Penelope*. I didn't mean for this to be awkward. I didn't mean for any of this to happen, really."

"What? You didn't mean to run into me or to have to spend your summer with me—probably remembering all the appointments you didn't go to with me?"

He stabbed his fingers through his gelled hair, letting her see it unkempt for the first time since she'd known him. "Come on. You know it's not like that."

She crossed her arms but kept her glare level. "Like what?"

"It's . . . I never meant for any of this to happen. You know that, right?"

It wasn't quite an apology, and something inside her wasn't willing to let this go without one. Maybe it was the way he'd spoken to her at Tucker's dinner. Or the picture-perfect tulip centerpieces that Emmaline had chosen, just a little too similar to her own. She could let it all go. Or she could make him feel just an ounce of the discomfort that had come from returning every one of their wedding gifts—half of them in person. No amount of checking things off the list to get over Winston could make her forget the look on her grandmother's face when she'd returned the hand-embroidered pillowcases.

"Any of what?" she prodded.

He shuffled his big leather shoes and smoothed down the front of his gray slacks. He straightened his belt and made sure his shirt was tucked in. Always out to look his best. But the wary glint in his eyes made all of him look off center. Which made her smile. And tap the toe of her shoe.

His gaze stayed somewhere in the vicinity of her high heel as he tugged on the collar of his shirt. "You know, it hasn't been easy for me either."

Her burst of disbelief came out without warning. "You've got to be kidding me. You're blaming me for this summer? For how awkward and uncomfortable it's been?"

"It's not like I can tell Emmaline the truth."

"Why not? It's not that hard." She dropped her tone to mimic his. "'Emmaline, I stood Penelope up on our wedding day.' See? Not that hard."

Dragging a hand over his face, he sighed. "Man, I know I messed things up between you and me, but I love Emmaline."

The implication in his words rang loud and clear. He hadn't loved Penelope. Not really. At least not enough. She pressed a hand to her chest and stumbled back, knocking the pictures she'd prepared to show Winston and Emmaline from her desk. They fluttered to the floor, so smooth and graceful. Penelope could only manage a wobbling stoop and clumsy fingers to pick them up.

"And she really likes you."

Did he have to go on? Penelope had heard enough, and she turned her back to him, leaning on the big wooden desk as she took deep breaths through her nose.

"She thinks you're great. She thinks you're friends. I can't stand to hurt her like that."

"And you think that somehow my not telling her is going to be worse than your betrayal? Why haven't you told her?"

The air in the room shifted. It was a silent change, but Penelope felt it up and down her skin, and she knew before Winston said anything that she had crossed a line. She'd accused him of betraying Emmaline the way he'd betrayed her. He might not have ever given her a true apology, but she had no doubt he knew the depth of the pain he'd caused.

"It hasn't been easy for me either, what with you . . ."

She spun back to face him, wanting to lash out but lacking the words.

"You've been parading your—your—your boyfriend around here."

"*My* boyfriend? This is not about me."

With a single step he advanced into her space, his shoulders wider than she remembered, his eyes darker. "Of course it is. You've been rubbing my nose in the fact that you always did—and always will—pick Tucker over me. Even when we were together, you chose him over me. And Emmaline thinks you're just the cutest couple, but I know the truth."

The world narrowed, her vision fading until there was only Winston before her and this boiling rage in her chest. "What are you talking about? It was never like that. How dare—"

"If he needed you, you were more than happy to run off together. Midnight strategy sessions to get his business off the ground. Spending hours helping him paint his house. Going to his family's house for brunch after church. Why didn't you ever come to my family dinner?"

"You never asked."

"I shouldn't have had to."

Her breaths came through clenched teeth, loud and staggered. Somewhere outside the realm of her consciousness a bell tinkled. "I did *not* end our engagement. You took care of that all on your own."

A sudden gasp filled the room, and Penelope's lungs stopped working. She didn't need to look around Winston's shoulders to know that Emmaline had joined them. Penelope risked a glance anyway. Emmaline's eyes were wide and glassy. Trembling fingers covered her mouth, but other than that she could have been a statue.

"Babe, I'm so—"

"Emmaline, please—"

Winston and Penelope spoke over each other, unable to finish their thoughts. In unison they stepped toward Emmaline, who finally blinked. She shook her head slowly. "You were engaged?" Though her words were muffled behind her hands, they stopped Penelope where she stood.

"I'm so sorry," she whispered. "I didn't mean for you to find out like this." Emmaline had deserved to find out the truth from the man she loved—not from a fireball hurled by his ex-fiancée.

Winston grabbed Emmaline's hand, holding it close to his cheek, but she tugged it free. "Babe, I didn't want to hurt you."

"Hurt me? And you think this doesn't hurt?" Her gaze shifted between them until a single tear escaped, rolling down her cheek, leaving its silver mark. "You've had two months to tell me—no, we've had a year and a half together. Why didn't you tell me the truth?"

Winston's mouth opened and closed, but no words came out.

When it was clear he couldn't find the words, Emmaline turned on Penelope. "I thought a friend would have told me . . . something."

"Babe—"

Emmaline cut Winston off. "And you. Don't call me 'babe.' I can't believe you didn't tell me you'd been engaged before." A soft sob escaped her lips, and she clapped her hand over her mouth.

"I should have. You're right. It's just that I hadn't ever felt anything like I do with you. I was afraid of messing it all up. But I should have been honest. Please forgive me."

Emmaline's eyes shone, and it was clear that she wanted to accept his apology, that she wanted to rescue the sinking ship of their relationship. But with a quivering lower lip, she shook her head. "I don't think I can." She walked away, the door jingling behind her.

Penelope wrapped her arms around herself. But it was Winston's gasping sob that undid her.

Tucker jogged down the sidewalk, dodging several tourist couples as he made his way toward PJ's office. Aunt Shirley had called, and they had a treasure to find. And if an anticipated kiss upon his arrival put an extra pep in his step, so be it. He couldn't think of anything better to look forward to.

But when he pushed open the door to her office, he had a feeling she wasn't going to kiss him anytime soon.

PJ stomped behind her desk, straightening papers and slamming filing cabinets. Frizzy patches of her hair had escaped her usual ponytail and curled about her ears, and her skirt was twisted off center, her sweater discarded and shirt wrinkled. She muttered something under her breath as she leaned over to wedge another file into a drawer that didn't seem to have room for one more. Then she kicked it and it crashed closed. Standing up, she huffed some hair out of her eyes and pressed her hands to her hips.

That's when she noticed him.

He gave her a small wave and cocked his head to the side. "Hey there."

"Hi." Her lower lip trembled, and he rushed toward her, his arms open. But she held up her hands and shook her head.

Dropping his offered embrace, he looked around for some sign of what had set her off. Her office was clean and organized. Her to-do list sat on her desk, half checked off. Everything seemed in order. "You want to talk about it?"

"No." Her eyes were wild as she spun toward a perfectly clean shelf and reorganized it, shifting pictures and knick-knacks around for no apparent reason.

"Okay, can I—"

"Winston came in earlier this morning. And now everything's ruined." Her voice wavered somewhere between anger and sorrow, a tremor just below the surface.

Everything inside him wanted to pull her into a hug, to make the rage or pain or hurt disappear. But he couldn't magically eliminate it. He had to do the thing you did when you loved someone. He had to just be there. Because he did love her, and there was nowhere else he'd rather be.

Sitting on the arm of one of her guest chairs, he crossed his ankles. "Do you want to tell me more?"

She shuffled and sorted for a silent minute, every movement tense and abrupt. "It was just that he was early, and Emmaline wasn't here yet, and then he blamed me for not being able to tell her about our engagement."

Oh, there were so many things he wanted to say to Winston. But he bit back every single one of them and waited for her to say more, only offering an encouraging nod.

She turned her back to him, jerking a drawer open and then banging it shut. Her heels clicked against the floor as sharp as typewriter keys. "As if his being a coward is my fault. Or somehow my friendship with Emmaline was a problem for him." Spinning back toward him, she advanced like a woman with a mission. "And then—I mean, you're never going to believe this. He *accused us* of being the reason he broke up with me. Get this. He said I always picked you over him. Can you believe that?" She slammed a stack of folders onto a shelf, shoving them into a corner in no particular order.

"Was he wrong?"

Oh no. He'd been doing so good. She needed this to be a one-sided conversation, and he'd butted right in where he didn't belong.

"What?" She grabbed her stapler, waving it in his direction. "Are you serious? Of course I didn't. I loved him. I've just known you forever. You're my best friend, and . . . and . . . and sometimes maybe you needed me."

He stood and strolled across the room toward her, deftly avoiding her flailing office supply. "PJ, maybe he saw what's between us before we did." Cupping his hands on her shoulders, he slowly pulled her in as her features softened.

"Yeah, well . . ." She licked her lips. "That wasn't even the worst part."

"What happened?"

She crumpled before him, her whole trembling body falling into his arms. Tears filled her eyes and splashed onto her cheeks. Her nose turned red, and her lips shook. She wrapped her arms around his waist, burying her face against his collar.

PJ, always so strong and smart, felt frail. She suddenly seemed like she might fall apart in his arms, and he tried to scoop her up, stumbling back until they dropped into a chair and he could hold her properly. Her arms encircled his shoulders as the wet spot on his shirt grew.

"I di-id the worst thing," she sobbed against his neck.

His gut clenched, his head spinning. He knew what *he* thought the worst thing she could have done with Winston would be, and it made him want to cry too. But she hadn't gone back to Winston. She wouldn't have.

Clamping his mouth shut, he simply held her, rubbing a figure eight on her back, whispering nonsense into her hair. And oh, it was soft. It smelled like citrus, and he wanted to bury his nose in it forever. But he forced himself to just hold her, to rock her gently until it all came out.

"I didn't mean to, but I was so angry with him, and I blurted it out—that it had all been his fault. And she was there!"

"Who?" But even as he said it, he knew. "Emmaline found out you were engaged?"

She nodded into the hollow of his neck.

"And she was angry?"

PJ began to nod again but stopped and shook her head instead.

"She was sad?"

With an affirmative motion, she took a gasping sob. His arms tightened around her in a reflex. It was the only thing he could do—aching for her heartache yet so very grateful that his own worst hadn't been realized.

"I'm so sorry," he said to her temple.

He thought she mumbled back, "I am too."

"But you know it's not your fault, right?"

She gave a little hiccup as she shook her head.

"This isn't on you. Winston should have told her before he ever proposed."

She hiccuped again, but this time she nodded into him.

They sat together as the clock on her desk ticked by the seconds, each movement of the hand echoing in the stillness. Slowly, softly, her tears faded, her breathing returning to normal. Her shoulders relaxed, and she leaned into him. Resting.

Oh, he could sit and hold her for ages. And suddenly he could see their future, decades down the road. He could see himself holding her, holding their children, holding their grandchildren. This love he hadn't even recognized had been there for so long. His future had always been about PJ.

Now he needed to be worthy of her. He needed to show her he wasn't the man Jepson painted him to be or the kid he'd once been, barely able to graduate from high school. He'd never told her that he'd been afraid the Marines wouldn't take him either. He thanked God even for the tours in the Middle East. At least he'd had a chance to do something that mattered, to serve with honor and earn the respect of the men in his unit.

But one question remained. Would PJ ever think he was enough? Or would she realize that some other guy was a better match, equal in smarts and success?

Tucker owned a business, but she knew he'd never have gotten it off the ground without her help. She'd literally written the whole business plan and showed him how it could work. He'd had the idea. She'd had the know-how.

They sat together in silence for what felt like an hour. He could have gone another, but when she finally looked up at him, her eyes were rimmed in red, her mascara smudged all the way down her cheeks.

"I feel terrible. I just wish she hadn't heard it from me. Not like that. And I wanted to show Winston that I have my life together." She threw her hands in the air and shook her hair out of her face. "Which clearly I do not."

He brushed a silky strand of her hair off her forehead, smoothing it back into her ponytail. "Maybe sometimes you have hard days, like today. But you have your stuff together more than anyone else I know."

She rolled her eyes. "Right. Because people with their stuff together generally almost lose their jobs and definitely lose friendships."

"I'm pretty sure that humans do both of those things. And that's what forgiveness is for."

She leaned her ear against his shoulder. Maybe she could hear his heart thudding a strange rhythm, the one reserved for when she was near. It was all he could hear for a long moment, and he gave her a tight squeeze.

"Thank you," she said. She gave him a peck on his cheek. It was tender and sweet, and he would have liked very much to turn his head just a couple inches to really connect with her. But that wasn't why he'd come to see her.

"So, my aunt is back."

"What?" She launched to her feet, rubbing her thumbs beneath her eyes. "Why didn't you say something sooner?"

"And interrupt your very impressive meltdown?"

She made a fist and moved to punch him in the shoulder, but he caught her wrist before she could make contact.

"I'm happy to hold you during any meltdown you like. And you're still the prettiest woman I've ever seen."

Her neck flushed pink, and she bit her bottom lip.

"But you might want to look in a mirror before we leave the office."

Tucker had barely given a solid thwack against the door when it flung open, his momentum nearly sending him to the ground.

"Tucker! Peej! Come in, come in! How y'all doin'?" Aunt Shirley took a closer look at Penelope. "Y'all better come on in now." She threw her arm wide, clearing an invisible path for them to enter her home, but her gaze remained fixed on PJ.

He greeted his aunt with a quick hug and then watched her swallow PJ in an embrace. When she pulled back, she adjusted her short brown hair and glared at him. "Is this," she said, pointing at PJ's puffy eyes, "because of you?" Her finger swung back to him, and he shook his head fast.

"No, ma'am."

PJ quickly backed him up. "Tucker didn't do anything wrong. I'm the one that messed up."

Aunt Shirley's gaze went up and down slowly. "But the two of you are still . . ."

Tucker reached for PJ's hand and squeezed it. "Yes."

"Good, good." Aunt Shirley plodded down the hall toward the kitchen, her stockinged feet rustling against the rug. Her bright yellow costume—it couldn't be called anything else— lit up the entire room, sleeves and skirt billowing about her slender form. Her cheeks were pink and her skin tan, and her eyes were bright with a thousand adventures.

"Did you have a good time on your trip?"

"Grand, my boy! It was nothing but grand. Mount Fuji is everything they say, and Prague and Vienna—don't get me started. The only part I did not like was coming back home."

She winked broadly at PJ. "At least the customs agent was a little bit handsy."

PJ cracked a broad smile, the first he'd seen since he'd met her at her office, and he released a full breath. She'd be okay. They'd be fine. He'd find the treasure, and they'd be together, and that was all that really mattered.

Aunt Shirley's arms waved about as she motioned toward the table where three glasses of tea sat on a pink place mat. The table looked like it had been salvaged from a fifties-era diner, and its matching metal chairs with shiny black vinyl on the seats and backs had been pulled out for them to sit. But Tucker wasn't there for a drink. He wanted the letters. He wanted to know the truth about the treasure.

"I thought you'd seen all the letters. I mean, they were all together in that box."

Only then did he realize that the table held a shallow yellowing box as well. He had a sinking feeling she wanted him to read the letters it contained, and his gut clenched at the very idea.

PJ stepped in. "The letter—it was in a trunk. I didn't see another box."

"We just saw the letter about Caroline running off with Lieutenant Haulder," Tucker said.

Aunt Shirley's smile twisted, one eye closing almost all the way. "Running off with who now?"

PJ looked at him, and he nodded. "Well, we just assumed," she said. "Caroline had kissed Haulder, and I assumed she'd fallen in love with him. Isn't that why she thought her father would be so angry with her?"

"Oh, dear child. There's so much more to every story."

"What do you mean?" Tucker asked.

"Here. Read it for yourselves." She held the box out to him, and his arm twitched, his fist clenched at his side. It was hard enough reading silently. There was no way he was going to read out loud in front of PJ.

He didn't have to. She stepped up to his side and reached for the box. "May I?"

June 3, 1865
Dear Mama,

I wish you could have been there. I carried a bouquet of wildflowers, and Mrs. Tillman lent me her veil. I wore a regular day dress and scuffed boots. It was not at all how I dreamed my wedding day would be. But I am certain I married the right man, and that is all that seems to matter.

I am sorry that my marrying him will take me far from home. By the time you read this, we will have already left on the train, first north toward Missouri and then west as far as the tracks go. I am not sure where our journey will end, but it seems such a grand adventure when you are beside the man you love.

I believe you tried to tell me once before about the love between a man and a woman. You must have, but I did not understand. What I felt then was just a passing fancy, an innocent flirtation. But now, after hearing all he has to say, I'm beginning to understand the truth. He faces so much with integrity and conviction. He is honest and trustworthy. How could I not trust him with my heart?

Perhaps love means facing the hardships together. For life is not easy, and he has a terrible burden to bear. I wish to help him carry it. I wish to help him make peace and see him returned to the fullness of joy. There are glimmers of it every now and then when our eyes meet. Last night he laughed, truly and fully, and it filled me to overflowing. If this is indeed love, then I am fully immersed. I pray the waters of it wash over me every day. May I love him well and care for him with my whole heart.

Please do not be angry with me. I will write again once we are settled. I hope to explain it all. But you may trust that my love takes perfect, tender care of me, and I him. Trust that the Almighty will protect and provide for us.

Rest assured that you are missed and loved by your only daughter and her new husband.

With love,
Caroline and Josiah

August 2, 1865
Dear Mama,

The longer I have thought on it, the more certain I have become. You must be terribly angry with me, and I do not blame you. I only wish I could somehow explain my actions without bringing further question upon our family. I fear there is no explanation that would suffice, but I must try.

I must begin by confessing that not even I could have foreseen how much I would miss you, and Papa and Bradford as well. We have settled here in the Arizona territory, but I cannot reveal just where. Some yet feel that Josiah's actions were traitorous. I do not believe that, and I do not believe you do either. Still I must be careful in what I write.

Please, let me start at the beginning, or rather at a new beginning. Our history goes back so many years, and I have loved him for so long. Josiah tells me now that he has loved me for just as long. He had longed to tell me of his feelings, to ask me to be his bride, but when the war came, he had no choice but to fight and dared not leave me with foolish promises.

When he was assigned to his regiment, his commanding officers recognized a certain way about him. I knew it from our childhood. How often he sneaked into the house and stole Bradford away when he should have been studying, only to disappear into the city. I tried to follow, but they were forever vanishing almost before my very eyes. When Josiah's commanding officers discovered this skill, they set him to sneaking through enemy lines, evading capture, and collecting information. He says he was called a scout. I think that is a ridiculous name, for it sounds as though he were a spy.

My heart nearly seizes when I think that he was in such danger, but he is well and truly good now. I thank the Lord Almighty for just that. And that he is by my side.

I've known for some time what terrible choices he was forced to make, but I was not free to speak of these things until I knew he was safe and far from those who might want to do him harm.

Please do not be distressed when I tell you that I stole from home many nights to see what Bradford and Papa were about. Do not be angry with Papa if he has not shared all of my secrets before now. But when I knew that Josiah was with us once again, I could do nothing but offer my help. I knew even then that I loved him. I only doubted if he—a man of such experience—could love me.

But I have gotten ahead of myself. Undoubtedly you have read my diary and discovered that Josiah did indeed return to Savannah. He was not the boy I had known but a man of action. Sometimes I believe I still see regret in his eyes, though

I know not if it comes from the Confederate loss or the role he believes he played in that.

For three years he served as a scout, and I believe he did so with honor and integrity, though he says his identity was all but erased. Then he was called upon to take delivery of a shipment running the blockade. The goods and materials were of the finest quality from France. Would they have made a difference if put in the hands of Jefferson Davis? Could such a shipment have won the war? I do not believe so.

Regardless of its potential impact, the shipment was never intended to help the Southern cause or her people. Josiah's superior officers intended to line their pockets with the gold and silver. And Josiah was left with little choice. Either he would do as he was ordered or he would have to disappear, allowing his officers to think him dead.

He chose the latter, commandeering the smuggled goods and intending to take them to Charleston as soon as possible. But with so many troops in gray working with the smugglers, he had no choice but to ask his other friends for help. Bradford and Papa and some of the others from our neighborhood stepped in, and I saw those men the night the treasure was first received.

Surely Papa has told you as much by now, how he and Bradford then helped to move the smuggled treasures to Mrs. Fitterling's so late that one night. How Josiah's name could not even be whispered about town should one of the soldiers hear it and know who had taken the goods. If anyone had discovered he was in Savannah, all he loved could have been in danger. Oh, how he worried about his mother's safety. Mine too, he claims now.

But when Hardee's men fled the city, there was not a safe

corner for him to find, and he had no opportunity to evacuate the goods. As you know, the war ended before the goods could be handed over to the government. But there are those who still want to find it. Those who wish to see him punished for stealing from the officers intent on making illegal gain. I pray only that the good Lord would spare us such suffering and that justice will be served.

I know he worries for me that someone will come looking for him. But I can only say that I have never felt safer than I do with Josiah. When we stood before Reverend Tillman and spoke those sacred vows, I knew that I should have nothing to fear now.

Please give Papa my love. I wish that I could give you my mailing direction, but Josiah has asked me not to. Not yet. I will write to keep you informed of our lives out west. So far it is hot and dry, but when I am tempted to miss the river, I remember that Josiah is worth a great many oceans.

With love,
Caroline

September 25, 1865
My dearest brother,

Josiah bids me write to you, and I gladly will. We both miss you. I confess that I pray often that you have found the courage to ask sweet Agatha for her hand. You were not one to hide your affections well, though I know the war seemed to take all that we had. Now I pray that you are able to offer her your whole attention. If you have not asked her to be yours, do so lest another man beat you to it. I know now the pain of delayed longing and the joy of a perfect union. I pray you are blessed with one as well.

Josiah and I have spoken, and we fear there may be other men searching for the hidden goods. You know that Josiah used only a portion of what was taken from that ship in order to help the people of Savannah. Though I believe if there had been more food and medicine to buy, he would have gladly used it all to care for the hungry and the widowed.

My heart aches as I remember the camps outside the city, the freed men and women and children. What poverty they lived in, and how I wish I could have done more to serve them. We leave that to you now. Please, I beg of you, take what is left of the treasure and do good with it. I believe there is still a diamond necklace there. While I would love nothing more than to see it draped around Agatha's neck, I am certain that her gentle heart would want you to care for others. Please find the goods and share them with those precious souls in need.

As you know, Josiah moved the shipment after it was first secreted away. He moved it only once more, four hundred feet south. You will find his mark there.

Be well, my brother. Josiah and I miss you and speak often of your kindness and loyalty. You were good to him, such a faithful friend. And you have been a wonderful brother to me. My one regret is that I will not get to meet your children and their children. What lucky scamps they will be to have you as a father.

With love,
Caroline

SIXTEEN

Well, that's it." Penelope laid down the final letter and stretched the kink out of her neck. "The treasure was supposed to help the people of Savannah, and Bradford cleaned out the last of it 150 years ago. So it's gone."

Shirley nodded slowly. "That's what it sounds like." Her words were clear, but they carried a heavy cargo of doubt.

Penelope clapped a hand to her chest as her heart thundered like horses' hooves. "What do you mean? If Bradford didn't take the rest of the treasure, where is it?"

"Well, isn't that the million-dollar question." Shirley leaned back in her chair, resting both of her hands on the back of her head.

Tucker leaned forward, stacking his hands on the place mat in front of him and staring directly into his aunt's face. "You know something you're not telling us."

Shirley let out a low chuckle. "I know a great many things I haven't told you. Some of them you've figured out." She waved a finger between them. "Some of them are still a mystery."

"Please," Penelope said. "Will you help us?"

She nodded, seeming to choose her words carefully. "You're not the first generation to go looking for that treasure."

"But why would they go looking for a treasure after Bradford used it to help Savannah's people?"

A sad smile worked its way across Shirley's features. She stood silently and walked across the kitchen and halfway down the hall. Were they supposed to go after her? Penelope looked at Tucker, who shrugged.

Before Penelope could decide if Shirley wanted them to join her, the older woman returned carrying a large black book. It was bigger than a dictionary, its fabric corners frayed. But she carried it with dignity and reverence. When she set it on the table before them, the faded gold letters on the front cover became clear. HOLY BIBLE.

Opening the front cover, she revealed a series of names and dates, and it was clear that this family Bible was the record for marriages and births and many joyous occasions. But the numbers after the dashes recorded a sadder history of loved ones lost and the broken hearts left behind.

"Caroline must have known her brother well." Shirley tapped her finger against a line joining Bradford Westbrook and Agatha Spencer in holy matrimony in June of 1865.

A warmth filled Penelope's chest, and she smiled at the thought of Bradford, who must have been Tucker's ancestor, finding love. After the war and all that Savannah had suffered, there had been hope too. Caroline had found it, and so had her brother. But if this was the evidence, why did Shirley look so somber?

Penelope leaned over the page, her eyes scanning the contents as quickly as she could, trying to make sense of it. The lines were blurry after so many years, and she traced them with the tip of her fingernail.

"Bradford married Agatha. And then . . ." She found the corresponding entry, and her breath caught in her throat.

"What?" Tucker's shoulder bumped hers, and she could see he was trying to put the pieces together too, his forehead a sea of wrinkles as the pieces didn't connect.

"Bradford died. That summer." She looked up at Shirley. "Before Caroline's letter was even sent."

"But Daniel Westbrook must have looked for the treasure," Tucker said.

"Oh, I'm sure he did," Shirley said. "The problem is that four hundred feet due south of Mrs. Fitterling's is . . ."

"Washington Square." Penelope could see Savannah's historic squares laid out like a map in her mind. Washington and Warren and Reynolds Squares all a couple blocks south of Bay Street. All had been there long before the war. But there was no way Josiah could have hidden his treasure in such a public setting. Not without gaining the attention of the men he was hiding from. If, indeed, he had whisked Caroline away for her own safety, he would not have risked his own neck in such a way.

Tucker leaned back, pressing a hand to his forehead. His eyes moved back and forth behind closed lids, and she could almost feel the waves flowing from him as he worked out the truth. After a long silence, he said, "The treasure was never found because Bradford was the only one who knew where Josiah had moved it. The rest of the directions—knowing it's four hundred feet south—doesn't help if you don't have a starting point."

"That's about the sum of it."

Tucker made a fist on the table, and Penelope could do nothing but reach for his arm and press a cool hand to the tense muscle there. She knew what this meant for him and for the election. For the second time that day, she could see a man's broken heart written across his face.

Also for the second time that day, she wondered how much of it was her fault.

Sure, she hadn't hidden the treasure, but she couldn't help but wonder if she might have missed a clue. Or maybe she should have tried to find a Fitterling heir among the city's population. Savannah was old homes and old families. Shirley was evidence of the way they held on to their history. Could there be anyone else out there who remembered the midnight visitors to Mrs. Fitterling's and what happened to the cargo?

"Here's what I don't get," Tucker mused. "How was Josiah getting to the stash in the dress shop without being noticed? If he was trying to protect his identity, was he sneaking around only at night? Wouldn't someone have noticed? Wouldn't Mrs. Fitterling have complained?"

He made a good point, but Shirley didn't seem to have answers. "You know as much as I do now," she said.

Tucker gave a soft grunt. "This doesn't make sense. If Bradford died, how did the Westbrook line continue? How are either of us even here?"

"Oh, that." Shirley flipped to another page in the Bible, this one a continuation of births, a branch of the family tree. And there was Bradford Westbrook Jr., Agatha's son.

"She was pregnant before he died," he said.

"Bradford Junior had five boys, so he made sure the family name would carry on," Shirley said as she closed the Bible and hugged it to her chest. "We have a lot of family history—and our ancestors were, in fact, smugglers and thieves. But perhaps they did it for the right reasons. And they helped a lot of people along the way." She patted Tucker's hand. "I wish I could tell you where to look to find it all."

"Do you know if Mrs. Fitterling has any descendants in the area?"

Shirley's face added a few dozen wrinkles as she considered the question. "I don't know that anyone's ever asked. But I'll tell you who would know. Jethro Coleman."

That name again. Carter had mentioned him from the beginning. And Jethro had cornered Tucker at the picnic. But if he was this magical font of information, he should have found the treasure on his own.

After offering their good nights to Shirley, Penelope and Tucker stepped into the still evening air. They'd talked for ages and uncovered the rest of Caroline's story, yet she didn't feel any closer to finding the treasure.

Even worse, she wasn't sure what they should do with it if they ever did. She'd been so sure that the very act of finding the treasure would be enough to clear Tucker's name and win him the election. But he needed more than that. He needed the money.

Only now that she knew the money had been intended to help the people of Savannah, she thought of who it could help today. It wasn't for lining the pockets of the already wealthy or even winning political elections. Josiah had risked everything to use it to help the poor and downtrodden. Could they do any less?

Tucker wasn't sure he wanted this old farm to be the right place, but the number on the door of the dilapidated home was the same one PJ had gotten from Carter Hale.

"You sure this is right?" he asked.

"Nope." PJ leaned over the dashboard of his truck and squinted at the house before them. It looked about ready to crumble, its shutters hanging at odd angles and the door half open. "But it'll be worth a check, don't you think?"

He pushed his door open with his foot, and immediately the sound of a hammer against a board reached them. Maybe Jethro was trying to spruce the place up.

They made their way up the uneven front steps. Even in her sneakers, PJ's foot slipped when a board rocked, and he grabbed for her. Somehow he ended up with his arms around her waist, holding her against his chest. Which he did not mind at all. "Hey there, pretty lady."

She beamed up at him. "Hey yourself, handsome."

The even rise and fall of her shoulders and her soft murmur of content were enough to make him never want to move. He'd wanted this his whole life. He just hadn't known it. He was such an idiot. How had he never noticed PJ when she was literally right in front of him?

Or had he been worried he wasn't good enough for her back then?

Well, he was going to lay all those questions to rest at the election. If he won. Which he would. He had to. Because going back to the way it had been between them wasn't an option.

Unfortunately, that meant letting go of her for the time being. He had to think long term like he had during boot camp. Keep going because the reward would be worth it.

Releasing her slowly, he said, "How about we pick this up later?"

"All right." She stepped back and rapped her knuckles on the door. "First the treasure."

She got it. She understood why this mattered. She understood him. And he had to physically cross his arms to keep from reaching for her again.

Her knock produced no response, save another round of hammer to nail.

"Jethro," he called. But the hammer drowned out the sound. He waited until it stopped. "Jethro, you here?"

"Who's there?" The question was as gruff as the one who asked it. "What do you want with me?"

"It's Tucker and Penelope."

Jethro's head popped around the corner of his home, a frown squarely in place beneath his crooked nose. His narrowed eyes suggested suspicion, and his cheeks were smeared with enough dirt that he matched the peeling paint on the rotting walls. "What do you want? I ain't donating to yer campaign. And I'm not buying nothing neither."

"We're not selling anything," Tucker said.

Jethro took a breath and leaned a full shoulder past the corner of the building. "If you say so."

"We were wondering about . . . you said you might know something about the lost treasure."

He snorted. "You want to find the money. You ain't the first."

"Right. You said that others had looked, but we think there might be—"

Jethro cut him off with a wave of his hand. "We ain't

gonna stand 'round here jawin'. If you want to know what I know, it'll cost you."

Jethro's gaze swept over PJ, and Tucker stepped in front of her, blocking the view and making it clear she wasn't going to be part of any bargain.

"Can she swing a hammer?"

PJ scooted out from behind him, her arm extended. "Point me to it."

Jethro cocked his head and gave her one more assessing gaze. Then he nodded, turned, and stalked away. They ran to catch up with him.

When they reached the backyard, they both stopped, mouths open. The lot had been filled with a massive one-story home, completely blocked from view by the old homestead. The new house had been painted slate blue, its trim and shutters clean white. Square corners and inviting gables made Tucker want to run his hands along the perfect edges. A big bay window beside the front door gave a glimpse into a tidy living room.

Jethro bent over an unfinished staircase that led to a porch spanning the whole front of the home. "I'll tell you what I know." He nodded toward the boards ready to be nailed into the steps. "If'n you'll help me finish up my stairs."

Tucker wanted to agree, but he couldn't quite wrap his mind around what he was looking at. How had a man living in *that* made something like *this*?

Maybe Jethro's skills went beyond carpentry to clairvoyance, because he answered the question without being asked. "The old one keeps most of the riffraff away. Don't get many of them solicitors trying to sell me magazine subscriptions and whatnot. I started building my new place last year.

Moved in last month." His hands on his hips, he gave his home a proud smile. "Did most of the work on her myself."

"Your home is lovely," PJ breathed.

"Thank you." He spoke like a proud father. "Now, you gonna help me or what?"

Tucker grabbed a hammer and handed one to PJ before they shifted a board into its slot and began driving in the nails that would hold the step in place.

Between thwacks of the hammer against the nail heads, Tucker looked toward Jethro, who was fitting together the two-by-fours for the handrails. "So what do you know about the lost treasure?"

"Less than some. More than others, I guess."

Tucker took a deep breath and gave his nail a solid hit. Better the stairs than Jethro. The man couldn't give a straight answer to save his life.

"You said others were looking for it?"

"Oh, sure. There've been lots of them. Ever since my aunt—"

PJ's head whipped up, her hammer raised to her shoulder. "Who's your aunt?"

"Ah, she's a few generations removed, I s'pose. But my great-granddad was her nephew. And he told me all the stories."

Tucker caught PJ's gaze. He was pretty sure they were thinking the same thing. Were Tucker and Jethro related?

"What kind of stories?" PJ asked, her voice soft and curious, her eyes filled with humor.

"'Bout the midnight callers. 'Bout how half a dozen men stomped through her home and hid some smuggled cargo."

PJ's eyebrows raised. "Mrs. Fitterling? The dressmaker? She was your aunt?"

Jethro gave a hard glare at their stilled hands. "Less talking, more working."

PJ jerked her hammer down, clearly not paying attention to where it landed. Which happened to be right on Tucker's thumb. He nearly screamed as pain shot up his wrist and past his elbow, but he bit back everything he wanted to say and turned away, holding his thumb to his chest.

"I'm so sorry." PJ dropped her hammer on the ground, ran around the base of the steps to his side, and cradled his red thumb in her hands. When she looked up at him, her eyes were wide and filled with sadness. "I didn't mean to. Are you all right?" She pressed a kiss to his thumb, gentle and soothing.

"I'll live." But as his thumb throbbed, he wondered if he'd rather live without it.

"Maybe I can make it up to you." Batting her big blue eyes at him, she pressed onto her tiptoes. Her T-shirt was softer than a kitten against his arm as she snuggled against him, her breath warm on his neck.

And he was lost. She could have hit every single one of his fingers and toes with that hammer, and he'd still have pulled her right back into his arms.

Jethro cleared his throat, but Tucker didn't move. He was just fine where they were.

"Seems like y'all might be more trouble than help," Jethro said.

"I'm fine," Tucker replied, showing off his thumb by wiggling it over PJ's head. But he stopped as soon as fire shot up his arm again. It was going to turn purple soon, and he could only pray he didn't lose the nail.

"Yeah, well, you ain't gettin' much done." Jethro put his

hands on his hips. "Guess I shouldn't have figured you to be the home-building type. Now tell me what you want so I can go back to work."

"What do you know about Mrs. Fitterling and the treasure?"

"I know she owned a dress shop over on Bay Street. And I know a group of men came knocking on her door at midnight. My great-grandpa told me stories when I was a kid about how brave she'd been. About how when she heard what it was being used for, she gave her own diamond necklace to help the cause."

PJ leaned toward Jethro. "What was it being used for?"

Jethro looked shocked that she would even ask. "To help them folks after the war. Sherman didn't burn Savannah, but its people sure was hurtin'. They was hungry and many of them homeless. About the time the war ended, that's when someone started caring for those most in need. Your family, they still had a roof over their head. But there were lots of families not so lucky. That's when flour and salt and fruit started showing up at the camps."

"A man named Josiah, he was behind that. But did your aunt just let him through her shop every night?"

"Through her shop? Why would she do such a thing?"

Tucker caught PJ's gaze, and she shook her head. "When did they move the treasure?"

Jethro put down his hammer. "What kind of nonsense are you talking? They never moved the treasure. Not as far as I know."

"But Caroline wrote a letter to her brother," PJ said. "She said it had been moved four hundred feet away. But that would place it in Washington Square."

Jethro picked his hammer up and turned his attention back to the railing, piecing it together one sure blow at a time. Finally, he looked up at them with a confused expression. "In Washington Square? Or below it?"

Tucker's jaw worked back and forth as he tried to make sense of Jethro's words.

PJ, on the other hand, didn't wait to ask for clarity. "What's that supposed to mean?"

Scratching his gray whiskers, Jethro chuckled. "Oh, you kids. So skeptical. Don't you know how many old stories of Savannah are true?"

"Old stories . . . like—"

"The treasure was put in my aunt's cellar. But the house wasn't the only way to reach it. There was another way. Underground."

SEVENTEEN

*P*enelope had heard the rumors about Savannah's shanghai tunnels since her childhood. Wild stories abounded of sailors taken to sea and conscripted to pirate ships. It was all part of Savannah's charm. Its storied history. Old men sat about checkerboards and laughed about what the tunnels had seen, all the history that had been witnessed below the city's streets.

As the stories went, the tunnels had served as escape routes and hiding places. Some even said they had been part of the Underground Railroad. The series of tunnels supposedly zigzagged beneath the city streets, cool and damp and dark.

If Penelope was completely honest, she had thought they were an urban legend, a myth. Until right this very second. Because the beam of her flashlight went well beyond the back wall of the cellar before her.

Her breath hitched in her throat, and for a sweet moment she let herself believe they were almost to the treasure.

It had taken several days to get as far as they had, though, so none of this could happen soon enough. With the election only a few more days away, she'd wanted to push and prod

Jethro to make this all happen. But the man was not one to be rushed. After he'd revealed that the treasure had never been stored *inside* Mrs. Fitterling's shop, the truth was so clear. It had always been in her cellar, accessed by a hidden door into the tunnels.

And as it turned out, Jethro knew just the man to help them gain entrance. Carter Hale.

The beam from Carter's flashlight illuminated his smile as they stood at the entrance to the tunnels. "Guess it pays to have connections in the historical society." His words sounded glib, but the truth was that Carter was something of a local legend. He'd somehow managed to find a sunken shipwreck that proved the truth of a journal more than 250 years old. And then he'd gone and donated much of his reward back to the city. His museum was the exclusive home to all of the nearly fifty pieces that had been discovered—so far. They were still finding more.

All of that had made Carter Savannah's favorite son—even if he was from Connecticut. He'd proven his dedication to the city, and certain doors had been opened to him for that. Including the door before them.

"Y'all all right?" Sean Cutter, the proprietor of a local eatery down the street from Jackson's Hole, peered at them from the top of the stairs.

"We're good. Thanks, Sean." Carter waved as he held a low door open and Tucker led the way into the tunnels.

The darkness seemed to eat the light, so much stronger than the four heavy-duty flashlights they carried. The tunnels appeared to be endless, stretching as far to the east as the west. Only darkness there. A halo of light illuminated a wall of brick and stone across from the entrance. It was pale and smooth and surprisingly cool as Penelope ran her hands along it. It was the middle of the afternoon and hotter than the sun outside. But beneath the sidewalks the tunnel was cool, and she shivered, leaning against Tucker's back for his warmth.

She hung on to his arm for an entirely different reason—to keep herself upright on the uneven ground. And also because sometimes she still couldn't believe she was free to hold on to him at any time. He didn't seem to mind, holding his elbow close to his side and her with it.

"Are you ready?" she asked, her steps cautious.

"Yeah. I think so. You?"

The truth was she didn't have nearly as much riding on this search, but that didn't explain the pit in her stomach. It was a strange mixture of nerves and hope, excitement and terror. What if they did find the treasure? What if it won him the election? What if his work had to come first? What if he decided the city was more important than her?

The questions shot through her so fast that her head spun, and she had to lean on him even more. He didn't complain, but her stomach knotted all the same.

What if he wasn't there? What if he walked away? He could easily decide she wasn't worth his time. Just like her dad and Winston had.

She tried to push the thoughts out of her mind, but the questions continued.

"There's the old door to Mrs. Fitterling's—I mean Jackson's Hole." Tucker pointed toward the wall ahead and on their left as they moved east. It had long since been boarded up, but the wood had been weathered by time and nature. In some places it looked to be hanging on by a sliver, a mere breeze capable of crumbling it to dust. Yet it remained.

Josiah had walked these tunnels, secreted away from all that had hunted him. But where had he moved the treasure?

As though he could read her thoughts, Tucker looked to the right—toward the south—and another stone wall. But Caroline had said the treasure was four hundred feet south. How could it be if there was no tunnel?

Carter and Jethro joined Tucker at the wall, each of them pressing their free hands against the curved wall and mumbling about what should be there. An opening.

But it wasn't there.

Penelope let out a soft sigh and shuffled her shoe against the ground. Her toe caught a pebble and it skipped down the tunnel. She looked up to follow its trajectory before her flashlight could make the arc, and her eye caught a tiny patch of light on a sparse patch of grass. That wasn't supposed to be there.

"Don't leave without me," she said to the men, who were clearly consumed with the physics of Josiah moving and replacing a tunnel wall 155 years before. Pulling out her phone and opening her GPS app, she dashed down the corridor in the same direction they had been walking. She lowered her flashlight every few steps to make sure she didn't miss that drop of light.

It took her several minutes to reach it nearly a hundred feet down the way, according to her phone. When she did, she saw what she hadn't been able to before—an offshoot of the main tunnel. The entire wall to her right disappeared into more darkness, save one beam coming from above. She flicked her light upward. It looked like the underside of a manhole cover, metal and slimy. A guard had probably been built over it too—around the time the city decided it wasn't safe to have random access to these tunnels.

But whatever was four feet overhead, it had let in enough light to catch her attention. And it had shown her a new path.

The men's voices still echoed down the tunnel. Waving her light, she hollered at them. "Hey! Guys! I found another tunnel."

Their voices stopped, and then a cacophony of bouncing lights and heavy footfalls roared toward her.

"Whoa!" She held up her hands as if that could fend off their onslaught. They stopped just in time, breaths coming out in quick gasps.

"What'd you find?" Jethro asked.

She nodded toward the cavernous entry to their right, and that was enough. Tucker charged forward, the others following close behind, every light on the walls. They searched for any sign of a mark that might be Josiah's. Caroline hadn't specified what it looked like, but along the unadorned walls, anything would stand out. The tunnel narrowed after a short while, and by two hundred feet in, they were forced to make their way single file.

The walls remained blank, and only the roots of plants that had forced their way between the stones and their earthy smell remained. They had gone nearly five hundred feet when the tunnel ended in a T intersection. Each narrow outlet was dark, each holding little promise. They could run around for hours and never find what they were hunting for.

Penelope bent her head and said a quick prayer. She wasn't quite sure if she should pray that they'd find the treasure and Tucker would stay with her or if she should pray they wouldn't find it so she never had to know if Tucker would choose another life.

But there was so much good that could be done with that money. There were so many hearts that could be given hope. She couldn't help but see Jordan's face in her mind's eye. Those kids needed the kind of help this treasure would bring.

Even if she and Tucker were given only a finder's fee by the city, it was so much more than Jordan had right now.

Lord, let us find this treasure and use it for good.

She already had a plan, a way to put it to good use. And it began with an open date on the calendar at the Hall. Her stomach threatened to heave her lunch as she thought about what had happened between Winston and Emmaline—and how she could have made a different choice.

Maybe she could do something good enough to make up for that terrible mistake.

Penelope looked to the right and then to the left of the intersection, following the other flashlights going in the same path. "Well, if Caroline was correct—and we're wagering everything on her here—and the treasure was four hundred feet south of Mrs. Fitterling's, then maybe we have to take the long way. Right now we're about five hundred feet southeast of the old entrance to her cellar."

Tucker stilled, his eyes bright even in the shadows. "That makes sense. I guess."

The other men grunted their agreement, and they plodded to their right. After a hundred feet, they turned down another offshoot to their right and went a couple hundred feet north. They were in a maze, and Penelope had never been so thankful not to be alone. Especially when she stepped on something that squished. Loudly. And her shoe slid across something slimy.

"What *was* that?" She nearly jumped on Tucker's back as he swung his light to her feet.

"Just a slug. It's dead now. Can't hurt you."

Until she had to cut off her own foot, because no amount of rubber between her toes and that slug was enough. She looked up at Tucker to tell him as much, but his head was cocked to the side, his gaze intent on something over her shoulder.

"What's that look like to you?" He pointed, and three heads whipped in that direction.

There, at eye level, was a red mark that might have once been the letter *J*. It was faded and worn, its crossbar all but gone. But it was something that couldn't be ignored.

Penelope hopped out of the way, dodging the dead slug as the men ran their fingers around the stone, dislodging a century and a half of mud and dirt and finding an edge. When Tucker's fingers found purchase, he pulled, and the whole wall seemed to fall away. They shuffled back farther, Penelope's light directly on what was behind the crumbled stone.

Two wooden crates marked in French. And through the slats, something brilliant glittered in the light.

Tucker couldn't stop his heart from hammering in his chest. It slammed against his rib cage and dropped to his stomach and then did it all over again. This was it—what he needed, what would win him the election. He pulled one of the crates forward. It wasn't as stable as it once might have been, but it had protected what was inside for a century and a half.

And now he prayed what was inside was enough. He prayed he'd be awarded a big enough share.

He risked a glance away from their find toward PJ, whose features were tight. He'd assumed she'd be as excited as he was, but a hint of a frown around her lips set him on edge.

"Tucker? You ready?" Carter had taken one end of the lid, and Tucker hurried to join him, lifting it away and revealing what had been hidden.

Three bars of gold, a couple bottles of amber liquid, and a diamond necklace.

Jethro cackled like he'd won the lottery, slapping his hand across his thigh. "That's hers. That diamond necklace was my aunt's. I'd wager my whole house on it."

Carter looked skeptical—probably because he hadn't seen Jethro's new home. But Tucker knew it was real.

"My great-granddad said she wasn't going to let all the help come from across the ocean," Jethro said. "But I guess there weren't no buyers for a piece like that."

Tucker shook his head. Caroline's journal had said that food was hard to come by in the days after the war. No one in Savannah would have had the money to pay what the necklace was worth. Except maybe other smugglers. And Josiah would have kept his distance from them.

But Savannah was a different city now, and there were deep pockets and old money. Someone would love the story of that necklace.

Tucker picked up the dusty piece, his thumb rubbing off a layer of grime to reveal the true gem beneath. It was beautiful. It also belonged to Jethro.

He held it out to the other man, but Carter clamped a hand on his forearm. "We've got to document this first. Can you hang on? I'll go get my camera. Jethro, help me get the cart. We'll be right back."

They ran into the darkness as Tucker put the necklace back where it was. Squatting beside the crate, he poked at its contents. "Look at this, PJ." He picked up a silver jewelry box half out of its paper wrapper. Inside were pearl earrings.

She leaned over his shoulder, her hand resting on it. "I can't believe it's been here all these years. I can't believe we actually found it."

He laughed. "I know. I was starting to think we were on a fool's errand."

She pulled away, and he pushed against his knees to stand. "Thank you." Pulling her into an embrace, he kissed her quickly. "This is going to . . . This is huge."

It was everything his campaign manager had said they needed. This was the election. And it was the rest of his life. All in two wood crates and the woman in his arms.

"I know." She jumped from his embrace, her eyes filled with wonder. "It's going to do so much good for the people of Savannah."

"Right. Wait, what?" He must have misheard her. Maybe it was his pulse still pounding in his ears. "For the election."

PJ made a face that matched what he felt in his gut. "For the people of Savannah."

"Right. When I win the election."

She shook her head slowly, and the shadows from his flashlight made the lines of her face longer, eerier, sadder. Her mouth pinched together as her eyes darted toward the box then back to him.

"For the people of Savannah." She repeated the words slowly as though she thought he'd misheard her. But it wasn't that easy.

"PJ, I need this money for the election. At least whatever is legally mine. It may not have belonged to my family, but we never would have found it without them. There's got to be a reward for that."

"But you heard what Caroline wrote in those letters. This money was for Savannah, for the downtrodden and the broken."

"Right. To rebuild after the war. We've rebuilt. The city doesn't need the money like it used to. I do." He ran his hand over his cropped hair, wishing he had a beard to pull on. "Beau says that if I don't flood the local stations with ads in the next two days, I can't win the election. This is my only chance to beat Jepson and make a name for myself."

"I don't think this is what it was meant for. I think we could put it to better use."

Her words ripped through him, tearing at something deep in his chest. He knew what "better use" meant. He knew from years of his father suggesting that his college fund would be better invested in stocks and bonds.

It all boiled down to one thing. PJ didn't think he was worth this kind of money. Everything he'd done in this race to prove to her that he was worthy hadn't amounted to a hill of beans.

That fire, that pain-fueled rage, that had burned in him the first night he'd kissed her leaked out of him one word at a time, this time lashing out instead of pulling her in. "You were all well and good with me taking money from Mrs. Saunders and the others at the dinner. Funny how

279

your tune changes when you think there's something in it for you."

She smoothed her hands down the sides of her jeans, taking a deep breath. "They donated money explicitly for that cause. This"—she waved at the crates—"was never intended to be used for political elections. Why can't you see the difference?"

"Why can't you see that I can do some real good for this city? Or don't you believe I'm capable of that?"

She reached for his shoulder, but her touch burned, and he pulled away. "Of course I do," she said. "You'll make a wonderful sheriff, but isn't finding the treasure enough? I mean, the media is going to have a heyday with this. You'll be on every station, every news show. This treasure and the journal and Caroline's letters should be enough to shut Buddy down."

Dragging a hand over his face, he let out a low sigh. "I can't risk it."

"Tucker." She dragged out his name, every syllable pleading with him to change his mind. "Would it be so bad if you didn't win?" She slammed a hand over her mouth, but the words hung between them, sharper than a knife.

"Yes." He hadn't expected to be so blunt, but it was the truth. "I have to win."

She looked him straight in the eye and asked something she hadn't before. "Why?"

"You know why." She had to know. She was smart and savvy, and there was no way she didn't know that this had all become about her. He may have decided he couldn't back out because of his father, but after their first kiss, he had needed to prove his worth to her. No one thought he was good enough, but he'd do everything in his power to show them they were wrong. Especially Penelope Jean Hunter.

Penelope shook her head. This man, the one she'd loved most of her life—the one she'd just realized she loved with her whole heart—wasn't making any sense. "No, I really don't." He tried to back away, but she grabbed his arm and held him stable. "What's the worst thing that could happen if you lose?"

"I'll prove to my dad and everyone else that I'm not worthy of—" He looked stricken, like he'd said the absolute last thing in the world he wanted to.

"Of what? Of a badge? Of winning a contest? Of the respect of this town? News flash, Tucker! You already have that. Winning this election can't change a thing about you. Becoming sheriff isn't going to set you on some invisible course for success."

He blinked hard, his head slowly shaking. "I can help the people of Savannah. As sheriff, I can help them."

"Yes, you could. You could also help them not as sheriff. Imagine how many bellies this money would fill with good food. Imagine how many homes this would build for those without a roof over their heads." *Imagine how many kids this might help land on their feet through Jordan's organization.*

She couldn't bring herself to speak the words. They were somehow too dear. Even imagining what this money would mean for kids like Jordan made her eyes burn and her throat feel full. The words were blocked somewhere near her heart, somewhere near the painful thudding deep in her chest.

Taking several deep breaths, she tried to find what had been lost, a way to tell him the truth. "I want you to win, Tucker." Her vision suddenly turned watery, and she clenched her shaking hands before her. "But maybe using whatever money comes from finding this treasure in order to win is too high a price."

"It can't be."

In the second that it took for him to say those words, her heart split in two. She'd known an ache in her heart when her dad had chosen another family, when Winston had chosen another life. But this wrenching in her chest was unrepairable. She pressed a hand over her ribs, but the searing, writhing pain only continued.

It was just as her mom had warned her. Like every other man in her life, he'd chosen something over her. She should have known.

And then she did something she'd sworn she would never do. She turned her back on Tucker Westbrook and walked away.

EIGHTEEN

*P*enelope knocked on the door of the old home, her hand stiff and her body aching. She hugged the book in her arms to her chest, bowed her head, and waited.

"I'm a'coming," hollered the familiar voice from deep inside the house. The door burst open. "Peej? What are you doing here?"

When she looked into Shirley's kind eyes, everything she'd been holding together so tightly fell apart. Her eyes leaked, tears streaming down her cheeks and dripping from her chin, precariously close to the diary in her arms. "He-ere." She shoved it toward Shirley, who took it without even looking at it.

"Honey-girl? You look far too upset for someone who just discovered a lost treasure. Where are your dancing shoes?" There was another question in her voice that Penelope had heard a dozen times from her mom in the last two days, and she prayed Shirley wouldn't ask it.

She was not all right. And she had no desire to explain why. Not when she'd already gotten the I-told-you-sos from her mom and beat herself up with the same words more than a few times. This was why people didn't fall in love with their best friends. Because when it didn't work out, the only person she wanted to go to for comfort was the one person she wasn't speaking with.

Instead she stood on his aunt's doorstep, a sweaty, blubbering mess, every other breath catching on a sob. "I-I'm sorry. I'll go."

"Now hold on just a second." Shirley scooped her into her arms and pulled her from the heat into the cool of her home. "You'll go nowhere until you tell me who has upset you and we decide just what to do to make them pay."

Penelope could manage only a limp shake of her head. She couldn't have Shirley plotting against her own nephew. Although if there was anyone in the world she would want on her team, it was Shirley Westbrook.

"Sit," Shirley said, dragging her into the kitchen and pushing her toward a chair. "I'll make tea. You tell me everything."

"I can't. It's . . . I can't get you involved. It's about . . . well, I can't ask you to take my side."

Shirley set the diary on the table before pressing her hands to her hips and facing her head-on. "You tell me what my nephew has done, and we'll figure out how to deal with it."

"Have you talked with him?" She couldn't meet Shirley's gaze.

"Don't need to. Only one person could make you look so heartsick."

Oh dear. She covered her cheeks with her hands, burying her puffy eyes and red nose. If she looked even half as broken as she felt, she should find a tunnel and hide there for 150 years.

"I want him to win the election." She glanced up to make sure that Shirley was still listening. "I really do."

"I don't think anyone doubts that."

Penelope took a stuttering breath. "I think *he* does. And maybe rightfully so."

Shirley picked up the kettle, filled it with water, and set it on a burner. "And why's that?"

"Because I told him I thought we should use the treasure to help people instead of funding his campaign."

Shirley's eyebrows rose slowly. "Did you now? I assume he did not take that well."

"No."

"And how did you get to that point?"

Penelope steeled herself to tell the truth—the whole truth. She and Tucker hadn't gotten to where they were because of one silly action. A lot of decisions had landed them in this spot. And it had all started with one terrible decision to allow their community to believe they were dating.

Choice by choice, Penelope laid out the truth. From Winston's return to Emmaline's intimation. From Buddy's letter to the editor to their hunt for the treasure. From the picnic to his fundraising dinner and that incredible kiss. She held nothing back. By the time the kettle whistled and Shirley poured the steaming water into a pink floral teapot, Penelope had revealed it all.

"I left him in the tunnel, and I haven't talked with him since."

Shirley pursed her pale lips as she set out matching teacups and poured some for each of them. "Sugar?"

Penelope nodded.

"And Tucker hasn't reached out to you yet?"

"No."

Shirley clucked her tongue. "Silly boy."

He wasn't silly. Maybe he was even right. But without that treasure, she had no hope of helping Jordan.

"He insists you pretend to date and then goes and falls in love with you." The note of humor in Shirley's voice couldn't be ignored, but Penelope couldn't stand to talk about it more at that moment.

"It gets worse." She blew into her tea, rippling the surface. "Winston and Emmaline broke up too. And I know I'm not to blame, but I can't help feeling like it."

"Oh? You must have some power."

Penelope tried for a laugh, but it came out dry and strained. "No, just plenty of failures. I yelled at Winston about leaving me at the altar, and Emmaline walked in. I never meant for her to hear the truth like that."

Shirley patted her hand. "Sweet girl. You're carrying some weight on your shoulders right now, aren't you?"

"I had all these plans, and none of them have worked out. I just don't understand. I thought God was supposed to have all these grand plans for me. Right? He's supposed to have a hope and a future for me, but here I am still alone with no one in my future."

Shirley's gentle smile turned sad. "If you think God's promise is for a husband and a family, you might want to reread that Scripture."

"Oh, Shirley." Her cup clattered as she dropped it onto its saucer. Shirley had never married or had kids. She'd chosen a life of independence, traveling the world and serving across oceans. As a nurse, she'd gone with a medical missions team that spent five weeks every summer caring for the broken and impoverished. Her life was anything but hopeless, and Penelope had belittled it with one careless word. "I'm so sorry."

"No need to apologize, but I'd hate for you to go through life thinking that not being married means you have no hope or future. Or that God does not have plans for you."

"But I had a plan. I was going to be married by thirty, have my first baby by thirty-two, and be ridiculously in love with my husband for the rest of our lives. And now my future doesn't look anything like I thought it would."

"Of course not. You thought you'd be with Winston forever. It would seem God has another plan."

Penelope nodded. "But what is it?"

"Isn't that always the question? And wouldn't life be boring if we knew it?"

"But then I could know how to prepare. I could be ready."

Shirley laughed out loud. "Sweetheart, it doesn't work like that. You don't have to be ready to enjoy the adventure. That's what makes it an adventure." She patted Penelope's hand, her eyes filled with wisdom that came from experience. "The adventure is in the unknown. God has amazing things in store for you, but if you knew what they were, you'd miss out on the anticipation of discovering them."

Could that possibly be true?

Of course it is, you nincompoop.

Falling for Tucker had entirely blindsided her. And except for the last few days, it had been the most fun she'd ever had. She hadn't planned on Tucker—in fact, she'd actively planned not to fall for him. But he'd showed her a love she'd never imagined. She hadn't known she could feel the passion she felt when he held her close, when his lips brushed against hers. Even now, the mere memory made her insides melt.

He was so tender yet strong. Protective yet empowering. He believed she was the best version of herself—and he made her want to be that person. He'd do anything for her. He'd shaved his beard for her, for heaven's sake.

"So then, what am I supposed to do?"

"I can tell you with certainty that the Good Book says God has a plan for you. Right now. Right this very minute. That you should live in harmony with others as much as it's up to you."

"You mean Tucker?"

Shirley nodded.

Penelope's throat closed around whatever words she might have found, and she shook her head. It was too hard. She couldn't start there.

"Make peace with him."

"I don't know how." That was entirely true and downright terrifying. She'd never not known how to talk with Tucker. And the truth left her reeling.

Shirley squeezed her hand. "Then start somewhere easier. Perhaps Emmaline and Winston?"

She was finally able to take a deep breath. "Yes. But what if they don't forgive me?"

Shirley poured herself another cup of tea and plopped a sugar cube into it. "Well, I suppose that's the 'as much as it's up to you' piece of the puzzle. You can't make them, but you can ask. And you can offer your forgiveness."

"Emmaline hasn't done—"

Shirley raised an eyebrow in a look so similar to Tucker's that it nearly stole her breath.

"Winston."

"Have you truly forgiven him?"

"Of course I have. I did all the things I needed to get over him." She waved a hand to cover a sad chuckle. "I have a whole checklist to prove it."

"I'm not talking about doing all the things to convince yourself." Shirley thumped her chest. "I'm talking about forgiving. Deep in your heart. Choosing to let the hurt go."

"I—"

"As long as you hold on to the hurt—from Winston, from your dad—you're always going to expect the next guy to hurt you too."

All these years she'd been expecting to be hurt. She'd been afraid Tucker would walk away, so she'd pushed him away.

Suddenly the tears returned in earnest, rivers down her face, splashing into her teacup. She'd never put the truth together. She'd never even considered that her broken engagement would impact her future relationships. Yet as Shirley sipped her tea, patiently waiting, Penelope connected the dots. From her father to Winston to Tucker.

Elbows on the table, head in her hands, she said, "What am I going to do?"

"If I may offer a bold suggestion."

Penelope looked up.

"Ask God to show you *his* plan. It'll be better than any plan you could make."

The tiny spark in her chest promised that this too was true. But could she trust God's plan instead of her own?

Penelope twisted the paper napkin in her lap until it was almost unrecognizable as such. The ends frayed and the middle turned to a damp mess. Still she twisted it to the rhythm of her tapping toe.

The door to Maribella's coffee shop jingled as it opened, and she nearly jumped from her seat. But it was just a college kid, his backpack slung over one shoulder and his eyes at half-mast.

She slumped back into the wooden seat, her toe resuming its beat, her heart thundering in her throat.

Dear Lord, please give me the words. I don't know how to make this right, but I believe you can.

Her prayer had been consistent since she had talked with Shirley the day before, and she knew that God had been at work or she'd never even have been able to set up this coffee date.

The door jingled. Her stomach swooped. That was her date. Right on time.

Emmaline wore a flowered sundress and a somber expression. Her usual smile had vanished, and her steps were stiff.

Hopping up, Penelope waved at her friend—her former, hopefully soon-to-be-restored friend. "I got us a table, and I ordered you a sweet tea." She pointed at the plastic cup sitting in front of the empty seat.

For a moment she feared Emmaline would make a run for it. In her high heels she was usually graceful as a swan, and Penelope had a feeling her slender legs could whisk her away. She offered her softest, most welcoming smile. "Please. Join me?"

With a glance around the nearly empty room, Emmaline gave a curt nod. As she settled into her chair, she eyed her drink like she was afraid Penelope had poisoned it.

There wasn't much Penelope could do about that assumption, so she took a sip of her own tea, swirling the ice around the cup. "How are you doing?"

Emmaline's eyes went wide, her lower lip quivering. What a stupid thing to say.

Penelope needed some supernatural help. Taking a deep breath, she prayed the same prayer. As she released her breath, she said, "I'm so glad you agreed to meet me."

"I have no idea why I'm here."

"I know. I was just hoping for a chance to apologize." Emmaline's eyebrows rose, and Penelope quickly added her qualifier. "In person." The dozen or so phone messages she'd left weren't enough.

"All right." Emmaline crossed her arms over her stomach. "Get on with it."

Get on with it, indeed. Hadn't Shirley said that this was God's will? That should mean he'd give her the words, right? Well, here she was, still no words. So she sent up another prayer and opened her mouth. "I don't have any excuses, only an apology. And more than one at that."

Emmaline's eyebrows pinched together.

"I'm sorry I lost my temper with Winston, and that that was the first time you heard about our past. I should have pushed him to tell you we had a history. The truth is, I was so surprised to see him that first day in my office that I didn't know what to say. I hadn't talked to him in three years—not since I gave him back his ring." She couldn't help a glance at Emmaline's ring finger, his grandmother's diamond still prominently on display. That had to be a good sign, right?

She didn't give Emmaline a chance to interrupt. "But I lied to you about something else. The truth is that Tucker

291

and I had never dated. Up to that point, we'd never even talked about it."

"But I saw you at his fundraiser. That wasn't fake. It couldn't be."

"It was and it wasn't." She twisted in her seat and gulped another drink of her tea. "Um . . . the truth is that I didn't want Winston to think my life was empty without him. I didn't want him to think I fell apart because he'd walked away. I wanted him to know I was strong and capable. Someone better than the woman he'd left. So Tucker and I agreed to . . . let everyone assume there was more going on than there really was."

"But why?"

"Because I didn't want my ex-fiancé to think I was stuck right where he left me."

"Because . . ." Emmaline prompted her, but Penelope wasn't quite sure where she was supposed to go.

"Because I thought my value was tied up in what he thought of me." She took a sip of her tea.

"Because . . ."

Penelope chewed on her bottom lip for a long moment. "Because I wanted to show him I had moved on."

"Because you wanted to make him jealous and win him back?"

Penelope nearly spit out her drink, choking on it instead. "Who, Winston? No! I wasn't trying to win him back." She waved her hands quickly to wipe away even that thought. "He's a good man and I cared about him a lot, but the truth is that he never loved me the way he loves you."

Emmaline dropped her head. "How do you know?"

"Because all those things he did with you to prepare for

your wedding—taking dancing lessons, planning every element of the ceremony and reception—he never did with me."

"Really?" Emmaline chewed on her thumbnail for a long moment, her eyes focused on the glass before her.

Everything in her life felt like a derailed train, but Penelope was sure of this. "Really. He used to hate it when I wrinkled his shirts with a hug, but he's never said anything to you about that, has he?"

"What? No. Never."

"You bring out the best in him—a part of him I never could. He's so relaxed with you. He and I just made each other more tense, more high-strung." She took a quick breath. "Love isn't about it always being easy but about trying to help the other person become the best version of themselves. It's about caring that their life is better for having you in it, and Winston is definitely better for having you in his life."

Emmaline's cheeks pinked, and she ducked her head, taking a sip of her drink.

"Besides, I have a feeling that you like who you are with him more than who you are without him."

With a sad giggle, Emmaline said, "I'm a little bit flighty. You might have noticed." She shrugged a shoulder. "I've never been expected to be more than my daddy's little girl. You know how it is."

Actually, she didn't. Penelope had always been expected to do something with her life despite her father's absence. Maybe because of it.

"But when I met Winston, he believed I could be so much more than the girl shopping with her daddy's credit card. And I am. I mean, I want to be that person. When I told him

I wanted to be more than what the Ladies' League expected me to be, he helped me find something I'm passionate about and a way to get involved. I'm going to be volunteering at the hospital, and I'm thinking about becoming a nurse for babies. I really like kids."

Penelope didn't know what prompted her, but she reached across the table and squeezed Emmaline's hand. The other woman didn't pull back, and Penelope gave her a rich smile. "I think that sounds wonderful."

"And we were going to—"

The bell on the door jingled again, and they both turned toward it. Penelope nearly swallowed her tongue, and Emmaline looked just as shocked. But Winston looked more surprised than both of them.

"Oh, excuse me. I didn't know you'd . . ." His eyes shifted back and forth between them as he took a hesitant step backward. Then he stopped, the steel growing down his spine almost visible. He squared his shoulders toward them and stepped forward. "I'm glad I ran into you. Both of you."

Emmaline stood, staring into his face, batting her long lashes. If that wasn't a sign of her feelings, Penelope didn't know what was.

Penelope scooted her chair away from the table, not sure if she should leave these two to work it out on their own or hang around to see it for herself. They didn't seem to mind either way, their eyes locked on each other.

"Emmaline, I'm so sorry. I've been calling you all week, and I just wanted a chance to apologize. I love you so much, and I know my actions don't back that up."

"Why didn't you just tell me about Penelope?"

He hung his head, but when Emmaline reached for his hands, he sighed. "I was so embarrassed." His gaze shot toward Penelope, and she nearly tipped her chair over in an attempt to get away from the weight of it.

He'd been embarrassed to be engaged to her. It made the air thick, suddenly too heavy. She fought for a breath against the pain in her chest, but his eyes never wavered.

"I treated Penelope terribly."

The air suddenly returned to normal, filling her lungs. But it did nothing to stop her head from spinning.

"I wasn't honest with her when I started having doubts about getting married. I embarrassed her in front of a couple hundred friends and relatives. I know I hurt her, and I hate that. I hate how I treated her." His gaze shifted back to his fiancée. "I didn't want you to think badly of me or worry that I would treat you that way. I love you so much, Emmaline. I'm sorry I wasn't completely honest with you about my past."

Emmaline blinked several times, her mouth opening and closing in silence. Finally, she sank back into her chair.

But Winston wasn't done. "I owe you an apology too, Penelope." He sat in an extra seat at their table and faced her. "And not just for how I acted three years ago. I shouldn't have said those things to you at Tucker's fundraiser or in your office the other day." Folding his hands on the table before him, he shook his head. "I guess I was always a little bit intimidated by your relationship with Tucker, and when I saw y'all together, it brought up all those reminders of how I felt when we were engaged."

Her hands shook, and she tried to cup them around her sweating glass of tea. That just made the ice rattle and her drink slosh. Letting go, she tried to focus on what he had said. "How you felt when we were together? About Tucker?"

"It was hard to get close to you, hard to be special to you, when you had Tucker around. How could I compete with twenty years of history? All those inside jokes and shared memories. I couldn't catch up because you were making memories with him as fast as you were making them with me."

"Oh, Winston. I'm so sorry if I ever made you feel like Tucker was more important to me." She could have told him that they weren't together any longer, but she wasn't sure she could get the words out of her throat.

He held up his hand, waving off her apology. "I appreciate it, but it's not necessary. I'm the one who wrecked things between us, and I'm the one who owes you an apology. Can you forgive me?"

"Of course." It came out quick and easy. And more importantly, it was true. She had forgiven him. And not because she'd adopted Ambrose or punched a blue bag until her arms no longer functioned or checked off any of the other things on her list. She'd forgiven him because of time and grace. And because she'd been forgiven plenty too.

When she stood, she felt ten pounds lighter. While she'd have been happy to lose any ten pounds, this made her feel more alive than she had in over three years—except for when she was in Tucker's arms.

"I'll leave you two to . . ." She glanced at Emmaline and then back at Winston. "Well, whatever."

As she slipped out of the cafe, she looked over her shoulder to find Winston holding Emmaline's fingers to his lips. Her cheeks were bright pink, a light in her eyes that hadn't been there before. Penelope didn't have any doubt that they'd find their joy together.

She just wasn't sure if she'd ever find hers. Or if God's plan even included that kind of joy in her life. But she'd be okay if he had other plans for her.

NINETEEN

*T*ucker knocked on the door of the old home, his hand stiff and his body aching. He'd been sleeping about as well as a cat in a washing machine. In the three nights since PJ had walked out on him, he'd tossed and turned until the wee hours of the morning, flopping across his bed, kicking the sheets free, and then grumbling when he had to find them in the morning. He'd gotten a grand total of three hours of restless sleep, and he felt every minute he'd missed.

Scrubbing a hand down his face, he scratched at his whiskers. His three-day-old beard was a reminder that he had no one to kiss, no one to care if he had a beard or not.

Forget that. It wasn't about just anyone caring. It was about protecting PJ's sensitive skin. It was about making kissing as pleasant for her as it was for him.

Pleasant. Ha. Yeah, right.

Okay, it was more than pleasant. It was darn near earth-shaking.

And he'd kissed it goodbye with one stupid decision.

"Hold yer horses. I'm on my way." The familiar voice

reached him just as the door swung open and Aunt Shirley greeted him with a scowl. "What are you doing here?" Hands on her hips, she looked like a soldier holding the fort. No entrance. No exceptions.

He mumbled something and pointed over his shoulder in the general direction of the eatery where they'd entered the tunnels. Where his whole life had changed. Just not in the way he'd imagined.

"I figured you'd've sold some treasure and bought up all the spots on my television by now. But as far as I know, you haven't even announced the truth behind Buddy Jepson's letter."

Everything she said was true, and he didn't have a good response. So he hung his head, crossed his arms, and hunched his shoulders. "I don't know why I'm here. But I can't make myself announce that we found the treasure. I guess I thought you'd understand."

Aunt Shirley's laugh was low and humorless. "You and Peej make some pair."

"PJ? She was here?" He whipped his head around, searching for any sign of her. "Do you know where she went? I haven't seen her in three days. I stopped by her office, but she wasn't there."

"Calm yourself, boy. She was here yesterday."

With a deep breath, he nodded. "Sure. Okay. Well, I guess I'll go."

"Don't be absurd. Get in here." She opened the door wider and held her arm out toward the kitchen. "Let's have ourselves a glass of sweet tea, and we can figure this all out."

When they were settled with tall glasses filled to the brim with tea sweeter than PJ herself, Tucker stared at the dancing ice cubes and waited. He wasn't exactly sure for what. He only knew that he didn't know where to start.

"So?" Aunt Shirley prompted him.

"It's been a couple of rotten days." That was an understatement if ever he'd said one.

"Peej let on as much. She told me everything."

He choked on his drink, just about ready to swallow his tongue. "Everything?"

She nodded. "She told me about you two fake dating." Her fingernails drummed against the Formica tabletop. "Stupid, stupid move. I wouldn't've thought you'd need to fake it."

The disappointment in his aunt's tone made him rush to respond. "I didn't." But then the words stopped. They were too raw, too painful to make it out of his throat.

"What did you do?"

He'd made PJ think his election was more important than she was. Not exactly the way to win a woman's heart—especially when that was all he really wanted to do.

Heaving a deep sigh, he began with a story Aunt Shirley had already heard from PJ. But this was his side of it.

"I know we shouldn't have pretended to date—well, we didn't even really do that. We just let everyone think what they wanted to. We spent a little more time together, held hands a little more often. And kissed."

"So it was all fake?"

"Oh, no! I mean, it started that way. I just wanted to help her deal with the situation with Winston. But then . . . I don't know. It became real. It was like I saw her in this new light. For years she'd just been my best friend, the one person I knew I could always rely on. Then one moment I looked up, and she was all beautiful eyes and silky hair, and she fit into

300

my arms like God made her just for me. It wasn't just that she was an amazing woman, but she was meant to be *my* amazing woman. And I couldn't stop looking at her legs." He hadn't meant to be quite that honest, but there it was.

Aunt Shirley's laugh was contagious, and he let himself chuckle. It was that or a total breakdown. He'd been fighting the latter for two days straight.

"And then you kissed her?"

"Yes, ma'am. I did."

"Of all the things that Peej told me, that's what surprised me the most."

"That I kissed her?" He was wondering why it had taken him so long.

"No. Don't be ridiculous. I knew you'd figure that out soon enough. Why'd you pick that moment? Such a public place?"

Right. That made more sense. He'd asked himself that more than once too. "I guess because . . ." He'd rather keep this particular truth to himself. But if he was to have any chance of fixing things with PJ—and he desperately wanted that—he needed Aunt Shirley's help. "It was my dad, actually."

"Travis?" She nearly jumped from her seat. "Not my brother. He doesn't have a romantic bone in his body."

"Not romantic, no. But he did say something that made me take action."

The corners of her mouth turned down as she leaned an arm across the table. "I'm so sorry. I know y'all have a tense relationship."

That was a nice way of putting it. "He was—he was trying to set her up with some lawyer at my party, and I lost it. I'm telling you, I saw red. He was going on and on about how she wouldn't want the whole town thinking we were dating—even though it wasn't quite real yet—when she could have someone like Flynn Rutledge."

"Rutledge? That pretty boy? Oh, no. Peej would never end up with someone like that. Not with the likes of you around."

"I could have used you there that night. Maybe I wouldn't have lost my temper and kissed her." Then where would he have been? Still pretending when all he wanted was real and true and forever. No, he'd made a choice that night, and it may not have ended well, but at least he'd had a taste of heaven on earth. And he knew it was worth fighting for. He just didn't know who to fight. "Then again, I'd have hated to miss out on that kiss."

Eyebrows waggling, Aunt Shirley nudged his shoulder as she got up to refill their glasses. "That good?"

"So good." But if she had to ask, had PJ told a different story? "PJ wasn't—she didn't say something else, did she?"

"Oh, I'm not going to spill her beans. A woman never tells when another woman kisses and tells." She winked. "But Peej was *not* disappointed."

He let that fill him with warmth from his heart to his toes, but a cold rush showered over him just as quickly. He'd had his last taste of her lips, his last feel of her in his arms, unless he could fix this. He had to fix this.

"Then why doesn't she want me to win this election? Does she think I'm as incompetent as my father does?" *Please, Lord, no.*

"I think she does want you to win. She just wants you more than that."

His knee started to bounce as he swiped a hand across his forehead. "That doesn't make any sense."

"Why *is* winning so important to you?"

He jumped to his feet, pacing a line in the linoleum of her floor. "Nobody likes to lose. I mean, I want to win. What's wrong with that?"

"I think it's something a whole lot more than that. And I'm guessing it has something to do with the reason you kissed her in the first place."

"My dad? No, I mean, this isn't about him."

At her full height, Aunt Shirley was about five and a half feet tall, and she'd returned to her seat after refreshing their sweet tea. But even standing across the room, Tucker felt like he was facing down a giant. One he'd been avoiding since he was a boy. One who looked an awful lot like his father.

"My dad, your grandfather, believed in making something of yourself. He didn't finish high school and worked a warehouse job he hated his whole life, but by golly, his kids were going to be educated and well respected. He hammered that into your father and me every day. Did we do our homework? Were we making good grades? Had we applied to the right colleges? He was relentless, and your dad probably got it worse than I did. I was supposed to go to college to get my MRS degree. Instead I went after my nursing license and never looked back. But your dad only learned one thing from our dad—love is contingent on success."

Aunt Shirley twirled the ice in her glass, her gaze focused on the pink place mat at the seat he'd vacated. "I'm afraid you might have begun to believe that. I'm begging you, don't buy it. Don't live your life that way. Love is love because it is freely given. It may cost everything, but it is free to give. God loves you that way. I do too."

"And I love PJ that way. But I have to show her—and my dad and this whole city—that I'm worthy of her. I don't want to spend the rest of my life hearing people tell her she could have done better than me." He shut his eyes as though that would make it easier to tell the truth. "Because I'm afraid that one day I might start believing it. Then I really wouldn't be worthy of her."

Aunt Shirley slammed her hand on the table. "Tucker Westbrook, you listen to me, and you listen good. You don't have to be anyone but the man God created you to be. You are loved, and you are enough. No badge or public office will change who you are."

PJ had said something similar in the tunnels, and he wanted to believe it now as much as he'd wanted to believe it then. But after hearing a different story for thirty years, he couldn't get the cadence out of his head.

"I was never much of a reader. Couldn't get the letters to stay where they were supposed to. And if it hadn't been for PJ, I would have dropped out in junior high." He resumed his pacing, his steps even and measured, but the room wasn't big enough, and the walls felt too close. "She was the best thing that ever happened to me. There's no way I could have opened my business without her help. Or even made it through my tours. She's been there at literally every important event in my life. Knowing she's here in town but I can't talk to her . . ." He hit himself in the chest. "It physically hurts. I don't know if I know how to do life without her. And I don't think I want to."

"Has she ever once made you think you had to earn her friendship—her affection?"

"No, but—"

"What makes you think she'd start that now?"

He scratched at his beard, suddenly hating everything it stood for—every wall between him and the woman he loved.

"You are a derned fool if you can't see how much that woman wants to love you. Badge or no badge, she wants to know that you're going to stay by her side. Forever. She stuck by you through all of that school stuff, the Middle East, and even this election."

He jerked back, her words like sniper fire, sharp and to the point. She might be right. Could it be possible that PJ wanted the same thing he did? The two of them. Together. For always.

"How can I . . . What can I do to show her?" He already knew she wouldn't answer his calls, and chasing her down at her apartment wasn't likely to win him any brownie points. Besides, she was probably staying with her mom to avoid him.

"I'm going to let you in on a little secret. This family isn't perfect, but it's filled with a long line of courageous people. When you went on your first tour, I thought about Caroline's diary and her letters home. She didn't choose the easy path. She could have stayed in Savannah with her parents. But she chose the one God had for her, even when it meant angering her father. She took off for parts unknown with the man she loved, not because it was simple but because she knew she could face anything with Josiah by her side."

Aunt Shirley stood and walked toward him. Her hand on his arm stopped him midway through another step, and he met her bright blue eyes. "Tucker, I love you like a son. I'm proud of you no matter what. But you need to be courageous right now and win her back." Her small hand patted his shoulder. "Or I might never forgive you."

There was no question about it. He had to win her heart. End of story.

He was pretty sure he knew how to do it. If it required courage, he knew how to use that. He just needed a few allies to make it all come together. Usually he'd call PJ right about now, and she'd set up all the details. But not this time. This was up to him. And she was worth it all.

Grabbing his aunt by the shoulders, he kissed her cheek. "Thank you. I've got to go. I've got calls to make."

"Go get her, boy."

When Tucker pulled his car into the driveway of the home he'd grown up in, he waited for that sense of dread that always arrived. But it didn't come. He marched to the front door, pushed it open, and hollered inside, "Hey, anyone home?"

"Tucker? I'm in the kitchen."

His dad was standing on a stepladder, power drill in one hand, a freshly painted white cabinet door with decorative scrolling in the other.

"You need a hand?"

"No, I'm f—"

The cabinet door wavered, and his dad leaned to grab it, teetering on the second step of the ladder. Tucker lunged for him, catching the door and pushing his dad upright before he landed on his mom's new granite countertops.

"Whew. Thank you. Your mom would kill me if I damaged one of these doors."

Tucker rested it on the floor and nodded for his dad to get down. "Might as well let me give you a hand since I'm here."

They switched places, Tucker taking the spot at the top of the ladder and screwing the hinge on the top of the door. The cabinets didn't quite reach the ten-foot ceilings, but they were close.

"I heard you found the treasure—proved our ancestors weren't smugglers."

"Yep." He fit the next hinge into place. "But I'm afraid we were definitely thieves. Thieves with good hearts."

His dad grunted, maybe from the weight of the door he was still holding in place. Or maybe from the hard truth that the Westbrook ancestors weren't quite as upstanding as everyone would have hoped. "What are you going to do with all that money?"

"Well, the authorities are still working to verify ownership, so I don't have much of it. Jethro's been awarded his aunt's necklace, based on the letters from Caroline that Aunt Shirley had." He paused as the power drill whirred into action. "The city might try to claim the rest of it— but there'll probably be a finder's fee. At least, that's what Carter said. There may even be a book deal in it. Imagine me writing a book."

His dad didn't laugh. "Why haven't you gone to the media? They'd eat that up. The election's tomorrow, and you haven't given yourself much time to spread the word that Jepson has been wrong all along. Better hurry up."

Tucker heard the chastisement in his father's words and counted to ten until the tension in his muscles eased. Aunt

Shirley had been right. His dad had bought into a lie that love could somehow be earned. Tucker wasn't interested in anything that resembled that.

Somehow that freed him to feel sorry for his dad. And that made it a whole lot easier to let his jabs fall by the wayside.

"I guess I found something more important than the election," Tucker said as he climbed to the bottom rung of the ladder and tested the door. It was sturdy and swung smoothly. "I wanted to talk to you about Penelope."

Just then the door from the garage opened, and his mom strolled in, colorful shopping bags in hand and a wide smile splitting her face. "Well, I didn't expect the two of you to be here together."

"Tucker was helping me put up the cabinet doors. They look good." His dad turned back toward him. "You always were good with your hands."

Tucker nearly fell off the ladder. He could remember the number of times his dad had given him a real compliment. Zero. He couldn't help but wait for the backhand to follow.

When his dad was silent, Tucker asked, "What do you mean by that?"

His dad shrugged. "Only that you could fix nearly anything when you were a kid. You took apart a computer when you were twelve and put it back together without a hitch. I always thought you'd make a great surgeon."

"I wish you could have loved me even though I'm not."

"Tucker!" his mom cried, her bags falling to the ground.

His dad cocked his head. "Are you serious? You think I don't . . ."

Tucker swallowed the urge to bolt, stepped off the ladder, and looked right into his dad's eyes. "I always thought

I didn't measure up. You made it seem like if I wasn't book smart, I wasn't worth your time and I wasn't worth much."

"Oh, Tucker." His dad's face was hard to read, the lines around his mouth pained, his eyes shadowed. There was a war battling within, a fight that Tucker could see. The man he knew his father to be versus the man he thought his father wanted to be.

It took everything Tucker had not to let his dad off the hook, not to sweep things under the rug. After all, love might be free, but it was incredibly costly.

"Dad, I love you. But sometimes you make me feel like you wish you'd had a different kid."

"A different kid?" His dad cleared his throat. "Did a different kid serve his country with distinction for two tours? Did a different kid start a respected security company? Did a different kid find a treasure that no one else has been able to find for 150 years?"

Tucker ducked his head, suddenly a twelve-year-old boy longing to hear his dad say he was proud of him. "Well, I couldn't have done any of it without Penelope."

"Even so." His dad clapped him on the shoulder. "I am so proud of you and the man you've become. Win or lose this election, I'm glad you're my son."

Tucker let out a half laugh. He'd waited so many years for this, and now that it was here, he didn't know what to say. So he didn't say anything. He just hugged his dad, pounding him on the back.

"I'll try to do better," his dad said.

"Thanks, Dad. I love you."

"Me too."

A sob suddenly tore through the kitchen, and they stepped

apart to find his mom crying over the counter. "You have no idea," she mumbled. "Been waiting so long. You boys . . . I'll make snacks." She scooped up her bags and disappeared down the hallway before both men chuckled.

"I guess Mom's happy."

His dad shrugged. "Guess so."

"Listen, Dad. Before she comes back, I need to talk to you about something else."

"Is this about Penelope?"

Tucker grinned. "I need your help."

TWENTY

*P*enelope expected the hotel ballroom to be filled with guests, bursting with balloons and excitement as the election results rolled in. But when she pushed open the side door to the party she'd planned weeks before, it was silent, empty. Sad.

The dais at the front of the room, cloaked in blue fabric, was dark. And a lone figure sat on the edge, head bowed and legs swinging. Tucker.

Her stomach did a flip complete with an unimpressive landing, and she wanted to run. But she'd worn heels and a sundress. This was supposed to be a party. Maybe the results were already in—and they were worse than she even imagined. After all, he hadn't used the treasure to discredit Jepson's claims and that terrible letter. He hadn't plastered his face all over every television screen in the county.

As far as she could tell, he hadn't used finding the treasure to help his campaign one iota. Which made exactly zero sense given their last conversation.

She slipped across the carpet, her shoes silent, the whisper of her skirt the only sound. Tucker must have been fully invested in whatever he was thinking about because he didn't look up until she lowered herself at his side.

"PJ?" He nearly jumped up, then reached to hug her, stopping just before he touched her. "What are you doing here?"

"I thought there was supposed to be a party." She tried to sound matter-of-fact, like she hadn't been craving his touch for days. His hug. His fingers locked with hers. His kiss. Any would do for the time being. Any rope could help a drowning woman.

He let out a dry laugh, his eyes focused on her face, the weight of his gaze like a gentle embrace. "I've missed you."

"It's been four days."

"It feels like forever." He bumped her shoulder with his own. "You probably didn't even notice."

Oh, yeah. Like she hadn't noticed the midnight crying jags that had interrupted her sleep each of those nights. She kicked his foot. "Not likely, Westbrook. Apparently you've become an important part of my life, and your nonsense is my nonsense."

A muscle in his jaw jumped.

"So, where is everyone?"

"I canceled the party."

Her mouth dropped open. "But you paid all those deposits, and everyone was planning on it. And how will you make your announcement? You can't just cancel the party at the last minute like that."

"Well, I did." He shrugged. "And I returned as much money to my donors as I could."

"Tucker?" She could barely get his name out. He sounded absolutely ludicrous. "What is going on with you?"

He looked away from her, facing the big, empty room.

He leaned against his hands on either side of him, his body rocking ever so slightly. "Penelope, I'm not going to win the election."

She didn't know which was more shocking, his solemn resignation to loss or that he'd used her full name. "But you could have. Why didn't you buy some ads? You had a plan. You could have beaten him."

His head bobbed. "Maybe. But I thought about what you said, and you were right."

"I was? Er, I mean, I was. But . . . I don't understand what changed your mind. You were so set."

He closed one eye and pursed his lips. "A truth bomb from Aunt Shirley definitely helped. And somewhere along the way, I realized that there was never a deadline on clearing my family's name. I can do that after the election."

"Shirley. She has a way of making it all so clear, doesn't she?"

His chuckle was deep and echoed about the room, a sweet embrace. "She's something else. She made me face the real reason I was running for office."

"To help the people of this county?"

He cringed, his flexed shoulders stretching the fabric of his blue dress shirt, the color perfectly matching his eyes. "I told myself that so many times, I think I began to really believe it. But it wasn't quite true."

Reaching for his hand, she planned to give him a reassuring squeeze. Instead he flipped his hand over and captured hers, his palm warm and steady. It made her heart beat faster and her breath catch in her throat.

"Penelope Hunter, I've spent an awfully long time thinking that I had to do something to prove to you that I was worthy."

"Of what?"

"Of you!" He sounded surprised that she didn't know. But he wasn't making a whole lot of sense.

"Tucker, I mean—what?"

"Well, it started with my dad. I couldn't back down and have him think worse of me. But then Winston came back into our lives."

"Yes, but it didn't mean anything. There wasn't something between us again."

"I know, but it was still enough to shock my system to remind me that you could end up with someone like Winston or Flynn Rutledge or any other guy—who wasn't me. And suddenly I had to do something to show you and everyone else in our world that I was worthy. That I was better for you than all those other guys."

His words were everything she'd longed to hear and couldn't quite believe. She wanted to bask in them, to let them cover every wound she'd carried for so many years. But she couldn't be sure this was God's plan, and anything else was just another broken heart waiting to happen. "What does Flynn Rutledge have to do with any of this?"

Tucker waved his free hand dismissively. "Only that my dad said Flynn would be a good match for you."

"And you think I'd take dating advice from your dad?"

"No, but I couldn't risk staying friends—only friends. What if you suddenly realized how smart and successful those other guys are? They don't need your help putting together a business plan or clearing their family's shady name."

"You think I didn't *want* to do those things with you?"

"Someone else might be easier. They might make more money, have more clout."

"Tucker, I don't want those other guys. And I especially don't want Flynn Rutledge. He's prettier than I am."

Tucker laughed out loud. Good. That's what she'd been hoping for, but it didn't let her off the hook for answering the question buried deep in his confession.

"I like being that person for you. I like helping you be the best version of you. Because you help me be a better me. You help me lay down my lists and live in the moment. You help me find adventure when I'd rather stay inside. But I'm scared."

He squeezed her hand still trapped in his. "Of what?"

"There's a line of guys who have chosen something or someone else instead of me. I've been afraid that you'd realize the same thing they did and walk away. I think I pushed you away before you could do the leaving. I'm sorry."

"Penelope." He breathed her name like a prayer, pulling the back of her hand to his lips. His kiss was gentle, chaste, and stirred something in her she'd only known with him. It was a longing, a promise for a future she couldn't plan, dreams she had yet to imagine.

Cupping his cheek with her free hand, she ran her thumb over the tiny cleft in his chin, across all that smooth skin.

He leaned toward her, and she followed his lead until their breaths mingled, only light between them. She closed her eyes and held her breath and prayed to know that this was God's plan, that this was his adventure just for her.

Suddenly a side door crashed open. She jumped back, and Tucker gave her a half grin. "I'll just be a minute," he said, hopping off the stage and sliding his arms into the suit jacket that had been by his side.

"What's going . . ." She looked toward the three party guests, only to realize they weren't there for the party at all.

The man leading the pack carried a video camera on his shoulder, and the woman behind him was looking at her phone, thumbs flying over her screen. She didn't even look up as they neared the stage. "Sorry we're late. You ready, Mr. Westbrook?"

"I'm just waiting on one other—oh, there she is." He leaned around to spot the last member of the procession. "You ready, Jordan?"

Jordan? The cameraman set down his tripod, and the woman—who looked vaguely familiar, from a local news channel maybe—picked up a microphone, stepping aside to reveal Jordan Park. She was wearing a soft dress and a wide smile, her hair curled and her makeup heavier than the last time Penelope had seen her.

"Jordan?" Penelope rushed forward, clasping her hands. "What are you doing here?"

"Mr. Westbrook asked me to come."

"Tucker?" She looked over her shoulder as he straightened his tie and ran a hand over his hair—not that there was enough of it to be out of place.

He didn't say anything. He just shrugged, the cameraman pointing to the spot where his light glowed.

"Both of them in the shot?" the cameraman asked.

"Yes. One on either side of me." The newswoman took her place, freshened her deep red lipstick, and fluffed her ebony hair. Then she indicated where Tucker and Jordan should stand.

Penelope grabbed his arm before he moved to his mark. "Tucker? What is going on?"

With a wink and a smile, he said, "I've got an ace."

Rats. She had a choice when it came to trusting him, and she did.

Taking a few steps back so her shadow was far from the camera angle, Penelope looked at her watch. It was almost six. Were they going live with this? Maybe it was a last-ditch effort to win the election. Except Tucker had sounded so certain he wasn't going to win—almost like he didn't care anymore. And none of that explained why Jordan had joined him.

She caught his eye, but there were no answers there, only a calm certainty.

Tucker had to fight the urge to loosen his tie or clasp his hand over his heart, which threatened to break free at any moment. Instead he found PJ's gaze and held it. And he could breathe again.

The questions written all over her face would have been comical, save for the magnitude of the results. This had to work. It just did. He could not spend his life without her. He wouldn't.

God, please let this work.

"Ready?" Anita Hickam, channel eleven field reporter, asked. Her movements were crisp as she addressed Jordan and him. "I'm going to start with Mr. Westbrook. Then I'll ask Jordan some questions. Keep your answers concise. Remember this is live."

Jordan nodded, her neck and shoulders strung tighter than a clothesline.

"Thanks for doing this," he said to her. "You'll be great."

She didn't look like she believed him, but he took a deep breath that he hoped would calm down both of them. He'd already had his face and every failing splashed across the local networks for the last few months. A disastrous interview couldn't harm his standing in the community. But he didn't care so much about that. He only cared about the woman standing a few feet away, chewing on the edge of her thumbnail.

The camera guy pressed a finger to his ear. "Ready to count down. Five. Four. Three." He counted the two and the one on his fingers and then pointed at Anita.

As though on Broadway, Anita put on a show. Her smile dazzled, her eyes shone, and her dark curls seemed to gain volume. Pressing the mic almost to her red lipstick, she said, "I'm here with Tucker Westbrook, candidate for Chatham County Sheriff. Mr. Westbrook, the election results haven't been confirmed. In fact, some reports have you within a few points of Buddy Jepson. Why are you making a statement so early in the day?"

He smiled despite the pressure in his chest. Losing wasn't easy, even when it was his choice. Especially when he didn't know how this would all turn out. "I called Buddy this afternoon and conceded the election."

"Why'd you make that call so early?" She shoved the mic back in his face.

"Well . . ." He looked right into the camera. "While trying to disprove Mr. Jepson's claims about my ancestors, I discovered a few truths about my family. It turns out they did steal smuggled goods during the Civil War, and they weren't always on the right side of the law. But they left a pretty hefty treasure behind too."

He reached into his pocket and pulled out the necklace on loan from Jethro. Its stones sparkled and shone under the camera light, and Anita's eyes grew huge.

"Where did that come from?"

"Toward the end of the war, the people of Savannah were struggling—hungry and hard up for hope. That's when Josiah Hillman, a Confederate spy, asked Daniel Westbrook to help him steal a cargo that was intended to line the pockets of Confederate officers. You see, Josiah thought the goods could be put to better use—helping Savannah's people."

"Something of a Civil War Robin Hood?"

"Exactly."

"Where did you find the treasure?"

Tucker kept his smile coy. "Right where Josiah left it when he ran off to marry my great-great-great-great-aunt Caroline."

"And what will you do with it?" Anita's even tone couldn't cover her excitement.

"Josiah and Caroline were adamant that the money be used to help Savannah rebuild and recover. Well, we've pretty well rebuilt after the war, but we still have a lot of friends and neighbors who could use a helping hand. Like my friend here who runs Stepping Stones, a nonprofit that helps kids aging out of the foster care system thrive." Tucker nodded toward Jordan, and Anita whipped her mic to her other side.

In the moment of silence, he heard a small gasp. PJ pressed her fingers to her lips, but he could still see her trembling.

"Jordan Park, tell us about what you do," Anita said.

Jordan gave a brief summary of Stepping Stones, but Tucker didn't hear anything she said. His focus was only on PJ, so beautiful in the halo from the warm light. He loved how much she cared about Jordan's organization. He loved how her heart broke for kids she'd never met. He loved her.

"So, Mr. Westbrook, what are you going to do now that the election is over?"

Tucker forced himself to concentrate on what Anita said. "Well, I'm going to do everything I can to make sure that the treasure we found is used for the good of Savannah's people—especially the young adults in Stepping Stones. Then I'm going to offer five jobs at Westbrook Security to those in the Stepping Stones program. I challenge my fellow small business owners to help these kids get a strong start. If you have an open position, use it to set up one of these kids for success."

Anita's smile flashed toward the camera. "You heard the man. We have the Stepping Stones phone number on the bottom of your screen and on our website. If you've got a job for one of these young graduates, call Jordan today."

No sooner had Anita made the invitation than the unmistakable ring of a cell phone echoed in the room. Jordan turned pink, fumbling in her pocket.

"There you have it," Anita said. "Savannah is stepping up already and making good on a 155-year-old promise to help the people of this city rebuild and recover."

Anita froze, and the cameraman gave her a wave of his hand as he shut down his equipment. "Good job," she said to Tucker and Jordan. "I couldn't have scripted the timing of that phone call any better." She shook Tucker's hand, smiled at Jordan, and wished them both luck before marching her two-person parade across the room and out the door, letting it slam closed in their wake.

The room felt suddenly dark in the absence of the camera's light, yet somehow PJ shined brighter than ever.

"So? What'd you think?" he asked.

Her only response—a loud hiccup—made them both chuckle.

"Were you surprised?" Jordan's cheeks were still pink, her smile a little hesitant.

PJ dropped her hand from her mouth. "Very much so."

"But happy?" Jordan clarified.

"Very happy."

Jordan spilled the beans about how Tucker had called and set the whole thing up. How he'd asked her to keep it a secret, how she couldn't believe they were helping Stepping Stones, and how some guy named Jethro had donated his aunt's old necklace and all those diamonds to her organization. And maybe now they'd have enough money that they didn't even need a fundraiser.

PJ nodded as Jordan rambled on, but her gaze never left his, her heart shining in her eyes. He knew Aunt Shirley had been right. This was what it looked like to be courageous—to lay it all on the line for the woman he loved. And boy, had it been worth it.

The distinct ring of Jordan's phone stopped her endless chatter. She glanced at the screen. "I think I better take this." She darted toward the door. "Um . . . thank you both. I'll talk to you soon." Then she was gone, the crashing door the last reminder that they were alone. All alone.

Finally.

"Why did you do this?"

"PJ, I would do anything for you."

"You did all this—for me?" Tears washed down her face even as she swiped at them.

"Aunt Shirley said if I wanted to win your heart, I'd have

to be courageous. So this is me—just me, no badge or title or anything special—saying I love you."

"Nothing special?" She punched him playfully in the arm. "What is wrong with you? Don't you know that you're the most special? Don't you see how no one has ever—*ever*—given up something like that for me? Tucker, you are my best friend and the best guy I know." Her gaze dropped to the tops of her pretty red shoes. "And I really like kissing you."

He might not have been the smartest guy in any room, but he knew an invitation when he heard one. Scooping her into his arms, he pulled her flush against his chest. Arms around his shoulders, she played with the hair at the back of his neck, her fingers running a lazy path that sent fire all the way through him.

She chewed on the corner of her lip for a moment, still not meeting his gaze. "Can I assume that you do too?"

"Penelope, I like anything having to do with you—anything except fighting. And I promise I'll be better. I won't be such a knucklehead in the future. I won't make you mad. You can win every argument. I never want to fight with you again."

She must have liked something she heard because her fingers found their way beneath his collar, and she shivered in his arms. That was fine with him. Any excuse to hold her close.

Pressing his lips to her cheek right at the base of her ear, he whispered, "Does that sound like something you'd be interested in?"

"Not fighting?" She arched her neck to give him a different angle, and he inhaled the scent of her citrus shampoo. "Definitely."

"How about not fighting forever?" He pressed his lips in a trail down her jaw toward her chin, each kiss calling a soft mumble of appreciation from her.

"We'll probably fight—sometimes." She sighed the last word, her eyes closed and her head falling back. "Most friends do."

Moving to the corners of her mouth, he kissed each side, the lightest breath, the softest brush. She tasted of raspberries and cream, she was better than cake and sweeter than frosting, and he wanted to drink her in. Every minute of every day. For the rest of his life.

If he could get her to understand that.

"I think you're missing the point. What about the forever part?"

"Like BFFs? When did you become a twelve-year-old girl?"

"No." He gave her waist a quick squeeze, and she squealed in laughter. "Not like best friends forever, or whatever. Like man and wife. Like I love you and I want to know if you'll spend the rest of your life with me. If you'll marry me."

Her eyes flew open, her hands dropping to the front of his chest, resting over his racing heart. This was just one of those things that took courage. And for her—he'd find it every time.

Except her big blue eyes turned gray, clouded. "You— what? You want to marry me?"

He reached into his pocket and pulled out his great-grandmother's ring, the one his dad had had in the safe. The one that reminded him of a family legacy of bravery and sacrifice. And love. Always love.

"Penelope Jean, I want to marry you tomorrow."

"But we just started dating."

"So what? You know me better than anyone. You know exactly what you're getting if you say yes. And you know—"

"Yes. Yes, I'll marry you." The words came out in a rush, but he wasn't about to give her a chance to change her mind.

"Tomorrow?" he asked.

She rolled her eyes.

"Or as soon as you'd like."

That made her laugh, and he pulled her closer, drinking in the sweet sound—the sweetness of her.

As her giggle faded, she looked right into his eyes. "So . . . that agreement we had about you kissing me?"

"About how I won't kiss you again without prior written consent?"

"I don't remember it quite like that, but yeah."

"What about it?" He held his grin at bay, but just barely.

"Maybe we could suspend it, you know, indefinitely."

She'd get no argument from him. He intended to kiss her every day for the rest of their lives. Spinning her around, he pulled her hand free and slipped the ring on her finger. "I love you, Penelope."

"I love it when you call me that."

Pressing his forehead to hers, he stared at her closed eyes, the fan of her black lashes making her cheeks even more porcelain. He whispered her name again, and she shivered against him. Fireworks brewed deep in his belly, his lungs ready to burst. Her hands on his chest were small and delicate and stirred an emotion that was anything but.

He'd never held joy and life and such a sweet gift all at once. Until now. How had he ever come to deserve such a treasure?

He didn't. It was that simple.

Maybe that was the point. He wasn't worthy. That's what made it a gift.

She pulled back just enough to catch his eye. "Are you sure you want me for forever? You know Ambrose comes with me. We're a package deal."

Kissing her again, he showed her exactly what he thought. He wasn't going anywhere, and he sure wasn't going to let her go. Ever.

EPILOGUE

Six Months Later

"Have you decided what you're going to do?"

Penelope looked up from the intricate pattern of crystals across the bodice of her dress into her mother's eyes. "I'm going to put on my veil and walk down the aisle toward the man I love."

Her mom laughed. "Of course you're going to do that." She made it sound like a foregone conclusion, although there had been a few heated discussions before she believed Penelope and Tucker were committed to making this marriage last for the rest of their lives and she didn't have to worry about her only daughter's heart being broken again. "I meant about the job offer."

Penelope smiled. Since her role in finding the treasure had been revealed and the gold and diamonds valued and put to use supporting some key organizations in the community—including Stepping Stones—she'd received more than one job offer. Even Anabelle Haywood had called after the resounding success of the Ladies' League fundraiser at the Hall, which had brought in more than twice its usual donations. And she'd offered Penelope the position of executive director of the Ladies' League—working closely with Anabelle as president, of course. She didn't even demand that Penelope sever ties with Tucker and his "nonsense." In fact, she'd suggested Tucker might want to run for sheriff again—since the county was investigating Buddy Jepson for fraud, and he'd stepped down barely six months into his tenure.

Tucker had had the poise not to laugh at Anabelle's suggestion—but he'd quickly shut down the thought when Penelope had passed it along to him. "I have more important things on my mind these days," he'd said. "Plus I have a wedding to plan." He now had a booming business and a handful of new hires from Stepping Stones to train. Every day after work, he'd fill her in on their latest achievements and funniest moments, pride in his eyes and joy in his voice.

Penelope had told Anabelle that she'd consider the offer, and she had. Along with the one at Carter's museum and another at the university. But truthfully, she wasn't looking for a new job. She'd managed to keep the one she already had and loved.

The only title change she wanted was from Miss to Mrs. And only if that came with a new name, thieves and smugglers though they were. Westbrook.

"Mom," she said, smoothing the cinched-in waist of her wedding dress. It wasn't exactly the corset she'd worn to the Fort Pulaski picnic, but she hoped to get a similar reaction from her soon-to-be husband. "I'm going to make one decision about my future at a time. And right now, marrying Tucker is the only thing on my mind."

She wasn't worried about her future, Tucker, or anything

else. Nearly ready to walk down the aisle, she knew that whatever lay ahead for them was going to be better than anything she could have planned. Because this wasn't about the plans she made but the ones God had in store for her. Knowing she could trust him with her future was better than any list she could make, any task she could check off.

That he'd picked Tucker for her forever—well, that was proof God knew her well. He knew what she needed, and he delighted in giving her so much more than she'd dared to ask for.

"Come on, Mom. Ready to walk me down the aisle?"

As they stepped arm in arm onto the red runner, Penelope took a deep breath, and her mom squeezed her hand.

"I'm so happy for you, honey."

"I am too," she said, unable to contain her giggle. She looked out over the small crowd of guests as they rose. For her.

Carter and his wife, Anne, stood near the middle, Anne's hand cradling her growing baby bump—both of them beaming. Jethro had found a spot close to the front, directly beside Shirley, who looked far too smug. After all, she said she had known they'd end up together. Maybe she really had known. Or maybe she'd just known that the good Lord loved to give good gifts. Love, perhaps the best one.

Near the back stood Winston St. Cloud in a crisp navy-blue suit and a broad smile. When he met her gaze, he gave her a slow nod before his eyes darted to the front of the chapel, where Emmaline stood in her lavender bridesmaid dress. Winston and Emmaline had said their "I dos" back in August, right on time and just as it should have been. And Penelope had found in Emmaline the best characteristic of a friend. She was quick to forgive and eager to move forward.

Penelope had been honored to put the finishing touches on their wedding reception and see them dance away into the night. It had been lovely.

But not nearly as perfect as this wedding. Tucker Westbrook stood in a charcoal-gray suit and black tie at the end of the runner, and he looked at her just like he had in the tailor's dressing room all those months ago. Only this time, she couldn't miss the silent words on his lips. *I love you.*

Her heart nearly burst as he stepped forward to take her hand, his grip strong and sure. She'd never worried that he wouldn't show up, because he'd been showing up every day for the last twenty-five years. And she had no doubt he'd show up for another sixty-five more.

I love you too. She mouthed the words back to him, and the rest of the room disappeared. It was just the two of them vowing before God to honor and cherish each other, to love and laugh and sacrifice for each other. They were a strand of three together for the rest of their lives, a cord not easily broken.

And then Pastor Guthrie announced, "You may kiss your bride."

No one had to invite Tucker more than once. He kissed her like he had that first time in front of a ballroom full of people, warm and sweet and full of promises she hadn't recognized then. But, oh, how she knew them now. And she kissed him back with all the love in her once broken heart.

The reception was perfect, and the food was pretty good, if their guests were to be believed. She never got to taste it, too busy hugging her friends and family. The cake she did enjoy—a bite of the perfect white cake with raspberry filling fed to her by her husband. No mess, no muss. The orchid centerpieces were stunning, and the Hall was perfectly decorated.

The band played their song, and she swayed in her husband's arms, tucked beneath his chin, hand pressed to his heart.

He held her palm against his chest. "You're always right there. You always have been."

"I'm glad you finally figured it out. Took you long enough."

His laugh rumbled beneath her ear. "Maybe if you hadn't been busy making other plans, we both would have noticed sooner."

"Are you sad about that?"

He kissed the top of her head, his hand on her back making a lazy circle, pulling her ever closer. "We got here at the right time. How could I be sad about that? We have the rest of—"

"I knew it when you were eight." Shirley charged up to them and pulled them into her embrace. "Consider this my 'I told you so.'"

They both laughed, holding on to the dear woman.

"Caroline would have been mighty proud of the both of you. And she would have loved to see what that money is doing for this city. What *you're* doing for this city." Shirley clapped Tucker on the back. "I heard that every single one of Jordan's kids has been offered a job in the community, and there are several openings waiting for graduates of the Stepping Stones program." She tucked an envelope into Tucker's hand. "I'm pretty proud of you too. Both of you. And since you're not keeping any of the money from the treasure, I'd like you to use my airline points to buy your plane tickets. Anywhere you'd like to go. Your honeymoon's on me."

With a quick kiss on both of their cheeks, Shirley disappeared into the crowd on the dance floor, leaving them speechless. They'd decided to postpone their honeymoon until they'd saved up a few dollars, but they'd never expected anything like this.

Penelope wiped a tear of joy from her cheek. "I love you, Tucker, and I love your family."

"I love that you're officially my family now, PJ."

Penelope Jean Westbrook loved every wedding she'd ever been to. But hers was the very best.

A NEW
PRINCE EDWARD ISLAND
SERIES FROM

LIZ JOHNSON!

COMING SUMMER 2021

ONE

Morning had a terrible habit of arriving far too early, at least as far as Meg Whitaker was concerned. And it was far too fond of adding a chill to the summer air at the shoreline.

She hunched into her oversized sweater and shivered against a gust of wind as a pair of headlights topped the hill and bounced down the red dirt road toward the dock. Finally. Her dad was already five minutes late, and she had only dragged herself from her bed at such an absurd hour because he'd told her he needed to see her.

As the vehicle rolled to a stop in the dark and flipped off its lights, she could see even in the darkness that it wasn't her dad's cherished red truck. This one was baby blue and sported over half a dozen rust spots from more than one harsh winter.

Squinting hard at the truck, she could make out the form of a man sitting behind the wheel. His shoulders were broader than her dad's lanky form, his neck straight like steel. But she couldn't see his features and didn't recognize his vehicle.

He didn't open his door. He didn't turn his head. He didn't move. He just sat there. Staring at her.

Meg could feel the weight of his gaze, every ounce of it. She cringed at a memory she'd tried so hard to forget. Only one other man—well, he'd been a boy then—had ever stared at her so intently she'd physically felt it. Then he'd destroyed her science fair project, her chance at a prestigious fellowship, and all hope of being accepted to Yale. But when she asked him why he'd done such a cruel thing, he only shrugged. He'd never looked her way again.

No way *he* was sitting in a truck at her dad's dock at 4:45 in the morning, staring at her through the darkness. He was barely a silhouette behind a windshield. But she couldn't look away. She could only wrap her arms about herself and pray that this man wasn't the one she remembered.

Only the lobster crowd was out so early in the morning. It was madness. She'd never understood the call to the sea or joy of fishing. Besides, she didn't particularly see the fulfillment in looking a little lobster in the eye and preparing it to feed someone unknown. Her students at the high school, on the other hand . . . well, she could look them in the eye and see that she was making a difference.

Meg was grateful for lobster fishing, of course. Her dad's hard work had made it possible for her to go to the university, to pursue science. Even if it wasn't exactly the school and ultimate career she'd dreamed of.

When the low purr of her dad's truck finally broke through the songs of the morning birds and the gentle lapping of the sea against the beams of the dock, Meg jerked her head up, ready to run to his side. He slung gravel as he skidded to a halt and threw open the door, the truck's shiny coat glittering even in the low light.

"Sorry I'm late, hon." Her dad's long strides ate up the

ground between them until he greeted her with a peck on the cheek. "Your mom had a rough morning."

Meg cringed. She hadn't even thought about why her dad might be late, what he'd been doing in the morning hours that most people still considered night. "How is she?"

"Tired."

They all were. Tired of late nights and far too early mornings. Tired of praying for an answer that never seemed to appear. Tired of the mystery illness that was stealing her mom's mobility and very life one breath at a time.

Meg squeezed his big hand, ignoring the calluses from years of pulling in lines and tying his own traps. "How are you?"

His fingers gripped hers, and his gaze dropped to the space between two pale, battered planks. "I'm ready to let go."

"Let go? Of what?" Surely not her mom. He hadn't asked her there to make some grand announcement about how he was throwing away thirty-seven years of marriage because life had become something other than it was supposed to be. He wasn't that kind of man.

He shook his head, his shoulders slumped under a weight she couldn't see.

"Dad?"

"It's too much for me."

She grabbed his elbow. "What's going on?"

He brushed an errant lock of her hair back from her face, even as the wind whipped more of it free from her ponytail. "I thought I'd be able to wait until you were married."

What was he talking about? She hadn't had a serious boyfriend in years. And even then they'd discussed marriage exactly once—just long enough for them to both know they weren't ready. They hadn't been particularly in love either.

Maybe that was why their relationship hadn't lasted much past that conversation. There certainly wasn't anyone special in her life at the moment.

"Dad." Her voice turned firm. "You're not making any sense. What are you talking about?"

"After you said you didn't want the fleet, I hoped you'd marry someone who did. Or maybe you'd have kids who wanted it."

"The fleet?" Her gaze swept over the fishing boats rocking in the narrow dock. Pale blue and white, all four of them pristine and free of barnacles.

The realization sat in her chest, heavy and painful, slipping south with each creak of the mooring lines until her feet were rooted where she stood. He was selling his business. He was selling his livelihood. He was selling her birthright.

Okay, technically he'd asked her a few years ago if she wanted to take over the business. But how could she run a fishing company when she couldn't stomach stepping on board a boat? She'd never earn the respect of the crew—or enjoy a day at her job. Still, there was something terrifying about the idea that the license her great-grandpa had bought would go to someone without the Whitaker name.

"Dad! You can't. Not yet."

He held up a hand that stilled her outburst, but it was the calm shake of his head that tore her heart apart. "You said you didn't want it." Confusion seemed to add a question to the statement, his eyes sad. "Have you changed your mind?"

She tried to form a response, but her tongue couldn't shape it. She managed only a slight shrug.

"Your mom needs me now. She can't wait . . ."

There was no need for him to finish his thought. She knew. While the income from the sale would allow them to enjoy the days her mom had left, he only cared about spending them with her. The money would be nice later. After.

Lobster fishing fleets were in high demand—mostly because there were a limited number of fishing licenses around Prince Edward Island. They rarely came up for sale, and when they did, they went for small fortunes. A fleet and license on the east side of the island had sold for over a million dollars just a few years back, and her dad had been approached by brokers many times over the years.

Her eyes swung toward the blue truck. Was that a broker sitting inside?

She quickly dismissed the idea. Brokers on that level didn't drive rusted clunkers. So who was he and what did he want with her and her dad?

This had been her father's heritage, passed down from Grandpa Horace and from his father too. Fishing was the family trade. He wouldn't give his license to someone else, would he?

If only she'd grown to love the ocean and its creatures the same way her dad had. If only she wanted to pick up where he left off. If only a short jaunt on the boat didn't make her insides initiate a revolution.

"There has to be another way." But even as she said it, she knew it wasn't true.

"I've decided to sell. Your mom and I have talked about it. I want to spend every moment I can with her." His mouth twisted on the words, his facade beginning to crack, and she could do nothing but throw her arms around her dad and hold him tightly.

"I'm so sorry," she whispered into his shoulder. He didn't need her grief too. He needed her to be strong and sure.

She'd heard fishermen talk of ships in distress looking for any port in the storm. But her mom and dad didn't need just any port. They needed to be able to lean on her in the face of the unknown. She couldn't buckle under her own grief. She wouldn't.

With a gentle pat on her back and a sniff just above her head, her dad pulled away. His long legs carried him back a step just as the glow of the morning sun lit up the ocean where it met the east, turning the water from black to inky blue. "I have to tell you something else." His furry black eyebrows drew together, meeting over his crooked nose.

Her stomach sank. There was no way this was good news. But what else could he possibly add?

"I'm going to sell it to Oliver Ross."

Was there another Oliver Ross on the island she didn't know? Maybe this one was from away. From far, far away. Maybe he wasn't the boy she'd gone to school with or the one she'd actively been avoiding for more than a decade. And it did require some concentrated effort not to run into him in tiny Victoria by the Sea. It was worth it for her sanity.

But when her dad motioned in the direction of the truck, she knew. She knew with utter confidence that he was selling his business to her arch nemesis.

Oliver Ross took a deep breath, squeezed his eyes closed, and yanked on the handle of his old truck. The door swung open with a loud groan. He'd have made a similar noise if he wasn't sure it would just add ammunition to Meg Whitaker's arsenal.

He leaned his hip against a rust spot, and a creak was quickly followed by the soft catch of the door closing. Then all was silent save the rolling of the water and the morning birds trilling their song.

He only imagined he could hear the steam coming out of Meg's ears. The thump-thump-thumping was his heart, not the unpleasant rhythm of her toe against the dock. True, her hands had found their way to her hips, elbows at right angles, and even at this distance, the shadows from the light above didn't hide the fury of her features. Eyes narrowed. Nostrils flared. Pretty pink lips turned into a thin line.

She was mad. She probably—no, definitely—had a right to be. But he couldn't avoid her forever. Not anymore. He'd been doing a pretty good job of dodging her the last ten years. Or maybe she was dodging him. He shrugged to himself. It didn't matter. He'd come face-to-face with her every day if that's what it took to take care of his family.

The gravel gave way beneath his first step. Then his second.

He picked up his pace, closing the distance before he could come up with a smooth opening line. Or even a bumbling one. So he said nothing.

Mr. Whitaker held out his hand, and Oliver returned the firm shake. "Morning, Oliver."

"Sir." He dipped his chin toward the father and then the daughter.

Meg did not respond in kind. Her eyes were stone. He'd seen them laughing once when she was sixteen. She hadn't uttered a sound, but her green eyes had glittered at a joke one of their classmates told. Oliver wondered then just what it took to make her laugh.

And then he'd wondered if he could do it. They'd been friends back then. Not close, but they'd run in the same circle.

A month later everything changed, and she'd never spoken to him again. That didn't seem likely to change as she addressed her dad.

"You can't be serious. Why would you sell it to *him*?" She gestured toward him with a dismissive wave of her hand. "There must be a hundred people interested in buying your fleet. You don't have to settle."

Her words stung for a moment, like winter wind whipping ice at his cheeks. He steeled himself against a further attack, squaring his shoulders and staring her down. He wanted to articulate every single one of his finer qualities, but the truth was, he didn't know exactly why Mr. Whitaker had chosen him. Oliver had been on his crew for six years, and a year before, Whitaker had asked him to take over the day-to-day management of the business. He'd said he needed more flexibility. More time to make sure his wife got the medical care she needed.

It had been an absolute failure. The crew continued seeking input from Whitaker, interrupting his wife's appointments to question Oliver's decisions. Long-time vendors called Whitaker directly. There had even been a buyer who refused to negotiate with anyone but the older fisherman.

Whitaker was too ingrained in the business. Oliver had known almost immediately that he would eventually sell. He'd started saving for a down payment, praying that Whitaker would be willing to sell to someone who needed a loan.

Oliver had learned everything he knew from the fisherman. The week before, Whitaker had clapped him on the back and called him "son." And then he'd given him the best gift in the world. A stable future.

Mr. Whitaker pushed his fingers around his frown in slow

motion, starting in the middle of his mustache and ending at the point of his chin. "I thought long and hard about who I wanted to pass our legacy on to. Did a fair bit of praying too."

Oliver's stomach clenched at the very suggestion that he might be the answer to that prayer. He'd been called a lot of things in his life—mostly by his dad—but never an answer to prayer.

"At the end of the day, I wanted to give it to someone I knew I could trust to continue it well. Someone who would follow the rules—the written and the unwritten ones."

Meg's eyebrows jumped to the middle of her forehead. "But, Dad, you know what he did." She waved her hand in his general direction but jerked it back before her fingers could brush against his arm.

Mr. Whitaker did know what he'd done. Oliver had made sure of that on the day he'd been offered a job. He'd known even as a twenty-one-year-old kid that hiding the truth about his last interaction with Meg was no way to earn trust. So he had gulped a breath and let out the truth in one stream.

Mr. Whitaker, for all his quiet dignity, hadn't even raised an eyebrow. He'd known. And he'd still chosen to offer the job. Oliver had never been more grateful for anything in his life. He refused to let Mr. Whitaker regret it.

Shoving his hands into his pockets and hunching his shoulders—more to have something to do than because of the breeze—Oliver nodded slowly. "He knows."

Her eyes snapped toward him, and he could almost hear a hissed, "No one asked you, boy." But the voice in his head was deeper, meaner than hers. She hadn't even spoken those words to him when they'd faced each other down in the principal's office. Oliver had mumbled an unintelligible excuse for his actions. He'd steeled himself against the stinging smack of his dad's hand against the back of his head and the hiss in his ear.

Only it hadn't come. His dad hadn't showed up that day. Or any day after.

Oliver expected an accusation from Meg. But she didn't speak. He couldn't quite read the look in her eyes, but her posture had turned stiff, her arms locked around her middle.

Mr. Whitaker held up his hand. "I made my decision with a full view. The past can't be changed, and I don't think he's the boy he once was."

She flinched. Oliver tried not to notice.

He'd been trying not to notice her for more than a decade. It hadn't worked very well in the high school halls either.

"Dad, have you talked with—"

"Your mother and I had a long conversation about this. Several of them, actually." Mr. Whitaker slapped him on the shoulder. "She agrees with me about Oliver."

The pinch of Meg's nose and her stumbled step back revealed the betrayal she felt, and a sudden punch to his gut almost made him refuse the offer. Maybe it should all go to her. Although her dad had said she didn't want it. And she couldn't keep her legs beneath her even in the shallows. But maybe she should still have some say in who took over the fleet and her family's fishing business.

"But there's no way he's saved up enough money to buy it outright," she said.

Whatever inclination he'd had to decline the offer vanished. So he wasn't wealthy. And he'd wondered more than once how he was going to feed his mom and little brother.

He was the one up at four every morning, reeling in traps and breaking his back. And if he worked two jobs in the off-season to make sure he paid every one of his bills and his mom's lights were never again turned off? What concern was that of Meg's?

He worked hard, and he'd make sure the Whitakers' legacy wasn't tarnished.

Mr. Whitaker's bushy eyebrows lowered over his eyes, his gaze hard on his daughter. "I'm going to give him an interest-free loan. Let him do the job and earn what he needs. He'll pay me back in five years, and then we'll be square."

Oliver patted the folded square of paper in his jeans pocket. He'd worked the numbers, figured out just how many pounds he'd need to sell each season to pay each of the crew and pay off the loan. The numbers checked out. The fleet would be his by the time he was thirty-three.

A slow grin inched across his mouth. A man couldn't ask for much more than his dreams.

But the glint in Meg's eyes promised him it might not be as easy as he'd hoped—not that six years of back-breaking labor and pinching every penny the last year just to make a down payment had been easy. There was a light in her, a fire that made him shuffle back. Her eyes were wild, unfocused. Every breath she took sounded like it had been scraped over gravel.

Then she opened her mouth and ruined his day.

"Don't sell it to him. Sell it to me."

ACKNOWLEDGMENTS

Just as I finished writing the book you now hold in your hands, I celebrated ten years of publishing, ten years of sharing the stories of my heart with readers like you. What an incredible privilege it has been to be part of your lives. You've been an escape and encouragement during difficult times, a sweet friend in the quiet hours. I wouldn't get to do this without you, and I'm grateful. Thank you for reading!

As this book releases, I will celebrate ten years as a client of Rachel Kent and Books & Such Literary Management. What a wonderful ride it's been. Thank you for believing in my stories. Thank you for believing in me. Thank you for your steady guidance and calm assurance over these years.

The amazing team at Revell has made this journey brighter and my books so much better. I'm honored to get to work with Vicki, Jessica, Michele, Karen, and the rest of the team. Thank you for all you've invested in me and my books. Thank you for sharing messages that matter.

Even with this amazing team, the actual writing journey can be a lonely one. So I'm beyond grateful God brought a special group of writers into my life. They encourage and challenge me every day to be a better writer and a better woman, and I look forward to our writing sessions every other week. Thank you, Lindsay Harrel, Tina Radcliffe, Sara Carrington, Jennifer Deibel, Tari Faris, and Ruth Douthitt. Your examples and perseverance inspire me.

A special thank-you to reader Jordan Sims, who suggested the name of Penelope's favorite nonprofit and received a character named after her. I'm so grateful for all my readers and love to connect with you on social media, through email, and at reader events. You make writing these books even more fun!

Having a writer in the family isn't always easy—like when I tell my family they can't visit or call me so I can write. It happened many times while I was working on this project, but they still love me, and I'm so grateful for them. They're always there as I climb out of my writing hole, ready to be part of the world again. Being part of this family is the best. I love you guys.

And finally, to my good, good Father, who threw a wrench in my plans this year and showed me once again that his plans are so much better and his lovingkindness never ends.

Liz Johnson is the author of more than a dozen novels, including *A Sparkle of Silver*, *A Glitter of Gold*, *The Red Door Inn*, *Where Two Hearts Meet*, and *On Love's Gentle Shore*, as well as a *New York Times* bestselling novella and a handful of short stories. She works in marketing and makes her home in Phoenix, Arizona.

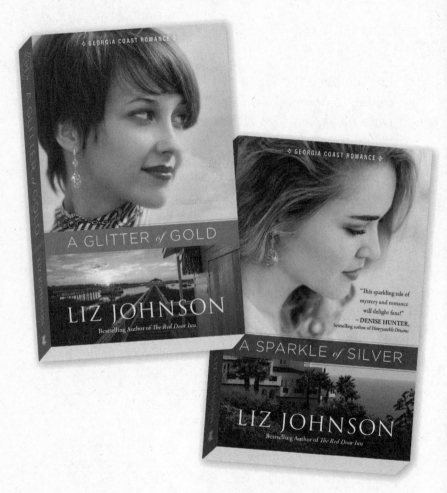

Escape to
PRINCE EDWARD ISLAND . . .

"A charming inn in need of restoration, Prince Edward Island, and a love story? Yes, please! I thoroughly enjoyed the vicarious visit to the Canadian Maritime Province of Prince Edward Island. I could almost feel the sea breeze!"

—BECKY WADE,
ECPA bestselling author of the Porter Family series

If you love **Liz Johnson**,
GIVE THIS A TRY!

Britt and Zander have been best friends since they met thirteen years ago, but unbeknownst to Britt, Zander has been in love with her for just as long. When the death of a relative brings them back together to uncover a tangled past, will the truth of what lies between them also come to light?